CHANGECHILD

ONCE UPON A TIME a changechild was born to the Windrunners, a nomad people roaming the northern Grass. When her skin began to go green, they sold her to the most powerful sorcerer alive, Ser Noris, who had secured for himself a kind of immortality—a cessation of the processes of growth and decay within his body.

ONCE UPON A TIME the most powerful sorcerer alive soured on life and challenged it to a duel. Serroi was one of the tools he used in his challenge, but she turned in his hand and he threw her away—then discovered that he needed her in ways he hadn't dreamed and tried to lure her back.

ONCE UPON A TIME there was a great war between CHANGE and STASIS. Change won, but not before much suffering and death, not before magic was driven from the world. Serroi and Ser Noris faced each other in a deadly dance and when it ended, were both transformed, Serroi to a graceful lacewood, Ser Norris to a brooding conifer.

ONCE UPON A TIME two trees dreamed upon a cliff. . . .

THEN ONE OF THEM WOKE.

DANCER'S RISE

JO CLAYTON

DAW BOOKS, INC.

DONALD A. WOLLHEIM, FOUNDER

375 Hudson Street, New York, NY 10014

ELIZABETH R. WOLLHEIM

SHEILA E. GILBERT

PUBLISHERS

First Printing, September 1993
1 2 3 4 5 6 7 8 9

DAW TRADEMARK REGISTERED
U.S. PAT OFF AND FOREIGN COUNTRIES
—MARCA REGISTRADA.
HECHO EN U.S.A.

PRINTED IN THE U.S.A.

DANCER'S RISE

PROLOGUE—
The Awakening

Warmth.

That's what she felt first. A warmth spreading from an irregular blotch to fill her.

More sensations.

Pain. Stretching. Twisting.

Change. Wrench, immediate, all-encompassing.

Then there was cold stone under her hands.

Hands?

She lifted her head. Head? Eyes? Knees cold with the chill of the stone? How long since she'd had any of those?

How long?

It came back as if it had never left, how to move legs, how to stand. How to speak.

She tugged her tunic down, feeling the worn black cloth with a muted wonder, turned on booted feet to face the woman whose touch had wakened her.

The stranger was tall and thin with slanted red eyes and soft pale skin delicately scaled. An Incomer she must be, but one with magic in her touch. "I thank you," Serroi told her. "A tree's a splendid form to rest in, but two centuries' sleep is long enough."

"What?"

"No matter. My name is Serroi. Who are you and how came you here?"

"I am Kitya of the Moug'aikkin." The woman stood

rubbing her wrists, the right, then the left. The lines in her face were sagging despite the firmness of her flesh; her world must be lighter than this. "I have no idea where here is."

"Incomer. I thought so." Serroi turned around, stood looking down at the confusion below, her hands clasped behind her. "Damn. Coyote's Incomers have really been busy while I was dreaming up here."

Among the old stone buildings a forest of tall, angular, weblike structures hummed in the wind, their stay cables singing. There were odd constructions on the roofs, plates slanted to the south, covered in shining black squares that seemed to swallow the sunlight. Among the buildings, on patches of green lawn, there were groups of young people sitting, talking, eating, pairs intent on each other, individuals reading, sleeping, stretched out and staring into the sky, young people everywhere. No children, very few adults visible. In the valley beyond, a yellow dust haze hung over a checkerboard of fields. On roads between the fields enclosed carts like black water beetles darted about, more of the light collectors pasted over their bodies. Carts of a different shape moved methodically through the fields, the men in them plowing and otherwise working the crops.

Beside her the Incomer Kitya glanced at the sun, glanced again, surprise on her narrow face, then resignation. "How can we get down from here? I don't fancy spending the night curled up by that tree." She flicked a finger up, then curled it back, indicating the rugged conifer growing at the edge of the cliff. "Besides, I'm getting hungry."

Serroi scratched beside the oval green spot between her brows. "There used to be a path of sorts. Over here," she nodded to the left, started picking her way across the cracks in the stone and the weeds growing in them.

Kitya followed her a few steps, then swung round as the conifer began to creak and shudder as if it were trying to come after them; she took a step toward the tree, her arm lifting. . . .

Serroi leaped at her, slapped her hand around the Incomer's wrist. "Nay!" She moved until she was standing between the Incomer and the tree. "Kitya of the Moug'aikkin, don't listen to that one; stop your ears and mind your soul. He'll swallow you in a gulp if you let him and you'll loose a great evil on this world."

"What?"

"Come, better to leave quickly. He'll creep through the tiniest crack given time enough." As Kitya moved her wrist, seeking to free herself, Serroi stopped her. "Nay, let me hold you as long as I can. It's safer, I promise you."

The path was in adequate shape, weeded sometime in the fairly recent past and edged with small bits of stone; it wavered back and forth across the weathered cliff, made descending more tedious than risky, but by the time they reached the valley floor, Serroi was stiff and tired. *What should you expect, woman, you haven't walked for two hundred years.*

She stood with her hands clasped behind her, staring at the wall that marched across the valley. The merlons were crumbling like a mouthful of rotted teeth, there were cracks in the massive stones of the facade, moss and weeds eroding holes deeper with every season, trees and brush growing up close, their roots attacking the base. *Generations of peace, that's what that means. Worth a few years vegetating, I suppose.* "We'd better get started, it'll take a while to reach the gate."

* * *

Ten days later Serroi stood on the cliff again, the conifer bending and groaning behind her as the woman who'd waked her from her long sleep went whirling off into nowhere, arms clasped about a dark-haired, gaunt-faced man.

When the clifftop was quiet again, she turned and stood with hands on hips, scowling at the ancient conifer. "This time, this moment, we won."

The tree's branches stirred, the needles rustled briefly, fell silent.

"I know. There'll be another time." She turned away, walked to the path down the cliff and into her second life.

1. On the Sinadeen (Two years after the Awakening)

M O TH TH THERRR— — — —
*A figure emerged from the fog. Bones with
shreds of flesh and sinew still clinging to them,
a rotted cotton shift hanging from denuded
clavicles. Its eyes were oozing holes, decay
dripping like tears, light shining phosphor green
from deep within the skull.*
The head turned, seemed to stare at her.
The lipless mouth opened.
MOTHERRRRR. . . .

The change in motion brought Serroi out of her nightmare even before the ship's boy began banging on the
door, shouting for them to wake and come on deck.
The boy moved on to Adlayr's cabin, beat on that, then
ran up the ladder, the sounds of his feet vanishing in
the shipnoises.

Zasya Myers swung her feet from the lower bunk
fitted like Serroi's against the hull, stowage shelves for
human cargo, and stood in grim silence buckling on
her weaponbelt. A moment later she was gone, the
gyes from the next cabin rushing past after her.

Serroi kicked off the blanket and slid to the floor;
she'd slept in her clothes, only taking off her boots.
She didn't bother pulling them on, just whipped her

cloak from its peg, turned it white side out, and left the cabin.

She climbed to the quarterdeck and settled out of the way beside the stern rail, watching with bleak interest as Zasya and Adlayr took in the situation, watching the Fenek Shipmaster standing at the quarterdeck's forerail, his eyes darting over his crew as they moved about below, getting ready with somber determination to fight to the death. Nijilic TheDom was low in the west, as gibbous as Camnor Heslin's belly, his light coming uncertainly through puffy cloud drifts, rimming their round edges with silver.

Zasya Myers left her companion and leaned on the rail beside Master Am'litho. "Swampkrys?"

"As you see, meie." He rolled a broad hand at the sea around them, the waves lifting and falling with an unnatural heaviness while the *Wanda Kojamy* wallowed in a trough, sails slatting uselessly against the masts. "With a windsnuffer in one of those phingin' garbage scows or they'd be watching Wanda's backside dip o'er the horizon."

"You're calm enough."

"Nowhere to go, meie. We just wait for them to get close, then do our best." As two men came from below, carrying crossbows and bolt sacs, he immediately contradicted himself by shouting at them, "Sakh! Jy, hustle, man! Into the shrouds, you and Herks. A silver huz for every rat you skewer."

A short distance off half a hundred low black outriggers ringed the merchantman, torches uncovered in their bows showing black shadows doing a precarious dance in those tottery shells. Fifty boats with at least ten Kry in each.

"Skaiy, not there! Haul those umdums to bow catter." Am'litho swore under his breath, then turned to

Adlayr Ryan-Turriy who was a pale shine in the darkness, naked except for his weaponbelt and a skimpy loincloth. "You better get some clothes on, gyes, those phingin' warts have barbs on their spears and smear them with sleepooze."

Adlayr raised shaggy black brows. "Not poison?"

"Don't want to miss their fun."

"I fight like this, Master. You'll see." Adlayr grinned at him. He had a pleasantly ugly face and a smile of surpassing charm.

"You know your business."

The drums began to beat faster, the swampmen added growling voices to the sound, a basso chant from five hundred throats that clubbed the ears and tried to numb the mind.

Master Am'litho turned back to Zasya. "Anything you can do 'bout that windsnuffer, meie?"

"Afraid not. No mages here, unless you count the Healer."

Am'litho blinked heavy lids over eyes that were almost yellow, blazing in his dark face. "Glad I'll be to have her later on, but a magicker of any other kind would be of more worth this moment. Haya, I've passed out edges and shooters, we'll take as many as we can. You know about the swampers?"

The chant and the drums continued, but the dancing stopped, the rowers dropped to their benches and the outriggers began gliding in a slowly narrowing spiral about the becalmed *Wanda Kojamy,* confidence and blood-thirst hooming in guttural pulses from the Krymen's throats.

"We've heard."

"Take what you've heard and fold it twice and twice again. If you're alive to the last, cut your own throat before you let them get you. I've seen what's left of a sailor they set adrift, they sliced the lids off his eyes and broke his arms and legs and put fayar in cages on his chest and left them to eat themselves free. Cut your own throat, meie, you'll do a kinder job.''

''Asha. Where do you want us?'' A grin thrown at the gyes. ''I can shoot the left eyebrow off a flea at forty paces and Adlayr'd be as good if he practiced a little.''

Adlayr snorted. ''In your dreams, Zas.''

Am'litho's nostrils flared, his eyes narrowed in their nests of laugh-wrinkles, then he was serious again. ''I'll not be ordering about meien nor gyes, you know the work better'n me nor my men.''

Round and round the outriggers went, round and round, as the windsnuffer's charm forced the air into smaller and smaller compass until breathing was as much labor as walking.

Serroi got to her feet. She licked her lips, tried to speak and could not, tried again, her practical side in conflict with the imperatives of the Healer. ''Zas, if I spotted the windsnuffer for you, could you take him out from here?''

The meie considered the distance between the *Wanda Kojamy* and the outriggers, turned and held out her hands to her companion. Handfasted they stood for a moment, then Zasya smiled, ''Think so, once they're a little closer.''

The drums throbbed louder and louder, the beat quickened as the outriggers circled nearer, though not nearly in spear distance as yet. The chant was louder and more ragged as the swampmen grew drunk on anticipated pleasure. The triumph in those Kry voices rasped across the nerves as the *Wanda*'s crew worked to get ready or waited the order to fire catters and crossbows.

Am'litho grunted, smoothed a hand over his bald head, then tugged at his short beard. ''Gi' a moment 'fore you do't. Let me get placed. There'll still be attack, y' know. *Wanda* is a steady girl, she don't jump 'bout like a phingin' lappet.'' He leaned over the rail, yelled to his first mate who was getting the fore-catapult locked in place. ''Bullah, get up here, leave that to Tagg'.''

A moment later he swore with fervor and fluency as a bulky shape came from below, swerved aside with surprising grace as the Bull came lumbering past, then followed the mate up the ladder to the quarterdeck. ''If this an't trouble. . . .''

As he stepped onto the quarterdeck, Camnor Heslin was furious but not showing it except in the stiffness of his bow. ''I thank you, good Master, for not disturbing my sleep.''

Serroi suppressed a smile. He was a foot taller and fatter than Hern had ever been, even at his plumpest, but he reminded her forceably of his ancestor; it might have been the Domnor speaking right then, with that acerbic bite in words polite on the surface.

Am'litho grunted. ''Any good with those?'' He nodded at the sword the Vorbescar had strapped on, the handgun holstered beside it.

''When I wear decorations, Master, they're ribbons, not steel.''

''Then you'd best get down on deck and get ready to use 'em.'' He grabbed the Bull's arm, pulled him close, and began talking to him in a rumbling undertone, his words coming so fast they blurred into each other.

Camnor Heslin snorted and stalked down the ladder. Adlayr followed with a grin, mocking the Vorbescar's walk with a cheerful insouciance that brought a chuckle from Zasya as she drifted across to join Serroi at the rail.

Serroi wrapped her hands around the smooth polished wood, steadying herself as she concentrated on the outriggers, trying to pin the center of that vortex of magepower that was circling the ship.

Serroi sighed and opened her eyes. "That one." She pointed, shifting her finger as the outrigger passed along an arc of its tight spiral. "You see the lump crouched over that firebowl? He's the windsnuffer."

Zasya smoothed her hand along the stock of the longgun in an absentminded caress. "Find a place to hang on, Healer."

Serroi nodded and moved away.

The quarterdeck had cleared while she was in search, the crewmen following Heslin, Adlayr, and the mate to the main deck. Only Am'litho was left; he stood, fists on hips, watching her.

"Ready," she said.

"As are we. Meie," he called, his voice low and tense. "Do it!"

Zasya Meyers settled herself, her booted feet a short distance apart, her narrow body responsive as spring steel, finding the heart of the ship's sluggish wallow. Her hand tightened in slow, controlled increments.

A hard spitting sound, muffled by the tortured air.

In the outrigger the hunched figure was flung back and a howl of consternation and rage went up from the Krymen rowing him, then from the Krymen in the other boats.

The suddenly released wind shrieked in a whirl about them all, tossing the outriggers like dead leaves, heeling the *Wanda* over one side, then the other, sending her bow down, stern down, sending Serroi rolling from rail to rail like an off-center skittle until she finally managed to wrap her arms about a stanchion and hold on through the worst of the bucking.

And all the while Zasya rode the bounding deck as

if she grew there, wholly intent on what she was doing, squeezing off one shot after another, emptying
one outrigger, turning on the next, shot after shot,
each timed to the sway of the deck and the targets of
opportunity, shifting clips so smoothly there was no
gap in the steady crack-crack.

Despite the tossing of the sea, the outriggers came
slicing at them, the arms of the rowers moving like
parts of a machine, taking great bites of the water, a
Kryman standing at each mast, waiting, a pod of
spears by his hand.

The *Wanda*'s bow catter clunked, thrummed,
dropped a missile to one side of the high carved bow
of a canoe; when it hit the water, it burst and burned
with an evil greenish fire. More of the missiles flew
from the other catters, getting the range better, though
they were slow and clumsy at best. Two outriggers fell
to the umdums, two more were grazed and left with
fires clinging to the wood, eating at it, fires that the
rowers didn't attempt to put out.

In the shrouds Jy and Herks were loosing bolt after
bolt, getting some hits despite the wild swaying of the
masts, shouting the count so Am'litho would hear and
pay their bonus.

The spearmen snatched spears from the pods and
hurled them at the crew and the quarterdeck.

Herks shrieked and fell, hitting the deck near Zasya,
who took notice of him but went on shooting since
there was nothing she could do. She concentrated on
the spearmen, leaving Adlayr and the crew to take
out the rowers.

Serroi let go of the stanchion, crawled on hands and
knees to the man's side. When she touched his neck,
she felt a pulse under her fingers. "Zas," she yelled,
"leave that a moment, help me."

The meie grunted, turned, sliding her arm through the longgun's sling. "What you need?"

"I'll lift him. Push the spear through so I can break off the point."

Zasya raised thin blonde brows. "Hurry," she said, "another breath or two and they're on us."

Serroi ignored that, rolled the man on his side, and held him while the meie gripped the spear. Zasya took a deep breath, pressed the shaft down so the point would be more likely to miss vital organs and shoved.

"That's enough."

Zasya grimaced. "More than enough," she said. "Yeuch!" She rubbed her hands on her sides, then swung back to the rail, unslinging the longgun and slapping a new clip home.

Serroi concentrated, drew strength from sea and wind into her hands, broke the jagged point loose and let Herks fall back. She pulled the shaft free, pressed her hands over the spurting blood and time stopped for her.

Blood welled out, covering hands and wrists with red, then it stopped, then warmth flowed out of her hands into the body; they sank into the flesh, her body sucked strength from the sea, used it to make new flesh, new blood. As the wound repaired itself, layer by layer, her hands emerged, glowing, translucent green glass with no blood on them.

When the glow faded, she looked up into confusion. Krymen were swarming over the rail, their painted faces contorted with hate for those who'd killed or maimed so many of them. One of them drew back his spear to skewer her—then fell, his head exploding as Zasya saw what was happening and put a bullet in it.

An immense black sicamar roared, leapt among the Krymen slashing with claws and teeth, his pantherish body avoiding knives and spears as if the attackers waded through quicksand.

Camnor Heslin thrust his sword into a Kryman's throat, slapped aside a spear, kicked another Kryman in the groin as he wrenched his sword free. He slashed the edge across the downed Kry's throat and went after the next.

Clip empty, no time for reloading, Zasya had her sword out; she knocked a spear aside, turned the sword in its arc, and severed the hand from its arm.

Am'litho and the Bull fought together, roaring Fenekel curses, lashing out with cutlasses, fists, heads, feet.

Serroi slapped Herk's face, got him onto his feet and hauled him toward the quarterdeck's ladder; she got him down to the deck, stuffed him under the ladder, out of the way of the fighting; she squatted beside him, shuddering with the pain/rage/fear that swirled around her.

Shouts from the shrouds brought her head up.

A swarm of Silkars came suddenly over the rail, their bronze knives slicing Kry flesh as if it were butter.

In minutes the last of the Krymen was dumped over the side, dead from a dozen cuts.

The Silkars followed except for one, the tallest and brightest of them all, scaled like a viper and green as the new leaves of spring. He wore a linked belt of beaten bronze with a bronze knife clipped to it, a short leather kilt, and a heavy bronze medallion on a chain about his neck. He stared a long moment at Serroi, his glowing golden eyes moving from her face to her hands and back, then he took the knife from his belt, the blade clotted with Kry blood, turned the hilt and thrust it at her.

Serroi hesitated.

He waited with the sea's patience.

She sighed and touched the hilt.

He smiled, clipped the knife back, and went over the side.

Serroi combed her fingers through her hair. "Saaa, silkars live long."

Am'litho roared, his laughter filling the hollow of the sky. "Old friend?" he said when he'd sobered enough to speak.

"I think so."

"I thought I knew you, Healer, now I'm sure of it. The father of my father's father was one Olambaro whom you may remember." He grinned at her, his eyes squeezed to slits above chunky cheekbones. "A grand teller of tales."

"So it seems."

"Pho! I'll say nothing till I, too, have grandchildren, if so you wish, Healer."

"Maiden bless, it would be more comfortable for me." She lowered herself onto a step of the ladder. "You've a slash on your arm, Master. Give it here, then send the rest of the wounded to me."

> > < <

When Serroi settled to sleep, her body aching, her mind troubled, the fetch walked in her dreams again.

Calling her.

She knew it.

Somehow that thing owed its life to her.

The thought horrified her.

Her mouth moved in a silent scream.

Go away.

Leave me alone.

Go away.

She could feel those bony fingers scrabbling at her. She tried to thrust the thing away, but it wouldn't go, it slobbered at her, cried to her.

MOTHTHERRR—DON'T DENY ME—DON'T PUSH ME AWAY—DON'T LEAVE ME—MOTHTH-ERRRRRRR. . . .

2. Assassin

Treshteny Falladin walked in her garden, circled a fire built on that spot a thousand thousand years ago, before Dander was even a dream; the shadowy figures that bent over it looked up, eyes wide as if they saw her. She lifted a hand, gave them her blessing, then chirruped to a crimson jesser chick who spread his newly furred wings and opened wide his leathery beak, awking for food; he wouldn't be hatched for years yet and the tree he sat in was a seedling by her foot, barely a hand's width high. She saw them both, or rather she saw a palimpsest of trees, translucent at the edges, blowing variously in winds that were and would be. She blessed the jesser and passed on.

Like the tree, her nurse, the nurse Peylar who walked beside her, was a multilayered vision, fetus, toddler, teen and woman, crone and corpse, sometimes simply that, sometimes exploding in an infinite variety of might-have-been, could-still-be.

When the would-be ghosts crowded too thickly about her, Treshteny rounded her shoulders, folded her arms tight about herself, and whimpered; this day the throng went quickly away each time it appeared and she strolled on, blessing things that were and were-not.

She stopped suddenly, her body jolting as waves of premonition hammered at her.

The nurse caught her by the shoulders, pushed down

until she was kneeling, then held her hands and called for help, her voice multiplied to a clashing carillon of sound.

The Marn's own Healer Bozhka Sekan came at a heavy trot, knelt beside her. "Say," she said, her voice low and firm.

The word came whole into Treshteny's ears; it was a pole she clung to. "Boom," she whispered. "Fire and force. Boom. Old woman flies in pieces, Mask wheels away. Young woman . . . hair . . . crinkled fire . . . flies . . . she flies . . . she flies . . . she falllls . . . she breathes . . . she dies . . . she dies not . . . she breathes . . . she dies . . . . she breathes . . . woman . . . meie . . . not-meie . . . healer . . . touches her . . . hands on her . . . green hands shining . . . she lives . . . she lies . . . she dies . . . alone . . . moans . . . blood . . . boom. . . ."

Hands under her, carrying her. . . .

What she called premoaning dried up the ghosts but left her so depleted that she couldn't take any pleasure in living a single line for the brief time allowed her.

The nurse bathed her hands and face with damp cloths, then undressed her and laid her on the daybed, drew a knitted coverlet over her, and tucked it in.

A man's voice: Anything new?

Bozhka Sekan's voice: The same vision with this difference, the Marn dies without any alternative, but the Dedach lives if the meie healer is there.

Man: Any better idea of where or when?

Bozhka Sekan: Nik for where. When: Possibly after the healer gets here. Might be two different times. The Dedach dies if it's before she comes, lives if it's after she's here.

Man: Will you tell the Marn?

Bozhka Sekan: Yes. She's faced death and accepted

it from the thing that's eating her; she won't be broken by a sooner, quicker end.

Ansila Vos the Marn went walking in her favorite garden on a golden afternoon when the bees were humming from flower to flower and moth-sprite childings swung on gossamer webstrands among the crooked branches of the broshka trees.

She walked without obvious pain or stiffness, but with a slow care that was a more subtle testament to her age and infirmity. And she wore the Mask of Marn, the ancient ivory shell carved and painted to imitate life with a certain stylized perfection, born at Cadander's birth, Cadander's Soul. And she wore a wig of braided gold wire, very fine wire, almost as fine as real hair. When she was young and filled with potency and stamina, the despair of her counselors and the wall against which the greedier of her merchants beat, she ran about like a wild thing and left the Mask and the wig for ceremony, but those days were long past and now she found the Mask a convenience that minded her face for her and left her free to think and act.

She walked alone through the garden, having commanded that it seem so. Her maids and her guards waited behind the carved wooden screens set up at intervals to maintain the illusion of her solitude. They had scented cloths and ivory fans, wine chilling in a sunken basin fed with water from an artesian well cold enough to bring on chilblains, hot cha, kava, hot chocolate, and piles of little cakes. And they had shawls, mirrors, clothbrushes, perfumes, needles and thread. Everything was there to maintain the perfect surface. And everything hidden.

The Marnhidda Vos walked a while among the fountains and the sweet-smelling flowers, watching the butterflies flutter from bloom to bloom, listening to

the hum of the bees and the varied songs of the skarivas, the modaries, the v'lashers that spent their summers here, nesting in the fruit trees and the conifers,
walked until she grew tired.

Over her shoulder, she said, "Tingajil, sing for me.
Sluzha, bring me my chair and my chocolatier."

She stood very straight though her knees were shaking and behind the Mask her face was drained of color;
she'd pushed herself too far, she knew it, but she didn't
really regret it. It was one of the few games she had
left, this flirting with discovery. She was dying, but
only she and her healer knew and Bozhka Sekan swallowed secrets like a well.

The Marn Maid Sluzha bustled her forces forward
with the chair, the elbow table of carved cherdva wood,
the chocolate urn, and the two-handed goblet with the
glass tube that would pass between the parted lips of
the Mask. They placed the chair where she pointed,
waited for her to settle herself, then brought the table
and put it where she could reach it easily. Sluzha
shooed the other maids away, poured chocolate into a
small silver cup and drank it down, then stood with
her hands folded on her solid round belly for the pre-
scribed fifty heartbeats. Then she filled the goblet,
bowed and backed away, vanishing behind a screen.

Tingajil came with her lute and dropped gracefully
on the prickly brown mat of old needles spread beneath a sosbra tree, her black singer's robe stark
against a broad patch of zhulas, their flowers yellow
as the springtime sun, yellow as her own bright hair.

As the singer plucked the strings to tune the lute,
her head bent down, her face rapt, Marnhidda Vos
sipped at her chocolate and smiled behind the Mask
in gentle appreciation of the total artifice of the per-
formance, the scene planned to the last fold of heavy
black silk draped over a fine white arm.

Another singer might ask Marnhidda Vos what she wished to hear, but Tingajil was where she was because she was adept at reading moods. Sometimes Marnhidda Vos wondered if this were intelligence or merely magic, but she liked the result; the song the singer gave her always matched her humor and never probed so deeply as to be embarrassing or painful.

This time it was a slow and melancholy tune and the words were sweetly sad. "Memory's wings," Tingajil sang, her rich bright voice filling the garden. . . .

> *Memory's wings beat in my head*
> *   Sorrow sorrow whispering*
> *Love's glory's sweet but soon it's fled*
> *   Morrow's dulcet lute unstring.*

> *See me clad in winter white*
> *My harp is mute, my heart's took flight*
> *My love his trust has broken quite*
> *   He lay him down at a jiny's side.*
> *   In a jiny's bed he's gone to bide.*

> *Memory's wings beat in my head*
> *   Sorrow sorrow whispering*
> *Love's glory's sweet but soon it's fled:*
> *   Morrow's dulcet lute unstring.*

> *I shall nest with the skarva's child*
> *Drest in rags, my hair gone wild. . . .*

Surrounded by commotion and protest as she almost always was, K'vestmilly Vos came striding around a clump of cherny flowers as violently red as the energy she exuded and the explosion of copper hair that sprang from the pale freckled face with its hawk's nose and hatchet contours. Marnhidda Vos' daughter had never been pretty, not even as a child, but she had much of her mother's force and all her mother's charm when she chose to exert it.

Some years ago, when she still cared passionately about Family Vos and Cadander, there were times when Marnhidda Vos despaired because the girl seemed to have no common sense at all. She was bright enough, but forever tumbling into muddles and aggravations that a moment's thought would have prevented.

Bozhka Sekan was the only one she spoke to of her worries and the old woman had hugged her knees, rocked back and forth, and nearly swallowed her tongue she was laughing so hard. I see you've forgot, she said. Forgot what, Marnhidda Vos asked. Bozhka Sekan ignored the annoyance prickling in her ruler's voice. She coughed to clear her throat, shook her head. How did you learn your own wisdom, dama? You were, perhaps, not quite so silly as K'vestmilly, but I would not swear to it. Do you remember during the Slan Houba in your nineteenth Spring when you flew so high on techka mushrooms that you. . . . And Marnhidda Vos held up her hands to stop the tale. For years after that whenever she saw a techka she was hard put not to blush. You score that point, she said. But at least I never made the same mistake twice. K'milly. . . . Bozhka Sekan laughed again. Would you rather leave your people a delicate blossom wrapped in cotton wool who has no notion of how life can bite one's backside? Zdra zdra, Marnhidda Vos said then, but when will she learn the limitations of power and the games she'll have to play to maintain it? Again Bozhka Sekan shook her graying head. She'll learn fast as you learned, Sila, or she won't and Marn and Mask will move to another line.

Now with death so close, Marnhidda Vos watched with detachment as her daughter erupted into the peaceful garden, shattering that peace without a second thought.

K'vestmilly stopped in front of her, scowling at the Mask she made no secret of hating. "I went to the mews and my jessers are gone. All of them! The Keeper said you did it. Why?"

"Because you are my Heir, my only child, and I don't want to lose you." To stop the words she saw trembling on her daughter's lips, she lifted a fine white hand, still lovely in its shape despite the erosion of the flesh beneath the skin. "It isn't your fault or mine, K'milly, that belongs to the times we live in. I'm a target of these shadows, so are you. Would you swear to leave your birds bemewed? Nik, and if you did, I wouldn't believe you." Her hand turned, expressing what her hidden face could not. "The birds are being cared for. When this is over, they'll be brought back." Some of her weariness seeped into her words and K'vestmilly heard it.

There was a roughness in her voice when she spoke, an anger that was no longer focused on her mother. "Put a boot in Jestranos' backside, Marn. If he can't find the plotters, get someone who can."

The silence that followed while Marnhidda Vos dealt with her impatience and weariness was broken by faint rustles and a busy snip-snip as a small gray man moved around the end zhula bush, clipping off dead leaves and withered flowers, so intent on his business he didn't seem to realize where he was.

"It is a more difficult situation than you realize, K'milly. I'd be a fool to cast aside years of experience and loyalty. . . ." A flash of gray caught her eye. "Who is that? Why is he here?"

The gardener straightened, stared at her, bewildered, his mouth dropping open, the color draining from his face as he began to realize what he'd done. Then his eyes lost all expression, his face sagged on the bones. He dropped the secateurs, reached into his shirt, and brought out a shortgun.

Shrieking outrage, K'vestmilly leapt at him, putting her body between him and her mother, her hands crooked into claws. He managed to get off two wild shots before she wrenched the shortgun from him; then, his eyes turning back in his head until only the white showed, he went limp and collapsed at her feet.

Her face ashen with rage, a line of blood slanting across her temple, K'vestmilly was about to put a bullet through his brain when Marnhidda Vos called out, "Wait. Don't be a fool, we need to question him."

"Saaa. . . ." It was a long hiss of disappointment, but K'vestmilly stepped back, handing the shortgun to one of the guards who had come rushing from behind the screens when they heard the shots. Lips pressed into a thin line, she stalked to her mother and stood scowling down at her. "Lot of use those guards were." She blinked as a drop of blood trickled into her eye, drew her fingertips along the scratch and stared at the red stain on them.

"Here, Dedach, it is brandy, sit you down and drink it." The singer Tingajil held out a glass half-filled with a dark amber liquid; when K'vestmilly glared at her from narrowed eyes, she smiled, poured a little of the brandy into the hollow of her palm and tilted it into her mouth, proffered the glass again when the fifty heartbeats were done.

Fighting a weariness that seemed to melt her bones, Marnhidda Vos locked her fingers together, drew a deep breath. "That was well done, Tingajil."

The garden dissolved into chaos around them, more guards rushing in, beating the bushes to see if they could flush another assassin. Treddek Prime Tecozar Nov came striding in with his clutch of aides; their notebooks out and stylos busy, they trotted after him as he circled first round Marnhidda Vos, held off by her daughter and her healer who'd just arrived, then round the abject figure of the assassin who lay without moving on the needles, barely breathing, his eyes glazed, a thread of drool oozing from his mouth.

Ignoring the angry, hostile stare of K'vestmilly Vos, the Inquisitor Jestranos Oram planted himself before Marnhidda Vos. After a perfunctory bow, he said, "You'd best go in and leave this to us, O Marn. I expect to learn nothing here. This isn't the first we've taken alive." He shrugged. "If you can call it alive."

K'vestmilly stirred, but kept silent as the Marn caught her by the wrist. She freed herself, took her mother's hand, and waited.

"I will stay," Marnhidda Vos said. "Send these other idiots away. You know as well as I do there's no danger now."

"Neither of us knows that, O Marn." He turned, surveyed the garden. "But I doubt a songbird will suddenly turn feral. Tratch," he called. "Clear the garden. Tecozar Treddek Nov, we appreciate your concern, but at the moment there's nothing you can do here, so. . . ."

"Tecozar Nov, go home," Marnhidda Vos said. "I'll speak with you tomorrow; right now we must leave this business to those learnéd in such things."

The Treddek Prime scowled at Jestranos Oram, but the Marn had spoken and he couldn't ignore that. He bowed, called his aides to him, and stalked out.

Marnhidda Vos laughed, a faint whuffing muffled further by the Marn Mask. "I hope you have copious files on him, Jes. He won't be liking you the next few months."

"He never has, dama. Vasyly, where's that shortgun? Get busy on it now, see if you can have more luck tracing this one."

Vasyly was a short plump man with a face like a

dishclout left to dry in the sun. He dropped the short-gun into a canvas bag, touched his brow, and left.

Jestranos Oram swung back to face the Marn. "I'll have my men go over his clothing later, and everything in his rooms to see what connections they can pry out. I've already had the family brought in, Preets is doing the first questioning. Krajak is working his warren, trying to discover any contacts."

"Then you know who he is?"

"One of your guards recognized him right away, O Marn. A Nerod called Vytor Synovin. He's been a gardener here in the Pevranamist since he was a boy, thirty years, the guard said. A quiet type, not very bright, but a good worker."

"Saaa, is anyone safe?"

"I don't know, O Marn." He turned to Bozhka Sekan. "Healer, if things go as before, the moment we begin probing that man, he'll die. Is there anything you can do to prevent that?"

Bozhka Sekan walked to the man, stood looking down at him. She held out a hand to one of the guards; he took it and eased her onto her knees. She reached out to touch the gardener.

"Best not, Healer."

"Pek! How am I supposed to . . . never mind, we do with what we have." She bent close to him, sniffed at his nose, his mouth, hovered over him for several moments longer, then held out her hand again. The guard hauled her onto her feet and a maid came scuttling from behind a screen to brush off her skirt. "Send me his body after he's dead, perhaps I can tell you more then. For what it's worth, I suspect there's no poison here, no drug, only a mage curse." She scratched at a shaggy gray brow. "Telling him to die if he's questioned in any way. Telling him with Power Words that I have no way of countering. No herb or physic can touch that. The next one you catch, and I'm sure there'll be another, if you can find an honest mage, though I've not heard of any in Dander or Calanda, have him there. Or her."

The Mask on the table beside her, Marnhidda Vos lay on her daybed, bundled into a loose silk robe with a wool lace blanket over her legs, moistened pads on her eyes, Sluzha the maid brushing the still abundant white hair that hung over the back. Bozhka Sekan stood at a table by the window whipping eggs, milk, and honey with a thick red gel from a small jar. K'vestmilly Vos fidgeted on a low stool by her mother's feet, tying knot after knot in a length of cord.

"Thank you, Sluzha, that'll be enough for now."

When the door closed after the maid, Marnhidda Vos said, "K'milly, I've been lazy for months now and I've let you slide with the rest. There are things you need to know."

Bozhka Sekan brought the drink she'd made, closed the Marn's hand around the glass. 'Drink this, Sila, there's no need to rush. You've survived again, Maiden bless K'vestmilly's quick hands, so don't be in a hurry to kill yourself."

Marnhidda Vos took the pads off her eyes, raised herself, then leaned back on the pillows Bozhka tucked behind her shoulders. "Zdra zdra, Bozhkina, hold your fuss. And bring me the dispatch box on the bed-table." She sipped at the drink, wrinkled her nose. "No matter what you do with that tonic, the undertaste always stays."

Bozhka's voice came from the other room. "And I keep telling you the taint is in your tongue, not my posset." She came back with a small box covered with steel mesh. "This is what you wanted?"

"Yes." She held out the half-empty glass, a brief wry curl to her lip that said what she'd taken was all she could manage and she'd appreciate silence on the subject. She took the box on her knees, used a key she wore on a long chain about her neck to open it.

K'vestmilly stirred, leaned forward, her thin red brows drawn down. "Mother. . . ."

"Patience, daughter." Marnhidda laughed, the faint whuffle that barely agitated her breath. She took two folded papers from the little heap, laid them beside her on the chair, and locked the box again. "When the pattern of these attacks became clear . . . nik, that's not right, when I saw there was a pattern, not just random eruptions. . . ." She coughed and Bozhka brought her a glass of water which she sipped at and set aside. "I sent this . . ." She lifted the first paper, held it out, then settled back as K'vestmilly took it. ". . . by a courier I trusted. Read it. Silently. I know what it says."

The paper crackled as K'vestmilly spread it on her knee; after a minute she looked up. "Communicators?"

"The Biserica has developed more than guns. Oram has been after me for months to import those things, the Treddekkap wouldn't hear of spending that much money, so I dipped into the Marn's Purse. Spojjin Treddeks, now I'll have to figure a way of squeezing the money out of them to replace what I've spent. Zdra zdra, it's worth it, I suppose. The need is obvious. Oram's got agents in Govaritil and as far down as Shimzely, but it takes forever to hear from them. Despite that, he's found out much more than you know. Talk to him, K'milly. I'll make sure he answers you. Go on reading."

A few breaths later, K'vestmilly looked up again, startled. "Treshteny? But she's crazy. I mean, she has fits, sees things that aren't there and doesn't even know what year she's living in. I thought she was just one of your charities."

Marnhidda Vos smiled and sipped at the water. "I'll explain later. Finish the letter. Then take the answer . . ." she touched the other paper, ". . . and read that."

K'vestmilly folded the second letter and set it on the table with the other. "Who else knows about this?"

"At the Biserica, the Prieti Meien Nischal Tay. She's told some of it to the companions she's chosen to send me, left the rest for me. As you can see from her letter, she's given a story of sorts to the Council of the Mijloc—it seems that's necessary now that they assert their control over the Valley—something about complicated negotiations around your marriage, K'milly, and a neutral party to handle details. It's nonsense, of course, but clever nonsense." Her eyes closed. "They may have believed it but they're still sending us a Vorbescar. That's what they call him, Agent of the Council; in truth he's a spy, sent to keep an eye on us. He'll be a friendly spy, though, and a clever one." She chuckled again, a faint whuffle quickly gone. "Clever is probably an understatement, K'milly. He's a Heslin, which means he can see round corners that aren't even there. We can use that kind of mind."

"Prak, so we get a few meien, a tricky spy, and some fancy toys. I don't understand where you're aiming, Marn."

Bozhka Sekan took the glass from Marnhidda Vos' slack fingers, stood behind her stroking her temples. "Let me explain, Sila. If I mistake myself, correct me, otherwise, just listen. And you listen, Dedach.

"Treshteny is not insane, she's just different. Very different. Disturbing to people. She reads might-be as easily as you read words, K'milly, as easily as you read those letters. It was what drove her to take to her bed,

I think, seeing every day split into overlapping ghosts
of what's real, what was, and what might be, if real
has any true meaning and after listening to her a while
you begin to doubt it . . . Pek! I know, I ramble. Let's
see, where was I? Ah! yes. Treshteny said that if the
Company of meien and others come here, Cadander
may survive or it may not, but it certainly will not if
they do not come. Two years ago, before any of this
started, she said a Dark Soul rises, the Dancer rises,
pregnant with evil, consort of Death herself perhaps,
laying hands on men to steal their wills from them and
talk them out of living. What the Dancer is or who she
can't or won't say. There will be death and blood and
change and this Dark One will dance the stars from
the sky and play with them like a cat with an anise
ball. Zdra zdra, Dedach, I know how it sounds, but
Treshteny sees true, though she never sees single, you
have to untangle the mess and hope you've found the
right strand. The Marn is good at that, Oram, too. Me,
I'm never sure what's the right thing.''

Marnhidda Vos chuckled again. ''I would have said
it in one tenth the words, Bozhkina.'' She closed her
eyes, sighed as the healer's touch soothed away some
of the aches that beset her these days. ''The companions from the Biserica should be here by the end of
the month. I'll leave them to you, daughter.''

K'vestmilly leaned toward her, her hands clenched
to fists, her face strained with anxiety. ''What are you
saying? What did that woman tell you?''

''That, daughter, is the Marn's affair. We won't discuss it, now or later. Just you use our visitors wisely
and see that we have an ambitious mage at the stran-
gling post before the year is out.''

3. Memories and Life Tales

"You're changed, Serroi."

"You're dangerous, Serroi."

She sat on the bench in the Shawar pit in the Cavern deep beneath the Biserica, looking up at the arc of veiled women, hearing the sadness in their voices, angry because the Shawar owed her their lives and their Biserica. It was theirs now, no longer hers. "Why am I dangerous? What have I done?"

"Nothing, Serroi, nothing but be what you are."

"You draw an Evil toward us, Serroi."

"You disturb us, Serroi."

"You're talking about the dreams. They're only dreams," she said, a grinding ache in her entrails. "Stop them. Shut them away from me."

"We can't, Serroi."

"The Sender of the Dreams is too strong for us, Serroi."

"Little less than a god, Serroi."

"With the mind of a child, Serroi."

"With the hungers of a child, Serroi."

"Willing to swallow the world to reach you, Serroi."

*"If you leave, we can keep the Valley safe,
Serroi."*
"For a while. Only a while, Serroi."
"Whatever you do, be careful, Serroi."
"The Sender is not sane, Serroi."
"It can turn on you at any moment, Serroi."
"For something you do or don't do, Serroi."
*"We have determined the Sender's main
pressure point on this continent, Serroi."*
*"It can't touch us, or do more than plague you
with the dreams, Serroi."*
*"It will destroy everything between It and us so
it can reach you, Serroi."*
"It is insane, Serroi."
"And terribly powerful, Serroi."

Serroi stood at the *Wanda*'s bow watching silkar children playing in the bow curls and thinking about this
journey and the one she'd taken with Hern two centuries before. They were a lot alike. Yael-mri had found
a task for her, a quest without much hope to it, but
one that would rid the Valley of her and Hern; they
were irritants to the Shawar and trouble for the meien.
*I'm an irritant again. And I make people nervous. They
liked me when I was a tree. I was safe. A legend they
could make sad songs about. If they knew what the
Shawar knew. . . .* She shivered. *Nischal Tay was delighted to be rid of me. Did the Shawar tell her about
the Sender? They made me swear to say nothing. So
much I don't know. What you don't know can kill you.
Would I mind?* She closed her eyes, lifted her face to
the sun and the wind. *I can't think of dying on a day
like this. Or complications and misery. It's too good
to be here.*

* * *

''Dragons fly.'' It was a shout from the lookout riding the mast.

Serroi glanced up, smiled in sudden delight, her worries banished for the moment.

A shimmering form drifted above the ship, a glass dragon undulating in vast loops, delicately etched against the clear blue of the sky. More of the giants floated past, singing intricate, silent chorales of colored light, the faceted bodies pulsing with light, winding about each other in knots of celebration.

''They're honoring your return, Healer.''

Serroi turned her head.

Zasya Myers stood a half step behind her, cradling a shimmer in her arms. ''Ildas knew you before I did.'' She scratched at the shimmer, which pulsed as if it purred. ''You'll remember Tuli Gradin from the war, she bore my father's grandfather. From the daughters of her line, the Fire-born chose me.''

''Myers . . . hmm . . . there was a man. . . .'' Serroi gazed up at the glass dragons dancing in shades of ruby and amethyst. ''Georgia Myers . . . an Incomer.''

''Yes.'' Zasya blinked dark blue eyes, looked past Serroi at a silkar girl leaping in long arcs away from the ship, her green hair flowing like weed. ''The story goes that Bunmama Tuli was out scouting for the Council when she ran into Georgia Myers who'd quarreled with the woman he usually lived with. They came together just in time to face the rogue Sleykyn she was tracing. . . .'' She chuckled. ''You knew Bunmama, you can imagine how ticked she was at being discovered, and it didn't help when the Sleykyn turned and came at them.''

The dragons caught the sun's light and spun gold from its rays, ocher and amber, saffron and citrine, topaz and cream and a thousand other yellows which had never had a name.

"On Maidenfete Vigils," Zasya said, "there's always someone in the family to tell the story of the fight, it goes on and on as long as the speaker's imagination holds out. Vai, I'll leave that part to your imagination. They were pretty well chewed to rags by the time the Sleykyn was finally dead and they had to lay up until they could travel again." She grinned. "You know mijlocim, this is the part of the story they don't tell aloud.

The dragons paled until all the colors were absorbed into an icy white, pure and unshadowed. Diamond dragons they were, too bright for human eyes.

"A-ric," Zasya said, "some months later, after they'd gone their separate ways, Bunmama found she was pregnant. She decided to keep the baby, and when he was told about the child, Georgia insisted on giving it his name, but he was as little enthused about getting back together as she was, so they wed, registered, divorced, and never saw each other again. That isn't the end the storytellers give you, but it's the truth. Ildas told me and he should know."

The glass dragons ended their silent song and blew away to the north.

Zasya sighed as they vanished in the clouds; she looked around, shook her head. "It's like they took brightness with them."

When the *Wanda* stopped at Paristo, Adlayr Ryan-Turriy came to talk to her. "The Ajjin Turriy lives in my bones," he said. "What she knew, I know. When I was five, my mother cut flesh from her thigh and gave it to me to eat raw, saying, *you are my only and you must know.* She was barren after I was born, you see; ordinarily it would be daughters that got the flesh

and the lore, but she couldn't have any. So it was me
who got it. She died the next year and my father was
a difficult man with too many disappointments and a
heavy hand, so soon as I was old enough, I came away
to be gyes, I came where I would find a place to be
valued for what I am. You saw me fight as sicamar,
but I have two forms, not one. I can ride the wind and
scout for you in the shape of a trax with hanguli gas
sacs to lighten me so my wings can lift me. Only Nischal Tay knows that, and now you.''

Serroi was silent a moment, watching the busy traffic moving about the harbor. She smiled as she saw
Darmen moving from ship to ship in their tiny outriggers, trading swamp ivory, bulbs, and spices for the
thousand things they needed, from needles to spear
points. More memories, good ones this time. Crossing
the Dar, on a quest for the changeman who called himself Coyote. She turned round, hitched a hip on the
rail, and steadied herself by holding onto one of the
shrouds. ''I remember,'' she said. ''I remember them
both, the Ajjin and Havier Ryan.''

At Yallor Am'litho stood by the plank, bowed as
Camnor Heslin, Vorbescar of the Grand Council of the
Mijloc, stalked ashore, one of the sailors following,
laden with his cases and other gear. The Fenekel shipmaster put out his hand as Serroi started to leave. ''I
don't know the Prieti meien's arrangements, but in case
you need a name. . . .'' He took a small brownish
card from his sleeve. ''Chamgadin, Master of the Battatai, a man as honest as may be. Cousin of mine.
When you get to Shinka, show this to him. If he can't
carry you, he'll find you a ship where you won't be
robbed and dumped overboard.'' He took another
card. ''And here, in case you need a place to stay in
Yallor while you're fightin' the clerks for a seat on a

canal barge. Tatamai the Widow. She rents out rooms.
Cousin of mine. She won't cheat y' too much over the
price. You want to watch out for land zarks, Healer,
the Neck's their prowlin' ground and in Yallor they're
cruisin' every street 'n alley. And if y' come back this
way when y' Ward's done and I'm in Yallor, I'll take
y' as m' guest to Southport, cabin and found, free
as the air.''

Serroi turned from the window of the sitting room
to find Camnor standing in the doorway, watching her.
''I've always been curious about you,'' he said. ''My
father took me up on the cliff when I was seven. He
had me touch the lacewood; I must tell you, it felt like
any other tree and I was disappointed. Then we made
a fire and he brewed some cha and melted cheese over
some bread and he told about the great battle and the
trek you and Hern made to save the world.'' There
was a dry note in his voice, a touch of dislike that
surprised her. His resemblance to Hern kept getting
between them and she realized suddenly that she knew
nothing about Camnor Heslin. Who was not Hern. Who
was born in another time. Who had a different history.

She settled on the worn divan pushed up against the
wall next to the window. ''I was dreaming,'' she said,
''the long slow dreams of trees; there wasn't much of
me left to feel.''

He came into the room, found a chair, and sat facing
her. ''When I realized who you were, I was . . . annoyed. It seemed like a slap in the face of my Bunmama, the grand passion of Hern Heslin's life walking
into the room and looking at me from those big orange
eyes. A tiny thing, wouldn't come up to my first rib,
and odd, not pretty at all.''

Serroi chuckled, amused by his acerbic and unflat-
tering description. She was seeing Hern again, hearing

him; it was eerie, yet oddly comforting. "Grand passion, tsaaaa, what a fistful of nonsense. Hern never said any such thing, I'm sure of it."

"That's the way my father told it; a grand passion and a glorious fight. It's the kind of man my father was, that he believed it." He eased the tails of his coat over his bulging thighs, leaned forward, his hands on his knees. "When are you going to tell me the truth about this business?"

She didn't bother denying the implication in the question. "The Marn has always been a friend to the Biserica, she's hired meien, sent Cadander girls to us, sent money, too. You don't need telling that there's trouble in Cadander, you need even less to know what it is. Marnhidda Vos will give us the details when we get there. That's the truth, Camnor Heslin, do you want me to swear it?"

He lifted a hand from his knee, let it fall back. "There's a reason I asked, not simple curiosity."

"Yes?"

"The bureaucrats here are being peculiarly obstructive. I've been through here before and a discreet bribe or two was all it took to smooth out difficulties. There's a large difference between their usual malice and sluggishness and what I faced today. It's as if they'd been given orders not to let us through. Not to deny passage outright, they don't want to make trouble with the Mijloc or the Biserica, but to nibble at us, niggle and carp, find fault wherever they can, invent it where they can't. I played the game a while and then I came away before I added irritation to orders." He straightened. "So I ask again, Healer. Do you know anything I don't about what we're getting into? If I'm to be of any use to you, I need to know where to set my feet."

She looked down at the hands she was rubbing together, palm against palm. "Something's eating at Cadander, and Marnhidda Vos doesn't know what it is. There were few details in the letter Nischal Tay showed us. For obvious reasons.''

''Something?''

''Wasn't mentioned, either by name or implication.''

''Not much help.'' He grunted onto his feet. ''I shall go and see what strings I can pull.'' In the doorway, he turned. ''I've already picked up something that might be useful. The Galyeuk has a daughter with a withered leg. Could you fix that?''

''Yes, I think so. It's merely a matter of reshaping and regrowing.''

''Good. I won't play that card unless I have to. The Galyeuk is a greedy man.'' He went out, closing the door behind him with a soft, decisive click.

Serroi stood and stretched. *Not fair to you, is it, Hern's somethingson? I don't like this lying by omission, but I am Sealed to silence. And I don't see a reason yet to break that Seal.* She went to lean on the windowsill, smiling as she saw Adlayr and Zasya strolling toward the house, the fiery shimmer running before them. ''We're an odd lot, Maiden bless, we are. But I like you, meie, I like the gyes. And you, Camnor Heslin. You make me feel alive.''

MOTH TH THER. . . .

Coming when she was awake this time, the whisper echoing around the room chilled her out of her brief happiness and rewoke her anger.

''Go away,'' she muttered. ''Leave me alone.''

MOTH TH THER. . . .

She wasn't ready to confront the thing, not yet. She didn't know enough. She went back to the couch, curled up on it, her arms folded over her eyes.

4. Court Dancer

The drums throbbed, lute and flute wove melody around the beat and he danced—Treshtal the Dancer, Treshteny's twin, though he'd escaped the curse that struck her down.

He was slender and flexible as a river reed and far stronger than he looked; he had to be stronger to leap and seem to hang aloft as he did, to throw his partner into the air and catch her as he did—and make it all seem effortless as breathing.

Marnhidda Vos sat on the high bench, her daughter fidgeting beside her.

The Treddeks sat lower, their benches on two curved wings that spread on each side of the dais, seven women, six men, their families to the third degree spread around the room, come just to watch him dance—Treshtal the Dancer, Premier in all the Land.

He hated them, some more than others and with good reason, hated them all.

He swung Fialovy round and round, her feet tapping and kicking in the intricate steps of the dance. They parted, turned in exact accord in separate circles, heels clicking in unison against the fine floor the Marn had laid down for them.

When their heels came down on the sounding floor, he whispered a name as if it were a roach crushed under the metal tap. Achkolias Pen of Steel Point,

Calanda-south. Treddek Pen. Her youngest son raced
with his friends through a crowded street. Treshtal's
wife was knocked down, his daughter dead of a glancing blow from a hoof. Pan Pen, the Head of Family
Pen sent him the blood gift, he took it with a bow, his
eyes on the ground so the messenger would not read
the fury in them, a fury fed when his wife threw herself in the river two months later.

Their heels came down, he whispered a name. Druzhadlo Treddek Bar of Leatherworks, North Dander.
Pan Bar raised the rents in the Leatherworks warren
and cast Treshtal's father and mother into the street
when they could not squeeze more money from the
meager earnings of their struggling candy store. His
father cut his mother's throat and hanged himself. Bar
killed them, but there was no blood gift then or later.

Their heels crashed down and he whispered the
names, one after the other. Tecozar Treddek Nov, of
Shipper's Quarter, South Dander. His brother had got
Treshtal's cousin pregnant and denied the child. Zhal-
atzos Treddek Sko from the Glasshouses of East Calanda, Podriddar Treddek Zav from The Potteries,
Calanda's River District. Dukladny Treddek Vyk, The
Paperies, West Dander. Sabbanot Treddek Ano from
the Zemyadel. Marazhney Treddek Osk from the Merr-
zachar Foothills and the Mines in the east. Vilavinit
Treddek Ank from the Hayadel Harozh. Oppornay Tred-
dek Ker from the Hayadel Bezhval. Shapatnesh Treddek
Hal from the Foothills and Mines of the Travasherims
in the west. Eleven Treddeks from eleven Families, with
Vos on top to make an even dozen.

You will die, he sang to himself inside his head
where they couldn't hear it, matching his words to the
beat of the drums, the stamp of his feet. *You will die
the line-death, root and branch I will purge the land
of you. I and mine will do it. I am your Enemy. I have*

*the Power. Pan and Treddek, root and branch, I will
purge the land of you.*

He swung Fialovy high, ran with her—her arms out,
filmy draperies fluttering in the wind he made for her.
Tossed her into a gliding loop, caught her, stretched
her on the stage and leapt in wide circles about her,
riding his rage, soaring for the folk he hated with a
corrosive passion. Leap, arch, catch himself on his
hands, throw himself up, then down in an extravagant
split as the music rose to a crescendo, then died. He
rose, lifted Fialovy to her feet (though she needed help
as little as he, her muscles were steel wires); holding
hands they bowed as applause crashed around them.

5. Snags

The anteroom to the Burkam's Office of Petitions was filled with people squatting on the floor and leaning against the walls and columns with the patience of those who knew their turn wouldn't come for hours or perhaps days. As the Mushta moved through them, thumping his staff importantly on the stone flags to shift those who were in the way of his progress, they stared at him and the two he was escorting with the dumb resentment of weary beasts—resentment and resignation mixed, because this was just one more occasion when they saw money and importance buying precedence over patience and earned right.

Walking a half step behind Camnor Heslin, Serroi drew her cloak tight about her, careful not to show the white lining that marked her as a healer. Along with that anger and that resignation, there was sickness here, weariness, hunger, all plucking at her nerves. She kept her eyes on the floor and her mind on the admonitions given to every meie pair when they went to take their first Ward.

> Do not interfere with local custom, no matter how strange or abhorrent you find it; in your ignorance of local circumstance you will always do more harm than good.

If you must try mitigating some flagrant
injustice, do it invisibly if possible, or within the
play of custom; if you search hard enough,
you'll find a way.

If you can do nothing, leave.

She could see the paper the words were written on,
she could see Yael-mri's elegant forefinger pointing to
the line where she was expected to write her name,
the line just below her shieldmate Tayyan's scrawl.

Tayyan. Her lips moved with the name of her lover
and shieldmate, but it only evoked a wispy sad ghost
of a memory. That ancient hurt was gone, erased by
time and the newer griefs that had been painted over it.

The Mushta circled the Nametaker's desk and used
the end of his staff to tap with delicate restraint at a
door deeply recessed into the wall.

It was opened by a silent man in a narrow black robe
belted close to his body by a braided leather rope also
black. He stared at them a moment, then stepped aside.

The Mushta stood in the doorway, bowed deeply,
then intoned, "The Vorbescar Camnor Heslin, on detached service for the Grand Council of the Mijloc.
The Healer Serroi of the Biserica." He bowed again
and took a long step to one side, where he stood as
erect as his belly would allow, the staff placed pre-
cisely beside the small toe on his right foot and held,
stiffly vertical, beside him.

Camnor Heslin didn't wait for a summons from inside the room, but marched through the doorway with
the arrogance of a man who knows he must be welcome. Serroi followed, a small dark shadow in her
black cloak.

The Temmek Yasikov Garip kept writing with slow deliberation for several strokes of the stylo, then he set it down and leaned back in his chair, his hands flat on the desk. His black eyes flicked over Camnor Heslin, passed from him to Serroi. He frowned. "THIS is the Healer?"

The Vorbescar looked down his long nose. His bulk seemed no longer fat but mass, exuding so much authority that the Temmek automatically started to cringe—before he recalled their relative degrees of power and grew red in the face with anger he didn't quite dare express.

"Perhaps," Camnor Heslin said in a voice that would cut glass, "you'll explain to the Galyeuk that you weren't satisfied with the Healer's appearance and insulted her into leaving."

Without bothering to answer, the Temmek pushed his chair back and got to his feet. "Follow me." He rounded a screen and went through a door in the back wall, taking them into the Galyeuk's private quarters, through a maze of intersecting corridors and into a walled garden.

A pale-faced young girl, eleven or perhaps twelve years old sat on a bench by an intricate fountain, her hands knotted in her lap. Two attendants stood behind her, waiting in stolid silence to be told what to do.

"Search her." The Temmek put up his hand to stop Camnor Heslin's protest. "It is necessary, a command of the Galyeuk."

Serroi took off the cloak and dropped it to the ground. Over her shoulder, she said, "It is a sensible requirement, Vorbescar. As long as the searchers spare my dignity, I don't mind."

The search was mostly a matter of probing fingers and quickly over.

Satisfied, the Temmek left, taking Camnor Heslin with him.

Serroi spread her cloak on the ground, black side down and knelt on it. Hands resting lightly on her thighs, she smiled at the girl. "Will you tell me your name?"

"Zayura. Is it going to hurt much?" The girl's mouth trembled and she looked down at her clenched hands; she seemed younger in mind than her physical age, though Serroi found her rather hard to read. Even when she'd traveled as a meie, she hadn't had much contact with the enclosed daughters of the wealthy. "They always say it's not going to hurt and it always does. Tell me the truth, Healer. Please."

"No, it won't hurt. Might itch a little, that's all."

"Oh." It was a polite little syllable, totally devoid of belief. "Do you want me to take my dress off?"

"No." Serroi reached out, put a hand on each of the girl's knees. "Just sit still and be patient. Did you know that it was I who asked for you to be outside, in a garden?"

"Yes. My father said. Why?"

"Well, it's a beautiful day, the sun is bright, the breeze just cool enough to be comfortable, but that's only me pleasing myself. The real reason is my strength comes from the earth. You see my skin, I'm like a plant drinking milk from the breast of the Mother of us all. What I'm going to do is pass that milk into you, Zayura. Your body already knows its proper shape. A part of it forgot, that's all. I'm going to remind it and the Mother and I and you together will make the wrongness right. That's all, Zayura. Relax. It's already begun."

Hands glowing, her fingertips sank through the cloth and into the girl's flesh.

She closed her eyes, felt the wrongness in the left

leg, the withered muscles, the misshapen bones; using
the good leg as a pattern, she regrew muscle and
sinew, straightened the bone, strengthened it, reformed the sockets. It was more difficult than healing
a wound because the girl had a powerful, though unconscious, resistance to all manipulation, built up from
the countless bungling attempts to straighten and
lengthen the leg, the pain she'd been forced to endure,
the handling of her body which had bruised her soul
as well as her flesh. And she had gifts that it was
apparent she didn't know about, gifts that both fought
and helped the healing.

Serroi felt the heat leave the leg; the flesh under her
fingers was cool and healthy. She sighed, dropped her
hands onto her own thighs, and knelt, head drooping,
while earth power flowed up into her to replace what
she'd expended in the healing, filling her with that se-
ductive, almost addictive, warmth—that joy, that alive-
ness, that vibrancy which she got with every difficult
healing.

"Well." She lifted her head, opened her eyes.
"That's done. Be careful when you try to walk, Zayura. You're probably going to have to relearn how to
hold yourself."

"But . . ." The girl frowned. "You didn't DO anything."

"There's an easy way to decide if I'm playing games
with you. Look at your leg."

Zayura took hold of the soft white cotton of her long
skirt; her hands were shaking, the color was coming
and going in her face. She lifted the skirt slowly at
first, then snatched it up and stared.

The leg that had been withered and bent was fleshed
out now, and straight, a perfect match to the other.

Zayura reached down, touched her thigh, tentatively, as if she thought she might be dreaming what she saw—then she drove her thumb into the muscle and laughed aloud when she felt the pain. She pushed onto her feet and stood swaying a little as she sought for a new balance. With another laugh she flung out her arms and ran a few steps, stumbled and fell, then was up again, grass stains green splotches on the white of her skirt, up and running, awkwardly, unsteadily, but freely, with lengthening strides.

In among the plants tiny green and gold elvins coalesced from the air, danced and clapped their three-fingered hands, dashed into shadow and behind flowers when Serroi turned to look full at them, drawn by the tickling they made on her skin with their skittering thoughts and silent giggling. The others didn't seem to notice these newcomers to the garden, though the girl stopped and stared, then shook her head and went back to her play.

Serroi got to her feet, shook out the cloak, and draped it over her arm. She smiled at the mute maids watching anxiously as their charge ran in the sunlight with a child's grave joy, gaining grace with every step she took. "Zayura," she called. "That leg is new-made, it's not used to all that work. Come rest a while. If you keep running like that, tomorrow morning you'll be so sore, you'll think you have the old one back.'

Zayura stumbled and fell again, picked herself up and came more sedately back to Serroi. "I won't, will I?" Her face puckered with worry.

"No, of course not. Could you run on an illusion? But you'll find as you start learning to ride and dance, every time you use those new muscles, you'll ache a while. It's a natural thing. Ask your father."

Zayura's face went pinched and suddenly much older. Eyes down, she settled herself on the bench. "Of course," she said. "I will."

* * *

The Galyeuk was a lanky man, his coarse black hair loosely plaited into two braids that hung to his belt as he lounged in the massive audience chair. His face was deeply lined, there were dark pouches under dull black eyes that looked as if he hadn't laughed since he left his mother's breast. "You don't have the aspect of power," he said. He rubbed his thumb against one fingernail after another, pushing the skin back, his eyes fixed on Serroi.

She knew what he had in mind, put a hand on Camnor's arm when she thought he was going to say something; that rooster on his throne would react violently and permanently to a challenge from another male.

He glanced at her, nodded, the corners of his mouth twitching.

Maiden bless, he has Hern's quickness. It's so comfortable not to have to explain things, so useful when one can't explain. "If you will have your bureau issue our passes, O Galyeuk." Her voice was quiet, firm. "It's more than time we were leaving."

"Prieti Meien's g'blessed havin' you about the place," the Galyeuk said thoughtfully and popped a knuckle.

"The Prieti Meien finds me useful," she said. "My Talent is a sword with two edges. What I give I can also take." She curled her lips, spread her empty hands.

He stared at her for a long tense moment, without blinking, without moving a muscle of his face, then he closed his eyes. "I can see it would be hard to hold you where you didn't want to stay, but if someone offered you sufficient inducement?" He cracked an eye, raised a brow.

"I am content to serve the Biserica," she said. "It is home and hearth and family."

"Too bad, it would have been interesting, having

you about the place.'' He straightened in the chair, tugged on the bell rope hanging beside it. When the Temmek appeared, he said, ''Provide our friends here with the passes they need, arrange with the Kanalbureau to have a barge placed at their disposal, inform them that this is to be done as gift to my daughter.''

The moment the companions came aboard the *Pogasha* and settled in the narrow cabin, the rain came lashing down. The wind swept along the Neck, howling like a hungry soul, driving rain before it into nearly horizontal lines that beat monotonously against the walls and windows and made leaving the shelter of the cabin close to impossible.

In the face of that relentless storm, it took five days to make a three-day trip. By the time the companions stumbled out onto the wharves of Shinka, they were close to hating each other. And the bargemen were looking slantwise at them and making avert signs when they thought no one was watching.

Serroi huddled the cloak closer about her body, tucked her gear sac tighter under her arm, scraped rain from her face, and followed Camnor Heslin and the porter he'd hired, a wiry little man loaded down with his gear, using their bulk as a windbreak.

She wasn't happy about the way things were going. The Fetch was too strong and getting stronger—when they reached Cadander, what was it going to be like then? She began to understand why the Shawar were so frightened. *I will touch you like I touched Ser Noris, Fetch. I will stop you. . . .* She shivered at the strength of the revulsion that filled her at the thought. Ser Noris she'd half-loved. He'd been the only father she'd known since she was a child barely walking. This, though . . . it claimed it was her child . . . no!

". . . here . . . tavern. . . ." Camnor shouted, the wind snatching the words and blowing most of them away. He turned into a recess, shoved open a swing door, and led them into the smoky, odorous taproom that was mostly empty because it was only an hour or so past dawn.

Adlayr Ryan-Turriy pointed the porter to a table by the wall, slipped him a coin when he'd pushed their gear under it. "Have yourself a todda to keep the chill away." He pulled out a chair for Zasya Myers, then sat across from her.

Camnor marched to a table close to the fire, turned the chair so it faced the hearth, and dropped into it with a sigh that came up from his heels. Serroi settled across the table from him, her cloak draped over the back of the chair, her gear sac by her feet.

Having taken the measure of the group with a professional eye, the Host hurried to Camnor's side and hovered there, waiting for his order.

"You serve food here?"

"Plain food, Seref. Fried tarmas, fish hash, toast, butter, honey. To drink, cha and kava, poral juice, boiled milk."

"Splendid." Camnor beamed at the man and began ordering.

"Aaah, I do feel more myself." Camnor looked at the cup in his large hand, set it gently on the table as the door swung again and another group of men came in, shaking out their cloaks and complaining loudly as they crossed to the fire. "Still raining," he said.

Serroi folded her hands. "Something doesn't want us in Dander, I think."

"And you really don't know what?"

She shrugged, letting the movement lie for her.

"Mmp." He looked around at the room that was

filling up with wharfers, seamen, and noise. "This isn't the place to talk. . . ."

"There's nothing to talk about."

The corners of his wide mouth tucked in and his eyes twinkled at her. "You insult my invention, Serroi Healer, we could discuss the weather, speculate on the cycle of the moons, trade tastes in lovers, chacakes or edged weapons, denigrate politicians we have known. I could go on."

She chuckled. "Nay Vorbescar, that's more than enough. To say true, I think we can count on miserable weather and other attacks of the sly sort."

"What you're saying is, the Enemy hasn't the strength to kill us outright, but he's going to do his best to nibble us to death."

"Hasn't yet the strength."

"Yet?"

"Ildas says the Dark is getting thicker."

Camnor snorted. "The meie's imaginary pet. Mmp. Riddling admonitions about things we already know."

"Ildas is no illusion even if you can't see him, Camnor Heslin. He has his uses. . . ."

The Fireborn squealed a high, piercing call that had every sensitive in the room rubbing his ears, then he leapt like an arc of firelight from beside Zasya's elbow to land on the head of a man walking stiffly toward the fire.

"Hern," Serroi cried, "Watch. . . ."

The man swung round at the first word, a knife in his hand. He leapt at Camnor, caught him across the arm as the big man moved with surprising speed; on his feet, the chair crashing behind him, the Vorbescar kicked the man in the gut, then brought his fist down on his attacker's head as it came forward. The man collapsed at his feet.

Camnor swayed, his face paling. The effort it took

visible in the stiffness of his motions, he bent, jerked
the knife free and lifted it to the light. The blade was
stained with his blood and with a gray-green, gummy
mess. "Poison."

Adlayr Ryan-Turriy leapt from his chair, caught
Camnor Heslin as he toppled, eased him onto the floor.
Zasya moved the table aside so Serroi would have room
to work, set the lamp on the floor beside her, then
joined Adlayr and went on guard, shortgun in her
hand, head turning.

All this took only seconds, clicking smoothly into
place as if they'd practiced it for years, and was completed by the time Serroi was on her knees beside Camnor Heslin, fighting the hold of the poison, struggling
to transform it into something innocuous, Ildas coiled
on Camnor's chest, feeding her strength from the fire.

The Host pushed through the circle of staring, mut-
tering men, stopped as Halal growled. "What is this?
What's happening?"

Zasya Myers spoke, her voice in its deepest notes,
cutting through the mutter like a hot wire through ice.
"We are meie and gyes of the Biserica and one of our
number has been attacked with a poisoned knife."

"Why? What did you do?"

Zasya snorted. "What a stic! You saw us sitting here
peacefully eating your food and getting warm."

"Su halda, what I say is, take your quarrels somewhere else, meie, leave us our peace. Go on, git!"

"We'll go when the Healer's finished, so back off
and leave us to our business."

Camnor Heslin opened his eyes and looked up at
her, laughter dancing in them. "Hern?"

Ildas made a small spitting sound and backed off as
the lamp oozed translucent forms that mimicked his,
tiny mouse-sized fireborns who perched on the base a

moment, then went scampering for the hearth, one after the other as if each flicker of the burning oil birthed another of them.

"Idiot. On your feet. We're not welcome here any more."

He caught hold of the chair and pulled himself up, then stirred the attacker with the toe of his boot. "Dead?"

"Nay, between you and Ildas and whoever put the geas on him, the poor man's addled. He'll be out a while longer. We should leave; I don't want to be here when he wakes. He'll have friends." She looked at the silent, sullen crowd watching them. "And we have none here."

Camnor Heslin took two silver pieces from his belt, dropped them on the table. "That should more than cover what we've eaten," he told the scowling Host. He swept the others with a glance, stalked for the door.

Chamgadin stood under a tarp pulled over a stack of crates, sheltering from the rain and scowling as he watched the ladesmen streaming on and off his ship. He was a short wide man with a beard he wore twisted in thin long coils that reached to his breastbone and a scrubby little mustache more like a smear of ash than hair. "No no no," he bellowed. "I said the ones with the red paint go last. Put that down, you jugh." As the startled ladesman nearly dropped the barrel over wharfside, the Fenek's roar grew several degrees louder. "Ah Maaaas! If you put that in the water, I'll boot you in after it. Leave it lay, fool, and go for the green ones."

"Chamgadin, Master of the Battatai?"

"So I be, who t'Ibliz are you?"

Serroi pushed the hood of her cloak back off her face, blinking the rain out of her eyes as she thrust her hand into the relatively dry space under the tarp and showed him the card. "A cousin of yours gave me this. Am'litho, Master of the *Wanda Kojamy*."

Straining to see in the half-light of the storm, he brought the card up close to his eyes; when he finished puzzling out Am'litho's scrawl, he turned it over, inspected the nameglyph. "Haya, 'tis Am's card in truth. And the Crone ha' kiss yer backside this time. Two sets m' passengers ha' take a look a the storm and decided to wait out the blow. How many y' be?"

"Three besides me. Two women, two men."

He frowned at her, stroking his fingers down the stiff coils of his beard. Abruptly he nodded. "I'll do it. Two silver apiece here to Govaritil. And that is the best price you'll get from any along this bay, Healer. If any would take you which I doubt after that business in Hakoman's Tavern."

"We'll pay when we come aboard. When are you leaving?"

"With this night's tide. I'll want you aboard by sundown." He tapped the edge of the card against his thumbnail, his eyes looking past her. "Sundown. Yes. That's the best time. No one's about. Stay in the shadows and come quick."

The Battatai was rocking on waves that were rolling in to crash against the piles, groaning and rubbing against the heavy leather fenders lashed to the timbers of the wharf. The stormlanterns aboard danced like courting fireflies, shadows moved swiftly about, adding more netting over the cargo piled on the deck, double lashing everything that might possibly break loose.

Chamgadin was waiting for them as they came up the boarding planks. He took the purse that Camnor

Heslin held out to him, roared, "Follow me. I'll show you your cabins."

As soon as they were out of the wind, he said, "Weren't it for m' cousin asking, I'd boot the lot of you off my ship. I figure this storm is your doing and it's apt to send us all to the bottom." He flung open a narrow door on his left, then turned to his right and slammed his fist on another. "Two in each, up to you how you sort it out." Without waiting for a response he went stumping back up the ladder.

Serroi shivered. "Half my weight is water. I don't know about you all, but I'm going to crawl into bed and see if I can get warm again."

When she woke the ship's movement was smooth and steady as if it rode the waves instead of struggling through them. She looked over the edge of the bunk and discovered that Zasya had waked before her and gone out.

When she stepped onto the deck, she stopped, amazed. The wind was still out of the north, crisp and cold, but it was just a wind. The sky was a deep clear blue with a few horsetails of cloud near the horizon. She smiled her pleasure and crossed to the rail.

Silkar children waved to her, went back to playing in the bow wave.

Out near the horizon she saw a spurt of steam break against the blue and several great curves of glistening black rise and fall. A broad tail that looked to be as wide as the Battatai was long flipped from the water, stood against the sky like an abstract image of a tree with two leaves, then slid with awesome inevitability into the sea.

Adlayr Ryan-Turriy was leaning on the rail watching the silkars play, now and then looking beyond them to the great maremars that seemed to be escorting them. There was a deep hunger in his dark amber eyes. The hands that gripped the rail flickered almost imperceptibly, the skin acquiring ghost lines as if trying out fishscales instead of flesh.

"The Sinadeen is a tame place," he said without looking around. "I've never seen ocean before, water from horizon to horizon, knowing that it goes beyond, farther than any eye can measure, running free as the wind."

"The Ajjin loved the mountains," she said.

"I know. But she never left them, did she?"

"Nay." She stroked a hand along his arm, feeling the tension in him. "Sicamar for earth, trax for air, will it be silkar for water?"

"I don't know. I'm afraid," he said. "If I went to water, would I ever leave it?"

She squinted into the wind; it smelled of the sea, clean and cold, with none of the heaviness she'd felt on the land. "We're in a Shield Circle," she said. "The silkar and the maremars are holding back the Enemy, so the wind and water will be wholesome a while. I know something of what you feel, Adlayr. I feel it, too." She leaned on the rail and smiled as a silkar girl rode the bow wave high into the air, her fine green hair fanning out, her sleek olive body closing then springing open; the girl's laughter reached them over the sounds of the sea and the ship as she waved a hand at the two watching her and vanished into the foam-streaked water. "We'd best enjoy it while it lasts."

6. Tough Times in Dander

Vyzharnos Oram

Vyzharnos yawned, blinked at the sun that was still only a red bead on the jagged line of mountains. " 'Nother day, Kub." He grinned sleepily at the man who'd come to relieve him on the tiller. "Good flow, no snags, easy night. The Chasm awaits, my friend. Filled with dayglare. Better you nor me."

Like many Nerodin bargeveks Kublics was a small wiry man; his mustache drooped past his chin and his lugubrious long face was a lie in every line since he had a quiet but intense enjoyment of the idiocies of life. "But I won't be listenin' to y' verse, Marn's Blessing on the Ner who made the schedule. Gawn, get y' some brekka, Poet."

The *Rekkavar* was a long low riverbarge, her triangular sail sometimes the only thing that showed above the levees that ran along the Red Dan to keep its surge confined and out of the Zemyadel and the crops on the farms in that fertile district. She was bound south to Tuku-kul and the great Spring Fair the Fenekel called the Sawasika Sik, with a load of Calanda steel and leather goods from the North Dander shops.

More and more Nerodin merchants were sending their goods by barge rather than caravan, though that did limit their markets and increase their expenses; the bloody raids on everything that moved outside the cities were making those limitations less important. Who could get at the barges out there in the middle of the Dan? And why would they try it?

The Marn was taking no chances; during the past two years, she'd had towers built in the few places where the river bent and the channel came close enough to one bank or another to bring the barges into reach. At first there were four Guards in each tower; now, as calls on the Marn's Guard grew every day, there were only two, one to watch and one to sleep.

Vyzharnos stood on the deck a moment longer, enjoying the wind in his hair and the loose sway of his body. He was tired after his stint at the tiller, alone with the night and the slap creak of the sail, watching the banks, reading the marks as he'd been taught. His learning trips he'd spent chanting them out blindfolded while old Velechny stung his arm with the varb whisk whenever he missed a call until he knew the Red Dan better than his own face.

The smell of hot kava rose from the cabin, woke his hunger again and he left off dreaming, caught hold of the lintel and swung down into the narrow common room. Mohutny was still at table, leaning back, half asleep, his mug on his chest; now and then he lifted it, sucked a mouthful of kava past the brush that grew on his upper lip. Kublics' plate and mug were washed and stowed already. On most barges it was turn and turn for who did the cooking; on the *Rekkavar,* they left that job to Falshev. He was so neat and so persnickety and so loud about it, the crews he worked with would have drowned him long ago if he weren't a mage with a frying pan and a treasure of a housekeeper. He stood a watch in emergencies, but mostly he cooked, kept the living quarters spotless, and did little jobs for the crew: mending things, washing, whatever finicking, irritating business needed doing. It meant longer watches for the others, but they didn't mind. Thanks to Falshev, they lived very comfortably aboard the *Rekkavar*.

"Don't stand round dreamin', Poet, there's some got work to do." Falshev's long nose twitched and the bristles beneath it pretending to be a mustache changed color like leaves in the wind. He set the steaming plate in front of an empty chair, filled a mug with kava and stood back, waiting for praise.

"Ahhhh," Vyzharnos breathed, "I should write an ode to your breakfasts, Falsha-eggmage." He settled in the chair and began eating; for several moments the only sounds in the cabin were the click of his fork and Mohutny's loud breathing.

When the first edge of his hunger was gone, Vyzharnos pulled a small, leatherbound notebook from his sleeve and began noting down the lines the night had produced for him, writing with his left hand and eating with his right. Behind him Falshev snorted, increased his clattering.

Mohutny finished the last of his kava, clanked the mug down, and got to his feet. He had to stand hunched over, a bear of a man whose strength was useful when the river shifted on them down in Fenka Plain and they had to winch themselves off a sand bar. He set his big hand on Vyzharnos' shoulder. "Don't be too long at that, Poet. We'll be in Chasm soon and come nightwatch, I've no mind to be pluckin' m'self off a rock 'cause y' shut y'r eye a bit and lost it."

"Pek, Moh, when 've I ever done anything like that?"

Mohutny grinned, the coarse black hair of his mustache spreading like a pulled spring. "Allus a first time.'' He went clumping up the steps and moved out onto the deck.

"Fancy's fine facility fades/in the face of ropes that fray the hands,'' Vyzharnos read aloud. "Not right. Chert!''

"Fancy, sprosh! Too fancy.'' The growl came from Mohutny who'd stuck his head into the hatch to check on Vyzharnos. "Thought you was still at it. Vyz, old's you be, do you need you mama to whip you tail and send you to bed?''

"Praka prak, Mama Moh, I'm goin'. My head's sucked dry now anyway.'' He frowned at the mess of scratches and cross-outs. "Too fancy? Maybe you're right, got too wound up in sound and forgot what I meant. . . .''

"Poet!''

"Prak, I hear y'.'' He glanced at the page again, hesitated then shut the notebook firmly and tucked it back into his sleeve.

Mohutny watched until Vyzharnos got his hammock hooked in place and was in it, wrapped in his blanket, the muffler wound round his eyes and ears, then he slammed the hutch shut and went clumping away.

The *Rekkavar* jolted, heeled over, swerved violently.

Still half-asleep, Vyzharnos rolled out of the hammock, fought clear of the blanket, and stumbled toward the steps to the hatch.

It slammed open, a black-painted face appeared, an arm swung and his head seemed to explode. He fell on his face, fell into blackness. . . .

He woke in a hell of fire and stench, burning flesh, burning leather; his left eye was swollen shut, his right stuck together with dried blood until he rubbed it away and his head throbbed with a deep grinding ache that erased every thought but that pain—until the burning wall !popped! and a spark landed on his arm.

The agony brought him up, trying to focus his one working eye on the arm. A tiny black bead sat on the skin, no bigger than a pinhead. Vuurvis oil. He knew about vuurvis from his early training and his father's tales, so he clawed a burning splinter loose from the wall and set the coal on the oil, rocking back and forth, groaning, teeth clenched, pain washing strength from his fingers as the oil bubbled and burned; he forced himself to keep his hold on the splinter, to keep the fire pressed against the bead until it was consumed.

Half out of his head, he charged up the steps, burst through the flames, and fell on his face as his foot slammed into Mohutny's body. He rolled over, forced himself up again, fire all round him, his clothes burning, stumbled to the nearest rail and plunged over the rail into the river, by chance taking the side of the barge closest to the bank.

The shock of the cold water blanked his mind for a moment, then the current slammed him against the hull, rolled him along it until his feet caught in the watergrass growing on the levee. He hunched there a moment, gathering himself, then staggered up the bank, using the rope that held the barge nosed into the mud; it was tied into the eye of a metal spike driven deep into the levee not far from the squat Marn's Tower supposed to protect this bend. His hand closed over the spike and he remembered what pain and panic had chased away—the soot-streaked face in the hatch.

"Raid." His legs shook and he crashed onto his knees, vomiting his breakfast in spasms that brought more pain from the place where he'd been hit. When

he tried to get up, he couldn't. The black iron spike
and the thick knot at the top of it doubled and doubled
again, his head throbbed, his muscles felt like water.
"Raid," he whispered; he started crawling toward the
Tower.

Two blackouts and an infinity of misery later, he
reached the door, started to go through the hole burned
through the massive planks, then drew back.
"Vuurvis." He began shaking, the memory of the
vuurvis burn flooding through him. He couldn't bring
himself to go inside and a moment's labored thought
convinced him there wasn't much point to it anyway,
the place would be gutted, the Guards dead.

Shivering from pain and shock, he crawled round
the Tower to the stables and in the door. There were
two macain in the stalls and a heap of hay down at one
end. He crawled toward it, meaning to climb into the
hay and get warm, but when he reached the first stall,
he stopped. "Fa," he said. It seemed to help his faltering brain when he spoke the words aloud. "I have
to tell him. . . ."

He touched the huge lump over his left eye. The
swelling was getting worse. "Now," he said. "Do it
now . . . if you wait . . . can't. . . ."

Fueled by rage and fear, driven by will, he got a
saddle on one macai, a halter, and managed after several failures that drained almost all the strength he had
left to lever himself onto the beast's back. He sat for
a moment, swaying, nausea roiling an empty stomach,
then he backed the macai from the stall, took it at a
walk out of the stable and up onto the levee road.

The *Rekkavar* was smoldering still, burned almost
to the waterline. He looked at it, then looked away,
unable for the moment to comprehend what had hap-

pened. Kublics, dead. Mohutny, dead. Falshev, dead.
And the raiders must have thought him dead, too. And
for what? Nothing. They couldn't have taken anything
from the hold, there wasn't time. They killed the Tower
Guards, then the crew, fired the barge—for nothing!

"Fa," he said. "Got to tell him. . . ." Gasping as
his head throbbed with the movement, he urged the
macai into the long glide it could keep up for hours
and fought to stay awake enough so he wouldn't fall
off.

Tingajil

The room in the mid-Dander warren was small, clut-
tered with a lifetime of little things brought into it,
little memories; a fire crackled on the hearth and the
Maiden Lamps were lit and placed on their brackets
on the walls, adding the fragrance of high mountain
conifers given off by the perfumed oil to the aroma of
spices from the Yearcakes and the rich plum scent of
the vasha punch. Gold paper was wrapped around her
mother's chair, silver around her father's, and they sat
grinning like happy babies at her when she gave them
their Yeargifts.

A quarter of a century ago on this day the Nerodina
Vyata Vyloush had wed the Nerodin Prevakan son of
Oromata. Five children they'd had in that time. Two
died before their second year, the one surviving son
was the master of a ship who came home only about
every third year (this not being one of them), one was
Retezhry Vyloush who married a butcher into the family and was here with him and her six children includ-
ing the newest, a boy still in swaddling, and the
youngest was Tingajil, released from her duties for the
day so she could celebrate the occasion.

Mama Vya untied the bright silk scarves Tingajil

had wrapped round the gifts, held up the ruby goblets so the light from the Maiden Lamps could shimmer on the deep red surfaces and glow in the depths of the glass.

Retezhry clapped her plump hands with pleasure and appreciation. "Halinny." She tapped her oldest daughter on the shoulder. "Fetch the wine, child. We'll have a toast in Tinga's glasses, Mama and Papa will each drink the other's health, and Tinga will sing for us. Go, go."

"Gift me a song," Tingajil sang and drew ripples of sound from her lute. . . .

> *Gift me a song and make it true*
> *Take the old words, turn them new*
> *As I do turn my looks to you*
> *And you do meet me with reply*
> > *You are mine*
> > *And I am thine*
> *As the swifting years slide by.*

> *Though year do turn, year fade to year*
> *Nor age nor ills will you unendear*
> *More sweetly love begins to be. . . .*

She broke off as a horrendous crash sounded outside, mixed with screams and shouts, the walls of the room shook, throwing several of the Maiden Lamps onto the floor. The older children hastened to smother the fires that started, Retezhry hurried to the window, her husband Harez got the door open and charged downstairs.

"It's Chetnery's grocery, those sprocherts blew it up." Retezhry said. "Ahh, 'tis horrible, blood and bone. . . ."

Vyata Vyloush stood. "Then they'll need help. We'd best go see what we can do. Halinny, you and the childer stay up here, you'd just be in the way, and we don't need to be worrying about you."

Tingajil set the lute down. "Halinny, watch this, it's Marn's Goods and important." She hurried after Harez, her parents and Retezhry following more slowly.

The carnage was worse from street level. They could see the scattered limbs and entrails of the dismembered dead, could hear more clearly the shrieks from the wounded.

Tingajil went pale and shuddered as the agony of the living rasped against nerves whose sensitivities she'd honed so lovingly for so many years. She swayed, put out a hand to steady herself—and saw a head resting against a wall, eyes open and staring. "Danaty," she whispered. Danaty was one of her cousins, nineteen years old, just married with twin babies. She swallowed, swallowed again, shut her eyes a moment, then followed her mother.

The dust from the shattered bricks filled the air. Her mother had tied one of the gift scarves over her mouth, Mama Vya practical as always. Following her mother's example, Tingajil tore a sleeve loose, ripped the seam, and tied it over her own mouth and began helping the neighbors dig out the dead from under the collapsed walls.

As she shifted bricks near the corner of the store, where the wall had folded over and there might be a small space inside, she heard a faint cry. "Someone's alive here," she called. "Help me."

Several Nerodin men she didn't recognize pushed

her aside and began gently, carefully easing the bricks
away. When they had a big enough hole cleared, one
of them got down on his stomach and reached inside,
easing out a baby that was red-faced and howling, but
blessedly alive. "It's Moddy, Danaty's daughter," she
cried and held out her arms for the child. "What about
Prumero, the boy? Can you see . . . ?"

"I can see a hand," the Ner said. "It's not moving,
but it wouldn't be, that's where the bricks are. Take
the baby away, we'll deal with this."

The rest of the afternoon Tingajil labored with the
other Nerodin of the neighborhood, gradually clearing
away the debris, bringing out the dead, carrying the
injured to the local clinic and the nursing of the Sekalaries, working dumbly, almost blindly, her feelings
and her senses reduced to a thread.

"Tinga!" The small hand was tight on her arm.

She turned impatiently, blinked as she saw her
mother looking up at her. Vyata Vyloush's face was a
mask of red brick dust above the rags of the silk scarf,
her eyes were watering, but still bright in spite of her
fatigue. "What is it, Mama Vya?"

"It's near sundown. You have to get back, don't
you."

Tingajil drew the back of her hand across her fore-
head. She'd forgotten about that. Her body slumped as
the weariness she'd been pushing away all the long
hours poured back into her. She groped blindly. "My
lute. . . ."

"Here, Aunt Tinga, I KNEW you'd need it." Halinny came round to stand in front of her, holding out
the instrument case. "I wiped it off and put it away
so the babies wouldn't get at it."

Tingajil blinked at the earnest young face, joy flooding her that Halinny and Mama and Papa and Retezhry and Harez and the babies were alive, when so many of her kin and her neighbors were not. "Yes," she said, "You took good care of it. Thank you, Halinny Caretaker."

As the child blushed at the praise, Tingajil felt once again that half-guilty joy. She tucked the case under her arm, touched her mother's cheek. "You'll be all right, you and Papa?"

"Tsaaa, we'll be too busy to fuss ourselves. You get on, Tinga, 'tis no time to fratchet the Marn."

Shuddering at every shout, flinching at each loud noise, Tingajil walked back to the Pevranamist through familiar streets turned feral in her imagination. By the time she passed through the Postern Gate she was sweating and shaking, with just strength enough to reach her room in the vast mews where the servants and the lesser functionaries lived.

She set the lute case on the table by the door, looked vaguely around as if she couldn't remember where she was, then lay down on the bed.

A maid came looking for her and found her lying in the dark, shivering and sobbing; the girl ran for the Healer who had her carried to the Pevranamist's clinic. Bozhka Sekan tucked her into bed there after giving her a drink of spanalek infusion to be sure she slept, sat a moment listening to her drowsy lamentations, then went to report to the Marn what she'd heard.

K'vestmilly Vos

K'vestmilly pulled her macai to a walk and waited for the Guards to catch up. She dug her thumbs into the spongy growths along the macai's neck; the beast

groaned with pleasure and put a syncopation in the
sway of his gait. "You like that, do you, my Stavvy?
Ahhh, I'm liking this." She shook her head, enjoying
the feel of the wind blowing past her ears, the smell
of the river and the dry dusty road along the levee. "I
was going crazier than Treshteny shut up like that,
walls coming in on me. Maiden Bless, old worm,
what's it going to be like when I have to be Marn? I'm
going to hate it. . . ." Her voice trailed off and she
shook her head. "Nik, that's a lie. Only parts of it.
Mother's dying, I'm sure of it. I wish she'd tell me,
but I suppose she's afraid to, afraid I'll do something
to let it out, then where'll we all be? T'k, Stavvy, we
NEED her. What do I know about anything?"

The Guards Zatko and Umremy slowed and rode
behind her at this more decorous pace, silent men in
Marn's Gray. The Marn's Guard was spread so thinly
across Cadander that it made her uneasy to take even
two men away from their posts, but seeing the Marn
so nearly killed had sobered her. This was no time for
the chaos of a line change, to have the Families ma-
neuvering against each other, undermining, even killing each other, destroying the Myth that held this Land
together.

*Myth. Mother's word. Nerodin myth. I know almost
nothing about the way Nerodin live their lives, nothing
about the people I've seen in streets and fields when
I've gone to fly my jessers. I don't know what they feel
about themselves, the Marn and me. I don't know what
they want, what they need. I'm ignorant.*

It wasn't a comfortable sensation, that. It was as if
she'd walked out over an abyss without realizing it until she looked down and saw she was standing on nothing.

I know you loathe this, her mother said and touched
the Mask, but it's part of our power, K'milly. It creates

a mythic distance between ruler and ruled. It is Myth itself. Not magic, that is altogether different. Myth grows in the minds of people and wraps around an ordinary man or woman and gives them extraordinary power. What are we, you and I, but people like these Nerodin, those who walk the streets, who worry you right now? Remember that, K'milly, because when you start believing your own fables, you're on your way to destruction. What was I . . . yes, those Nerodin out there, they don't want us to be like them. They want us strange and wonderful, it satisfies something in them. That's what the first Marn knew, she who had the Mask made for her. She knew, too, that she was a convenience, holder of the common conscience, a hat-stand where Rodin and Nerodin alike hung the things they didn't want to think about. Myth and Mask can make people comfortable with their inadequacies and their little meannesses, K'milly, and they grow very angry when anyone tries to take their Mask away. So the Distance has to be maintained. . . .

Her mother paused there, spread her hands in her substitute for a smile. But that doesn't mean, she said, that you won't work like all the demons in Zhagdeep to keep our place, you'll coax and you'll wheedle, you'll bribe and you'll punish, secretly and openly, you'll do the twisty dance the rest of your life. And if you're wise, you'll find lines into the cities and the farms so that, even if you aren't seen to know, you do know. And you must have men and women to serve you who'll tell you truth, even when it's hard and dangerous. You don't like Oram, but he does what needs to be done and he only lies a little to me—and never about impor-tant things. I value him and so should you, there aren't many like him. And you'll remember this, I hope, a tyrant can rule for one generation, but the Vos family has ruled for a hundred. Think on why that is.

* * *

Wild zhula flowers grew in profusion on the levee
slopes, the low bushes lying tight to the ground like
patches of melted butter, their sharp, sweet odor mixing on the wind with the river mud, the new green
leaves on the weeds and brush and the musky sweat
of the macain. Ahead, there was a long curve where a
thousand and a thousand years ago the Marn of that
time, who was Bar not Vos, had, out of spite and irritation, paid the Norit Washimin to dig a new channel
for the Dan so the restless, arrogant Govaritish would
be left sitting on a dry ditch. That didn't last long, but
the split remained. These days the Yellow Dan went
east and south to a chastened Govaritil and the Red
Dan west through Washimin's Chasm and south across
the Fenka Plain to Tuku Kul. Near that curve a grove
of brellim trees bubbled like blue-green smoke against
a cloudless sky—and from that grove a rider came, a
rider who lay low on the neck of his mount, a weary
macai in its resting walk, head tucked in and ears back.

Ignoring the yells of her Guards, K'vestmilly Vos
sent Stavvy racing toward the man. She reached the
weary macai a length ahead of the Guards, brought
Stavvy tightly round it, dirt spraying as his claws dug
in to slow him enough to pace beside it. She caught it
by the halter and pulled it to a stop.

The man struggled to sit up. An impatient wave of
her hand and the Guard Zatko caught his arm in a
practiced grip and eased him up while Umremy stayed
back, his crossbow out and cocked.

A great black bruise swelled across half the man's
face; one eye was forced shut, the other narrowed to
a slit; one arm had an angry red burn so deep the bone
was showing; there were other burns and bruises, the
rags he wore were slathered with mud and stuck to his

body. "Oram," he said. Though weak, his voice was surprisingly clear, as if he'd had declamation lessons sometime in the past; he had to take short panting breaths between words, but he forced them out, one after the other, as quickly as he could. "Must see . . . must tell . . . Rekkavar . . . barge . . . raid . . . last tower . . . 'fore Chasm."

"Oskliveh!" Zatko leaned closer. "The Tower Guards, what happened to them?"

"Vuurvis . . . Oram . . . must see. . . ." He swayed, the part of his face unbruised and unburned turned even paler, took on a greenish cast; K'vestmilly thought he was going out on them. He surprised her, closed his free hand about the pommel and squeezed so hard the pain from the burns must have been indescribable. Sweat beaded up all over him, but he stayed awake.

"Prak," she said briskly. "We'll get you to him. I presume it's Jestranos Oram you want." She frowned past him at the Guard. "Zatko, it was your brother at the Chasm Tower?"

"Yes, Dedach."

"We'll need confirmation and more details. You and Umremy go see what you can find. It's an order, Guard. I'll be all right. The raiders don't come this close."

Zatko hesitated a moment longer, then he nodded and started down the Levee Road at a long lope, Umremy close behind him.

That ride back to Dander was slow and terrible. There was nothing she could do about the man's injuries; she couldn't even talk to him because she was afraid of disturbing the fierce concentration that was keeping him awake.

He swayed when they reached the Guard Post at the beginning of the Mask Way, relief momentarily undercutting his will, but recovered and stayed in the saddle.

K'vestmilly waved to one of the Guards; he came running, then walked along beside her. "Get Jestranos Oram and tell him I want him to meet me at the Clinic."

He trotted off and after a look at the swaying man, she took her macai into the lead up the long slope to the Pevranamist.

"Oskliveh!" Jestranos hurried from the doorway where he'd waited. "Vyzharnos. . . . ."

The wounded man blinked and astonished K'vestmilly by smiling, only a half-smile because of the bruise, but one with genuine humor in it. "Fa. All your dreams come true . . . nik, don't touch me, not yet. Listen. . . ." In a clear but halting voice he gave his account of the attack, dredging his memory for every detail he could bring up about the raiders and their method. Then his face went blank and Jestranos caught him as he slid from the saddle.

Jestranos Oram stood by his son's bed a moment. "He was a stubborn fool even before he could walk." He looked up, saw K'vestmilly watching him. "My second son. He left my house when he was seventeen. We don't talk about him. Poet, that's what he went to be. Living in filth, breaking his back doing stoop labor. He didn't want anything from me. Stubborn. . . ." He bent and touched his son's cheek, then strode from the room.

"He's not the only one," K'vestmilly murmured. "Poet? Hunh." She crossed her long legs and sat watching the man sleep. He was shorter than his father, shorter than her, slender, though his shoulders

were broad enough. His burned and bruised hands
were wrapped in cloth and salve, but she thought she'd
never forget them, big hands for his size, callused and
rough from the hard labor he'd done for the past . . .
how many years had it been? Left home at seventeen,
hard to tell how many years since with that bruise in
the way, crow's-feet at the corner of his unmarred eye,
deep lines from his nose to his chin. Strong nose, like
his father. She smiled. Bits and pieces, add them up,
he's older than me, maybe a little younger than he
looks since he's lived hard. I wonder what color his
eyes are?

She blinked, stood. "Like your father, I've got
things to do. Not nearly so interesting. Spojjin' formal
dinner with that lot from Skafaree. Bath and fancy
dress, then sit for hours playing word games." She
leaned down and touched his cheek as his father had.
It was cool and a little damp, extraordinarily exciting.
Her nipples hardened and a familiar sweet thrill shot
up her body. "Tsaaa, this is a complication." She
managed a small smile. "If you do this to me when
you're asleep, what happens when you wake up?"

When she was dressed, she went to join her mother,
found her pacing about the sitting room, her cane
thumping angrily on the floor; she was silent part of
the time, part of the time spewing out a spate of whispered curses.

"What happened? Bozhka Sekan, was there another
attempt?"

"Nik, not exactly. There was an explosion in the
city. Tingajil was there; she wasn't hurt herself, but
she helped dig bloody pieces of her neighbors and her
kin out of the mess, so she's not feeling too bright at
the moment. What with your young man and his news
and this business, it's not been a good day. I've been

trying to get the Marn to relax. You can see what sort of luck I'm having.''

K'vestmilly strode into the middle of the room, stood with her hands on her hips. "This the way you're going to act, Mother, you might as well get those clothes off and go to bed. I'll deal with those would-be zarks.''

Marnhidda Vos swung round and glared at her, the eyes in the Maskholes like blue fire. After a moment, she sighed. ''Prak, you win.'' She thumped across to the bell cord, pulled it. When Sluzha appeared, she said, ''Tell the Domcevek to put back the gong for another twenty minutes.''

As soon as the maid was gone, Marnhidda Vos stumped to a straight-backed chair. When she was seated, she slipped the Mask off, tossed down the strengthener Bozhka Sekan gave her, and let the healer pat her mouth dry. ''Hah!'' She closed her eyes a moment, her head resting against the chair's back.

K'vestmilly was appalled by how old and feeble her mother looked; she relaxed a little as the tonic brought a tinge of color to the papery cheeks, walked to a hassock and dropped onto it, smoothing her skirt so she wouldn't crush the silk.

''I had a thought today,'' she said.

Marnhidda Vos opened one eye a slit and gave her breathy chuckle. ''Only one?''

''Only one I want to talk about now. If you don't mind.''

''Why should I mind such an auspicious event?''

''Bozhka Sekan, whatever you put in that stuff, I think it's gone sour.'' She flashed a grin at the healer, turned back to her mother. ''Who was my father? I assume I had one.''

Marnhidda Vos chuckled again, let the laugh fade into a smile. ''No WAS about Husenkil. He's a tough old Nerod, a potter on Keshtinac Street. I used to go

visit him when I could get about better.'' Her smile
widened a little, her face softened, her eyes were
glazed with memory. She blinked, came back to the
present. ''That's another blessing of the Mask, K'milly.
After a while it's only a few who know your real face.''

''Why didn't you tell me before?''

''You didn't ask.''

''I was afraid to.''

''Should I ask why you bring it up now?''

''You haven't the least need to ask, Mother. We both
know that.''

''Hmm. He's a very heroic young man. He doesn't
like us much, you know. And he doesn't care a fist
full of spit for honors or wealth or power. He sounds
a lot like Hus. If you want my blessing, you've got it.
It's him you'll have to be persuading.''

K'vestmilly sighed. ''Life,'' she said.

''True.'' Marnhidda Vos slipped the Mask back on
and held out her hand. ''Lend me your arm, K'milly.
It's time we were going.''

7. Govaritil

Drifting above dark figures kneeling on a darker floor, the Fetch floated in an oval of golden light, reaching down to touch one, then another of the kneelers, drawing moans of pleasure from them.

See, Mother, see how I cherish them, how I comfort them. See how I would love you. Why won't you come to me? Why won't you answer me? I am your child. I am born of your rebirth. Why won't you take my love? They come to me freely and with joy. Why must I compel you? I NEEEEED YOU, MO TH THE THERRRR. . . .

Two days before landfall at Govaritil the silkars vanished and the wild wind came back; rain lashed at the ship, the sea tossed it, slammed it, came pouring over the rails, inundating the decks.

In the cabin Serroi wrapped herself in blankets, stuffed a pillow between herself and the wall, and settled grimly to ride out what was bound to be a very bad two days.

Zasya cracked the door and slipped in, slamming it shut and dropping the latch before it could get away from her and bang against the wall. "Hooo! What a day!" She began stripping off her sodden clothing.

"Chamgadin's having fits, yelled at me, doesn't want any of us up there gettin' in his way."

Serroi turned onto her stomach, looked over the end of the bunk. "Any chance of something to eat?"

"Chamgadin was in no mood to talk about food. Trail rations will have to do us till things calm down a bit."

"Zhag! Pass me a trailbar, Zas, and hang the waterskin where I can reach it. Gnawing some nuts will take my mind off rare steaks sizzling in their own grease, tubers smothered in butter yellow as the sun . . . oof!" She reversed the bag Zasya threw at her and began digging in it for the foil-wrapped bars.

Zasya reached for a towel. "Bad enough we're going to be stuck in this cave for who knows how long." She began rubbing at her hair.

Serroi slung the gearsac onto the bottom bunk, turned on her back and lay worrying at the hard, sticky bar, listening to the sounds Zasya made as she dried herself off and climbed into dry clothing, to the howl of the wind and the creaking of the ship. For a while she'd been distracted by the beauty of tranquil days and nights, the sense that they were for the moment taken out of time into another place where nothing evil could touch them. There were always some maremars in the distance and at times others swam close enough to the ship that their size was truly apparent. The silkar children were continually around, playing, laughing, cutting through the clear green water. But the dreams kept coming, getting stronger every night despite the protections around them. *What am I going to do? Should I try to speak to that thing?* Her throat closed up and she nearly choked on a piece of trailbar. Everything in her fought against the idea, but she forced herself to think it through. *Not yet. I don't know*

*enough. Too many people could get hurt. I could get
killed. . . .*

Healing was good. The earth hadn't changed, that
was good. Those moments of sheer terror when she
had to scramble to stay alive, they were nicely unam-
biguous. No need to search the soul for purposes when
life was teetering on a delicate balance.

I don't want to die.

That was the answer, pretty or not. She didn't want
to die and she didn't want to cause the death of others.
And she was furious at the Fetch who sent these
dreams and made her look at herself and see these
things.

"Ildas says the blow is lightening up, maybe the
worst is over."

Serroi blinked, drawn out of her unhappy thoughts.
"I wouldn't count on that," she said. "Something
wants us sunk and won't give up so easily."

"Mm. He usually knows. Maybe your something is
getting a trap ready for us when we reach land."

"That's a cheerful thought."

Zasya chuckled, yawned. "Ei vai, Ildas and me are
going to sleep as much as we can. Let Ol' Something
gnash his teeth and plot his plots, we'll do him good,
time comes. Won't we, babe?" Her hand made a soft
silken whisper as she passed it along the Fireborn's
back.

Serroi listened to Zasya climb into the bunk and
ease out on the mattress, listened to the creak of the
web of rope beneath the pad. A few moments later the
only sound inside the cabin was the steady rasp of her
breathing.

*Time comes. I can smell the blood already. Maiden
avert!* Serroi lay staring at the ceiling so close above
her. *I suppose that's it, then. I've got no choice. If I*

die, you eat the world, so the death has to be yours.
To the death, Sender of Dreams.

Two days later, with great difficulty but also confident seamanship, Chamgadin brought the *Battatai* round the Horn of Gov and into the harbor at Govaritil.

"You! You there! Stop." The nachod came striding toward them, the six men behind him spreading into two wings and trotting to surround the companions and the shivering porter loaded to the tottering point with Camnor's gear.

"Papers," he said brusquely, his hand out.

Serroi pushed the wet hair out of her eyes and smiled as she watched Camnor Heslin pull importance over himself like a cloak, looming over the smaller man like a cliff about to fall on him.

His deep voice rolled out. "I am Vorbescar of the Grand Council of the Mijloc on detached service with diplomatic privilege and I have no intention of standing in the middle of a downpour getting myself and my credentials soaked. Take us to shelter, Nachod, then we'll show you what you need to see."

The nachod hesitated. His eyes flicked from Heslin to Serroi, then to the others.

Sodden and chilled, she watched his face and knew what he was thinking; privilege had a sting in its tail and he hadn't got where he was by upsetting importance. Camnor had likely saved them considerable hassling now—and later on by his insistence that they all be provided with transpasses, notarized and stamped with the official seal of the Council.

"Bikkah," the nachod said. "You'll come with us, then."

* * *

He led them up and down several precipitous slopes, through narrow winding streets that were turning into canals from the water pouring along them, past ordinary buildings and two Serroi found intriguing, houses whose shining white doors had radiant gold circles with faces painted on them, a mature, motherly version of the Maiden. *I don't see your bones, fetch. Is this the face you show when you seduce?*

Govaritil was built on hills; they weren't high, but they were many and steep and to get to the heart of the city took considerable climbing. By the time the nachod waved the companions and the frightened porter into an arched opening in a wall, Serroi's legs were trembling as much from weariness as from the cold rain that had soaked through her cloak and saturated her boots.

There was a curious dread in the massive stone building; the few people they met scurried past, eyes fixed on the floor as if even looking at someone might commit them to a cause and bring more than rain down on their heads.

Serroi glanced at Camnor's face and could read nothing there, but behind that mask she sensed tension and grim anticipation. *He's ready for trouble, he sees it, too. Something's happened here, something that's chilled them to the bone.*

The nachod threw open a door, stepped back. "Wait there," he said; he snapped his fingers and two of his gaveks went in and stood at attention beside the hearth where a small smoldering fire was trying to heat the chill out of the room. The porter dumped Camnor's cases on the floor and went scuttling away after the nachod waved him off.

Serroi tugged her sodden skirt away from her legs and followed Heslin into the room. He stepped in front of the guards. "Towels," he said. "Bring them. You want us to die of pneumonia?"

They looked at each other. "We s'posed to stay here," the shorter man said. He tugged at one of his rattail mustaches, his little black eyes sliding uneasily around.

Camnor moved closer to loom over him; his voice deepened. "Do you think we're going to attack this place? This great army of us? If you don't have towels around, bring us some spare blankets, before we freeze to death. And hot cha. Now! Move, man."

The short gavek turned to his partner, but the other gavek stared straight ahead, making it clear this was no business of his. He tugged at his mustache, chewed his lip, then he scuttled to the door, stuck his head out. A second later, his whole body relaxed. "Eeeeh, Tiru, c'm 'ere." He stepped into the hall, there was a murmur of voices, then he strutted back in and took his old place against the wall. "Blankets and cha, they comin'."

"Good."

Serroi settled into a worn wicker armchair with a high back; the pads were filthy and flat, the wicker was broken in several spots, stubs standing up like little knives, but it was surprisingly comfortable. She tugged her boots off, dropped them on the floor beside her cloak and gearsac; she was still soaked to the skin, but with the tight weave of the chair to keep the drafts away and her feet tucked up under her, she was warm enough to be getting sleepy.

Zasya Myers knelt on the hearth, slicing curls off a split section of log and setting them on the smolder, building it up enough so she could add a pile of the splits without putting the whole thing out. She looked up as Camnor loomed over her. "If they swept the chimney more than once every century, there might be a better draw.''

He inspected her handiwork, grunted, turned his back and stood warming himself, hands clasped behind him.

Adlayr Ryan-Turriy sat with his hip hitched onto the sill of the single window, head turned so he could gaze out into the gray sheets of driving rain; as he'd shown before on this trip, he didn't like confinement of any kind.

Serroi yawned, watched Ildas shimmer into the fireplace's cavity as Zasya began carefully stacking splits of wood onto the crackling blaze she'd got going on the pile of ash and feebly burning coals. The Fireborn circled about, then settled in the middle of the flames, boneless and limp as a cat sleeping in the sun. *Poor baby. How he must have hated all this water dropping on him.*

Zasya left the fire and perched on a bench pushed against the wall across from the guarding gaveks. Her cloak was a pool of wet wool beside bare feet; she took a cake of leather cream from her weaponbelt and started using it on her boots, working the herbal compound into the sodden leather.

I should do that or I'll never get my feet back in mine. Vai vai, too lazy and comfortable to move. . . .

Serroi blinked as the door opened and several men bustled in, carrying blankets and a tray with an absurd collection of mugs and glasses and a large bellied pot of coarse reddish earthenware with steam rippling from the spout. They deposited the blankets and the tray on the bench beside Zasya, fetched in Camnor's cases and stacked them beside the door, then left without saying a word.

Zasya looked at the tray, then at her hands, and went on polishing her boots.

Adlayr slid off the sill and padded across the room. He chuckled as he inspected the array of crockery, lifted the lid on a cracked sugar basin, then looked round. "Vorbescar, how do you want yours? There's sugar but no milk."

"Two spoons sugar. No lemon?"

"Nay." He filled one of the larger mugs, and took it to Camnor Heslin, then bustled about, delivering hot cha to the others.

A blanket wrapped about her, Serroi sipped at her cha, delighting as much in the warmth that filled her as Ildas relished the fire. She smiled sleepily at Camnor Heslin as he strolled across to her.

"More storm," he murmured, raised a brow.

Clever man. Sees the trap and reads the connections. "Rather a swamp," she said, "one misstep and we're up to our necks." She started to ask him if he'd noticed the tension, then changed her mind.

The brow went up again and he winked at her. "Less said, less we have to sweep up."

The afternoon trickled on and on. The gaveks grew restless, took turns walking to the door and staring down the hall. Serroi slept a while, then got out her own cake of leather cream and began working on her boots. It passed the time while they waited for something to happen.

The room was quiet except for the crackle of the fire, the burr of the herbal bars on the leather and Adlayr Ryan-Turriy's faint snores. He'd moved the tray, wrapped himself in a blanket, and stretched out on the bench to sleep the wait away.

The light that struggled through the unceasing rain

grew dim, shadows crept out from the walls and the
basket of wood was almost empty by the time the nachod returned with another man with a round face and
a small hooked nose, his resemblance to a night flying
sova enhanced by the large, round, gold-rimmed
glasses he wore.

The nachod stood at attention, shoulders rigid,
thumbs pressed against his thighs. ''The Menguzhek
Kambin,'' he intoned.

''Your papers,'' the Menguzhek said, held out his
hand to Camnor Heslin who produced his transpass
without comment.

Serroi unfolded the blanket from around her, thrust
her feet back in her boots, and sat with her hands
folded in her lap. Adlayr sat up, smoothed his hair,
Zasya pulled her boots on and stood.

The Menguzhek took his time examining the transpass, then went to each of the others.

When he was finished, he said, ''Everything seems
to be in order. However, we cannot permit you to pass
through the State, not until your mission is made clear
to the Radwan. Relations between Govaritil and Dander are . . . ahhh . . . delicate at the moment. If you
will follow me?'' He waited impatiently while they
collected their gear and put on cloaks still damp from
the soaking they'd got.

Drawn up to an improvised canopy of canvas and
spears a black van waited for them, a closed box with
no windows, only a few ventilation slits up near the
roof. A gavek drooped on the driver's box, holding the
reins to a team of four draft malekainin who stood
with ears flicking and tails switching as the rain ran
down their horns and soaked their thick black hair.

Serroi started for the steps, but Camnor Heslin held
up a hand, stopping her and the others. ''One minute,

Menguzhek Kambin, I'm a representative of a sovereign and powerful republic. . . ." His voice vibrated with indignation. "Not a carft fresh dug from a field to be tossed in a wain and hauled to market. Provide more suitable transport or we will go nowhere with you."

The Menguzhek's thin lips compressed into a colorless line. Light blinking from the thick glass of his lenses, he stared at Camnor Heslin for several moments, then relaxed his face, it seemed by an effort of will. "This is no insult, Vorbescar. The city is in a dangerous ferment." He hesitated, then went on. "Two days ago, agitators introduced a bomb of some sort into the Radwan Rum and by the greatest of ill-fortune, the Val Kepal was killed, along with a number of our Radveks. Until the new Val Kepal is properly installed, volatile elements will be active and the streets very dangerous. It is your importance that impels me to insist you allow us to protect you, Vorbescar." The word *insist* was oh-so-lightly stressed; the meaning was clear.

Camnor Heslin scowled. "I do this under protest," he said. "Let that be clear." He mounted the steps into the dark interior, lowered himself onto one of the benches, and sat gazing stonily at the wall as the gaveks tossed his cases in.

Shivering and soaked, Serroi climbed the steps and settled on a bench across from him, smiled briefly as Ildas flew in and circled the box like wind-driven fire. Zasya followed her familiar, sat and stretched her long legs with a sign of relief. Adlayr grumbled to himself, squeezed water from his braid and pulled his boots off.

As the driver snapped his whip and the box lurched forward, Ildas nosed around the gloomy interior, making whining sounds that whinged at Serroi's nerves; Zasya winced, began scratching at the inside of her elbow where the noises were raising a rash.

Ildas brushed past Serroi's legs, a gentle flush of heat that was a lovely and all too brief hiatus in the gnawing of the cold drafts that wandered around about the floor. His whines and yips grew louder.

Adlayr frowned. "What?"

Zasya looked up from the weaponbelt she was poking through. "Ildas has found something odd. I think." She located the jar she wanted, unscrewed the lid, and began spreading cream on the rash.

Adlayr grinned. "Ghost roaches?"

"Have to wait till he winkles it out. I've never seen him act like this before." She put the lid back on, tucked the jar into its pocket, and snapped the flap down.

Serroi heard quick scrabbling noises under her bench, felt half a dozen brushes of heat as the Fireborn darted about beneath her, then something whizzed past her knee and flitted to the roof—a delicate oddity like a moth sprite that had grown ten times its usual size. Gauzy wings fluttered, black eyes turned and turned, a translucent body shimmered in the light from the single small lamp burning on the front wall.

On impulse Serroi lifted her hand, held it out, palm up.

The sprite fluttered into it and crouched there, shivering in terror.

Now that it was sitting still and close enough that she could make out details, Serroi saw that it was streaked with gray dust and dried . . . liquid—the streaks looked more like sap than blood. Its wings were torn near their trailing swallowtails and there were rips in the membrane.

Not it. She. The sprite had the form of an adult female, her body exquisitely formed though she was no taller than Serroi's hand. She was hurting and so frightened. . . . Serroi crooned to her, "It's all right, baby, it's all right, no one's going to hurt you here, quiet, little one, yesss, that's right, curl up and rest and we'll see what we can do about those wounds. . . ." She closed her eyes and let the power flow through her hand into the tiny body, at once strange beyond belief and sweetly familiar.

When the healing was done, there was a prickle in her palm. Serroi opened her eyes.

The sprite was kneeling, her back very straight as she fluttered her gossamer wings. Her mouth opened in a triangular smile, then produced a high sweet humming that translated into words inside Serroi's head. Honeydew bless you, big person, magic person, Honeydew is going to stay very close to you, big person, this place is scary, Honeydew ran away from the big man who caught her and put her in a cage, he think Honeydew stupid 'cause she won't talk to him, but he stupid 'cause he can't hear anyway, but Honeydew can feel you hearing, you don't need to be 'fraid, Honeydew look like spiderweb a breath can blow 'way, but Honeydew is tough, tougher than HE knew, stupid man. Honeydew scared a minute of the Firething that snuffle at her, but big person, magic person, he won't snuffle at you, so Honeydew not scared any more. The sprite jumped to her feet and went running down Serroi's arm. She settled herself on Serroi's shoulder, looking with bright interest at the others in the box.

Serroi laughed. "Her name is Honeydew," she said. "I think we've acquired a new companion."

After an interminable jolting up and down the little hills of Govaritil, the box leveled out, rolled a short distance and stopped. It shifted as the nachod climbed down; he opened the door and waited in the rain for them to descend, water streaming from his thin black hair. Behind him several more gaveks hovered, holding umbrellas.

As befit his status in his own eyes and the eyes of the Govaritzers, Camnor Heslin was first down the steps. He turned with majestic deliberation and beckoned to Serroi, the short gavek assigned to him straining to keep the umbrella over his head.

As soon as the door opened, Honeydew ducked inside Serroi's cloak, clinging to the cloth of her white healer's robe.

Despite the sprite's boast about her toughness, Serroi was uneasy about this, fearing to crush the lovely little oddity; but Camnor Heslin had spent the drive here choreographing this business down to the smallest movement and she had no time to spend on fussing. She pulled her cloak around her, took Adlayr's arm, and let him help her down the steps. Zasya dropped down without bothering to use the steps, Ildas riding her shoulder, a shimmer that some of the gaveks saw and some did not. It was an honor guard to daunt the boldest.

With the gaveks holding umbrellas over them, eyes shifting nervously among Heslin, Serroi and the stalking bodyguard, more of them grumbling along behind with the luggage, the companions moved into the Val Kepal's Istapan.

"A suite has been prepared for you and your entourage," the nachod told Camnor Heslin. "You should find everything you need there, but if there is something lacking, then just open the door and tell the gavek on guard. It will be furnished immediately."

As soon as the door was shut behind the nachod, Honeydew flitted from under the cloak. She darted about the room, swooped through an open door, came fluttering out, and continued exploring every place she could get into.

Serroi swung off the dump cloak and dropped it on the floor with her gearsac. "Some good things about our new cell. It's dry, the floor doesn't move, and there's room enough to breathe."

Camnor Heslin walked to a window door that led into a small, walled garden, inspected the iron grate a hand's width beyond the dusty glass, glass that was speckled with stray drops that managed to get under the awning above the door. In the court visible beyond the poles that held the awning up, rain was beating down on a patch of flags and churning a dead lawn into a mire, the wind was whipping leafless, dead bushes about, breaking up the brittle ones and blowing those that were still limber flat against the mud. He tried the latch, but the door was locked. He moved to a table beside the door, picked up a small glass sculpture, drew his finger through the film of dust that covered it, and set it down again. "And if we get hungry, we can plant a crop in the dust."

Serroi chuckled, then broke off as Honeydew came darting to her, landed on her shoulder, and began humming in her ear.

There a man in the wall, Honeydew hear his noises, touch his heat, find a peep and look, he a little man like the ones that brought he and he and he and she and she and you and Honeydew here, he listening and making marks on paper, Honeydew does think that what the man who snatch her called writing. Honeydew thinks the man in the wall is writing down what you say. Honeydew talk to him but he don't write so Honeydew thinks the man is one of those who can't hear her. She fluttered her wings and looked smug.

What wall? Where?

Honeydew swooped toward a wall, hovered in one place, shook her head, fluttered sideways along it till she reached the corner, then went joyful all over her

body. She slapped a tiny hand against the plaster,
darted back and perched on Serroi's shoulder. He move
'round in there.

How do you know where he is?

Honeydew feels the hot place he makes; the heat makes shapes in Honeydew's head. Healer doesn't feel the hot?

Not as you do, that seems clear. Would you do me a favor, Honeydew?

Yes, yes, yes, ask Honeydew, ask. She bounced happily on
the shoulder, one wing tickling Serroi's ear.

I'll take Camnor Heslin into the other rooms one by one. You come along and see if the man follows us. If there's any place where he can't get, let me know right away.

Honeydew can do that, yes yes. She bounced on the shoulder
a last time, then took off, flew in an excited loop about the
room, then hovered above Serroi's head.

Heslin had been watching all this with a slightly
scornful amusement. He was still ambiguous toward
her and meant her to know it.

"Shall we examine the dust in the other rooms?"
She held out her hand and smiled sweetly at him as he
put his arm under it.

There were two large bedrooms connected to sitting
rooms by archways filled with a sort of hanging net of
shells threaded on cord, two smaller bedrooms, one
on each side of a short hall, the bathroom at the end
of the hall. Serroi grinned at the sound of splashing
coming through the closed door, raised her brows at
Adlayr squatting against the wall, waiting his turn; he
looked up, his grin echoing hers. "Hot water, Zas
trying it out," he said. "Doing us good, they are."

"Eh vai, let's hope there's some left after the two of
you get through with it."

"So didn't the man say, you want something, ask
the gavek outside?"

"So he did."

Honeydew fluttered about for a moment, then landed in the small round vent high up in the door, wriggled through it, using her arms to fold her wings down so they'd fit. A moment later she was out again, sitting in the circle, wiping the dampness from her face and arms. When she was finished with that, she beckoned urgently to Serroi, ran down the arm the Healer lifted to her, and crouched by Serroi's ear.

It worse'n a summer fog in there; Honeydew's wings got wet and Honeydew was scared to fly. Man can't go there, no holes in wall. The echoes tell it all, tell it true.

Maiden Bless, Honeydew, that's a big help. Now rest yourself, I have to think on this. She held up her hand and when Honeydew had a good hold on it, set her down beside Adlayr. *I suspect Adlayr can hear you, so tell him what you told me.*

She straightened, put out her hand for Camnor Heslin's arm, and walked with such stately grace as she could manage with her head bobbing along by his ribs.

Back in the reception room, she picked up a footstool and carried it to the middle of the room. "Vorbescar, find yourself a chair and bring it here."

He leaned down so his head was close to hers. "So are you going to explain?"

"I doubt I need to," she grinned up at him, "or you wouldn't be talking in whispers."

"Rats in the woodwork?"

"With pad and stylo, taking notes. Not just listening either. Rat's got holes to peep through."

"I imagine that was why they kept us waiting so long." He looked at the smear of dust on his palm. "It certainly wasn't so they could do some housecleaning. Your new friend?"

"Seems she can read his heat through walls."

"Useful." Camnor Heslin rubbed his hand along his chin, beard stubble rasping against the palm. "Relations are always somewhat tricky between Govaritil and Dander. If it really was someone from Dander who set that bomb. . . ."

"Does it matter?"

"Ah. Probably not—as long as they believe it was. There could be another complication. A dynastic struggle brewing. If the Val Kepal hadn't set seal on his heir, and from what I know of this place, which isn't all that much, he wasn't fifty yet, so he probably hadn't, that means there's no one ready to step in his shoes. Just to make it more difficult, his two sons are identical twins and there's a tale I picked up when I was put on this assignment, a whisper that there's something confusing about their birth so no one is sure which is the elder. I don't like it; outsiders get chewed up in situations like this."

"Especially outsiders each side could find a use for?"

"Yes, Healer. You more than most. Best to say very little about your Talent, hmm?"

"Who am I, then?"

"A healer of the Biserica. A lie would interest them more than a diminution of the truth. You do know your herbs and poultices and so on?"

"Nay, Vorbescar, no more than a meie's teaching. I never had occasion to learn more." She shrugged. "Or time. The Talent appeared in the middle of the Sons' war, and I was rather busy then."

"Mp. I'll do my best with law and custom, but they make a feeble staff to lean on; we'll need to be looking for a way to run." Once again he rubbed at his chin, then pulled his hand down, irritated at the stubble; even when the Battatai was yawing and dipping at its most extravagant, he'd kept his face shaved clean.

She found his smaller vanities endearing, they reminded her so much of Hern. "We'll need to know how the city's laid out, where the guard points are. Do you sail? I'm thinking the fastest and safest route north should be the river. Do you know how far Govaritzer influence extends upriver?"

"You finished?"

"I could think of more questions, but those are enough to go on with."

"As I said before, my information about this place is best described as meager. This is a wing of the Istapan. Which is. . . ."

"I know that much. I've been through here before, remember? Some things last longer than others. Handy fortresses more than most."

His mouth twitched. "True. Tree women, to name another. To go on, I'm acquainted with the laws and political structure of the city. Which, I admit, is no great help at this particular moment. There was a Cadander Custom's House here, and a Marn's Voice. The Custom's agents will be interned by now and the Marn's Voice sitting a few rooms off if he's still alive. The Marn collects taxes from the Val Kepal, but her agents are allowed to approach no closer than ten stades to the NorthGate. Ten stades. That should answer one of your questions. And yes, I sail. Among the lot of us, we could probably manage a boat fairly well, enough to get it upriver to Dander. The Yellow Dan used to be a busy river. Marnhidda Vos keeps it cleared of snags."

Adlayr Ryan-Turriy came padding into the room, Honeydew riding his shoulder. He squatted and looked up at Camnor and Serroi. "You'll need a scout," he said. "I can run the night on four legs."

Camnor snorted. "And how do you propose to get out of here?"

Adlayr grinned at him. ''Thought I'd leave that to you, smart man.''

Serroi patted a yawn, spoke in her normal voice. ''Bathroom free yet?''

''Of all but steam.''

''Good. I want a bath. I've dreamed of a bath for weeks now.'' She got up, smiled at Honeydew who was snuggling in Aldlayr's long hair; he'd pulled it out of its braid so it could dry and it hung in a black fall nearly to his waist.

The sprite waved a languid hand and settled back as Adlayr and Camnor shifted into a fiercely whispered argument.

> > < <

Zasya pressed more soap into the crude lock, worked the probe to spread it around, then tried again to move the stiff wards. Behind her Heslin and Serroi were staging a loud argument about how to deal with their captors; they moved constantly, but kept between Zasya and the peeps Honeydew had located for them, their voices and movements covering any sounds she might make. She increased the pressure a degree and the ward abruptly clicked over. She probed for another, found it, tripped it, tried the latch, and smiled with pleasure as it moved under her hand. ''Ready?'' she whispered.

A soft growl answered her and a warm black head brushed against her arm.

She got to her feet, pulled the door open just wide enough to let the huge sicamar pad through it, Honeydew sitting on the loops of rope round his neck, clutching at the loose folds of skin and the thick black hair. As soon as they were out, Zasya pulled the door shut, and wiped off the lock plate. She stood watching

as the sicamar trotted across the muck, turned and
raced the length of the neglected garden, and leapt at
the wall. His front feet slapped down on the top, his
hind legs kicked against the bricks and he was on the
wall and running along it, a black shadow in the intermittent moonlight.

> > < <

Adlayr leapt and trotted from wall to wall as Honeydew flittered ahead, warning him of sentries, finding
a passable route for him in the complex of courts and
keeps until they reached a section of the outside wall
near the back where the stables were. There were
plenty of guards around, some with green badges,
some with red, but these greens and reds were more
suspicious of each other than of any attack from outside; the watch towers were empty because neither
faction would allow the other that advantage, nor did
they trust each other enough to mount the towers together. He crouched in the shadow of the merlons,
watching until he was sure there'd be no one coming
along, then he shifted to his man form, looped the
rope around one of the merlons and half-fell, half slid
down it, landing on a scrubby slope. He checked the
rope, smiling with satisfaction as he had a hard time
finding it against the soot-streaked stone.

He shifted again, this time to his trax form. As a
bird he was too heavy and clumsy to get off the ground
within the walls of the court; he needed the slant of
the slope and the running room it provided. Too bad
he wasn't a more efficient flier, but one worked with
what one had. He waited for Honeydew to settle on
his shoulders, then went bolting downslope until he
had the speed he needed and his bladders were filled
with liftgas, then he snapped his broad wings up,

down, up, down, powered himself into the air and went soaring over the city, counting the gavek patrols, following several of them to check out their routes, drifting over to the river, counting the boats and barges tied up there, looking for the right kind of boat in the right kind of place, small enough for them to handle, away from guard routes, with bales and such around so the companions could steal it without raising the alarm.

He found several that met his requirements, swept on out to check the guard towers at the RiverGate, then came drifting back, watching for guards again, this time looking for badges to see where the greens were, where the reds walked, the abrasion points where they met, exchanged insults, and occasionally fought.

Bored with this, Honeydew spread herself along his back and went to sleep; he could feel the heat of her tiny sores in his neck fur.

He kept on circling. He had to know the pattern of the night watch, had to see it work over time so the companions could choose the best moment to follow him over the wall.

An hour before dawn he widened the glide to take him back over the Istapan, watched the gavek movements inside the walls for two turns, then decided he had all he was going to get for the night. It was time to go back. He hesitated a moment. It would be so easy just to land in the garden and shift there. But that would leave the rope in place and someone was bound to find it. Not only would it cause a fuss, it would burn one of the best spots to go over the wall. *Ei vai, we do what we must. Honeydew, wake up! Come on, sprite, rise and shine and hang on tight. My landings are never easy and I don't want to have to worry about you. Honeydew!*

She stirred, yawned, grabbed a handful of trax fur and pulled herself up. Honeydew awake.

Both hands. And if you can fly off as I hit ground, you'll have an easier time.

He expelled the gas from the liftsacs in a long jet, the intestinal smell hovering round him as he fanned his wings desperately, worked his legs as soon as his talons touched ground, and still ended up with his toothy beak in the dirt.

Annoyed at Honeydew's fizzy laughter, he got his face clear and shifted to manform as quickly as he could manage. Brushing the mud off, he scrambled to his feet. *Honeydew, check the wall.*

Honeydew do. Giggling some more, the sprite fluttered to the top of the wall, perched on a merlon, a tiny spot of moonlit white against the dark stone. A moment later she tipped off the wall and came spiraling down to land light as thistledown on Adlayr's bare shoulder, showing him how a landing should be done, giggling again as she caught hold of his hair. All clear, nobody there. She took off again, hovered in the shadow of the tower so she could warn him if someone showed interest.

The journey back across the walls and roofs was tedious but not dangerous in any sense. The courts were mostly empty, filled with the gray silence of the time just before dawn. There were a few torches burning, but they were little more than coals. Overhead only the Dancers were up, the three moons in their early summer configuration, an elongated triangle of glows drifting in and out of the thinning clouds.

He dropped into the garden with a wet squelch, slid in the mud, then picked his way over tilting step-stones to the window door. He didn't have to scratch at it,

Zasya was there and had the door open as he reached it.

One of the used bath towels was on the floor and she handed him another as soon as he shifted back. "Don't want tracks," she murmured. "Don't have to worry about rats—they gone home to bed. Ildas learned the trick for finding them from Honeydew." She smiled at Honeydew who was hovering between them, watching them and listening. "Get anything?"

Adlayr held his hand out, tilted it back and forth. "Poh poh, I'll need another night to confirm."

"Heslin thinks it could get tricky fast, if the factions come after us. You see any of that?"

"Red badge, green badge, baring their teeth at each other. Some of it inside the walls, some of it in the streets."

'Ei vai, you'd best get some sleep. No telling what's going to stick its head up come daylight."

8. Politics

Vyzharnos' door was half open and K'vestmilly Vos could hear him moving in the bed. She knocked on the door, calling out, "Ready for company?"

"Dedach?"

She walked in, her face composed though the sight of the colorful bruise that distorted his face, the patch over his left eye, and all the bandages wrapped round him made her stomach churn. "K'milly, please. In here at least, I can get rid of that." She settled in the chair by the bed. "You're looking a bit livelier today."

"A corpse would've been livelier than I felt." He frowned, winced. "The Guards you sent to the Tower, did they get back?"

"Last night. They brought back the bodies, your father took their reports. If you'd like to see them. . . ."

He lifted the arm that wasn't burned, winced again, and eased it back down. "Nik, Dedach, I saw enough to furnish nightmares for years, I don't need to read more."

K'vestmilly frowned as he used the title, used it deliberately, the unpatched eye fixed on her face, an eye bluer than a modary's wing. The swelling, the bruise, the bandages made it hard to read his expression, but there was something about the curve of his mouth that she didn't much like. "There were six of them. Raid-

ers, I mean," she said. "They found tracks of six
rambuts, footprints of six men."

He turned his head away, closed his eye. "I thought
so," he said after a short silence. "They didn't come
for loot, just for killing."

"Why . . ."

"Think, woman. Six men, six rambuts. No packers
when they're hitting a barge that carries heavy cargo?"

"Oh. Yes, I see."

"What's going on? Tell me what's going on here.
You know. Tell me." His voice rose as he spoke; the
last words were almost a shout. A sekalari came to the
door, looked in. She saw K'vestmilly Vos and left
without comment.

He saw that; the corners of his mouth drew down
again. "Tell me," he said more quietly. "Who's playing games with people's lives?"

"We don't know."

Once again he closed his eye, turned his head away.

"It's the truth, Vyzharnos Oram. Your father's doing
everything he can to find out, questioning Nerodin,
looking everywhere he can think of."

"But not at himself."

"Don't be an idiot. Himself? Marn says he's the
loyalest of all her administrators."

"He is that."

She winced at the contempt in his voice; it was
aimed at her as much as at his father. Her mother said
he didn't care a fistful of spit for any of them, but she
didn't know the whole of it. Those three simple words
. . . they sent a chill to her belly, then anger surging
through her.

"More than anyone can say about you, kicking your
family in the face like you did."

He wouldn't look at her; when he spoke it was to
the wall. "Rodin . . . you . . . you're all alike, charm-

ing as moth sprites on a warm spring evening, zhagdeep black behind your smiles.''

K'vestmilly stirred on her chair; she didn't have to
take this kind of abuse. But she didn't move. She stared
at the clean line of his jaw—the bruised side was down,
hidden against the pillow—the way his eye was set beneath the light brown brow that angled up as if it were
a black bird's wing, the arc of long, thick, gold-tipped
lashes that glowed against the tan he hadn't had time
to lose. *Maiden Bless, why does this have to happen
to me now? And to be him!*

"What did you mean," she said, "look at himself?"

She saw his throat move, as if he swallowed, then
he brought his head around so he could see her. "I
didn't mean he was behind it, only that it's likely one
of his friends is playing him for a fool."

"One of the Families."

"There's plenty of precedent. It's not something you
learn in school, that's for sure, zdra zdra, maybe you
do, but not the Nerodin. It's happened several times;
one of the Pans gets ambitious, wants to make a Marn,
but only makes pain."

"If he hasn't thought of that, the Marn has." She
looked down at the hands folded in her lap, trying to
keep her ignorance from him. She'd never questioned
anything she'd been taught, hadn't been interested
enough, just absorbed what her tutors gave her, spewed
it back at test time, and forgot most of it before a day
had passed. *I'll have to talk to Marn, read more history . . . if I can find honest books . . . Maiden Bless,
life is complicated, I wish . . . I DON'T LIKE FEEL-
ING STUPID! And it's dangerous . . . especially now
. . . dangerous. . . .* "Why did you leave home? Your
father said, the way you lived, hungry, hard labor,
filth, he couldn't understand you, not at all."

His mouth moved in something like a smile, as if

he were pleased she asked. ''I went to find my father
one day; I'd just finished a poem I was rather proud
of and he liked to hear me read, he was good about
that.'' He said the words slowly, separating them with
small pauses. ''And I saw him watching a Nerod being
tortured. Just sitting there watching. And listening.''

''You knew what he did. You must have.''

''Knowing and seeing . . . smelling. . . .'' His
mouth worked and he was green under the tan. ''It's
different''

''Prak, he irritates the zhag out me sometimes, but
he's not a cruel man. He does what he must to keep
you safe, you and those Nerodin you love so much.''

''He does what he does to keep your Family in
power.''

''What's so wrong with that? Marnhidda Vos is a
good ruler. Our dungeons aren't full, teachers can say
what they need to in the schools, we don't have beggars in the streets. These bombs, the raids, they HAVE
to come from outside. I don't care what you say about
the Families, the Marn handles them, pets them when
she has to and lays the whip on their sides when she
has to. A tyrant can rule by violence for a single generation, but the Vos Family has ruled for a hundred.
Think about that.''

He grinned at her, lopsided but charming enough to
melt her insides. ''Quoting your mama?''

''Don't patronize me, Poet.''

''Prak, that wasn't fair. Tell me something. You ever
been in any of those homes you're glossing over with
history lessons?''

''Have you?''

''Oh, yes, Dedach. Whatever you dream, Dedach,
there are Nerodin in Dander and Calanda who go to
bed hungry and wake up hungrier and quietly die after
a while.'' His eye dropped shut. ''There were times I

was close to starving.'' His mouth tightened and he
made an impatient movement of his hand. ''It wasn't
real, not like them. If it came down to dying or eating
some untasty words, I could always go home. They
were home. Home is where you die, even if it's only
a patch of street.'' Eye open again, he stared past her,
lost in memory for the moment. ''When they started
to trust me, the Nerodin I worked on the wharves with
would give me dinner with their families, those that
had families. I'd write a verse for them to say my
thanks. It was all I had, and they'd take it, giving me
my dignity. They know about dignity, those men.
Sometimes I'd sit with the kids so their wives and they
could have some time free on fete-eves. I liked that,
when the kids were in bed, it was quiet and warm, not
like the room I had in the hostel. I could write. . . .''
His face suddenly suffused with blood, anger hardened
that blue blue eye. ''They're dying, Dedach,'' he
shouted. ''Marn's doing nothing. NOTHING!''

Bozhka Sekan pushed the door open and stumped
into the room. ''That's enough of that. Dedach, go
home. You're agitating my patient.'' As K'vestmilly
stood, she added, ''And don't go fussing your mother
either, she's resting.''

K'vestmilly Vos kicked along the corridor, feeling
as if between them Vyzharnos and Bozhka had stripped
the past five years off her bones and she was a grubby
girl again, trying to slip out on her tutors. One treated
her like an idiot, the other like a child.

''Aaahhhh!'' She flung her arms wide, startling several maids, then speeded to a trot, enjoying the consternation she caused as she loped through the halls,
enjoying the shift of her muscles, singing to herself,
*I'm going to see my father, my father, I'm going to see
my father*. When she reached her own set of rooms,

she bounded inside, slamming the door, and began undoing the buttons on her tunic.

"Puzhee, where are you? I want going out clothes, something plain, dull, something that makes you yawn to look at it."

Her maid came from the bedroom, a big woman with a horsey face and mild brown eyes. She smiled at K'vestmilly. "Did you have a nice visit, Deda'?"

K'vestmilly opened her eyes wide, then she laughed. "Yes, I think I did, taking it as a whole. There's somebody in the city I need to visit, what've I got to wear that's boring enough to make me look like part of the wall?"

"Nyni, Deda', you not goin' out 'thout guards, are you? You promise y' Mum you wouldn't do that."

"Zdra zdra, I'll pick up somebody from Oram's office, someone who won't make a long shadow. Clothes, clothes, Puzhee, and then we have to do something about my hair."

A gawky gray shadow, K'vestmilly Vos hesitated before the door to Jestranos Oram's offices. Oram was probably going to be difficult about this. She squared her shoulders and pushed the door open.

Letenk Kouley, Oram's aide and acting gateguard, looked up as she came in, didn't recognize her, and went back to his scribbling. She scowled and sat down on the bench pushed up against the wall. The silence in the anteroom was broken only by the scratch of his stylo and the buzz of a fly on a windowpane. She shifted on the hard bench, crossed her ankles. She was used to going where she wanted, when she wanted. Letenk was all smiles and bows the other times when she came with her hair unwrapped, in the trousers and tunic she found most comfortable for informal wear. He'd rushed past others waiting on the bench she was sitting on right now, ushered her into Oram's sanctum. She crossed her ankles the other way. This was boring and time wasting. She started to get up, then settled back as she remembered Vyzharnos' words, *I starved a little in the beginning, but it wasn't real, I could always go home.* Her mouth twitched as she began to find the absurdity in the situation. *Letenk will vych rocks when he finds out who he's been keeping waiting, just to show off his importance.*

The aide set his stylo down, squared his papers. "Prak, jama, what business do you have with the Inquisitor? And do you have an appointment?"

She rose from the bench and sauntered over to him, bored with games, all pretense of humility wiped away. "Since when do I need an appointment, aide?"

He paled as he recognized her voice, scrambled to his feet. "Pardon me, Dedach, pardon me, I didn't realize it was you, of course you don't need an appointment. . . ." Still babbling, he flung open the door, bowed her into the inner office and retreated to his desk, so rattled he forgot to close the door.

K'vestmilly clicked it shut. "Why does he do that, Oram? He must know we don't drop idiots in the dungeons."

Jestranos Oram sighed, set the paper he was reading on one of the mounds heaped at the side of his worktable. "If you really want to know, ask him. What is it, Dedach?"

"I need to go into the city and I promised the Marn I wouldn't go out without a guard, but I want one in ordinary clothes with a little more intelligence than your aide out there. If he works out, I want him assigned to me." She raised a brow, felt the pull of gelled hair, and let it drop. "It'd make things simpler, wouldn't it. You'd get reports straight from the witness. Seriously, Oram . . ." she hesitated, scowled at him. She didn't like this or him, but the Marn trusted him and her mother's instincts were formidable. "I've been discovering the dimensions of my ignorance. It's not a comfortable state, but it's curable. I'm not going to do anything stupid, mostly just walk around, listen to Nerodin talking, see how they live, maybe talk to some merchants while I'm buying things."

His eyes narrowed, his face unreadable, he contemplated her for several moments, then, somewhat to her surprise, he nodded. "It's a good idea. To my shame, I must admit that with a guard you'd be as safe on the streets as you are in here. Just one caution, Dedach, if you see something you don't like, tell me. Don't try to right it yourself. You have a generous heart, but as you said, you lack knowledge. Good intentions have caused more damage than the evilest of motives." Without waiting for a response, he pulled the bell cord.

When the aide came in, a sheen of sweat on his face, Jestranos Oram said, "Send for Hedivy Starab, tell him to come in street clothes."

The aide started to leave, then turned back. "Hedivy," he said, "he's sleeping, Inquisitor, he only got back from Govaritil two hours ago, somewhat battered. It was apparently a difficult passage. The report's on my desk. I was copying it for the files."

"I see. Send for him anyway. He can sleep later. Street clothes, remember."

"Yes, Inquisitor."

When the door closed, Jestranos Oram said, "Hedivy's one of my best agents, but he's been going a bit too hard lately; this'll be a way of getting him to take a rest. You wanted intelligence, he has it. He's not much to look at, like a caricature of one of those farmers up from the Zemyadel for the day to see the sights of the big cities. You'll think he's clumsy and stupid, but he isn't. Far from it. If something comes up and he has to act, stay out of his way, he gets a bit heedless in fight mode, but I'd set him alone against a dozen hard types, bet on him to walk away and leave them on the ground.''

''Have I seen him? Where's he from?''

''I doubt it. He's usually somewhere else. From the Zemyadel.'' Oram rubbed his hand across his beard, a frosty twinkle in his light eyes. ''He has the look by right. He was the seventh son of a small farmer, his mother's pet, his father's punching ball, and bored by farming. Ran away when he was about fourteen, managed to join a pack of wharf rats in the Shipper's Quarter, here in Dander. In half a year, he was running the pack, turned them into more than snatch-and-grab lappets until he had a thriving business going in stolen goods and was moving into protection. I gathered in the pack round then, wasn't enough evidence to send him to the post and none of his lappets talked, though we did have a try at them. Fifteen, saaa.'' He shook his head. ''He's been working for me since, mostly because it's more intriguing than anything else he can do. He's not going to like trailing you around, Dedach. I offer you a challenge. Charm him, make him glad to do it.''

''Hunh! Sly man, keeping me out of your hair, hmm?'' She sighed. ''Zdra zdra, I have to admit it, you've interested me.''

He looked down at his hands, rubbing thumbs against forefingers. ''I hear you saw my son.''

''Hmp. He's healing fast and I must say, there's nothing wrong with his tongue.''

''Young idiot. His crazy ideas. . . .''

''I don't know, some of them made sense.''

He lifted his head, startled. ''What?''

''He told me I was a ball of fluff with maybe charm but not much else.''

"He what!"

"Not in those words, but it was what he meant. It's why I'm here. You yourself said that's a good idea."

A knock on the door stopped whatever he'd planned to say. He leaned back, hands on the arms of his chair. "Enter."

The bulky man slouched in, his light brown hair a frizz about his big head, eyes half closed, the dark patches under them extending halfway down his round, sullen face. "Soah," he grumbled, "what is it now?" The lingering echoes of the Zemyadel lilt in his voice went oddly with its rough rumbling.

"A few hours' work, it won't strain you. The Dedach here wants to go into the city without making a fuss. She wants to see for herself how Nerodin live, listen to them talk, you know the sort of thing."

Hedivy turned to stare at K'vestmilly Vos; his eyes were an odd gray-green, right now more green than gray, smooth and shiny like polished stones, frightening eyes because there seemed to be no soul behind them. "Why me?"

"We stopped another sleepwalker last night. One of the maids; she got to the door of the Marn's bedroom." He caught K'vestmilly's start, nodded. "That's the fifth. They're coming faster. I want the Dedach back whole and alive, but I want her to see what she needs to see. Who better than you?"

"Do I watch my tongue, Dedach?"

"Nik," she said. "I've got no time for anything but hard truths. You know them, tell me."

"Why?" Before she could answer, he grimaced and added clarification. "Why no time?"

"If the Marn is killed, I have to be ready. I've been dreaming, but now I'm awake."

"Prak," he said. "I'll do it." He looked her over. "First thing, change those clothes."

"These are the plainest things I've got."

"Mp. Shout slumming. Soah the color's dull, that is not what a Nerod would be looking at, they would be gauging the quality of the weave. No countrywife 'd have weave that fine. Oram, Zemyadinna's gear for the Dedach, Zemya for me. And a southron mix to the coin we spend, some rapeens from Gov, a few bits of Island copper, with the usual lot of medzas and stribs."

"Yes, I agree. That's good."

"Another thing. Goin' nowhere today."

"What!" K'vestmilly Vos jumped to her feet. "I won't have. . . ."

"You said you want truth." As K'vestmilly winced at the acid in his voice, Hedivy went on. "I thought so. A game. You want games, you get someone else. You want to learn something, you do what I tell you."

She sat down. "Explain, please."

"You can trust Oram, you can trust me. Anyone else, you should forget it. Hands of folk will be knowing you planned to go out, prak? Nik, be quiet and listen. This place swarms with Nerodin you never notice, Dedach. how many saw you drest like that? How much thought would they need to find the reason for 't? Then it's only to watch and guess where you go, and what'll be waiting for you but a dreamer with a bomb. And it'll not only be you that's killed but everyone around you."

"I see. And how do I avoid this tomorrow?"

"Good. You listen. You go to the mews, there's a gate near there, you know it. . . ."

"My birds have been taken away."

Hedivy turned his head. "You will have them returned, Inquisitor, that will be a better excuse than any we could invent."

Jestranos Oram laced his fingers together. "I'll talk to the Marn; I'm sure it could be done."

"You will go to the mews then, Dedach, and you will greet your birds. Spin the Keeper a tale for the yellow of his eyes; you know better than I what he'll expect from you. I will be waiting near the wall beyond; you will change your clothes there and we will go walking. And that is enough of that. Send for my report, Inquisitor. There are things in it the Marn should know and quickly, and the sending will explain why you called me here."

"Letenk is loyal as they come."

"So were they all, your sleepwalkers."

"Accepted."

K'vestmilly Vos pulled the scarf from her head, ran her fingers through her hair until she'd broken it free of the gel she and Puzhee had slathered on it. She grinned at Hedivy, knowing she looked a raggle-headed urchin. She was starting to appreciate him; in some ways he was like Vyzharnos Oram, he wouldn't give a handful of spit for all her titles and pomp, he didn't want to rule anyone but himself. And he was sharp. No feelings though, or if there were, they were buried so deep he'd forgot he had them. *I can't get too comfortable around him. Maiden knows where his loyalties lie. If he has any except to himself.*

The aide placed the report folder on the worktable, glanced at K'vestmilly Vos, and scurried out again, shutting the door carefully behind him.

Jestranos Oram tapped his thumbs on the folder. "I'll read it later; sit down and tell me the parts I need to know."

Hedivy lifted a chair and set it in front of the work-table, turned a little so his back wasn't fully toward K'vestmilly Vos, moving with that same controlled silence he'd shown from the moment he came in. Not turning his back on her was neither courtesy nor a compliment; it was obvious he never turned his back on anyone.

"You were right, Inquisitor, supplies for these attacks are most definitely coming in through Govaritil, mostly on Shimzely ships. I wouldna swear to it, I was hearing it from a drunken Shimzy sailor, toward the end of his ramblings before he happened to fall in the river, he said there were black ships that came into the harbor at Bokivada and transferred cargo directly to Shimzy ships, his ship for one, cargo they brought north to Govaritil, cargo that seemed to vanish without being unloaded once they were at wharf. He was saying they vanished in a swirl of black smoke, but Shimzys are like that, so it's hard to know just how much truth is there and how much hot air."

"From beyond Shimzely? That doesn't make sense. I could believe Govaritil playing games, but. . . ." He glanced at the folder, then fixed his eyes on Hedivy. "Where do these ships come from?"

"He didn't say. Wouldn't say. Whoever the Enemy be, he is not Govaritil. Unless the Twins are smarter—and twistier—than they look to be. Two days before I left Govaritil, a bomb blew the Radwan Rum and killed the Val Kepal. Notice pinned to the door with a three-edged knife, the Mask of Marn carved into handle. Said this: Marnhidda Vos is sending a message to bombthrowers; what they gave they are to receive. They believed it, hauled in every Cadandri in the city and locked 'em up. Told Marn's Voice stick your nose out and we cut it off, barges 'n cargoes 've been impounded. Gritz busy takin' other barges as they come in. 'T would be a good idea to send a relay downriver to warn those who aren't there yet to turn round and maybe head for Tuku-kul instead. 'T would be an even better idea to get in some of those communicators I keep askin' for.''

''I know, I've tried, but the Treddekkap won't come up with the money.''

''Now they losing hard cash with those barges, maybe they see reason. Or maybe Marn gets off the stump and does what she did ought to've done a year ago.''

Jestranos Oram shook his head. ''Too late. It'd take months to get a shipment here from the Mijloc and even then, the raiders could hit the barge and probably would; they haven't passed up much.''

''Send for them, Inquisitor. Send someone you trust. We gonna need 'em.''

''I'll see what I can do.'' He drew his hand across his mouth, then made a note on a slip of paper he took from one of the piles. ''Anything else?''

''Day I left, a source of mine said gaveks they arrested a meie 'n a gyes and some important types traveling with them. Coming here, he says. You know 'bout that?''

Jestranos Oram looked down at his thumbs tapping lightly on the slip of paper. ''I knew about them, yes. We'll talk about this later. I might want to send you back, see what you can do to pry them loose.''

''Send me now. Some of my connections are dead or locked up, but most of them they went to ground when scour started.''

''Nik, I have to talk to the Marn first and do some thinking. This isn't something to rush into. Even Govaritzers aren't idiots enough to make the Biserica put the curse on them, it might well mean they lose all the Mijloc trade to Tuku-kul and the land roads.''

''I tell you, Inquisitor, way they're stirred up down there, 't would be no surprise should they do something crazy.''

"Nonetheless, you'll spend the next two or three days taking the Dedach around. Show her what she needs to see and I'll let you know when I'm ready for you. Go get yourself some sleep, Hedivy, I'll have the Zemya gear waiting for you tomorrow morning."

Hedivy Starab got to his feet and stumped out.

K'vestmilly raised her brows. "From the look of him, he could eat nails and spit out needles."

Jestranos Oram leaned back in his chair, looking not quite so tired as he had been, the lines softened in his face, something like approval in his eyes. "He's a good man at his job, but that's all the good that's in him. Remember that, Dedach." He got to his feet. "I'd better see the Marn right away. Get me in to her, will you?"

"Yes, but don't send me away once you're there. Agreed?"

"Agreed."

9. Dancer on the Altar

The light had no source nor was it like other light—shapeless, expending itself in all directions equally. It was warm and yellow as butter-amber with sunlight behind it, and like amber there were shadows inside, shadows that hinted at something strange and marvelous.

It danced on the altar of the ancient shrine in the low curving hills outside Dander, moved and flowed to the beat of the tambours and the chant of those in the shadows of the walls. Kazim, kazim, they sang, meaning Glory Glory.

Treshtal danced before the altar, his bare feet scraping and splatting on the gritty flags, his body echoing the shifts of the light with a fidelity remarkable in a less fluid form. His eyes saw nothing but gold, yet he didn't miss a step.

The chant and the drums grew louder, swept him higher and higher until he leapt upon the altar and merged with the light.

For the first time he spoke, his voice echoing within itself as if many spoke, not one. "Come and be blessed, come and be healed."

He stretched out his arms and the drums fell silent, the chant ceased.

One by one the dark robed shadows came into the light; the robes were heavy coarse weave with pointed cowls that hid the faces of the men and women from each other and from him. They came and bowed, setting their hands on the altar, hands hidden in the overlong sleeves of their robes. He bent and laid his hand upon the hidden head and the golden light flowed round the figure, melding the two into a single entity, then it flowed back and the worshiper walked away, head down, quiet, but throbbing with a force that tickled at those still waiting, a promise of the ecstasy they remembered from the other times, hunger gone, sickness healed, sadness turned to joy, and over it all the communion with the Glory that was indescribable and more necessary each time they experienced it.

As each was touched, he or she left the chamber, stripped off the robe in the anteroom, tossed it in a corner, and hurried out to get lost in the night.

Several times as he touched, Treshtal murmured, "Stay."

These didn't leave like the others but went to kneel at the back of the chamber, merging with the shadows.

Treshtal throbbed as the Light flowed through him, stronger this night than it had ever been, more present; he exulted in the power of his dance, in the vigor of his spirit and the hope that was still unspoken and unshared with these who came to worship the Glory, the hope that the land would be purged of the Families and the evil they wrought on all around them.

The last of the worshipers went out.

He settled himself on the worn altar stone, legs in a lotus knot, the light shifting and flowing around him. He lifted a hand, held it flat, the fingers splayed. "Come," he said, his voice floating out across the room with the lines of golden light that flowed from his fingers to touch the four kneelers at the back of the room. "Come here."

They rose as one and shuffled stiffly across the flags to stand in a row before him. "Sit," he said. Once they were down, he said, "Sleep." Heads drooping, shoulders slumped, they slept. He closed his hand into a fist, pointed a finger at the first of the figures. "Kurzak Uspezhny, speak and answer me. Where do you work?"

"The Leatherworks. I am a tanner and dyer." The man's voice was hoarse, with a drag to it.

"I have Glory's ardor. Will you take it?"

"I will take it."

"Will you place it among the dye vats, where no one will see it but you?"

"I will place it among the dye vats, where no one will see it but me."

"If anyone asks you anything at all that touches on the Glory, you will not answer, your heart will cease to beat."

"If anyone asks me anything at all that touches on the Glory, I will not answer, my heart will cease to beat."

"Stand, Kurzak Uspezhny, hold out your hand."

The robed figure got stiffly to his feet, turned back the hem of his sleeve to bare his hand and reached out.

Treshtal gave him an ardor, a small round blackness like a child's toy. "Hide this in your clothes," he said. "Speak of it to no one, be careful that no one sees it, do not think about it once you have placed it, and when you have placed it, forget what you have done. Go now, go home and be as you always are."

When Kurzak Uspezhny was gone, he pointed his finger at the next sleeper. "Semesh Karovyn, speak and answer me. Where do you work?"

It was a woman's voice that answered this time, hoarse and dragging like the first. "In the laundry of

the Pevranamist. I collect dirty sheets and used linen
and take them to be washed.''

"Do you go into the Marn's rooms?''

"No one but Sluzha and Bozhka Sekan goes into
the Marn's rooms. It is not even permitted to go close.
The maid Sluzha leaves the sheets two corridors
away.''

"Do you go into the Dedach's rooms?''

"Until two months ago I did, but now it is the same
as with the Marn.''

"Can you get into the dining rooms?''

"On the morning after a state dinner, I collect the
cloths from the tables and the other linens provided
for the guests.''

"Do you know when the next dinner is?''

"It is two days on. They expect an embassade from
Tuku-kul. There will be dinners each night as long as
they are here.''

"I have Glory's ardor. Will you take it?''

"I will take it.''

"Will you place it at the Marn's table, underneath,
where no one will see it but you?''

"I will place it at the Marn's table, underneath,
where no one will see it but me.''

When the last of the new-made slaves left, Treshtal
jumped to his feet and gave a wild cry of triumph and
jubilation. "Glory, glory, GLORY!''

Then he stretched out on the worn rectangular altar
stone and slept.

10. Plotting and Execution

Camnor Heslin, Vorbescar of the Grand Council of the Mijloc, swept into the throne room on the winds of indignation.

As she followed him in, Serroi watched Ildas racing wildly about the huge room, worried briefly that he might set on fire the white-paper streamers that hung in corkscrew twists from every knob, bump, lump, and prominence on the walls. She glanced at Zasya, but the meie looked alert and unconcerned, so she forgot the Fireborn and tried to look as inconspicuous as she could while she took in everything around her.

The room was filled with groups of scowling men, no women visible. They were all dressed in the spotless white, mourning white, even the guards. The throne on the high dais was draped in more white ribbons and piled high, almost buried, in white paper sculptures, folded and glued into birds, fish, and beasts of all sorts, and all around the base of the chair, set in phalanx after phalanx, white paper soldiers stood at attention. And in the middle of all these soldiers, erect and menacing, was a life-sized, white paper sculpture of the dead Val Kepal.

A step down from the high dais there were two smaller chairs draped in white velvet, one to the left, the other to the right of the throne. Two young men sat on those demithrones and it was as if one were the mirror of the other, Takuboure on the right and Ta-kuzhone on the left.

The scowls were the same, the thatch of soft black hair, straight and thick, the golden eyes, the pale skin, the bony faces and big hands. When they looked at each other, Serroi could almost hear the sound of swords clashing.

The floor was an intricate mosaic, an undersea scene in blue and green tiles with thick gold and silver wire worked into the design; Camnor's bootheels clicked loudly on those tiles as he strode toward the thrones, drawing glares that smoldered hotter than Ildas.

Taken away earlier when their bodies were searched to the last smear of dust, their papers lay in a heap on a table beside the stairs to the dais. In white like the others, his hair braided with narrow white ribbons, the glitter of his spectacles hiding whatever expression his eyes had, the Menguzhek stood waiting beside the table.

Camnor Heslin brushed past the guard who stopped them, marched to the table, collected the papers, green eyes fixed on the Menguzhek's glitter, daring the man to object. He bowed to the Twins, stalked back to the companions, and stood waiting. Serroi bit her lip to keep from grinning.

Takuboure leaned forward. "What business do you have in Dander, Vorbescar?"

Camnor Heslin's deep rich voice rolled out, filling the room and making the young man's tenor seem a pale squeak. "There's no secret about it. I go in two roles. It is the present policy of the Grand Council of the Mijloc to send a Vorbescar with meien and gyes when they leave on Ward if the Land they go to has no official representative living there, which is the case with Cadander. It is a matter of standing witness for and offering protection to our citizens, since all meien

and gyes become citizens if they are not already so
when they contract for their first Ward. I will also serve
as trade representative and Council representative to
Marnhidda Vos and her advisers, reporting back to the
Grand Council on matters in which they would have
an interest.''

Serroi relaxed as she listened. *He knows his business, our Vorbescar. Pomposity on demand, how to
flatter by implication. Look at them preen, especially
that one on the right. The left one's smarter, I think.
We'll see. . . .*

''Ah.'' Takuzhone lifted his head. ''A spy.''

Camnor Heslin seemed to swell. ''Certainly not,''
he roared. ''Spy? Me? Never!'' More sedately, he finished, ''Everything will be done with the knowledge
and approval of the Marn.''

''Well, then.'' Takuzhone settled back, crossed his
hands on his flat stomach. ''The answer to this difficulty is simple. Just change your destination. We have
residences newly available, very comfortable, and I'm
sure we can find sufficient trade to make up for whatever Cadander would have provided.''

Camnor Heslin laid his hand on his heart and bowed,
then he said, ''It would be an elegant solution if it
were it possible, O KuaSar, but it is not in my power
to make such a radical change in my mission. And it
would be an unforgivable insult to a Land which has
been friend and ally to the Mijloc as long as history
has been written. I must present my papers in the
Marn's Court or not at all.''

Takuboure, who'd been fidgeting restlessly during
this speech, slapped his hand on the arm of his demi-
throne. ''Then it will be not at all. When they killed
our father, they declared war on Govaritil. Let them
take the consequences of their acts. As you will, fat
man. Take them out of my sight. They make me sick.''

* * *

As soon as the door closed behind their escorts, Honeydew came fluttering from the drapes and landed on Serroi's shoulder. Adlee, Serree, they come, they leave guns but they take bullets, they take them all, they take the knives and the swords, even the big man's; they argue and argue about it but they take it. They empty out belts and take everything in pockets, everything, even needles and thread.

"Saaa."

Chuckling at the way the others scattered after she'd reported what Honeydew told her, Serroi crossed to the window door to try the latch and found it unlocked; she went out and stood on the paving under the canopy. A brisk wind whipped the white healer's robe about her legs, teased her hair into a wild tangle, the ends snapping against her face. Still on her shoulder, Honeydew shivered, complained a little, then fluttered back inside.

The sky was a brilliant cloudless blue, the sun seemed larger, brighter, hotter after all the days of woolly gray cloud and dull gray light.

Zasya brought Ildas out, ran with him, played with him; they filled the court with her laughter and his squeals, silent sounds that tickled Serroi's mind. Finally the Fireborn skittered across the rapidly drying mud, dug his claws into the soft bricks of the wallface, and went up it like fire burning up a curtain; when he reached the top he stretched out in the sun and with a tiny sigh that only Serroi and Zasya heard, drifted into sleep.

Serroi chuckled. "He's not worried about much."

"Unlike our Vorbescar." Zasya patted a yawn. "He's in a real snit, that one. They made a glorious mess of his clothes and walked off with his store of canned goodies. When I left, he was out in the hall, yelling at the gavek about diplomatic privilege and thieves and things like that, confusing the poor guard no end."

The scowling nachod slammed the case on the floor. "You!" he said, jabbing a finger at Adlayr then at Zasya. "And you, come with me." He held up a hand as Camnor Heslin started to protest. "You've caused enough trouble, fat man, shut your mouth. You two, you can walk or we'll carry you."

At the nachod's first words Serroi backed against the drapes beside the windowdoor. *Honeydew, can you fly after them and see where they're taken?*

'Tis scary, Serree, but Honeydew can do, Honeydew will do.

Ei vai, get into the folds of my robe, quickly now, they're about to go.

As soon as Honeydew was in place, Serroi hurried across the room, miming agitation and anger, her small hands fluttering. "What are you doing?" she cried out, "Where are you taking them? It's not right, leave us alone, we haven't hurt you."

Wriggling, pushing, waving her elbows, Serroi maneuvered herself into the hallway despite the shoves and shouts from the guards; having accomplished what she wanted, she allowed herself to be soothed by Camnor Heslin and drawn weeping back into the reception room. Before the nachod slammed the door shut and turned the key in the lock, she glimpsed through her fingers the tiny figure of the sprite crouching almost invisible against the baseboard.

"Come into the garden," Camnor Heslin crooned to her, mindful of rats in the walls, "come into the garden, Healer, the sun will warm the chill away."

In the middle of the waste that had been a garden he turned loose of her and stepped back. "And what was that nonsense for?"

"Don't be an idiot, Heslin. How else could I get Honeydew out there without her being seen?"

"Ah."

"It was all I could think of. There was so little time." She stroked her eyespot, stared past him. "Clever bit, Honeydew, she'll tell us where they've been taken and what's happened to them." A blink and a shiver, then she turned, faced him again. "And you! Why such a fuss about a few comfits?"

"It was necessary," he said. "I don't like this separating us." He clasped his hands behind him and began pacing along the stepping stones, three steps east, turn, three steps west, turn again. "It's a delicate balance we hold. Govaritil lives off trade," turn, "The Mijloc has a monopoly on certain items, but it's a long way off," turn, "times are changing, but the Biserica's name still carries weight," turn, "on the other hand, passions are hot and those boys have about a half-wit between them," turn, "Takuboure especially, if he wins control, he'll be marching against Dander before summersend, burning everything ahead of him," turn, "Takuzhone seems a little less impetuous—and a lot more treacherous." He stopped in front of her, set his hands on her shoulders, his dark eyes worried. "Adlayr wanted to make another sweep, but we'll have to do what we can with the information in hand. If we don't get out tonight, I've a notion some of us won't get out at all."

> > < <

Honeydew was weary and desperately uneasy by the time the gaveks stopped marching down twisty stairs, through the maze of corridors and went into a stone-walled room filled with smoky light and stench from huge oil lamps hanging from the chains that looped across the high ceiling. Shivering with fear for herself, but also afraid she'd be shut out when they swung that massive door closed, she clamped tiny teeth on her lower lip, darted through and up as high as she could get before landing on one of the chains. The link she straddled was filthy with a mix of dust and oil from the lamp and other things she didn't like to think about. Careful to keep her wings free of the muck, her stomach clenching with disgust, she clasped the link and looked down.

Along the walls of the long room were *things* of black iron, twisty things, ugly and stinking of pain, and in the center was a cumbersome table, a dozen chairs placed about it, in front of them black iron cuffs rising from the age-dark, blood-stained wood. Adlayr and Zasya sat in chairs at the end nearest the lamp where Honeydew clung.

Two of the gaveks were tightening cuffs on Adlayr Ryan-Turriy's thin wrists. Zasya was already immobilized.

At the far end of the table a man stood watching, a young man with thick soft black hair and eyes that shone yellow as if they'd stolen their color from the lamps. He was leaning on hands flattened on the tabletop, his face a mask of hostility as he watched the gavek finish his work; beside his right hand there was a peculiar knife with a blade as broad as it was long— it looked at once clumsy and dangerous.

The nachod tugged at the cuff, at Adlayr's arm, then he straightened. "They are ready, KuaSar" he said.

"Good. Wait outside."

The nachod bowed.

"And this is no one's business but mine. I will NOT be interrupted. Do you understand?"

The nachod bowed. With a snap of his fingers he

collected the other gaveks around him and marched out.

The one they called KuaSar lifted the cutter, held the tip of the handle with one hand as he balanced the thick, flat back of the blade on his wrist. "When I was a boy," he murmured, "I used to run away to the kitchen. I was always hungry. They said I must have a tapeworm in me because I never got fat, not like that gross friend of yours. One of the cooks was a magic man, not a wizard or a norit or anything like that, it was just that he could do wonderful things with this. . . ." He grasped the handle, brought the cutter up and around, then down so hard it cut deep into the wood.

Honeydew gasped at the sound and nearly fell off the chain. Wings beating, she caught herself, grimaced at the black muck on her hands, but took hold of the link again and leaned down, watching.

The KuaSar jerked the cutter loose, stood bouncing the back of the blade against his palm. "He could slice a piece of meat into paper thin strips faster than breathing, tik tik tik, three heartbeats and it was done. Why did that bitch send for you?"

Honeydew was above and a little behind Adlayr so she couldn't see his face, but she saw his head turn, saw Zasya look at him and nod.

The meie leaned forward, lifted her hands as much as she could. "This isn't necessary, O KuaSar. Haven't we answered all the questions you asked us?" There was a subtle coo in her voice that made Honeydew smile and seemed to reach past the youth's hostility and calm him, at least for a moment. "All we know is Marnhidda Vos hired us. That's the way it works. Someone hires us, they don't have explain why, they just have to pay the fees. If we get there and find out it's something we won't or can't do, we leave and arrange that the money be returned. We've operated that way for a thousand years. We won't know what this's about till we get to Dander. You could cut bits off us forever and get no other answer.''

''And you can talk until you choke and I won't believe you, woman. You're supposed to train their army for them, aren't you. Fighting meien, fffuh! I've had stories about you shoved at me all my life. What else are you good for, you and those bosshy gyes, halfmen trying to turn themselves into women? What are you taking the bitch? What have you promised her? How do you mean to destroy us and snatch our city?'' While he talked he was walking back and forth, swinging the cutter, getting more agitated with every step, every word. Abruptly he broke off, rushed down the table, and held the cutter's edge against Adlayr's neck. ''Tell me, tell me, tell me,'' he screamed at Zasya, his voice shrilling to a squeak.

The door burst open and a duplicate of the youth strode in, followed by a swarm of gaveks and the Menguzhek.

''What are you doing, fool?''

''Getting answers, milk-sucker.''

''Making us pariahs, you mean.''

The two voices grew more and more identical as one youth got angrier and the other calmed. Wings quivering with frustration because there was nothing she could do, Honeydew squeezed the iron link and waited tensely as the two young men glared at each other.

''Creeping worm, this is OUR city, outsiders get itchy, they have to take what WE say.''

''You really think you can keep this quiet?''

''Dead don't talk, worm.''

''Dead'd have to be everyone who saw them, fool. People talk. You know how rumor blows on the wind, you've started enough of them against me, you brainless litjer." There was a degree of satisfaction, almost gloating, in the brother's voice—as if he were actually delighted with what he saw and heard.

"Litjer! LITJER!" The youth jerked away from Adlayr, nicking the gyes' neck as he swung the cutter out; he leapt at his brother, screaming incoherently.

The gaveks caught hold of him, took the cutter from him, and hustled him out, while the brother stepped aside and nodded to the Menguzhek. "Go with them," he said. "Takuboure is ill, that's the word. See that he's not allowed to harm himself or . . . mata mata . . . anyone else. And send Sakit back with the keys to those." He flipped a finger at the manacles.

The Menguzhek bowed and went out.

The brother picked up the cutter, set it on the table. "Meie, gyes," he said. "I ask you to pardon my unfortunate brother. Grief has turned his brain and we must do what we can to restore him to health."

Adlayr's hands were closed into fists, his shoulders hunched, his head down. Honeydew could see the tendons bulge in his neck, his wrists, his hands, could almost smell the rage that he fought to control. Her wings trembled as waves of it rose around her.

"We are not your enemies," Zasya said, the purr more pronounced in her voice. "We have our duty. Let us do it."

"I am sad that it must be so, but that is not possible, meie. Marnhidda Vos murdered our father. You must see that we cannot send you to strengthen her hand against us."

"How can you be so sure it was Marnhidda Vos who directed the killing? Did you catch the man who laid the bomb?"

"Oh, yes, we did, and we tried to question him, but he died. Before we'd even touched him, he threw a fit and died, saying only two words: Marnhidda Vos."

The annoyance in his voice was far more convincing that any oath he might have taken; he was really irritated by the man's escape, even if it was into death.

There was a knock at the door.

"Enter," the youth snapped.

A nachod came in with two gaveks, their pistols drawn; he offered the key to the youth.

He waved it away. "Unlock the cuffs and take them back to the others. If they try running, you needn't be choosy about your aim, but I won't have them knocked about, and if you kill them unnecessarily, I'll strangle you myself. Understood?"

The nachod bowed. "Understood, KuaSar."

> > < <

Honeydew perched on the washbasin, scrubbing her hands with a bit of cloth Serroi had ripped from a towel using her teeth because the knives were confiscated. She squeezed it out, dipped it in a mug filled with soapy water, started work on the inside of her thighs where they'd touched the filthy chain.

Serroi sat on the edge of the bath and watched her, amused and exasperated, impatient to know what had happened.

When the gaveks had shoved Zasya and Adlayr through the door, slammed it after them, Heslin took one look at Adlayr, caught hold of his arm and with Zasya's help eased him outside into the sunlight. Honeydew fluttered in a moment later, but refused to say anything until she got the filth off her body.

She rinsed the fragment again, dealt with the last smut, then began drying herself with another washcloth that for her was big as a blanket.

She dropped the cloth and fluttered to Serroi's shoulder, wrapped her hand in Serroi's hair and sighed immensely. He crazy, that brother, both of them, cracks in the head. D'you see them? The ones that look so much alike? He really craaaazy. I thought Kirrko was weeeird, he the man that net me and sell me, I mean, he straaange, but not like . . . his brother called him Takuboure, he had cutter up by Adlee's throat, if that gyes take a long breath, he dead, but the brother he come in right then and poke at him not with his finger, with words, poke poke, till this Takuboure he blow his head boom boom and go at his brother with this cutter, he gonna kill him, his own brother! Wish I had a brother, sister, somebody, wish it wan't just me and nobody like me. . . . She sighed again, her whole body shifting with it.

I know, I know. I'm alone, too. A tribe of one. Sometime, when we're out of here and not so pushed, if you feel like it, you could tell me about your coming, how it happened, how you lived, anything you want to talk about. But right now, my Honey, tell me what you saw, everything, even if it doesn't make sense.

Honeydew stroked Serroi's face, her tiny fingers like the touch of butterfly feet. Ei vai, I will, but let's go out of here now. The wet makes m' wings feel baaaad.

"If I see him again, I'll kill him." Adlayr Ryan-Turriy's voice was quiet, no passion in it, only a stony certainty. He looked up at Camnor Heslin. "Don't talk to me. I know everything you could say and it changes nothing." He moved his shoulders and stared past Heslin at the wall, his face set, remote.

The wind had died, the sun was warm and gentle on them as they ate a late lunch in the dead garden, a fancy lunch with seafood and fresh vegetables, kava and cha and a bottle of wine which Camnor tasted and claimed for his own. And a tall crystal vase with five crimson roses—Takuzhone's silent joke, a small tribute presented to them for giving him a large step up in his struggle with his brother.

Camnor Heslin poured the last of the wine into his

glass. "If this travels, it would make an interesting
addition to my cellar. Very unusual flavor. I wonder
where it comes from. Not here, I think." He sipped
at the wine, set the glass down gently, stared at the
straw-colored liquid a while, fingers curled around the
delicate stem. "Adlayr, most people are at their lowest
around two hours before dawn; I was thinking we
should wait to leave until around then."

Adlayr passed a hand across his face, the tension in
his muscles softening as if he wiped it away. "It'll
take longer to walk the distance and even that late there
are patrols out, so there's a good chance we'll have to
go to ground at least once."

Serroi sipped at her wine. *You keep surprising me,
Camnor Heslin, scaring me a little. You read people
too fast and too accurately. Big things and little. Seeing that it's easier for Adlayr to be dealing with details
about escape, takes his mind off the brothers and what
they did to him. Hern was good, but you're better.* She
blinked as she thought she saw a column of darkness
flit past, moving through the walls as if they didn't
exist. A bit of it touched her, chilled her to the bone,
then was gone. No words, just the presence. She
gulped the rest of the wine and forced herself to listen
to the discussion.

"Chance, that's the word. Anything could change
where they go, when they go, some traggit with a weak
bladder stumbles round a corner, bumps into us, yells
the alarm. Anything. And with only one night's scan,
there's no way to know the real patterns. TheDom is
up late this time of the month; I'd say we'd better start
close to Domset, that'd give us a little over three hours
before the streets start filling."

Zasya nodded. "I agree. Getting over the walls
won't be easy and this isn't a little town. We'll need
that time."

Camnor Heslin swirled the wine gently around the bowl of his glass, lifted his eyes past the others, focusing on the wall. "Anyone wish to add to this? Nay? Then it's settled. I suggest we all get some sleep this afternoon."

Zasya grinned at him. "Why not, there's nothing else to do. Sleep's as good a way of passing time as any I know."

"Serroi, wake up. Up, Healer."

Warmth sat on her back as the words drifted into the nightmare gripping her; together words and warmth pried her loose and brought her floating up to an aching head and eyes filled with grit. "Wha. . . ."

Zasya snapped her fingers, calling Ildas back to her. "These Zhagsent Govaritzers have had another bright idea. We're supposed to go eat dinner with the dear young prince, or whatever he is. Or maybe the two of them, though I hope not. We've got Adlayr pretty well calmed down, but he meant it, so if you see two of 'em, get ready to run."

"Two . . . ah . . . twins." Serroi rolled over, drawing the back of her hand across her eyes. "How much time. . . ."

"We let you sleep because Heslin took the bathroom prisoner, but he's out now, yelling at the valet the Menguzhek sent because he's messing up his jacket." She cuddled Ildas and grinned at Serroi. "He made the valet iron one of your robes for you. It's ready when you are."

"My brother is indisposed or he would be here to claim your pardon for his excess." Takuzhone smiled at them, the glow from the candelabras in the center of the long table turning his eyes to yellow shines. The light dropped soft and mellow on the crystal glasses clustered at each place, the white dinnerware with its blood-red rims, the gold eating utensils, the serving dishes piled high with exquisitely presented food.

It was, in its way, an informal dinner. Aside from the Menguzhek who sat at Takuzhone's right hand, they were the only guests. There were gaveks on guard within a step of each of them, but they were back in the shadows and could be ignored. The servers were young boys, twelve or thirteen at most, too nervously intent on their tasks to bother themselves with what was being said.

Takuzhone was served first and no one touched anything until he took a bite from his fish. Serroi noticed that he ate and drank sparingly, a little fish, some vegetables and a green salad, half a glass of wine, replaced later by water from a carafe at his elbow.

Camnor Heslin ate with an appetite as grand as his size, his face glowing red as the dinner went on; he rambled expansively in his answers to Takuzhone's delicate probes, ignoring the scowls from Adlayr and Zasya, scowls that gradually faded as they realized that in all the volubility there was no information at all of value to the Govaritzers. Several times Takuzhone tried to question the others, but Heslin's voice was always there first, with a mellow amiability that made it impossible to take exception to his chatter. He talked about macai racing and breeding, horses and hunting, swords and dance, the odd customs he'd come across in his extensive travels, the show that the glass dragons had put on over the Sinadeen, the predations of the Swampkrys, the virtues of the food before him, questions about the wine, where it came from, how much was available, the musical river of his deep voice flowing over and around them as remorselessly as the Yellow Dan in spate.

Serroi watched Takuzhone's face grow gradually

paler, his eyes start to glitter, and was afraid that all of Camnor Heslin's verbal tricks wouldn't get them out of this. She was sitting beside the Vorbescar, lost in his shadow, insignificant in all these strangers' eyes and she rather liked the feeling; it was a kind of freedom she hadn't had since she woke.

Eyes on her all the time.

The Fetch stared at her from oozing sockets when she slept, and when she woke the living sneaked glances at this legend suddenly come to life. When this is over, she thought, then her mouth twitched into a rueful half-smile, if I survive . . . and if I don't, ei vai, I won't care.

". . . trade representative," Camnor Heslin said, "I'm serious about this wine, O KuaSar, it has an unusual flavor, a pleasing difference. If you could arrange transshipment of several hundredweights of this and similar wines, we might be able to work out repayment in goods I'm sure you'd find interesting. We are developing something called a telefon, it uses copper wires to carry speech from one place to another. As an example, if there was a telefon in the Istapan and one in the Pevranamist and a wire strung between them, you could speak directly to Marnhidda Vos, demand an explanation of her acts, or say whatever you felt like saying."

Elbows beside his plate, hands clasped, Takuzhone leaned toward Camnor, the glitter gone from his eyes, his interest firmly caught. "Magic?"

"Not at all, it's a product of the new learning at the Biserica. Quite an amazing place, that is. You ought to send some of your young people there, you can get a better idea of what you could use here. The things we make are to a large extent made for our own people, although the guns have found a wide acceptance.

In fact, it seems like everyone's turning them out these days.''

''I see. How could I possibly give you leave to go to Dander with help like that for my enemy? I've had a thought, Vorbescar. We will send a letter to your Council, asking to have your mission changed. I'm sure they'll understand the necessity if you add your explanation of this emergency to mine. I'll want to read it, of course, before it goes out. Until the answer comes, you will be confined to the Istapan, but we'll see that your stay is as comfortable as possible.'' He touched the graceful glass bell at his side, rose to his feet as the nachod stepped forward. ''Take the women back to the suite, escort the men to the Conservatory. I will join them there for more conversation.''

Zasya kicked her boots off and paced restlessly about the room. ''Even Heslin can't be talking this long. What's going on?''

Serroi shrugged. ''We'll know when we know. It's getting late, why don't you go to bed? Fidgeting around like this won't help anyone.'' She walked to a table pushed against a wall, lifted a bit of wood carved into a crude representation of a fish. She ran her finger along the arched back, looked at the dust smeared on her skin. ''I think we should ask for a maid tomorrow, or at least dust cloths.'' She set the carving down, started to move away and stumbled, her hand slapping against the wall.

Zasya rushed to her. ''Serroi, you all right?''

Serroi said nothing, just leaned on her hand, her eyes closed, her body focused on the man behind the wall, trying something she'd only done a few times before, reaching into him, stealing away his consciousness, sending him into a deep sleep.

She sighed and opened her eyes. ''Fine,'' she said.

"It's all right to talk now, Honeydew says this listener's the only one and he'll be snoring away for half an hour, maybe more."

"I didn't know you could do that."

"Mostly I can't. But him, he wasn't suspicious, so he didn't push me out. Heslin should be all right, he had to do what he did, the Twin was about to blow, if you know what I mean."

"But if they don't get here soon, we're stuck for another night and who can tell what will happen tomorrow?"

"Mp, I know," Serroi ran her hands through her hair, started moving for the door, "while you're waiting, you could look over Adlayr's gear, get him packed so we can leave as soon as they do get back. I'll see what I can do about Camnor's bits."

His voice reached them before he did, belting out a raucous song, the words only slightly muffled by the walls.

The door burst open, and the gaveks who were hauling him along gave him a shove and sent him sprawling at Zasya's feet. They stepped back to let Adlayr stagger in. Then they slammed the door, turned the key, and marched off.

Camnor grunted, moved his arms and legs, and sagged into a boneless heap.

Adlayr swore, bending down to take one of the massive arms. "C'mon, Hes, let's ge' y' head under faucet."

Zasya added her strength to the effort to get Camnor back on his feet. "What happened?"

"Whatcha think?" He heaved, with her help lifted the body enough to get a shoulder under Camnor's arm. "I give 'im this . . . unh, got 'im? Good, move y' foot, Vor'scar . . . he hatta do't . . . now t' other

foot. Nay nay, don't try talking, Hes, keep y' mind on
you walking. That rinch was after everything he could
screw out of us.'Twas a thing to see how this furc slid
the drink down ol' Tak'zhone so sly he hadna clue how
much he was getting. 'M a little hazy m'self. Round
the corner, Hes. Zas, c'n you slip by? Cold water,
Zas, tub . . . start fillin' it . . . shut up, Hes. Nuh . . .
none a us c'n take 'nother night like this. Gotta get
you ready . . . to walk . . . vai vai, turn 'im sideways,
sideways, Hes, crab it, that's right . . . out the way,
Zas, when he goes down, he gonna take ever'thin' with
'im.

The crash brought Serroi hurrying from Camnor's
bedroom. She took in the scene in the bathroom, giggled, then marched in. "Why didn't you idiots think
to call me? This won't sober him, just make him cold
and cranky. Leave him to me, I'll have him on his feet
and coherent before you can sneeze twice. Now get
out of here."

"I thought I could count on you." Camnor looked
up at her and smiled, all sarcasm and doubt momentarily banished from his face, the smile broad and tri-
umphant. "Best hangover cure around."

"You didn't have a hangover."

"I would have. Move back a step, I don't want to
soak you." When she was out of the way, he muscled
himself onto his feet, collected every towel in sight,
and shooed her toward the door. "Come with me, I
need to talk to you. If you don't feel like viewing so
much flesh, you can look out the window while I
dress."

She heard a noise behind her as she was about to
follow him out, turned, and saw something small and
misty fall or jump from the rim of the tub and scuttle
for the shadows behind the commode. There was more

movement by the tub's rim. Whatever it was ducked down and went still when it saw her watching. She could feel it waiting, terrified, for her to do something. *Rats in the walls, mice in the plumbing. Ei vai, go on, you. I'm not going to waste time fooling with you.* She pulled the door shut and went after Camnor Heslin.

Serroi leaned on the windowsill, drawing faces in the mist her breath made on the dirty glass. "What's this about?"

"I presume you took care . . ." His voice was temporarily muffled as he pulled off his tunic, "of the rats."

"Sound asleep, no idea what happened to him. I put him out."

"Useful." The plop of wet cloth on the carpet, rasp of towel against skin. "Why now, not before?"

"Because it won't work if you're prepared for it. I knew I'd probably be able to manage it once; it was best to save it till it was really needed."

Soft pad of bare soles on the carpet. For such a massive man he was very light on his feet. "Nischal Tay told me a bit more than I suggested."

"I'm not surprised."

"Hmm." Creak of the bed as he sat on it. "Marnhidda Vos ordered some special communicators the Biserica has developed, but she didn't want them brought openly. Too easy a target for raiders. Not so good for us." More creaks as he stood, sound of cloth rubbing against skin as he pulled on dry clothing. "There are three of them packed in each of those comfit cans. If anyone survives this night, you will, Healer, it's your talent, isn't it? See that the cans get to Dander."

* * *

Outside, the wind had died to a whisper and there wasn't a cloud in the sky. TheDom had set and the Dancers were just clearing the rooftops as Ildas ran up the wall and along the top like a patch of mist, scouting for trouble. He was back in a breath and a half, sitting on his hind legs chittering impatiently. "No alarm, no one watching," Zasya whispered. "Let's go."

The black sicamar raced across the garden with the sprite clinging to his neckhairs, clawing his way onto the top of the wall and shifted to manform. Honeydew leapt from Adlayr's shoulder and spiraled up to hover above the court, keeping watch from a height that gave her an overview of most of the courts round theirs. Adlayr pulled Zasya up, looping the rope round the inner railing of the parapet, secured it with a quick half hitch, then dropped both ends. Serroi and Heslin tied blanket slings to the ends and loaded all the gear save Heslin's comfit filled case into them.

When the loads were halfway up the wall, there was a loud shout, then gunshots and curses. Zasya made a hissing sound and hauled her load up as fast as she could. Adlayr hesitated a moment, his eyes blanking, then did the same.

The sprite came flashing down, hovered over Serroi for a moment, then flew back to her post.

Speaking just loudly enough so they could all hear, Serroi said, "There's a fight between reds and greens a couple courts over, more of them running toward it. Honeydew says she can't see anyone else awake and paying attention, so maybe it's a bit of luck finally. They'll be good cover for the noise we're making."

Adlayr finished emptying his sling, dropped it again. "We could use a break to our side, we've had enough of the other kind. You finished there? Good. Heslin, we're ready for you. Let's go." He kicked the ropes over, took hold of his, and waited.

The sounds of the battle were intensifying. There were noises from other sections of the Istapan and a glow of torches reflecting from tower walls. Honeydew fluttered down a few lengths, shouted in her minivoice, hovered in place, her tiny body tense with anxiety.

Serroi touched Heslin's arm. "Fast as you can. Honeydew says the place is waking up."

Camnor cursed, stuffed his case into one of the slings, lifted Serroi up and settled her beside it. "You ready?"

"Asha. Haul it up, Adlayr."

Heslin took the other rope and walked up the wall as fast as any of them, his powerful arms lifting his weight with little visible effort. As soon as he was up, he took the case from Adlayr and thrust his arms through the straps he'd made for it. "Let's get out of here."

They trotted along the wall, bent over, concealed behind the parapet, accompanied by all the noises of a confused but vicious night fight, the increasing disturbance throughout the Istapan.

Honeydew *shouted*.

"Down." Serroi flattened herself on the wall, pulling the hood of the black cloak over her head. The others dropped at her low warning, lay flat on the stone.

She heard voices, then the clatter of boots as a clot of men trotted across the court below them, hammered on a gate till it opened, and passed into the court beyond.

Honeydew *shouted*.

Serroi pushed up onto hands and knees. "Clear for

now,'' she said, and scrambled onto her feet to follow the black sicamar.

They moved from wall to wall, progress slowed as again and again they had to drop to avoid gaveks that swarmed about like ants in an anthill some idiot had kicked into, but as they neared the outer wall, most of the disturbance was behind them and they made better time, fetching up at the deserted tower before the Dancers had reached zenith.

Adlayr was the last one down the rope, holding both ends, letting one slide through his hands so he was in a controlled fall; as soon as he was down, he whipped the rope loose, coiled it over his shoulder, then joined the others in a clot on the hillside.

"We're a toothless lot." Camnor Heslin shifted his bundle and glared down the weedy slope toward the row of hovels at the base of the hill. "Curse them to zhagdeep for filthy thieves."

Adlayr grinned. "Not toothless, not me."

Heslin's mouth twitched into a ghost of a smile. "True, I'd hate to turn a corner and see you there. Ei vai, you lead, I'll take the rear."

"Nay, Hes, that's mine." Serroi held up her hands. "If it's necessary, I can take instead of giving; all I have to do is touch. Besides, there's all that to haul," she waved a hand at the gear, "and you can carry a bigger load."

With the Sicamar trotting ahead of them, Honeydew in the air again, flying watch above them, Zasya and Camnor Heslin packing the gear, they wound into the town, keeping to narrow alleys between houses, moving down stairs so steep it was almost like climbing a ladder, changing direction several times as Honeydew warned them of gavek companies coming their way, huddling in doorways twice as clots of drunks staggered along the street, down and down, through increasingly dense tenements and shops, past more of the white doors with their gilded faces, reaching the multileveled warehouses along the river's east bank when a pearly gray predawn light touched the hilltops beyond the city, warning them that the three hours they'd allotted themselves had been swallowed in distance and tension.

"Money grubbin litjer! Creeping sedika worm lickin Dander klediks." "Crazy junkker gonna get us all killed, crack head, you crazier'n 'im to want that one seated." The wharf guards were nose to nose, red badge, green badge, shouting at each other, shoving, the shoves getting harder as the insults sharpened.

Zasya and Adlayr leapt from the shadows, caught heads and chins in strong hands, jerked and twisted hard and dropped two dead men on the wharf.

Fifteen minutes later the boat was on the river, running before a light wind, making slow but steady progress away from the city.

11. Exploring Dander

Houses were built pressed up against each other, three or even four stories high, the ground floor given to shops with bay windows on each side of the entrances, windows that glittered in the morning sun, not a trace of dust on the small glass panes, windows filled with whatever the shop sold, bright with color and tantalizing shapes. Where lanes branched off from the major streets there was no break in the upper stories, only a dark tunnel where little sun ever reached, wide enough for a team of vul and a two-wheeled city wain to pass along and reach the stockyards at the back of the shops where they could unload their goods.

The main streets of Dander were wide, paved with waste stone from the mines, a line of javories planted in the middle, their thick shade welcome in the hot summers, their tangle of branches a wind and snow-break in the winters.

The walks along the edges of the pavement were filled with hawkers, dancers, musicians, jugglers, fire-eaters, scam artists of a dozen kinds, all playing their changes for whatever crowds they could collect.

Wains squealed along the pavement, vuls nodding their heavy heads as they walked, the horns of some decorated with straw charms and fluttering ribbons, others painted or capped with copper knobs.

Traders from a score of lands strolled the streets or

sat in the sidewalk kavarnas bargaining or chatting over hot kava or cold piv. Dark Fenek men with tight-curled hair and long, frizzy beards up from Tuku-kul, dark Fenek women of regal bearing who moved with long, free strides through the crowds, wrapped in lengths of bright batik. Golden men from the Skafaree with amber and orange eyes, dressed in layered robes of profusely embroidered silk and sateen, with stripped turbans and heavy, intricate earrings dangling from the left ear only. Brown men and women dressed alike in patterned weave, tweeds, brocades, twills and honeycombs and a dozen others, trousers, shirts, blouses and skirts, up from the Shimzelly Islands. Sleykyn assassins in velater armor, guarding one or another of the visitors. Minarks with suspicious eyes. Even a few icily blond Sankoyse from the Closed Kingdom beyond the Mijloc.

Walking beside Hedivy Starab in her Zemyadinna's going-to-city garb, K'vestmilly Vos was fascinated by the scene. She'd never been on foot in the city before, never been immersed in the colors and the smells, the noise of it, voices chattering around her, words merging into words until only the cacophony of the whole was audible. A curious privacy this, so wholly public.

She stopped before an odd-looking shop. The door was covered with white enamel paint that had been sanded, repainted, sanded again until it was smooth and unflawed as a fine porcelain glaze; in the center of it was a face like that of the Marn Mask, but subtly older, a Matron's Face that looked with vast benignity on those who passed by; around the Mask there was a circle of gold paint with rays reaching to the edge of the door. The small panes in the bow windows were covered inside with squares of gold paper. The whole thing seemed to shimmer, almost swim, between the

darker earth tones of the stores on either side.
"What. . . ."

"House of Glory," Hedivy said. He took her arm,
moved her along, bending close so he could speak in
her ear and not be overheard. "We looked, but there's
nothing in it. Just a cult taking advantage of Nerodin
being scared, making promises the Temple Preöchmat
and her Setras won't because they know they can't keep
them."

Two lanes down from the House of Glory, she saw
a gaunt-faced Nerod woman seated at the edge of an
alley, a whining baby in her lap, holding out a cup for
coins. It was like a slap in the face. Her own words
spoken in ignorance to Vyzharnos Oram flashed up
before her: Our dungeons aren't full, teachers can say
what they need to in the schools, we don't have beggars in the streets. *Beggars in the streets!* Angry and
disturbed, she started to say something to the woman,
but Hedivy's hand tightened on her arm and he murmured, "Nik, Milla. Just walk on."

"Beggar," she whispered angrily. "Why isn't
she. . . ."

"Nik. Do you listen or do we break here?"

She scowled at him as he set a thick mug in front
of her and took his place across the small battered
table. This kavarna was little more than a hole in the
wall with half a dozen tables and stools at a counter.
He tipped a spoon of honey into his kava, added a
dollop of cream, and sat stirring it. "I hate kava," she
muttered. "I never drink it."

He shrugged. "Don't drink it, then."

"That woman. . . ."

He sipped noisily at the kava and set the mug down.

"I could read you a story for her easy enough. Husband dead, her tossed out of her rooms, they couldna been much, but at least shelter. With a youngling hanging to her skirt and another starting to run wild. I would say her man brought her up from the Hayadel Bezhval, she has the look, long and skinny with skin still dark from the sun, no family here and no way to get home. What else can she do?"

"The Marn has places for Nerod like her."

"Zdra zdra, but who'd tell her? Even should a Nerod do what most would not and give her the word, she'd have to sit for days waiting for a clerk to see her, a clerk who is most likely a little Rodin, some cousin thick between the ears slid into a place so his Family wouldna have to support him, because they are the ones who get those jobs. And they despise all Nerodin, especially those they see as worthless layabouts. And she would have to keep from starving while she waited—unless she could scrape together a few coins for a bribe. And then she would have to fill out a pile of forms, enough to paper a wall. Chances are she can't read, writes just enough to sign her name. And if she does manage all that somehow, the Marn would indeed take care of her, would keep her and her family just this side of starvation. So she begs and sleeps in the bushes; she is doing for herself that way and with a sliver of pride left to her—not in begging, but in playing the game, milking the suckers. If that infant is a boy, by the time he makes five or six, he will be running with the riverpacks. The river's close enough for that. She'll bury him when he makes seventeen, eighteen, that's when most of them get it."

"How many. . . ."

"Don't matter." He shrugged. "Just leave her be. She's doing well enough."

"How can I?"

"If you mean to be useful, then stir up the clerk cadre, give the boot to those who take the bribes, give the others a raise, and open the job to Nerodin. But not now. You need them loyal now and you won't get that attacking their perks. When we find the notney who lies behind these hits, that will be the time for your housecleaning."

She dipped her finger in the cooling kava, swirled it around, frowning at the dark brown liquid. "But if I stay silent, aren't I making myself responsible for. . . ."

"If you want to play games with words, that's one thing, if you want to keep your seat, listen and do as I say. Where now?"

Eyes still on the cup, she murmured, "He told me about you before you came in. Would you take me to the river and show me where you lived?"

After several moments without an answer, she looked up. He was gazing out across the dark, smoky room, a vacuous expression on his round face. His silence made her uneasy. "If you'd rather not," she said, "no problem. We'll just go somewhere else."

His gray-green eyes fixed on her face, shiny and opaque as waterwet stones. "Won't hang out my life to dry. And you shouldn't ask."

K'vestmilly wrinkled her nose, feeling as if she'd been slapped; she was annoyed, though mostly at herself for what was an obvious misstep once you looked at it. *K'milly puts her foot in it again. Chert! I hate feeling stupid.*

When he spoke again, he ignored the whole episode. "You can have your choice of stinks. There's a papery in West Dander, a leatherworks in North Dander."

"Paper stinks?"

"You'll see."

* * *

The wind was out of the northeast with a touch of
chill to it that surprised her since Midsummer wasn't
all that far off. The Zemya dress that had pleased her at
first was beginning to feel heavy and clumsy; the long
skirt and the petticoats wrapped around her legs and
came close to tripping her when she backed down the
ladder and stepped into the boat Hedivy rented for them.

She perched in the bow and watched him row,
knowing he was going to make her pay for intruding
on his life, rub her nose in every bit of filth he could
dig up. It was almost funny, that was exactly what she
needed—though she had thought to draw it more gently
from her father. *My father. I have to see him, I have
to know who he is, what he looks like, I was going to
wait . . . nik, this afternoon, I'm going to do the shops
this afternoon and Hedivy can lump it, trail me around
while I look at this and that. . . .* She chuckled at the
thought.

He glanced at her, scowling, his eyes chilled to gray.

She folded her hands in her lap, the chuckle fading
to a faint smile. *Yes, O smart man, it's going to be my
turn soon to make you sweat. Not too bad, though, I
need you.*

When he angled the boat closer to shore so he could
turn into the canal, she glanced at the water, saw a
sort of milky haze mixing with the yellow mud that
gave the Dan its name. As the boat nosed up the old
canal, the white thickened until it was as if Hedivy
rowed through dirty milk, not water at all. And when
the direction of the canal changed, turning more into
the wind, she began to understand what he meant when
he talked about stink.

He tied up at a landing around the bend from the
papery. ''There will be someone to wave us in if we

do go farther.'' He helped her onto the shaky little landing, sat down beside her. ''Fair enough reason for it; the logs to make the paper, they come down the canal from the Travasherims. They'd chew that up for sure.'' He nodded at the boat.

A gust of wind blew directly from the huge rambling structure partially screened by a thick stand of brellim and conifers; she gagged at the stench.

He smiled, enjoying her distress. ''You do not get down this way much, do you, Dedach? Nor do the Vyk come to see their work. They own this, but they don't live anywhere round here.''

''The Marn can't know. . . .''

He shrugged. ''The Marn pets the Treddeks to keep them sweet.'' He went silent and K'vestmilly wondered if he was going to say anything more. He seemed to be like that, either lots of words in that Zemya lilt of his, or a grunt or two. He scratched out an old bottle someone had left lying on the landing and tossed it in the water; the splash set him off.

''I am farm-bred, Dedach. I hated it, but I will tell you this, in my bones I feel a farmer's ties with land . . . they say in the old days, the Pan Vyk hired a Norit to clean up after him, that this water was so clear you could drink it.'' His hands moved about, found a loose splinter; he tore it from the plank, used the pointed end to clean his nails. ''Then there was the Sons' War and when it was over, the Nor were gone and the magic with them. It is said the Vyk did not know what to do, so they just let things go.'' He tossed the splinter into the murky water and the second splash dried the flow. ''Seen enough?''

''Enough for now. The Leatherworks next?''

''Why not.''

* * *

It was almost noon when Hedivy edged the nose of the boat against the pilings of a wharf on the upstream side of a line of bulky warehouses. The noise was a living thing, a beast that crouched growling over the river.

Swarms of men moved over the planks of the wharves, in and out of the warehouses, rolling barrows ahead of them, carrying immense loads on their backs, shipmasters and traders rushed here and there, their mouths open, their faces stretched into visible but not audible shouts, boys of all ages appeared and disappeared like figures in a puppet show, snatching whatever came to hand and vanishing down the nearest escape hole. Sometimes they were caught; if it wasn't a wharflek—one of the private guards the Pan Nov hired to patrol the Shipper's Quarter—the boy was stripped and tossed into the river, left to get himself out however he could. The wharfleks marched their catches off to more formal punishment.

By the time the boat was in place and K'vestmilly Vos had climbed to ground, she'd seen more than a dozen of these captures and enough thieving to stock a small store.

"Skirts up. Drag hems here, pick up more'n you want to know about."

Hedivy led her through a narrow, filthy alley between two warehouses and into the Shipper's Warren, a place close to exploding from the number of Nerodin packed into it. The noise was nearly as loud as that on the river; there were heaps of garbage and other filth in the lanes, pools of murky liquid, skinny chinin growling and fighting, the brown streak of a rat chivied from one hole, diving into another.

Children swarmed around them, chanting incomprehensible things at her, pulling at her skirt, taunting her and throwing bits of dried mud and garbage at her when she didn't give them anything. With Hedivy looming massively beside her, they didn't dare more, but it was bad enough.

Halfway along the street a House of Glory glittered amid the filth. This time the door stood ajar. As they walked past she could see a tall yellow lamp lit and glowing, standing on a block of common stone; there were women inside and a few men, all of them kneeling on dark cushions facing the lamp.

Beyond the warren there was a stretch of wasteland with soil that looked diseased from which grew scraggly, half-dead weeds, scattered sickly brellims, a few stunted javories, thorn vines growing abundantly around them, and through all this growth, heaps of decaying discards that even the Shipper's Warren couldn't find a use for. And furtive little paths like rat runs crossing and recrossing the waste.

"How much farther is it?" K'vestmilly tugged impatiently at her skirt, winced when it came free from the thorns with a tearing sound.

"See that row of brellims? Past them. . . ."

An intense flash of light interrupted him, then a roar. The ground shook and a blast of wind slammed into them, throwing K'vestmilly onto a discarded mattress that yielded under her with a soggy, sickening squelch.

"Zdra, Dedach," he grabbed her arm and pulled her onto her feet, "you've just seen what killed Govaritil's Val Kepal and flattened their Radwan Rum."

K'vestmilly Vos could hear the yelling two corridors away.

The Pan Bar was pacing up and down the Tradurad in front of the Marn's worktable, his long white hair teased into a wild tangle, his face red with fury and frustration. "Do something," he screamed at the Marn. "You sit there like a stump while Dander comes apart."

More sedately, Druzhadlo Treddek Bar said, "Yes, Marn, at least tell us what you're doing. These explosions are discouraging trade in addition to the damage they cause to our property. And, of course, the lives lost. There is a great deal of unrest in the warrens, seditious ideas passed around and gaining strength. I have a list of teachers who should be disciplined for the filth they're forcing into children's heads."

"Shhhyess! Filth! Sneaking in from . . . Mijloc!" The Pan spat the last word in a spray of saliva that splattered across the table.

Marnhidda Vos sat with her back straight, her head up, her hands crossed on the shining table top, the fingers trembling very slightly.

K'vestmilly Vos saw that and knew her mother was having a bad day, made worse by this stupid attack. Heels clicking on the tiles, she marched across the room, circled the table, and stood beside the Marn. She stared at the two men until they broke off their antiphonal chant and turned to her. "The investigation of these incidents is in hand," she said, keeping her voice as calm as she could. "Do you have anything to add to what we already know?"

Pan Bar was a little man and had to look up to meet her eyes—which he didn't like, but the counter-irritation had the result of calming him and lowering his voice. "It's not our responsibility, this running around nose to ground like some filthy chini. The Marn has agents, let them get busy and do something."

K'vestmilly held up her hands. "I said information, not argument. You're an intelligent man, Pan Bar. This is too public a place for such things. Go see the Inquisitor and speak in his private office.'' She laid a gentle stress on the word private. ''A few suggestions. Survey the damage and start repairs. Hire guards and tracking chinin, establish paths for your workers, then fire anyone who leaves them. The Marn and I will continue the search for the source of these attacks.'' She came back round the table, laid a hand on the Pan's arm and gently but firmly turned him toward the door. ''Come, tuhl Pan, you know we're doing what we can. I feel your pain and your anger, but those get us nowhere. What we need is courage and information. You have the one, see what you can do to get the other for us.''

Talking, smiling, teasing the Pan and the Treddek into a better mood, K'vestmilly Vos eased them out, then came back to stand glaring down at her mother. ''Where's Bozhka Sekan? Why isn't she here?''

''I sent her away.'' Marnhidda Vos' voice was husky, so low that K'vestmilly had to strain to hear her. ''My suite.''

''Then we'll get you back there right now.'' She hesitated. ''Can you walk, or should I call someone to carry you?''

''I'll walk, if you'll lend me your arm.''

''You're sure?''

The Marn didn't bother answering, just struggled to her feet. Her hand was cold against K'vestmilly's arm, achingly fragile. She walked slowly, but held herself erect and showed little outward sign of the weakness she was fighting with every resource of will.

As they moved through the corridors, past shadows that flitted back and forth in busy haste, members of the vast horde of domestic and state workers that lived and labored in the Pevranamist, shadows K'vestmilly wouldn't have noticed yesterday, she chattered brightly, adding her part to the show, talking about the things she'd seen that morning, describing traders male and female, a hitch of vul with larger charms than usual, knotted and woven from pale yellow straw into intricate designs, a juggler and his jokes, little things, bright things, innocuous things, playing the game till they reached the private section of the Pevranamist.

Bozhka Sekan came trotting to them as K'vestmilly kicked the door shut and swept her mother up, appalled by the fragility she felt in her arms. She brushed past the Healer, laid the Marn on the daybed, and took the Mask away.

Bozhka Sekan handed her a napkin moistened with oil warmed and perfumed. "For her hands and face," she said. "The tonic's ready, I'll get it."

K'vestmilly wiped the sweat from her mother's face, stroking as gently as she could because she felt her mother steel herself not to wince at her touch. The skin seemed thin as tissue paper, as easy to tear. As she began tending her mother's fingers, Bozhka Sekan slid her hand under the Marn's head and lifted it gently so she could sip at the drink.

Aside from the soft sounds of the ministering, the buzz of an unseen fly against a windowpane, the room was filled with a deep silence. The Marn's eyes closed and her breathing steadied. Carefully, so it made no sound, Bozhka Sekan set the glass on a straw mat, got to her feet, and nodded at the bedroom door.

K'vestmilly followed her through the room and out the door into the small garden beyond. "How much longer?"

Bozhka Sekan was staring at a clump of zhula flowers, her hands clasped behind her. She turned her head. "I don't know. A few months. If she'd rest. She won't."

"Chert! I've wasted so much time playing. . . ." K'vestmilly flung herself onto a bench. "Do you know, if I'd chosen to go to the Leatherworks first, I'd probably be dead now. I was close enough so that it knocked me off my feet. You won't tell Marn that, of course."

"Nik. But don't go out again."

"I have to. Just like Mother has to show herself to the Pans and the Treddekkap. You know that and you know why."

The Healer shrugged. "Her yes, you nik."

"In one day," K'vestmilly said. "One day! I found out more about the real Dander than I learned the past twenty years. I have to know these things myself, Bozhka Sekan. When the time comes, you know and I know it's going to be soon, I have to be able to go around the Treddekkap and the Pans when it's necessary and to do that, I have to KNOW!"

"After. . . ."

"After, I'll be busy kicking the Families into order, there's ambition out there, maybe one of them is behind this business or if not behind it, involved. I won't have time or freedom to wander then, I've got to do it now." She sighed and got to her feet. "Keep the Marn asleep as long as you can. I've got to go out."

"K'milly."

"I'm tired of arguing, Bozhka Sekan. I'll be back in time to dress for dinner, it's going to be private so that's. . . ." She paused, frowned. "Nik. Is the Marn's secretary around? I haven't time for this if I intend. . . . Find her, Healer, tell her I'll want invitations written out and hand-carried to the Treddeks asking them to join me for dinner and an informal discussion of these explosions. Make it the usual time, I should be back by then." She grimaced. "I hope you have a panacea for indigestion, Healer. If you can be present, I'd appreciate it, but the Marn comes first."

K'vestmilly Vos swept into the anteroom, stopped briefly by the aide's desk. "He in?" When he nodded, she pushed the door open and went in.

Jestranos Oram looked up, his mouth tightening. "What is it, Dedach?"

She ignored the weary patience in his voice, spoke briskly. "I've invited the Treddeks to dine with me. Should you be there? My first thought was nik, better not. Changed my mind, decided I should ask what you think."

"Why?"

"When I got back, the Bar Pan and the Bar Treddek were harassing the Marn, and old Bar was having a spitting fit. I got them soothed down a bit and out of there, then it occurred to me that I should do the same to the lot of them, the Treddeks, I mean."

"I see." He rubbed at his chin, looked past her, gazing at nothing as he turned the idea over in his head. "The Marn won't be there?"

"The Marn is tired. She needs to rest."

"I see. You've never handled something like this before."

"I've watched the Marn do it. Yes, I know, watching's far from being the same thing as doing and I don't know them like she knows them." She looked at her hands, lifted her head to meet his eyes. "The weight of the world isn't resting on this dinner and I've got to start learning sometime."

"Yes." The word hung between them like a pall covering the thing neither could say. "I am inclined to believe your first thought was the right one. If I'm there, they'll focus on me, be after me to find out what

I've got, which I don't want to tell them, not yet anyway. Better to have the focus on you."

"Prak. I've already told Pan Bar and his Treddek to hire tracking chinin and guards—I couldn't believe that they hadn't done that already, but that's what Hedivy said. What else can I tell them?"

"Chinin and guards cost money and until the Leatherworks went, the only big explosions were out at the mines. I have told them and told them. . . ." He sighed, moved one hand across the other. "The Enemy's got their attention, give him that. I'll make some notes and send them across so you can look them over before you go in."

"Good. Now, I want to go into the city for a while. Is Hedivy still available?"

"Why?"

"Personal reasons." She grinned at him. "You'll have to wait till Hedivy gets back."

He chuckled. "You'll do all right, Dedach. I'll order Hedivy to the Mews; you'll have to soothe him down, too. Good practice, mh?"

"Thought you had enough this morning."

"You worked hard enough at disgusting me. Just one problem, it's what I needed to see. Next time you might try boring me. Do you know Keshtinac Street?"

" 'Tis over in Calanda. We'll have to cross the Bridge. You are sure you want to do that?"

"I'm sure."

The Bridge joining the two parts of the Double City was a soaring structure of cable and brick almost as old as Dander.

It was thrown across the river by the Norit Washimin, spun out of dream and the solid piles of raw materials assembled at his orders. For five days he lay in trance on the riverbank, as stiff and lifeless as the bricks piled beside him. For five more days he rose and danced in circles, shouting at the heavens. On the eleventh day, steel and stone swirled into the air and between sunrise and sunset the Bridge was formed.

In the two hundred years after the War that destroyed the Nor, the Bridge had started to crumble, cracks in the towers and rust eating at the cables, but it still was a wondrous sight and carried thousands of walkers and hundreds of wains each day.

Calanda was a gray ghost of Dander, a city of manufactories small and large, of smelters and kilns, grain silos and farmers' markets. Gray dust clung to the walls of the shops and warrens, grit crunched under feet and wheels, even the air had a gravelly feel.

"Keshtinac Street," Hedivy said. He stood beside her, slumped and sullen, radiating annoyance.

"Husenkil's shop, a pottery. You know it?"

"Never heard of it."

"Zdra, find it."

He looked along the street; foot traffic was considerable, shoppers and workers, city guards strolling along swinging their sticks at the end of the short chains; vul wains creaked along both ways, piled high with lumber, clay, ingots of metal, barrels of liquids and powders and a thousand other things needed in the shops and manufactories.

"Stay with me," he said, "Keep your head down. Don't walk ticky-toht like you owned the place." He didn't wait for a response but started for the nearest guard.

"Husenkil's?" The guard swung his stick and screwed up his face as if thinking hurt him. Casually he held out his free hand, glanced at what Hedivy dropped in it, smiled as he slipped the coin in a pocket. "Number forty. Two lanes down, then count three doors."

She frowned as she passed another House of Glory at the corner of the second lane. *I have to find out what goes on in there. Prak, talk to Oram tomorrow.*

House of Glory, tailor shop, pottery.

The shop was small but neat, the front glazed with bright blue and green tiles with accents of red in a dancing pattern. The single bow window had a faint dusting of grit, but had obviously been washed that morning; in the window, a red pot stood delicately poised on a small stand; the door was painted a shiny black with blue ceramic numbers down the middle, four lines, a slash and a zero.

She pushed the door open, went inside and stopped, face blank with shock. A young girl, twelve, thirteen at most, stood behind a counter painting glaze on a large mug; she had a lean face and a nose that was a twin to K'vestmilly's own, an explosion of dark reddish-brown hair that haloed her pale face. A half sister? K'vestmilly ran her tongue over her lips, cleared her throat.

The girl looked up, smiled. "May I help you?"

"Is Husenkil here? I need to talk to him."

The girl turned toward an arch blocked by a curtain made of woven strands of green glazed beads. "Uncle, can you come out? There's some one to see you."

Uncle! K'vestmilly flushed, then paled as a wave of relief drenched her, followed by a wave of anxiety as she tensed to meet her father.

The curtain clattered as a man pushed it aside and came into the shop, wiping big, bony hands on a dark brown towel, a tall man with a fringe of frizzy faded red hair and her face.

He looked at her a moment without speaking, then he said, "Prak, come back to the workroom and we'll talk."

When Hedivy started to come with her, K'vestmilly held up her hand. "Nik, there's no need. Wait here."

"I have my. . . ."

She interrupted him. "I know. Just wait."

Husenkil dropped into a chair across the worktable from her. "Dedach," he said. "What do you want?"

She smiled at him, lips trembling. "Do I need a reason to talk to my father?"

"Yes."

"The Marn said you walk your own road." She looked down at hands laced tightly together in her lap. "I didn't know about you until a few days ago. I thought . . . never mind, that's not important. I need your help."

"I'm no spy."

She looked up, a flash of laughter in her eyes. "You're quick. Right in a way and wrong, too." She set her hands on the table, pressed them down to stop their shaking. "The Marn is dying."

He drew a deep breath, let it out, closed his eyes. "How long?"

"Bozhka Sekan won't say, but I doubt she's got a year left. I've been a fool in a lot of ways, playing when I should have been learning. Zdra zdra, I need to know what Nerodin want, not just the Families."

"She didn't tell me."

"She'd be angry that I did. But I had to. I need help I can trust. With these explosions, things are going to get a lot worse and the Pans and the Treddeks. . . ." She shrugged. "I'll need support dealing with them. I've got none now, I know that."

"I need to see her."

Chilled by his lack of response to her, K'vestmilly dropped her hands back to her lap, dropped her eyes to hide the tears gathering there; it was as if he didn't hear anything she said, couldn't even see her. "I'll see what I can do," she said when she could trust her voice. "Maybe tomorrow. She's sleeping now. It was a bad day."

"Prak. Now, you don't know me, I don't know you, so we don't play pretty hugs and kisses, not yet anyway." He sighed, ran fingers through the fringe of hair above his ears. "You willing to put some time in this?"

She looked up, trying not to show the hope that was starting to warm her. "What do you mean?"

"Come here an hour, say a couple of times a week. Work with me, talk with me."

"It will be dangerous. To you, I mean. I've been warned I could be a target, especially as I get busy with more than jessers and hunts. You know what happened at the Leatherworks and there've already been six attempts on the Marn's life."

His nostrils flared. "I won't be ruled by some sneaking cherv. You come."

"Yes. I will." She got up. "If I can't come tomorrow, I'll send that man out there to get you. He's one of Oram's lot, though I expect you'd guessed that; he doesn't know what this is about, and he doesn't have to unless you want to tell him." She giggled uncertainly, drew her finger along her nose. "Though it wouldn't be too hard to guess. Your family spreads its mark about with a lavish hand."

"Zdra zdra, that's true enough. Wait a minute. There's something I want to give you." He hurried through a door at the back of the workroom, was gone for several minutes, returned with a dusty box. "I made this when she told me you were coming. Never had the gumption to give it to her. Nik nik, don't open it now. It's not much, just a baby's milk mug. Keep it for your own, when you decide to have one. If you want.''

She took the box, couldn't speak, couldn't move for several breaths. It was as if he'd given her herself. She cleared her throat, found she had nothing to say. ''Thank you,'' she managed finally. She reached out, touched his face with the tips of her fingers, then swung round and marched out.

In the salesroom she nodded to the girl, waited for Hedivy to untangle himself from a stool, then strode from the shop.

12. Glory Hits

In the ruined shrine on the shoulder of Mount Nahera, Treshtal touched the altarstone, trembled as he felt the Glory in it.

Come. Sit. This time the voice was small and gentle, tickling through his bones, teasing him rather than commanding.

He swung onto the stone, folded his legs in a lotus knot, and dropped his hands on his thighs.

Misty light drifted around him, opaque enough to conceal the details of his face and form. The warmth flowed through him, tickling his mind as it searched for the words to speak to him, words already there, brought swimming up by the *desire* of the Glory.

Zavidesht Pan Nov comes this night. I have sent him dreams, have shaped him to my hand. Yes, I know, O Belovéd, he is the most corrupt of them all and you have good reason to hate him, but he is also the youngest, the cleverest, the richest—and the most arrogant. A pause while those words floated off and new ones arose. *He is restless and impatient with the restraints the Marn puts on him, a bear in a pit, fighting at walls he can neither climb nor break down, a weapon self-primed we will use to bring down the others and when he thinks he has triumphed, then it will be his time to know his fate. Of course he thinks to use us for his advantage, but it will not be, I swear to you, O Belovéd, it will not be.*

As the last words faded, Treshtal dreamed a new world, a world of music and joy, a world where he spoke and his words became fact.

He dreamed caresses and perfumes, tastes upon his tongue.

Time eddied past, not touching him.

A sliver of cold like a shard of glass stabbed into him—it broke his dream.

He comes. The small caressing voice of the Glory brushed his ears and thrilled across his shoulders. *You are my voice, my heart.*

The light thickened about him, clothing him in Glory, intensifying all his senses.

Footsteps outside, quick, impatient, something of the man's arrogance and drive even in the sound of his feet.

A dark figure came through the open arch into the altar room of the ruined shrine. The cowl of the black cloak was pulled forward, concealing his face as the cloak was meant to conceal his body. "What is this?" he snapped. When he was angry as he was now, his voice had a tendency to slide suddenly to the higher notes of his natural tenor.

"Pan Nov. . . ."

"No names!"

"There is no one here but us, no one on the mountain but us, do you think we wouldn't know?"

"Chert!" His hand disappeared under the cowl, his thumb stroking his mustache. "I haven't got time for foolishness. Get on with it."

Treshtal felt words sliding sweetly into his head; he disengaged and let them come without hindrance from his mouth. "There are four from the Mijloc sailing the Yellow Dan, coming here to join with Marnhidda Vos, to steal yet more of your right and your power and your wealth and slide it into her hands; they bring treason in their bones and blood. We have thought of sending a storm to wreck the boat, but we can't be sure of killing them all, they are a slippery lot. They should arrive early in the morning, day after tomorrow." He lifted a shining arm and pointed. "Look at that wall and listen as we speak their names."

In the circle of light, a man's face—heavy, round, eyes like a stooping jesser's; the fat did not conceal the danger in him. "Camnor Heslin, called Vorbescar of the Grand Council of the Mijloc, actually a spy and saboteur. More than one land has regretted his presence."

In the circle of light, a woman's face—thinnish, high cheekbones, dark blue eyes, hair a mix of blonde and light brown, cut to hang in a loose helmet, just long enough to brush her shoulders, not pretty, but attractive, especially when she smiled. "Do not be fooled by that air of fragility, she is Zasya Myers, fighting meie, and she brings with her a demon from the heart of zhagdeep that works her will for her."

In the circle of light, a man's face—an odd almost triangular face, hazel eyes, bold cheekbones, a jutting nose, long black hair gathered into a single braid which hung down his back; he had a wild air about him, as if walls were not made to hold him. "Adlayr Ryan-Turriy, gyes and shape-changer, he walks on two legs or four as a matter of choice and is a killer in both forms, man and sicamar. Be wary of that one, don't try to close with him, even with a gun; he'd have your face off before you pulled the trigger."

In the circle of light, a woman's face, oval and muted green, with a darker green spot between the level brows. "This one is nothing, let her be."

The light winked out.

There was a rustle in the silence; papers fell from the air like snow flakes, landing about the Pan's feet. Treshtal worked his throat; his voice was husky when he spoke—husky in his own ears, he had no idea what the Pan actually heard. "The images are there, we do not expect you to hunt out these killers yourself. You have agents, give these to them and set them to work."

Zavidesht Pan Nov looked down at the bits of paper scattered around his feet, then lifted his head. "Why should I?"

"They only delay us, they will destroy you. And the Vos hold on the Mask will be stronger than ever."

The cowl tipped forward as the Pan looked down; he squatted, gathered up the pictures, glanced at the top one, then stood, tucking the papers inside the cloak. "Is that all?"

"Nik. There is one other thing. Tomorrow night the Marn hosts the first of a series of dinners for some Fenek. You had best contrive an excuse—and be sure it is convincing—for not being there that night. Or the night after or the night after that. Ask no questions. If what is planned succeeds, you won't have to ask."

"Hmm. Then getting this lot. . . ." He tapped the pocket with the papers. "It's more important than ever. Give me one of your fuzzies to track them."

"Nik. Oram is sniffing everywhere. To do that would tell him far too much too soon."

"If you can get to the Marn. . . ."

"That is not certain. We have tried before and failed. We are not pursued because we have been careful to keep a wall between ourselves and our dreamers. We trust in your own good sense to be sure to maintain such separation between yourself and those you send after the targets. Or at least be very sure of their loyalty."

"Zdra zdra. And stay away from this place."

"It may not be necessary to come again. Pray that this time the dreamer wins. If the wonder happens, we will count on you, O Seeker of Merit, to protect the House of Glory and its children when you take the Mask to yourself."

"Nik nik, not to myself, to my daughter. If I laid hands on the Mask, the land would burn hotter than one of your spojjin' bombs."

"We bow to your wisdom, O Seeker. Walk with Glory."

Treshtal watched Pan Nov stride out, the arrogance in the cock of the Pan's head and the set of his shoulders churning his stomach, knotting his entrails. "Promise me," he whispered. "O Glory, promise me that one will die."

Belovéd, it will be so, it will be wonderfully so, I swear it by my Self in little and large.

13. Entering Dander

*Power. Enormous and unknowable. Coalescing
into a figure that clothed itself in flesh as it
came toward her, golden mists swirling about
it.*

*It was a beautiful woman's face bending over
her, with a touch of Yael-mri in it, a woman's
warm arms reaching toward her.*

> *I am Glory. I am all that you desire. Love
> me. Come to me. You have seen my children.
> They come to me, spend themselves for me,
> and I give them joy and I give them rest. I
> gather them to me as a Mother should.*

*The flesh on the face quivered and began to
ooze away from the bone. The dissolving lips
moved and the voice grew frantic.*

> *Mother, come to me. I NEEEEED you. I will
> make you come. I will.*

Shaking herself out of the first dream that had plagued
her since they left Govaritil, Serroi unwrapped the
blanket and sat up, moving carefully so she wouldn't
wake Zasya who lay sleeping on the deck beside her,
Ildas coiled on her chest. Of them all, the meie was
the most contented. Early on the second day out of
Govaritil they'd stopped at an Everything Store in a
farm village for food and water and a change of

clothes. When Zasya saw the boxes of ammunition piled on the shelves behind the counter, her whole body smiled.

Adlayr was sitting watch in the bow, Honeydew curled up on his shoulder, talking to him to keep him awake, her tiny voice a mosquito's buzz in his ear, an itch in his mind. He turned his head as he felt the shift of the boat, saw it was Serroi, and went back to staring at the water and the nixies who kept forming on the surface then melting again.

It was almost dawn and a strong, crisp breeze was blowing north along the river; the air had a fresh, new feel that eased the sweaty grunginess that made her skin itch. The boat was cranky, the wind strong enough to be dangerous; with the river's curves, sandbars, and snags, no one got much rest. And it was cramped; there was adequate space for two, but there were four of them. And Honeydew, of course, but she was too tiny to be a problem. The Everything Store was the only stop they made, so they were hungry, dirty and exhausted—and very tired of each other's company.

And no dreams until now. *Why? And why now? Something going to happen? I wish I knew what I should do. Is it as idiotish as I think it is, not telling Heslin about the Fetch?*

Watching where she put her feet, keeping her head down in case a bend in the river or a snag meant a sudden jibe, Serroi edged past the low hutch and crouched beside Camnor who was taking his turn at the tiller. She waved a hand at the shore. "Maiden Bless, it's beginning to seem familiar."

He grunted.

The water bulged and broke apart; yellow-brown heads pushed up, grew long weedy hair, cheek hollows changed to glittering brown glass eyes with nothing in them but a feral curiosity; though the nixies had never harmed them or even threatened harm, they made Serroi increasingly uneasy—the way they stared at her, their guggling laughter that she didn't understand.

There were two of them this time, swimming in such exact unison they might have been joined at the waist. As she watched, the face of one—such an ordinary face, that of a young boy—melted away, then rebuilt into the face of the other and for a moment identical twins swam out there, then the face of the second melted and reformed into the face the first had worn. Then both of them laughed and remerged with the muddy water.

Serroi shuddered, lifting her eyes from the river to the west bank levee and the road that ran along the top of it. "Hah! Look there. He's really moving." A macai was racing north, stretched into its long-reach stride; being smarter than most horses, it wouldn't keep that up for long without sinking into a rest squat so the rider had to have a relay arranged if he planned to maintain his pace. She leaned forward, trying to see more clearly in the cloudy darkness. "You think he's the Marn's man?"

Camnor Heslin glanced at the bank, then went back to watching Magoerno. "I think we'd better be ready to move fast once we reach city waters."

"Ahhh." She chewed at her lip, scowled at the nixies. "Or maybe before. I had a dream, I think it was a warning."

"Feel like talking about it?"

She hesitated. "Nay. Not . . . yet."

As the sun rose, they began to pass small landings with roads leading back through patch farms that raised vegetables for the Double City. There were few boats tied at the landings; most farmers had loaded and left

hours ago so they could be at the markets in Dander
and Calanda before the day began.

On the northern horizon a yellow-gray haze caught
the first rays and took on a touch of pink, the dust that
hovered over Calanda.

There was little barge traffic heading south. Serroi
could remember times when she'd seen barges moving
along the Yellow Dan so thick upon the water they
were almost nose to stern. Warning about the confis-
cations in Govaritil had evidently reached the merchants and they were redirecting their cargoes along
the Red Dan though that would mean they had to deal
with the land zarks on the Neck if they wanted to reach
their usual markets. A reduced profit was self-evidently
better than no profit at all.

Serroi moved to the front of the boat and sat watch
while Adlayr shifted to sicamar and used his rough
tongue to clean himself. Back in man form, he brushed
and rebraided his hair, then he took the tiller from
Heslin so the Vorbescar could shave and get himself
ready.

Serroi heard Heslin swearing over the limitations of
his wardrobe, glanced back, laughed and started to sing.

Caytyr went a-courtin', oo-ah oo-ay
Combed his teeth and scraped his hair, oo-ah, oo-ay

She broke off a moment. "Snag ahead. Left, quarter
point, count thirty and you're around it."

Set the cart afore his mare, oo-ah oo-ay
And rode afoot to his lady fair, oo-ay oo-ay aahhh.

Setting aside the tunic she was repairing, Zasya
joined with exaggerated soprano trills; from the stern

Adlayr came in with a baritone, Heslin with a boom-
ing bass. Surrounded by curious nixies, half giddy with
weariness and the realization they were going to be at
their destination in a very short time, they slid down
the river singing.

Caytyr went a-courtin', oo-ah oo-ay
Fell in the river, splash-a-splish, oo-ah oo-ay
Up in his pants swum a big fat fish, oo-ay oo-ay
 ahhhh
Caytyr come out with a drip and a scream, oo-ah
 oo-ay
Cod a wiggle like a maiden's dream, oo-ay oo-ay
 aaahhh. . . .

The wind dropped and their forward speed dropped
with it.

"Hes." Adlayr scowled at the slatting sail. "You're
the expert, come do something 'fore we start slippin'
back to Govaritil."

Camnor Heslin looked at the boots he was holding,
set them beside the mast, caught up a towel, and padded to the stern; he dropped the towel in Adlayr's lap.
"Spread that, will you? This is my last pair of clean
trousers." He took the tiller from Adlayr, settled himself, and began making small adjustments in sail and
heading, swearing as the boat lost more way. "Gyes,
is there a landing ahead? Sail's in my way, I can't
see."

"Grove of brellim and javories about half a stade
ahead, can you see that? There's a landing on the
downstream side. And enough nixies popping up to
staff a government office, they're grinning all of them,
waiting for something, I think, I don't know. . . ."

Camnor Heslin scowled. "Serroi, come back here,

that's right, now stretch out flat on the deck behind the hutch. The rest of you get down and be ready to jump. Maybe that lot out there are just having fun watching us squirm, but I wouldn't wager a tin uncset on it.''

He squeezed enough way out of the puffy gusts to angle across the current and ease the boat against the upstream rank of posts supporting the sturdy plant floor of the landing. Adlayr rose to a crouch, caught hold of the rope loops at the edge of the planks, and pulled the boat along until the nose was pressed against the mud. He straightened, reached for the nearest mooring post, then crumpled, blood spraying from his shoulder with the crack of a longgun. More shots whined across the deck, coming from the grove, some from up in the trees, some from the ground.

Camnor Heslin tipped over the back rail into the river and went swimming strongly underwater, heading for a patch of brush a little way along the levee that would shield him enough to let him get into the grove and at the shooters. Zasya sprang after him, Ildas leapt from the boat to streak along the levee, a ghost shimmer leaving a line of black pawprints where his feet charred the grass.

Adlayr lay on the deck, unconscious, not-so-slowly bleeding to death. Serroi crawled from behind the hutch to lie on top of him, pressing her hands on the ugly wound.

The noises of the ambush died away . . . she felt a strange echoing throb come into her through the boat from the river, from the nixies sculling about the yellow water . . . she heard voices, strange gobbling, glubbing voices like water bubbling through a pipe . . . the voices of the nixies . . . they were excited about something, she couldn't understand what . . . she wasn't trying to understand, she was focused on the healing . . . all the rest was peripheral . . . disturbing but distant. . . .

The trees *CHANGED*.

The shooters aloft screamed and dropped their weapons as branches went suddenly limber, wrapped around them, squeezing them like constrictors until bone and muscle were bloody pulp inside the skin; they were dropped to the ground below, roots came snaking up through suddenly loosened earth and pulled them under. And the trees ate them. The ambushers on the ground behind tree trunks were trapped in root-nets, squeezed and sucked under. A sigh passed over the grove as an ominous aura spread above the tree-tops, a purplish glow with the sulfury smell and hair-stiffening feel of air after a lightning strike close by.

The aura spread, met Serroi's green glow, and backed off.

As Camnor Heslin came surging from the water, Ildas screamed, started jumping about between them and the grove, trying frantically to stop them both from going into it. Zasya reached for Heslin's sleeve. "Wait. . . ."

He ignored her, pulled loose and plunged into the shadow under the trees. . . .

And a moment later was on the bank again, shivering and staring. "Ka-zhaggin' limbs were reaching for me."

> > < <

Serroi's hands came clear as new skin closed over the wound; she emerged from the heal-trance, pushed onto her knees and looked around, startled by what was happening around her.

Out in the river the nixies were having a wild time, playing and laughing, shouting to each other in their water voices, glubbing and gurgling; she listened and was appalled at what she heard.

The grove is eating men, isn't it fun? From now till they catch on and burn it, it will eat them all, every one who runs inside it, every beast and man, isn't it fun? She did it, our mother did it, the little green mother did it, she has the power, the OLD power, the great power, the power to wake and make and every time she uses it she'll birth new funnies, she can't help it, I and I and I wonder what the next will be, who it will eat, what it will do.

Serroi climbed to the landing, walked slowly, stiffly, along the planks, settled where she could feel the earth beneath her, closed her eyes. The trees were roaring, a soundless anger and hunger and need, but even that couldn't destroy the peace and the gladdening she felt as the Great Mother gave back what she'd expended.

But the respite was very short.

She sighed and looked up to see Camnor Heslin striding along the levee, cursing with every step because his good clothes were ruined and he had nothing else remotely suitable for a Vorbescar to wear. She smiled and out in the river the nixies giggled, the gusts of their laughter making the limp sail slat against the mast and enveloping her in a cloud of mud stink.

He stopped beside Serroi. "Adlayr going to make it? What's all this about?"

"My fault, I'm afraid," Serroi said. "Give me a hand, will you?"

He hauled her to her feet, glanced at the trees, their writhing and creaking growing louder and more threatening. "Weirdness," he said. "Those dreams you didn't want to talk about? Never mind, there's no time now, look at those clouds heading this way. The Enemy marches. We'd better get the zhag out of here.''

Serroi pointed. ''And there comes our transport.'' Zasya was coming around the rim of the grove, riding one macai, leading half a dozen others. ''I imagine those belonged to the shooters.'' She cupped her hands about her mouth. ''Paba paba, Zah-shee! Zah-shee!''

Zasya waved at her, stopped the herd on the landing road and held them there, waiting for the others to wake Adlayr, clear out the boat and haul the gear to her.

A short while later the boat was out in the middle of the river drifting south with an escort of nixies and they were riding north along the River Road.

Rain pelting them, wind snatching at them, trying to rip them out of the saddles, they rode into Dander in a noon so dark it might have been dusk instead.

The javories were whipping wildly, the streets empty except for a few struggling wains—the shoppers, traders and street people driven into kavarnas and the gloom-filled covered lanes.

The wind turned with them as they left Dander's center and rode up the Way of Masks between tall obelisks with the Marn Mask carved at the top; it lashed at them, trying to push them off the raised road. It was a steep climb and the macai were tired; they groaned and hooted and threatened to squat, but they could see the soaring bulk of the Pevranamist ahead and had enough sense to know that meant shelter, food, and hostlers rubbing them down.

''Who goes?''

''Camnor Heslin, Vorbescar of the Grand Council of the Mijloc and escorts to see Jestranos Oram.''

A shot wheengggged off the wall, another cracked immediately after, but by this time, the companions were crowding into the gate tunnel and out of reach.

A few moments later half a dozen men with a struggling prisoner came rushing along the slope from the trees where the sniper had been waiting. "Sahnout, open up. Get a move on."

"Eh Zaps, what about. . . ."

"Oram's expectin' 'em, we'll escort."

Jestranos Oram came out to meet them, ushered them into his office, and sent his aide scurrying to make sure their rooms were ready over in the main building of the Pevranamist, that baths were heating and dry clothes were laid out for them.

He seated the Vorbescar in the chair and waved the others to the benches along the wall, hesitating when he came to Serroi. "Healer?"

"Yes?"

He took her hand, led her to his own chair behind the worktable. "Ah. Hot drinks, prak? Would that be right to ward off sickness?"

"They can wait," she said, curious about the mix of emotions she was sensing in him; the strongest of all was a deep-seated anguish tearing at him. She'd caused it, but she had no idea why. Nor was this the time to ask.

"Nik, nik, it won't take any time to arrange and we'll all be more comfortable." He bustled from the room.

Serroi clasped her hands on the table, raised her brows.

Camnor Heslin shook his head.

Honeydew crawled from Zasya's gearsac where she'd been nestling next to Ildas. She worked her wings, then fluttered onto the chain of the lamp hanging above the desk. *Aaaayahhhhh, what a day!*

Serroi chuckled. *That it was, but it'll get better soon.*

Jestranos Oram returned a moment later, carrying a straight-backed chair and followed by two young men holding trays loaded down with steaming pots of cha, todda, and kava, with crispy waffle wafers piled on plates beside the pots. His brows shot up as Honeydew came spiraling down to perch on Serroi's arm and sip at the cha in her mug. "I wasn't told about the little one."

Serroi broke a wafer into pieces small enough for the sprite and set them aside for her. "Her name is Honeydew; she is one of us and not the least valuable."

Camnor Heslin sighed, set his cup on the table at his elbow, and got to his feet. "This courtesy is much appreciated, Inquisitor. However, there's a business we need to complete." He placed the case he'd brought from the stable in front of Jestranos Oram, opened the locks with a key he took from round his neck, and began lifting out tins of candied fruit, sweet rolls, toffees, and a dozen other sorts of comfits—according to their labels. When the case was empty, he closed it, set it on the floor and returned to his seat, smiling at the carefully blank face of the Cadandri.

"If you'll take a tin-opener to those, a sharp knife with a short blade will do if you're careful, you'll find three communicators packed in each. The Prieti Meien arranged the packing, so they should have survived the trip well enough."

Jestranos Oram lifted a can that had bright orange chays with pink cheeks painted on the label; he looked from the can to Camnor Heslin's ample form, a twinkle in his eyes. "Clever," he said.

"I was inclined to take it as an insult," the Vorbescar murmured, "included in this business as camouflage to a heap of tins, but Nischal Tay appealed to my love of country, so what could I do?" He sobered. "You've heard about the explosion in the Radwan Rum? That the Val Kepal was killed?"

"Yes. You had trouble?"

"We were detained, supposed to be interned until our loyalties could be shifted or the troubles were over." In a few crisp sentences he outlined the situation they'd left in Govaritil, the uproar in the city, the hostility between the twin brothers and between the red and green factions that supported them, the possibility that Govaritzers on their own would start attacking the border areas, wherever there'd been tension before, the further possibility that the new Val Kepal, whichever brother it was, might decide to get an army together to march on Dander. "If there is evidence of weakness here or too much confusion," he finished, "that might tip the balance toward attack. Takuzhone hates Cadander as much as Takuboure, he's simply more prudent and perhaps more intelligent than his brother." He sighed, got to his feet again. "If the Marn requests it, I'll give you a written report later. Now I'd very much appreciate a close and intimate acquaintance with that hot bath you mentioned."

"Of course. If you'll come with me?" He blinked as Honeydew flew to Serroi's shoulder, but he didn't comment, merely led them from the room.

Honeydew yawned and fluttered to the window where she sat making faces at the rain coming down, enjoying the knowledge that it couldn't get at her.

Serroi chuckled, teased out of her gloom by the

sprite's antics. She tossed the sodden cloak over the back of a chair, stripped off the filthy torn clothing she'd worn for far too long and went into the bathroom. The tub was full of warm water and scented bubbles, there were clean towels and a dish of soft soap that smelled of roses. "Blessings on your head whoever got this ready."

She eased herself into the bath, stretched out and closed her eyes as warmth crept through her and the delicate perfume of the bubbles wiped away the river stench.

When she woke, it was late afternoon. The shadows were long in the garden outside the window; the clouds had broken while she slept, the rain had stopped. The Enemy wasn't wasting his energy on people he couldn't reach. She curled up on the window seat, wrapped in a blanket from the bed, hungry but still too tired to do anything about it.

Nixies . . . they called me Mother. Maiden Bless. What kind of children are those? I wonder . . . Yallor, the elvins in the garden . . . my children, too? So to speak. The fire mouselets in the tavern in Shinka? And in Govaritil, those whatever-they-were in the bathroom? Carnivorous trees. . . . Odd. Sterile all my life, now I'm spewing children like a frog laying eggs . . . birthing and passing on, leaving them to take care of themselves. She chewed her lip. *And if that's so, then the Fetch IS mine. Maiden Avert! I can't . . . I have to do some. . . .*

The glass rattled in the window and the wall itself seemed to shudder. Serroi closed her eyes, pulled the blanket more tightly about her.

Her door crashed open; without waiting for permission a man came rushing in. ''Explosion,'' he gasped, ''we need you.''

He snatched her up, flung her over his shoulder, and ran out.

14. Getting to Know. . . .

Marn's only daughter and Marn-to-be, second in power and honor only to the Marn herself, K'vestmilly Vos beat at the lump of clay and cast envious eyes at the wheel where Husenkil's niece Narazha was throwing a pot.

For the past three days Husenkil'd had her learning the clays, the feel, the smell, even the taste, of the different grades and sorts; it should have been excruciatingly dull, but she surprised herself by finding the study of assorted piles of dust and lumps of goo fascinating, especially when he showed her pieces fired from the various clays. Today he'd set her to wedging clay for the wheel, driving the air out of it; even this tedious and tiring thump-ka-thump was curiously satisfying, though she was getting impatient, lusting toward the wheel as she sneaked glances at Narazha caressing and shaping the lump she was working with into a long-necked ewer, the clay following her fingers, taking shape so swiftly and obediently the ewer seemed willed not made.

Thwap. *I wish this was the Enemy's head. Or Tecozar, that thrunt.* Thwap. *Or that Pan of his. Zavidesht Pan Nov. For what he's done . . . nik, not done . . . to his miserable warren and the people who have to live there.* Thwap. *Or Dukladny Treddek Vyk. For souring the Land and mucking up the river.* Thwap.

Druzhadlo Treddek Bar for being an idiot and hassling Marn. 'Twasn't her fault his Pan let the Bar Leathery get blown up. Thwap. *Vyzharnos. Prokking Poet. Next time I catch him flirting with that.* . . . Thwap thwap thwap. *My arm's getting tired. What did Hus say? When you think it's done, cut it open and look.* Prak. *There's one cut, cross it with the second.* Spros! *There's an airhole, that looks like another. Now, stick your fingers in the muck and see if there're lumps. Zdra zdra, that's one thing right. Pile the sections up and whack them some more.* Thwap. *Hedivy, that not-ney, sweet-talking Oram into turning him loose.* Thwap. *I wanted to see his spojjin'* . . . *saaa!* Thwap thwap thwap. *Ah! That feels good. I'd like to play this tune on their skulls. All of them.* She glanced at Nar-azha, sighed, and brought the roller down hard enough on the clay to drive a deep canal through it.

Husenkil came into the long room, glanced at Nar-azha's ewer, tapped her on the shoulder. "Carve it loose, that's about perfect, Razhee." He crossed to K'vestmilly, inspected the cuts she'd just made, dug his fingers into the clay. "Good," he said. "Now go wash your hands and tell your watchdog to settle for a nap, I'm going to take you for a walk and I don't want company."

K'vestmilly glanced at the House of Glory as they went past. "Tell me about them," she said. "Hedivy wasn't interested in anything but turning my stomach, trying to make sure I wouldn't ask for him again and he could get back to his proper job."

"Seems to've worked."

"Zdra, he wasn't much pleased about fiddling around with me, but I'm reasonably sure that wasn't why Oram called him back." She kicked at a ball of paper someone had thrown on the walkway. "I think things have got so hairy he couldn't spare one of his best men. He doesn't tell me much, but that's what I think."

"Could be. Turn down here, there's a park a little way back there. We can talk a while without ears around to hear what we say."

The park was gray and dusty; even the water that flowed sluggishly in the old fountain seemed tired and smudged. There were Nerodin babies crawling about everywhere, tadlings chasing each other or playing in the big sand box, digging and patting the sand, all of this watched by two harried girls in white aprons.

"The kids' mums are working," Husenkil said as he dusted off a section of bench for her, then sat beside her. "Those are sekalari novices, it's part of their testing. The Sekalar Mistress figures if they survive a couple wards down here, their call is strong enough to hold them through their training. You want to see what life is like for us Nerodin, you ought to spend some time in their clinics in the warrens."

"Not now. It's too dangerous, for them as much as me." The lazy wind stirring up the dust and flicking the leaves about had an odd smell, not unpleasant exactly. Unfamiliar, though. Unhealthy?

"I know." He smiled as he caught her sniffing. "The wind's coming from Steel Point and the mills there, that's what you're smelling. In Calanda you can always tell the direction of the wind by the smell it carries. The Glasshouses, the Papery, the Leatherworks, they all have their smells." He sighed. "She wasn't happy to see me, but I'm glad I went. It's been an odd way to be together, K'milly. Not easy for either of us. Maybe you'll find a better, though I don't how it'd go. I couldn't live there, which is just as well, because I don't think your mother would've liked that, she's a woman who needs space around her. Zdra zdra, you wanted to know about the House of Glory. I'm not sure what I think of that lot.''

Two of the older children ran past, screaming and kicking up dead leaves and clouds of dust.

Husenkil waited until the novices had settled the argument and herded the tadlings back to join the others, then he moved his shoulders. ''Maybe it's just because I'm an old fossil who prokkin' well isn't going to go confessing his sins to some beardless thrunt or lettin' some notney stick a ring in his nose and lead him round like a castrated vul.'' He scraped a foot across the gritty concrete under the bench, twisted his mouth. ''A lot of weird things been happening, K'milly. Day before yesterday this woman I knew, Uzlana Patrat, she thought she saw her son swimming in the river and he's been dead three weeks and no mistake about that, I saw the little struv hauled out the water, not a pretty sight after the crawbabs had got at him.'' He clicked his tongue. ''Poor woman, she wasn't right in the head after those fools let her see the body.'' He tilted his head back and watched as a jesser glided by far overhead, the colors of its wing fur lost in the haze that hung over Calanda; after a moment's gloomy silence, he went on. ''She took a dive off the bridge last night, they pulled her body out down by the Papery canal, but some prokkin' fool was saying just this morning he saw her swimmin' round the piers with her boy. Other things. Rats in the walls that aren't rats, or not altogether, they look at you with knowin' eyes; gets you in the stomach when it happens. Kids being born weird, not to look at so much, but the way they act, the things they do. They say magic went out of the world after the Son's War, my feeling is it's pouring back now in ways that scare the. . . ." He broke off again, leaning forward, his hands cupped over his knees. "Look at her," he said, "the little girl sitting alone by the fountain, the one with the hair that's like melted copper. Watch her a minute."

K'vestmilly was slowly getting used to her father's sudden focusing on something she hadn't even noticed. He had an astounding peripheral awareness and he tended to switch his attention from the person he was talking to or the job he was doing to fasten on some little thing that caught his interest. It made talking to him at once fascinating and intensely irritating.

The child was two at most, a tiny thing, fragile, with huge eyes that seemed almost colorless, all the vigor in her gone into the bright hair that was pulled into two thin braids that framed her face. She sat very still, her hands clasped in her lap; her dress was faded, cut down from a larger one, but it was clean and well-tended, no tears or frayed places. Long coppery lashes fluttered as K'vestmilly stared at her.

K'vestmilly turned her head so she seemed to be watching another child, one pounding two sticks together. A moment later the little girl's mouth moved, rounding into a whistler's pout, though no sound came out. There was a shiver in the dusty leaves of the stunted javory growing beside the fountain; a small modary fluttered down, landed on her shoulder, rubbed its furry blue head against her cheek, and burst into joyful song. The girl looked up, stopped her whistling as she saw K'vestmilly watching her again. The faint color fled from her cheeks and she tensed, her body shouting her fear. The modary flung itself off the girl's shoulder and flew away.

K'vestmilly forced herself to smile, trying to reassure the child, then she turned so she was facing her

father, her back to the girl. "Poor little one. She's
petrified. Is there anything we can do?"

"My mistake," he said. "Ignore her. With a little
luck she'll forget; she's only a baby."

"But so afraid."

"That's her mother's doing; it's her mother's fear."
He wrinkled the beaky nose he'd passed on to her.
"There've been bad things happened to other such babies. That's something you should think about,
K'milly. The Biserica takes youngers like her, though
even they don't take babies; in any case, it's a long
way off and poor folk can't afford to travel, most of
the warreners barely get across the Bridge twice in a
lifetime. Maybe Cadander should start something like
the Biserica, to protect these kids, school or sanctuary,
I don't know, there're a lot of them already and there
are going to be more. Zdra, their mothers are scared
pink, that's one set goes to the Glory." He ran short,
stubby fingers through the frizz over his ears. "And
then there're these explosions, the thing that's worst
about them is nobody knows why. And when you don't
know why, you don't know who's going to get it next
or how to protect yourself. That's sending more people
to the House, the Glory gives them some kind of comfort. Krechin the Tailor keeps trying to get me to go."
He moved his shoulders again. "It's not to my taste,
that's all."

She smoothed her hair down, retied the scarf. "How
new is this . . . whatever it is? The first I heard of
Houses of Glory was when I walked past one of them;
that was the day I came to see you. I don't remember
anything like them when I went riding, though I have
to confess that I never noticed much about the city, I
was in too big a hurry to get to the hunting
fields. . . ." She grimaced. "So much time gone . . .
zdra zdra, as one of my teachers said over and over,

regret is a like a ghost with claws and about as useful. Do you know when they started showing up?''

"I saw one in a Glasshouse warren a year ago. It's the first time I heard anything about them.''

"Hmm. That's before the explosions started, but not the raids, those were already happening. Hedivy did say they were looked into, didn't seem to have any ties to the attacks.''

Husenkil shrugged. "Without knowing the details of those reports, it's hard to judge. There's something you ought to remember, Kimi, when it's your time to evaluate the reports you get. You'd think men like Hedivy who are born to the Nerodin would know better, but they take their cues from the top and Rodin basically despise Nerodin, don't think they have the intelligence to be dangerous. Even Oram looks through smoked glass. If he suspected the Houses might be a threat to the Marn, he'd have closed them down months ago. But they don't preach against the Marn. Or the Families. So he discounts what else they might be doing.''

She got to her feet. "Could you get your tailor friend to take me to a meeting? I'd like to see for myself what's happening. Get some feel about the people there.''

He stood. "Setting Krechin on me like a leech. Tsss! Tomorrow?''

Her mouth twitched, stretched into a grin. "Why not? So what was it you were going to show me?''

As they walked past the fountain, she stopped, knelt beside the child who was shrinking against the stone, almost fainting with fear. "You whistle pretty, bébé. I thought it was sooo nice that I'm going to keep it a secret between you and me, hmm?'' She pulled a strand of coppery hair from beneath her scarf and grinned at the child. "Just between us redheads, hmm?" She didn't wait for a response, but straightened and followed Husenkil from the park.

"That was well done," he said.

She glowed inside; she'd taken immediately to the man who was her father and she wanted rather desperately for him to like her. "We redheads have to stick together," she said.

He took her into the back streets of the city, showed her the life of the Glasshouse warren, the Pottery warren, took her past the schools, the communal ovens and laundries, the small artisans' shops tucked in among the teeming life of the mid-Calanda warren. He introduced her to a cabinet maker who'd fallen off a scaffold some years back; he couldn't walk, but he made the wooden tools Husenkil used in his shop, and others for just about everyone along Keshtinac Street, combs and cosmetic tools for women, exquisite small boxes, cups and other trade items for shops in Dander. In the corner of the room, two small boys who had comical small replicas of his face were sanding plain boxes, working with the intensity they'd inherited with their short noses and pointed, lobeless ears. What the woodworker was finishing was a cradle for a woman who expected twins and could afford the prices he had to charge for the work and the time he put into each thing he did. He was in the middle of a last rub on wood that glowed in the dusty light coming through the small windows.

There was a weaver who looked out the door when Husenkil called to her, nodded at them, and never stopped the busy jump of her shuttle, the clack of her loom, the jerky dance of the punch cards which ordered the pattern.

There was an embroiderer crouched over a frame,

needle flickering with swift sureness. A lacemaker. A glover. A cobbler. And dozens of others tucked here and there all through the busy warren.

There was a scissors grinder rolling his stone along the twisty ways, chanting his prices as he went, calling on the folk around to bring out their tools, he could hone an edge that would split a thought in half. There were fruit sellers and candymen, hot pie sellers and icemen, all of them with their own chants, calling to the men and women of the warrens to come out and buy.

The contrast between these and the Shipper's warren grew more powerful with every bend she turned; though she said nothing of this, she wondered some more about the Pan Nov. Why were his people so different from these?

At the end of two hours Husenkil circled back to Keshtinac Street and took K'vestmilly to a small kavarna near the pottery. He waited until she'd brushed the grit from her face and finished her first cup of cha, then he leaned across the table, speaking low so they wouldn't be overheard. "These Nerodin, they're your wealth, K'vestmilly Vos; they're the Marn's strength. If they're content, the Land is well. If they suffer, the Land suffers. It may not seem so at first glance, but it is so. Your mother has let things slip in the past few years. I can understand why now, but it has to be stopped, K'milly. Talk to her, persuade her to let you do more. And find someone you can trust who knows the ruling business. I can't help you there, but I'll do what I can elsewise." He reached out, touched her hand. "I wish I'd known you before this, but Ansila wouldn't have it, I don't know why. Zdra zdra, she is what she is. So we scratch the itches your clawed ghost has made on us and go on from here. You're a daughter

to be proud of, K'milly.'' He sighed and straightened.
"If you can, come tomorrow, you've smelled Steel
Point, I'll show it to you." He chuckled, his eyes
dancing. "And I'll screw my courage up and see if
old Krechin will take us to a Meet."

"You should've left this to me," K'vestmilly whispered, anger roughening her voice. Her mother's fingers were digging into her arm; even so, they shook
with the effort she was making to walk easily and hold
herself erect. "The Feneks are friendly."

"Weakness does not make for a good partnership,"
the Marn said softly, her words coming with short
spaces between them. "We went through this already,
K'milly, I don't care to repeat myself."

The Gold Room glowed with light and warmth; it
was the smaller of the two formal dining rooms, the
one they used when it was more important to show
friendship than to drive home Cadander's wealth and
consequence. The table was at the far end of the long
room, the near end was filled with stuffed chairs, elbow tables, lamps, several jewel rugs in shades of blue
and green. Two men and a woman waited there, bow-
ing as Marnhidda Vos entered the room, tall, angular
people with skin like the shell of a wanja nut, shiny
and dark brown, hair like steel wool, black streaked
with gray. One of the men was nearly bald with a close-
clipped beard and mustache, the other's eyebrows had
the shape and density of woolly worms. The woman
was wrapped in folds of heavy dark silk, her hair
braided into an elaborate confection of loops, gold
wire, and beads. She was austerely beautiful and when
her eyes met K'vestmilly's, the Dedach shivered at the
impact.

"Welcome, Hekandral, Olltarro, Malkia Hekka-

taran. It is a pleasure to greet you once again.'' Marnhidda Vos moved to the chair at the head of table and
eased herself down with K'vestmilly's help. ''Be
seated, friends, and tell me how Tuku-kul goes these
days.''

Pevranamist servants in dark clothes came like
shadows to pull out chairs and fill glasses, flitting about
in their felt shoes as soundless as the ghosts they were
meant to be, setting up the array of tall stemmed
glasses with the soups and purees forced on the Marn
by the exigencies of the Mask, and laying out the trays
and bowls for the other diners.

K'vestmilly glanced at the closed faces of the servants and wondered what lay behind those natural
masks; she thought about the weaver and the cabinet
maker, about her father and Narazha her cousin who
at the age of twelve was already settling into her life-
work. *When I was twelve, what was I . . . zdra, I was
climbing trees and learning to ride and running away
from my lessons.*

The Malkia Hekkataran set her jeweled hands on the
linen cloth, her teeth flashing in the candlelight.
''Tuku-kul does swelter these days.'' Her voice was
warm and deep, like melted chocolate. ''And it is not
even summer yet.'Tis an oddity, this year, and getting
odder as the days slide by.''

''Zdra zdra, we haven't felt that yet, but of course
we're much farther north here. How goes trade? You
should be doing well with Govaritil pulling shut.''

Hekandral stroked a bony, flat-tipped thumb along
his jaw, smoothing the soft springy beard. ''Ach'a,
that is a terrible thing. We will talk about it later,
needing your news to add definition to the little we
know. But this is true, trade comes so thickly we have
trouble finding room for it.''

The Malkia Hekkataran smiled again, that broad

glinting smile that seemed to heat the room with its glow. "It is not a trouble that troubles us much."

Worried about her mother who only pretended to sip at the glass straws as she talked with febrile vivacity, K'vestmilly sat silent listening to the exchange between the Marn and the Fenek envoys, fluent chitchat about nothing important, an exercise in wit that was its own reason for being, a time passer until the dinner was over and they moved to the chairs at the other end for after-dinner kava and the more serious talk, where they'd be as alone as they would ever be, the only others present the guards standing silent and disregarded against the walls.

While they strolled from the table to the talking area, the steaming kava urn was brought in, along with a cha service, a tray of liqueurs and delicate stemmed glasses from the Sko Glasshouses, bowls of warm, scented water and soft rolled towels; then the servants slid out, leaving them to their conversation.

K'vestmilly's anxiety was diminishing, though still there. Her mother was enjoying this, as if she fed on the flying words and drew strength from the delicate combat.

". . . of this heat has an unfortunate outcome; the Raider's Moon shines in Autumn, but the Majilarn clans are moving south much earlier." Hekandral's tenor sang smoothly along, despite his worrying words. "It seems that part of the North is even hotter than we; the grass is dry and their waterplaces are shriveling. No rains, you see."

Marnhidda Vos sipped at her tonic, medicine disguised as a liqueur; she set the glass down, leaned forward. "We haven't yet felt pressure against the High Harozh; the Dan is running at its usual levels, perhaps that's why."

Olltarro's woolly brows flew up. "But your barge-veks speak of raids?"

"Thieves, not the clans; chovan from the hills, a miserable concoction brewed from the worst of a dozen Lands. They raid the Majilarn as much as they do us—when the clans are about, that is."

The Malkia stroked her fingers along one of the tuk-ulware cups the Domcevek had set out as a compliment to the visitors, her dark brown hand a pleasing contrast to the azure glaze. "The bargeveks say other things, as do our traders who've returned from Dander. Fenka has worries enough with the Majilarn; we would be seri-ously disturbed if new trials descend on us."

"Zdra zdra, these explosions. They have caused relatively little damage to us since they're so widely scattered; that should have been evident as you came through Dander, yes? Where it hits us mostly is mo-rale, the random nature of these events, so pointless and so painful, bedi beda, it's disturbing, one can't plan, you see."

Malkia Hekkataran spread her hands, the jewels of her many rings glittering in the mellow lamplight. "Were these events confined to Cadander, we would commiserate and aid where we could, but not contem-plate a severance. The rumors from Govaritil disturb us greatly. Several of our shipmasters were caught there, but managed to get away—we have sent envoys to protest their confinement and demanded the release of others of our people, but we have heard nothing from the embassade. The captains tell us the Val Kepal is dead and the City torn apart as the Twins fight for the Seat. We have our own factions, as I'm sure you know, O Marn, though the situation is different, at once more stable and more fragile. Were a similar event to come to Tuku-kul, we would be forced to reconsider our options."

"My Inquisitor is laboring like twenty men to discover the source of these events and the reason behind them. He has learned a number of things—you understand, I cannot discuss these without compromising his continuing investigation, but I will say this. The source is outside Cadander, perhaps even beyond the Shimzelys. We find it difficult to understand the event in Govaritil since it shut down all traffic up the Yellow Dan and cut off what must have been an important supply line. It seems possible that the Enemy has turned his eyes on Tuku-kul and the Red Dan as an alternate route to bring in his devices. If that be true, it is highly unlikely he would wound himself again by arranging events to happen there."

Olltarro worked his brows again. "This is a semi-conforting thought, O Marn. Unfortunately the Kul Marshes breed smugglers as prolifically as they breed flies. They are Fenek, but they have little loyalty to Fenka and, in any case, would sell their grandmothers for a piece of hard candy."

"The smugglers of the Kul are indeed notorious; it might be possible, perhaps, to co-opt some of them to report activity if they won't interdict it. We do not expect Fenka to undertake a dangerous interference with these activities, but information as detailed as possible would be most welcome."

The Malkia Hekkataran tapped a fingernail against the cup, nodded, the gold beads on her wire loops clattering softly. "That would be feasible, I believe, though it needs consultation before it can be approved. Perhaps more information could be provided?"

Marnhidda Vos held out her hand; K'vestmilly gave her an arm and helped her rise. "We will talk again tomorrow, I thank you all for coming. May the old friendship between our Lands continue unabated."

* * *

"Don't go yet."

K'vestmilly turned. Her mother was stretched out on the daybed, Sluzha patting cream on skin with almost no flesh under it; her eyes were sunk deep in dark bruises, only half open. A moment before she'd seemed livelier, stronger than she had in days, but that was gone now. "You need your rest, Mother. We can talk tomorrow."

"Nik, K'milly, I don't think about tomorrow these days, the only thing I'm sure of is the hour I'm in right now. Sit and talk to me."

"Prak." K'vestmilly kicked the hassock over and perched on it. "Shall I tell you about my day?"

"In a minute." Marnhidda Vos shut her eyes, sighed. "I'm . . . pleased . . . yes . . . pleased at what you're doing . . . I was afraid . . . zdra zdra, never mind that. Tell me what you think happened tonight."

"Oral exams now? I thought I was out of school."

"If you've any sense . . . go on."

"Hmm. First, you know them very well indeed."

"The Malkia I've known since she was to my knee. Her mother used to bring her when she came to raid the Glasshouses. Glass is one thing we do that they can't, though I must say they've tried. The other two almost as long. Trust comes from time, K'milly. Time and attention."

"Yes. They came to let you know that Fenka is hearing things about our troubles and if there's the slightest threat that they could spread they'll bar Cadandri from entering Fenka. They also came to pick up whatever bits of information they could that might prove profitable. And, give them this, to be as helpful as they dared."

"Anything else?"

"Helpful . . . mm. They won't search cargoes for us or try to stop the Enemy; as long as he has a use

for them, he should leave them alone . . . you know,
I don't understand it either, hitting Govaritil, I mean,
and the way it was done, aiming at the heart. It's as if
he were telling us this is what's going to happen to you
the minute I get lucky."

"I hadn't thought of that." Marnhidda Vos winced,
then stroked the maid's hand. "It wasn't you, Sluzha,
your touch is gentle as thistledown. 'Twas only a sad
picture in my head. K'milly, you'll have to know them
all, the Pans and the Treddeks." She laughed, a
soundless whuffing that barely stirred her bluish lips.
"It seems I must deal with tomorrow whether I want
to or not. You go see your . . . hmm . . . teacher, but
when you come back, come straight to me. There are
things I have to tell you, things I've learned and kept
secret. I'm too tired now. Sluzha, would you bring me
a few drops of that foul brew the healer left?"

When the maid had bustled from the room, her
mother beckoned urgently. "K'milly," she whispered
when K'vestmilly was bending close to her, "Tell me
you remember. The Marn's Tower?"

"How to unlock the door from inside? How to find
the Marn's Treasure?"

"Yes, yes, tell me, in my ear. Quickly."

When K'vestmilly was finished, Ansila Vos smiled.
"There's one more thing, the Treddeks and the Pans,
what I know, it's written down. I've been writing every
night for weeks now. No one knows, not even Sluzha.
There's a place in my bedroom, Hus built it for me.
He knows and I know and no one else. You'll need it
. . . you'll need it soon. . . ."

"Mother. . . ."

"Go sit down, I hear her coming, she thinks she's
so quiet, but I always hear her."

K'vestmilly kissed her mother's hollow cheek,
straightened and walked away, but she didn't sit down

again, she needed to get away, to forget the smell of death for a while; much longer in here and her mother would see that; her body might be dying, but her mind was still sharp. "Mother, you've talked enough, now it's time to rest. And if I stay, you won't. Maiden give you peace."

The noise crashed across the wasteland, towering stacks belched smoke, fires flickered behind tall pointed windows that rose three stories high, some panes broken, others cranked open to let out more smoke and more noise. As K'vestmilly watched from the top of a small hill a short distance off, coke and other supplies moved in and out of the paved yard before the mill in a steady stream of two-wheeled vul wains; hand carts of rough-cast iron ingots rumbled along rails from the foundry built beside the steel mill; an ore train came clattering up to the foundry, nine huge drays with two drivers for each twelve orsk hitch, a cook wagon and a dozen of the Marn's Guard milling about, yawning and scratching.

Husenkil had been watching her face; he grinned, tapped her arm. She'd noticed that about him, people he liked he was touching constantly, as if he tasted them with his fingertips. He was doing it more and more with her; the brush of his fingers made her glow with happiness, it showed he was liking and approving her. "Pens are the wealthiest of the Families," he said, "the Marn's sturdiest support. And the most popular among the Nerodin."

She scowled at the sooty gray structures and found that hard to believe.

He chuckled, set his hand on her shoulder and squeezed gently. "Looks like working in Zhagdeep, doesn't it, but those men fight to pass their jobs on to their sons; some families from Steel Point warren have

three generations in there, Grandfather a Master, son a
Journeyman, grandson an Apprentice. The pay's good,
they aren't treated like idiots or potential thieves . . ."
he grinned and tapped her arm again, ". . . what they'd
steal or how I don't know, takes a crane to lift those
bars and sheets. And behind the mill, you can't see it
from here, there's a clinic with sekalari healers and
novices to take care of breaks and burns."

"That's fine . . . but it looks. . . ."

"Don't go by looks, Kimi. Your tutors must have
told you about Calanda steel. Pen could sell twice as
much if he wanted to and could make it, and at a good
price, too."

"I thought it was just the usual kind of bragging; I
was tired of wading through that kind of spros." She
grimaced. "I was a horrible student, Hus. No kind of
student really. Memorize stuff, spout it back, forget it
five minutes later."

"You seen enough?"

"If I'm not going to go down there."

"Better not, there's no telling when the next explosion will be or where." He began picking his way
down the slope toward the road atop the levee, talking
as he moved. "Haratocel Pan Pen is as hard and im-
mobile as the steel he makes; he hates changes, they
always mean trouble, he has to stir himself and figure
out how to cope when he'd rather march in the same
rut year on year. That's why I say he'd be the last to
desert you; there's a thousand years of Marn rule he
can look to when he wants to feel warm and secure."

They walked slowly along the grassy verge of the
road to avoid the wains and wagons trundling along
the cracking pavement, Husenkil talking around the
creak-rumble-thud from them and the vul and orsks
pulling them. That was another thing she'd noticed, he
loved to talk, to lecture, to run his voice, perhaps as

a reaction to the intense silence of his concentration when he was creating something new. She listened with one ear and after a while let her mind drift; her head was tired of all this intake. The river flowed past, lyrical wrinkles looping across the yellow-brown surface, now and then pushed into swooping vees by the blunt noses of barges carrying winter wheat and bales of hides down from the Harozh.

The water bulged and broke, shaping a yellow-brown head with a young boy's face; the nixy swam along staring at her. Another joined it, another and another.

They vanished as suddenly as they appeared, melting back into the Dan.

"There, you see," Husenkil said, "it's as I told you, more and more of them every day. And they don't just swim around now, this morning there were all kinds of stories about how they're nosing into things, breaking ropes, stealing boats and carrying them way upstream or just letting them float away. Old Hopilly said one with a woman's face tried to pull him into the water, but he's a drunk with delusions, so some believe him and some don't."

Noon rush and the Steel Point warren closed around them as they moved out of the Waste around the mill; the winding lanes were clamoring, busy, children running everywhere, let out from school, mixing with men and women coming home for their polda, the midday meal; the beggars were out full force, men with missing eyes, arms, legs, women with children, young boys who caught at sleeves and never stopped their beggar's cry, tové tové tovee. There were food carts around every corner, their owners calling their wares, steaming meat pies, sausages, flatbread cornus filled with chopped meat, vegetables and rice with cha and kava on the side.

At first K'vestmilly found the commotion enormously enjoyable; seen through this vivid screen, life in the Pevranamist was a pale imitation, drained of color and interest. After a few turns, though, with the beggar boys tugging at her sleeve, yelling their tovés in her ears, elbows in her ribs, the noise battering at her, the smell of hot oil mixing with sweat and other odors she didn't want to think about churning her stomach, all she wanted was to get out of there and find a little peace.

At the edge of the warren was a small cluster of shops, a grocery, a dry goods seller, a tailor, half a dozen more; they were all busy, filled with shoppers taking advantage of the midmeal break. Beyond this last crowd K'vestmilly could see the relatively clear width of Jevejisit Street. Jevejisit, Neprevac, then Keshtinac and the pottery where the wheel was waiting for her.

She walked faster, hurrying to get where she could unclip her elbows from her sides and breathe more freely.

A blast of heat.

A force lifting her from her feet, slamming her into Husenkil, driving both of them back and back till they crashed into a wall and crumpled to their knees, coughing, eyes streaming.

When she could see again, people were running, mouths straining wide, there was blood everywhere, pieces of building and people still falling, dust clouds boiling up and out, all of it in eerie silence. *I can't hear, I can't hear.* . . . She felt frantically at her arms and body, but all she had were a few bruises.

Husenkil's arms closed round her, stilling her jerking movements and easing her panic; she still couldn't hear, but she leaned against him, feeling his warmth, his solidity. After a moment of just holding her, he pulled away and got to his feet, helping her up as soon as he was standing. He pointed toward Jevejisit, led her past the bodies. Her hearing began coming back and she shuddered at the screams and groans, swallowed again and again as her stomach rebelled against the smells. What was left of the building was burning and the bodies of those caught in it were burning with the wood.

"We ought. . . ."

"Hush, Kimi, just walk."

"But. . . ."

"There's nothing you can do here. You can't stay, you know that."

Dizzy, shaken by the violence and death, she let him lead her away.

By the time they reached the pottery she was shaking again, but this time with a rage she could barely control, too angry to feel her bruises or understand the effects of the explosion on her, though her knees trembled and she had to lean heavily on her father's arm.

Narazha gasped and hurried round the counter as Husenkil settled K'vestmilly into the chair beside the door. "Uncle Hus, Milly, what is it? What happened?"

"Explosion in the Steel Point warren. Where's Thratt?"

"He went to fetch our polda, should be back any minute." She hurried out, returned with a glass of broshka juice. "Here, Milly, drink this. You're so pale you scare me. You weren't hurt?"

K'vestmilly's teeth were chattering so with the fury that filled her she couldn't talk; she shook her head and gulped at the thick sweet juice.

Husenkil stepped into the doorway, looked along the street. Over his shoulder, he said, "Razhee, do you know where he went?"

"Machudy's cart, you know, down past the Glory House."

Husenkil rubbed his hand across his chin. "Chert! I don't know . . . Razhee, go find him, bring him back. Be careful, it's a mess out there. Hurry, but don't run or we'll have Krechin over sticking his nose in our business."

He stood in the doorway looking after Narazha, his shoulders tense. K'vestmilly set the glass down, pressed the heels of her hands against her eyes. Images and strands of words flickered in and out of her head, escaping her whenever she tried to focus on any of them.

Husenkil relaxed. He came over to her, stood behind her chair, rubbing her shoulders. "Thratt's coming. He'll get you home and you can send help."

She shuddered, dropped her head so he could knead her neck. "I'm going to find him, Hus," she whispered. "The Enemy. The rest doesn't matter, I'm going to find him and stop this."

"Kimi, that's your blood talking; if you're going to be Marn and not a weather vane, you can't listen to the blood."

"I'm not Marn yet. Maiden grant it'll be a long time before I am." She leaned back against him, the work of his strong fingers easing the tension out of her. "Ahhh, Hus, that feels good. You keep telling me those Nerodin are MY people, well, I prokkin' well am not going to let some sproch wipe them out." She sighed. "Zdra zdra, spitting in the wind. I've been playing, Father, you know that. I've got to work now. I've got to do more than just dip into Oram's files, I've

got to read them, study them, really study them. I hate
that kind of thing, I've skimped it because I hate it,
now. . . ."

"Zdra zdra, it won't hurt and maybe you'll find
something." His voice was absent, he was listening to
the sound of feet clacking along the planks. "Pek! I
know that step. Can you stand, Kimi? Good. Scoot
into the back room, hmm? Krechin's nose is twitching
and I don't want him poking at you."

K'vestmilly Vos jerked the door open and swept into
the Inquisitor's office. "Get Guards and sekalari over
to Calanda, Jevejisit Street by the Steel Point warren.
There was an explosion in the shops there, just before
midday, I don't know how many dead and hurt—ah,
and there's fire."

Jestranos Oram swore, snatched a bit of paper,
scrawled on it, signed it. "Hedivy, barracks first, send
whoever's there out, then the Hospital, tell the Sekalar
Mistress about the fire, the sekalari will need the burn
supplies. Then get back here, talk to me about the
Steel Point warren." He turned to K'vestmilly. "You
saw it?"

Scowling and swearing under his breath, Hedivy
went striding out.

K'vestmilly pulled the door shut and dropped into
the chair. "More than saw it. I was walking past when
it went off. Blew me across the street and into a wall."
She closed her eyes. "I saw . . . ahhhh, what I
saw. . . ." She started shaking and crying again, the
tears squeezing through her lashes.

"Vych! Here, drink this." He hurried round the
worktable, pressed a glass of water into her hand.

She started laughing, gulping as he snatched the
glass back and threw the water in her face, then bent
over her, clucking, wiping the wet away with his hand-

kerchief. She caught his wrist, took the cloth from him and finished the job. "I'm not hysterical, Oram. It's just that the first thing everyone does is hand me something to drink."

"Have you seen a healer?"

"I don't need a healer." She straightened, tossed the handkerchief onto the worktable. "I want a room with a good lamp and a pot of cha, then I want you to send me your files, Oram. Everything you've done, everything you've discovered, all the dead ends, the missteps, everything. Not summaries, the files themselves. Start from the beginning and don't set up to cater to what you think are my sensibilities. If you try that, I'll have your hide."

"It'll take weeks to go through, Dedach."

"Then I'll spend the weeks. Probably I won't see anything you haven't. But I NEED to know that, Oram."

He frowned at his hands, steepled them, fingertip pressed against fingertip. "It is your right, Dedach, but as a favor, will you see Bozhka Sekan first?"

"Agreed, as long as she doesn't tell the Marn. I don't want my mother worried."

"Nor do I. I'll have you called when it's time to dress for dinner."

She grimaced. "Pek! I can't sit there playing with pretty words. . . . Zdra zdra, I know that's important, too, we have to keep Fenka open." She pushed to her feet, swayed a little, held up her hand when he started round the table. "I'm all right, Oram. The room first, then you can send for Bozhka Sekan."

A knock on the door.

K'vestmilly set the folder down, brushed at her eyes. "Come." When she saw Jestranos Oram standing in the doorway, she frowned. "Is it that late already?"

"Nik, you've about an hour left. The Company from the Biserica got in half an hour ago."

"From Govaritil?"

"With difficulty. Told your mother. She won't let me send them to her, it seems she's resting. Talk to her, will you? At least make her see the Healer."

K'vestmilly sighed, shut the folder, and moved it onto the out pile. "I'll do what I can. If she's feeling like that, she might not see me. Anything else?"

"Nik. I. . . ." He shook his head and left.

"She won't even let me in, K'vestmilly. I'm sorry."

"Bozhka, you and Oram, you know something. What is it?"

"Marnhidda Vos laid silence on us and as long as she is Marn, we are bound to her wishes."

Her mind a jumble of impressions and stories, her body stiff and sore, K'vestmilly Vos pushed open the door to her suite and grimaced as her maid swooped down on her, exclaiming at the torn and filthy clothing. "Don't fuss, Puzhee, just help me out of these things. The bath's ready?"

"As if I wouldn't have it waiting. Now, come sit and let Puzhee take care of you."

K'vestmilly slid into the warm, foamy bath with a pleasure made all the more intense by the horrors she'd seen and the others she'd read about. Her head on the rest, the rose perfume swirling round her, she lay and let the warmth soothe away the aches and the weariness. . . .

"Deda' Deda', t'k t'k, sleeping like that, you could've drowned yourself."

K'vestmilly yawned, sat up, still only half-awake. "What time is it?"

"Late, Deda', you've only ten minutes to dress and you'd best go straight to the Gold Room."

"Chert!"

K'vestmilly slowed, twitched a handkerchief from her sleeve, patted gently at her face, then walked more sedately through the grand hall to the double doors that led to the Gold Room. The attendant bowed, opened them for her, closed them behind her.

The Marn was seated already and the others were moving toward the table; they stopped and turned to face her as she walked toward them.

She smiled, spread her hands. "Forgive me if you will, I. . . .

The room exploded.

Once again she was snatched up and flung back. In the instant before she hit the doors, she saw her mother torn apart, the Mask of Marn sailing through the air. . . .

15. Triumph

Treshtal stood on the crumbling stone block of the altar and danced in Light and Glory. IT HAS BEGUN. THE MARN IS DEAD. THE MARN IS DEAD. IT HAS BEGUN.

When he'd worked the elation out of himself, he squatted on the block, crossed his arms and dropped his head on them. "Evil takes care of its own," he said. "The Dedach escaped. She should have gone. She should have been with her bitch dam and blown to the shag she's earned. Forgive your servant. I have failed again."

The Voice in his head was sweet as sex and soothing as a hot bath, flowing through him, tickling him to a quiet contentment.

I have considered the Path and I rejoice that the Dedach lives. We need a focus to build the fire around, O Belovéd. The Dedach is temperish, you have told me that, rash and willful, and she won't have the ties the Marn built to the Pans and the Treddeks. We will prod her and drive her and she more than anything will bring herself down and the whole edifice of rule with her. Rejoice, Belovéd, you have done wondrously well.

He stretched out on the altar, writhing as pleasure thrilled through him, waves of Glory beyond description.

* * *

Veiled in thick yellow light like melted butter, Treshtal sat cross-legged on the altar watching the dark figure come striding across the broken floor. This time the cowl of Zavidesht Pan Nov's cloak was flung back; the side panels flared out as he swung his arms. He stopped before the altar, sneering at the flowing light. "Games!"

"If you want to talk about games," Treshtal said, his voice altered and replicated into a tenfold chorus as it passed through the light. "You played and failed. The Company reached Dander unharmed and at the Pevranamist your longgun missed his shot and was taken alive."

"And I lost twelve good men, I don't know how. As if the earth opened up and ate them. You didn't tell me there was a witch among them."

"And there is not. We ask you to consider well. Is there any way at all the longgun can be linked to you?"

"Nik, not by divination or investigation. He knows nothing, not even the man who hired him."

"Good. We called you here not to praise or reprimand, but to inform you of our actions present and to come so that you may be ready to take advantage of them. The Marn is dead."

"What!"

"It was done this night, only a few hours ago. The Dedach escaped with bruises, nothing more. We are going to use that. We are going to goad her into unconsidered actions which will reap so much ill-feeling that she will fall of her own weight. Oram is a secret man and will try to keep the death and its manner quiet, but rumors will be out before the sun comes up, rumors that will grow wilder with the day. We have men ready to speak against her, to accuse her of ordering the explosions and plotting to kill her own mother. Men who will say this is the time to seize rule for ourselves, to build a more just society, men who call to action.''

''No one will believe that or follow them. And Oram will have them in his cellars before the first word fades.''

''So we hope. The more he tries to suppress them, the more credence he gives to what they are saying. And they will keep saying it. And you will defend her, but do it in such a way your words convict her more surely than any denunciations. We are confident you are quite capable of producing the proper effect. And you know her temper, think how she will react and how it will look.''

''I see.''

''By morning the Treddeks will know what has happened and will start to react. What is your assessment as to who the next target should be? The raids will continue as before, the random explosions and the other manifestations, but we also intend some directed removals. Whom do you consider the Marn's strongest defender?''

''No question about that. Haratocel Pan Pen. If you can get his Heir with him, so much the better. The next Heir's a baby and the brother who'd be appointed guardian, he's a fool. After him, Marazhney Treddek Osk and Pan Osk. With those gone, there'll be so much elbowing and backbiting, sweet K'vestmilly Vos won't know what hit her. And . . .'' He wheeled to face the altar, white teeth glinting in a wide grin. ''You'd best hit me at the same time, make it a near miss, hmm? And near miss Vyk. He's home right now, but a brush will send him scuttling for the horizon. That'll make sure Vyk is neutralized, cover me, and give me a reason to play the defender in the breach, waving my sword and convicting that skinny bitch with every word." He sobered. "You can get spies into Family Holds? I want to know what they're thinking before they know."

"It will be done. Come." Treshtal extended a glowing hand, beckoning the Pan to come and be touched.

"I think not." Zavidesht Pan Nov pulled the cowl forward, adjusted the lacings of the cloak. "I walk my own road. That way we both get what we want."

Treshtal watched him stride out, arrogance and ambition in every swing of his cloak.

You are angry, Belovéd. Don't be, the higher he rises, the more terrible will be his fall.

"He'll turn on us the moment he has what he wants."

I know that, Belovéd. Even if I could not counter that, persecution would only make us stronger. And we do need to be stronger. Our numbers are growing, but we need to move out of the cities and across the Land. We buy time and use that evil man as broom to sweep away the other filth. Leave despair to the unbeliever. That is your sin, Belovéd, you fall too easily into melancholy and hopelessness. I have promised you his death. It will come, Belovéd. Believe and endure. Our time will come. Believe and endure.

"I will try, O Glory, I am a weak man and unworthy, but I am yours to the roots of my soul."

Rest now, Belovéd, dream and enjoy.

Treshtal curled up on the altar while the Glory filled him and showed him dreams more wonderful than before.

16. Pieces

With a sound more animal than human, K'vestmilly Vos wrenched herself from Serroi's hands and ran toward the other end of the room, into the clouds of dust still settling, ignoring the tottery walls, the fires licking at floor and debris, the bits of ceiling breaking loose and falling around the hole where the table had been.

Serroi shuddered away from that anguish and let herself be drawn to a physical pain that she could do something about, crawling across the floor, through the shards of glass and porcelain scattered everywhere, the distorted pieces of metal that had once been serving trays, candlesticks, knives, forks, ladles, and the other ornaments and utensils from the table. In the end nearest the door, chairs were torn, overturned, smashed against each other, the small tables broken and flung toward the back wall, lamps were tipped over, most of them blown out by the force of the blast, but here and there fires were beginning to creep among the ruins; guards snatched drapes from the walls and began beating them out.

The Fenek woman had glass fragments sprayed across her face and shoulders, a bruise over one eye where something had slammed into her, a leg twisted, ribs crushed. Serroi straightened the leg, set her hands on the woman's body and focused on the glass cuts,

willing the fragments out of her, smiling as the bloody
splinters washed from the flesh and rolled off to tinkle
onto the floor. Then she closed her eyes and let the
warmth flow out of her into the battered body, cleansing and restructuring it from the heart outward.

Another body called her, a Fenek man with woolly
gray brows. As soon as her hands came free, she
crawled to him. Around her there were the moans and
screams of the servants, the shouts and pounding feet
as Oram's men searched what was left of the room and
went after other fires that were beginning to threaten
them all.

K'vestmilly came storming past, jerking away from
a guard who tried to stop her. She found the tablecloth
bunched up against the back wall, shook it out; by a
freak of the explosion it was almost unharmed, a few
smears of food, a single cut near the edge. She spread
it on the floor, ran back into the billows of smoke and
dust.

When she emerged again, she had her mother's head
and torso cradled in her arms. Oram tried to take them
from her, but she jumped back. "Nik." Her voice was
low and intense. "No one but me. Do you understand?
No one but me touches her."

> > < <

Treshteny looked up from the cup of soup her nurse
was coaxing her to eat. "Boom," she said. "I don't
want any more. Marn can't eat. She's dead."

"Zdra zdra, that says nothing." The nurse's voice
was professionally soothing. "You need food for
strength."

"I want to go outside. I'll eat it outside."

"It's dark and cold out there. You'll catch your
death."

"Death doesn't need catching. He comes when he's called. I want to see the trees." She pushed the nurse's hand aside and got to her feet. "I have to see the trees."

> > < <

In the river the nixies gathered and watched the glow that only they could see, the pulsing green aura spreading its arms out and out from the Pevranamist, touching the land here, there; where it touched it called forth the sleeping magic and stung it toward shape. They cheered in their eerie voices as it skimmed across the river and more of their own came to join them, along with merfolk like moth sprites with fishtails instead of wings and froggets, little warty green rivermen.

They went silent and melted into the river when a column of darkness took shape above Dander; it shivered there a moment, surging as if it was trying for shape and solidity, then vanished.

> > < <

Serroi glanced at the third Fenek, but he was dead, a sliver of glass glinting in one eye, its point driven into his brain. She got to her feet and looked around. Despite their broken arms, cuts, burns, and other injuries, Oram had herded the servants into a corner of the room where the fires had been put out and the debris swept away; two of his men were questioning them and writing down the answers.

The trembling ashen Domcevek stood by the door, struggling to answer the questions the Inquisitor was hurling at him.

". . . swear, no one but the cleaners, same cleaners as always, and the women who got the table ready.

Nik, I didn't search them, why should I search them? Why would they DO this?'' The last was a wail half of terror, half of grief. "The Marn . . . why?''

Serroi stopped beside a servingmaid who was groaning over a broken arm and trying to answer questions. Ignoring the agent's protest, she pushed the maid's good hand aside, soothed her fingers along the arm; the girl screamed as the bone slid into place, then gasped as the pain vanished and the bruises mottling her face and arms faded, then were gone completely.

Serroi moved to the next, a man who was bleeding at the mouth and hunched over cracked ribs.

> > < <

Treshteny sat on the bench absently swallowing the soup her patient nurse fed her, watching intangible invisible upwellings from the earth claim shape—her shape and that of the nurse, other shapes, all female— and merge with the trees. Each tree that got a dryad grew immediately more solid, as if their new tenants had taken their futures firmly in hand.

There was a sapling beside the bench, a young javory planted to replace one struck by lightning a few years back. One of the upwellings began near it; Treshteny could feel the warmth of the flow and it woke in her an urgent desire—for what she didn't know, but the need was there. She reached out, tried to touch the nothing that she could see, but it evaded her hand. For an instant she saw herself in it, saw herself sad but determined, saw herself shaking her head, then the newly formed dryad merged with the tiny tree.

She had no time for grief. She saw the darkness rise above the city and fell in a premoaning fit, crying out about terror and death, but no one came to listen to her.

> > < <

Serroi rose from the last of the wounded servants, exhausted and apprehensive, wondering what she'd done this time, what *things* she wakened or created. As she moved away, she could feel eyes on her, almost smell the awe mixed with fear. It was the Biserica again; the men and women she'd healed and the agents who were trying to question them, all of them held themselves carefully away from her as if she were a bomb that could go off in their hands. *Bomb? Am I going to make a shambles like this? I have to talk to Oram, to Heslin. There has to be something. . . .*

She walked away from the huddle of servants and agents, leaned against one of the incongruously shining gold drapes and watched K'vestmilly Vos wrap the cloth about the fragments of her mother's body.

When she was finished, the Dedach stood and looked around. Her face was pale, her eyes stony.

The fires were only smolders now, the dust had settled, the dead were collected, the two Fenekel Serroi had healed were standing beside the body of the third, talking in whispers.

Cowled and caped in black, holding a staff in her right hand with the Maiden's interlaced diamonds in wrought iron as its finial, a tall woman with long white braids came through the door and stopped beside the body, half a dozen more women clustered behind her, black scapulars falling over their white robes.

"Preörchmat. You and your Setras are quick off the mark. I suppose you've come for the Marn." The Dedach's voice was as cold as her eyes. "Oram sent for you?"

The room went silent except for creaks from the weakened walls and the patter of plaster breaking loose from the ceiling. The agents held their questions, almost seemed to hold their breaths; the Nerodin servants in their torn and bloodied black tunics straightened as if they were on duty again, then went to their knees, their heads bowed.

Serroi thought it was formal as a play, as if these words had been spoken before, many times before and the actors speaking them merely playing their parts.

"Yes and nik, O Marnhidda Vos," the Preörchmat said quietly. "Jestranos Oram sent word we were needed, but we come for Ansila Vos, not the Marn."

K'vestmilly Vos shuddered. "I am not. . . ."

"There must be no break, O Marnhidda Vos, the Masking will come later but the Truth is now, the Marn is yours. May we do what our duty requires?"

Face impassive again, K'vestmilly Vos stepped aside; for a moment she stared blindly at the wall, then she nodded.

Mute and reverent, the Setras lifted the wrapped body and laid it on a litter. Jestranos Oram and his agents joined the servants on their knees as the Preörchmat took her place at the head of the litter. "Ansila Vos has served her people long and well. She lays down this task at last, not willingly but at death's summons. May her rest be untroubled and sweet." The Preörchmat brought the ironshod butt of the staff down hard on the parquet, then swept forward in a long stride, the Setras carrying the litter behind her.

As soon as the procession had passed through the door, the two Fenekel approached cautiously, bowed, and waited.

K'vestmilly Vos brushed a hand across her eyes, turned to face them. "Malkia Hekkataran, Olltarro, I am happy to see you well, and sad . . ." She glanced

at the body laid out on the floor a short distance off
". . . that Hekandral is not."

"Our grief is great, O Marn, and will continue long.
We have lost two friends of many years." The Malkia
Hekkataran hesitated a moment, then gestured toward
the body. "We have dead to care for and family to
comfort. We ask your leave to take our brother home."

"It is granted. Inquisitor, Domcevek Aktov, come
here." When they reached her, she said, "We'll need
another litter and guards to carry the body. Domcevek, I want a length of virgin linen for a winding
cloth." She turned to the Malkia. "Will you wash and
prepare him yourself or would you want our sekalari
to do that for you?"

"We will care for our own, though we will need the
proper herbs and tools."

"Domcevek, you hear? Good. Malkia, if there's
anything more you need, ask and it will be provided.
Oram, are you finished with the servants? I'd like to
send them to bed; they've had a hard night."

"I'll want to go through the questions again with a
truthreader this time, and I'll need to see the cleaning
women and the table dressers, but we can do that in
another room. I suggest the Domcevek's offices."

"Good." She brushed at her eyes again. "Domcevek, stir up the kitchen, I want sandwiches and kava,
cha, hot chocolate set up in your offices, pallets and
blankets, the Inquisitor will tell you where to put them.
Healer."

Startled, Serroi came away from the wall. She
bowed. "Marnhidda Vos."

"Stay with me. I want to talk to you. Later."
K'vestmilly Vos closed her eyes, squeezing them tight,
her lips drawing back, the skin taut over her cheekbones. "Domcevek."

"Yes, O Marn?"

She shivered, but didn't reject the title again. "I want this room stripped to the stone. . . ." With a sudden violence she spat, "If I could destroy this. . . ." She beat her fist against her thigh. "Repair the walls . . . th . . . the ceiling . . . floor . . . lock the door. I'll decide what to do with it later," she finished in a rush. "Let's get out of here. Now."

Serroi followed K'vestmilly Vos, forced to trot to keep up with her as she moved with restless uncertainty through the halls, walking with long swinging strides, head turning and turning, looking at everything, everyone, as if she were seeing them for the first time.

There were few people about, servants, a guard or two. These stiffened and stared straight ahead as K'vestmilly Vos swept past, pretending not to see her. It confused Serroi at first, then she realized that the news of the Marn's death must have already spread throughout the Pevranamist and she remembered the Mask and the importance the Cadandri put on it. As the Preörchmat said, Ansila Vos was dead, the Marn lived and it was not proper to look on her true face.

They walked for more than an hour, passing from corridor to corridor, moving up flights of stairs, down again, covering the Pevranamist from cellar to attics and back again, all of it in silence and a kind of blind desperation. A search for the grief K'vestmilly Vos couldn't feel. That she wanted to feel. That she NEEDED to feel.

She stopped, located herself, then started off again, Serroi following, a small shadow running after her.

K'vestmilly Vos pushed open a door and walked in. A woman was sitting in a chair, a sturdy old woman with masses of gray hair; she was slumped forward, staring at the floor, her hands dangling between her knees.

"You've heard."

The woman looked up, her face was twisted with grief, silent tears dripping from wrinkle to wrinkle. "Oram sent word." She got heavily to her feet. "I shouldn't be here, I'm sorry. But I . . . I just couldn't make myself move."

"You can stay if you'd prefer it."

The woman straightened, ran her eyes over K'vestmilly Vos as if she were searching for something. "Nik, thank you, but it's best I go," she said finally. "Where is she?"

"The Temple by now, I imagine. The Preörchmat took her . . . ah, I don't know, a couple hours ago."

"I suppose I knew that." She looked vaguely around. "I had a cloak somewhere . . . ah." She collected it, folded it over her arm, paused in the doorway. "If you want anything . . . if you need help sleeping or . . . whatever, I'll be at the Temple for an hour or two, then at the clinic." She left.

K'vestmilly Vos walked to her mother's daybed, touched the white silk of the back pad, looked at her fingertips, drifted off, moving around the rooms of the suite. In the bedroom she stood for several moments staring at the bed where she'd been born, then went on with her prowl.

She came back to the bedroom, glanced over her shoulder to make sure Serroi was still with her, and went out through the door into the small walled garden beyond.

The Dom was up, just clearing the peaks of the Merrzachars, the three small moons called the Jewels of Anish were overhead; the grounds were still damp from the rain, the smell of wet leaves and earth came up around them, a calm smell, quiet and comforting.

K'vestmilly Vos walked about a few moments, then settled on one of the benches, ignoring the damp that came up through her silken skirts. "I loved her," she said. "I loved my mother."

Not knowing what to do, Serroi looked around, perched on the edge of another bench a few steps away and set herself to listen.

"She was almost forty-five when I was born, so I never knew her when she was young. Bozhka Sekan, that was the woman you saw in there, Mother's Healer and her oldest friend, maybe the only person she trusted completely, more than she did me. . . . Bozhka Sekan used to tell me I was my mother's echo, we didn't look alike, but that didn't matter, everything else was . . . I hated that for a time . . . a few years ago . . . I wanted . . . zdra zdra, that didn't last . . . after a while I was proud that I was like her . . . she was dying, did you know . . . of course not, how could you . . . if you'd got here a day ago instead of . . . you could have healed her . . . she knew . . . but she wouldn't see you . . . she wouldn't see me . . . why . . . I don't know. . . ." She looked up. "I've been remembering my history. You're that one, aren't you. The tree." The last words were sharp, almost hurled at Serroi.

"History . . . yes, I was here when your Bunmama wore the Mask. It was my first Ward as a meie."

"I was talking to Mother. . . ." She squeezed her eyes shut, tightened her hands into fists and went on. "About the Mask and things . . . a while back. She said people need Myth, which is what you are, you know."

"They might need it, but they don't want it living among them."

"Mother said that, too." K'vestmilly Vos leaned back, smoothed her hands down the front of her dress.

When she spoke, her voice was tired but calmer. "What are you going to do?"

"I don't know." Serroi lifted a hand, let it fall. "There's not much point in fussing about it now."

"Yes. You could always be killed. You can be killed?"

"It might take a bit of doing, but yes."

"Ah." K'vestmilly Vos closed her eyes, folded her hands.

A kanka passare glided past overhead, its mournful wail mixing with the rustle of leaves in trees and bushes, the sharp yips of chinin coming up from the warrens by the river. TheDom's light dimmed and brightened as the moon passed through horsetail clouds; the first of the Dancers rose above the javory growing in the corner of the garden. None of the commotion in the rest of the Pevranamist reached them there or disturbed the cool silence of the night.

"I can't feel anything," K'vestmilly Vos said. "I want to feel, but I've got no tears, nothing. I was angry, but even that's gone."

"Mm."

"Funny, this is the second time today I nearly got blown to . . . Hus! I've got to tell him." On her feet, she looked down at the dress she was wearing, torn, wet, smeared with blood. "Got to change my clothes, I can't go out like this." She inspected Serroi. "You, too, I want you with me."

"You should have a guard."

"Nik! Not this time." She started for the door. "You're the only guard I'll allow."

Serroi shrugged, followed her out.

In her bedroom Serroi pulled on a clean robe, buckled on sandals and flung her still soggy cloak around her.

Honeydew woke, stretched, ran tiny hands through thistledown hair. Going out? I want to go with you.

Come along, then, if you don't mind cold; we're going outside.

's long 's rain don' fall.

Adlayr blinked at Serroi. "What?"

"K'vestmilly Vos is going down to the city to see someone. I haven't got time to explain, I have to get back to her. Follow us, trax or sicamar, whichever's easier."

Dander was crowded, people filling the streets, milling about, talking in undertones or staring up at the lighted windows of the Pevranamist. From the fragments and phrases Serroi overheard as she followed K'vestmilly Vos, they knew something had happened and were waiting to be told what, waiting with apprehension and a touch of anger. There were knots of intense hostility, most of them centered about men talking in low voices.

There were more people on the Bridge, staring at the Pevranamist or leaning over the rail to curse the throng of nixies who swam below, laughing at the Cadandri, mocking them by taking their faces. The moment Serroi set foot on the Bridge, the nixies howled and flung their arms up in a parody of worship. She could hear those terrible liquid voices telling her what she'd done. *Mother of monsters*, they called her, and threw merfolk wriggling and screaming from the water so she could see them.

Their agitation transferred to the Cadandri on the Bridge, but no one noticed her, she was too small, too insignificant. Nonetheless she was glad when she followed K'vestmilly from the Bridge and could no longer hear the voices.

* * *

Calanda was quieter than Dander, the people drawn out of it to the city across the river. Keshtinac Street was almost empty until they reached the House of Glory. The door was open and the inside was packed from wall to wall with worshipers, living light pulsing and swaying on the altar.

The pottery was dark. K'vestmilly Vos yanked at the bell pull. "Maiden Bless, let him be here. Let. Him. Be. Here."

"K'milly? What're you doing here? You shouldn't. . . ."

"I had to talk to you. Let us in."

"Of course." The man stepped aside, blinking a little as Serroi hesitated in the doorway, beckoning. "A moment," she said. "Someone else has to come in."

There was a complicated thudding outside, then Adlayr slid through the door, naked except for a narrow breechclout, Honeydew perched on his shoulder.

K'vestmilly Vos's head jerked up. "I said. . . ."

Serroi pushed back her hood. "I wasn't about to leave you without a guard, not tonight. This is Adlayr Ryan-Turriy, gyes and were. He watched our backs coming over and he'll watch when we return."

The man chuckled. "Got you, Milly. Come upstairs, the lot of you. I've got some cha boiling and Razhee's mum sent over some wafers." His eyes were worried as he looked at K'vestmilly Vos.

"Nik, Hus, I can't . . . there isn't time. The Marn is dead. There was another explosion and. . . ." She started crying, her body jerking with sobs, her arms lifting, groping toward him.

17. Planning

Jestranos Oram paused in his pacing and frowned. "Why?"

It was late, an hour past midnight. They were in the Marn's sitting room, a single lamp lit on a table by the daybed where Ansila Vos had spent so much of the last year, Serroi silent on a hassock in a corner, lost in deep shadow, K'vestmilly stretched out on the daybed, lines of weariness etched in her face, one hand stroking and stroking the white silk of the padding.

"Because I want them here," she said. "Mother told me to use them and I'm going to."

"Prak, but you're asking for trouble. If the Pans and the Treddeks think you're listening too much to outsiders, those outsiders especially, you're going to lose them."

"Heslin, yes. I have to be careful about him. But the meie and the gyes, they're different, aren't they?"

"Considering what happened to your mother, bodyguards will seem reasonable as long as they act like bodyguards."

"Mother valued you, Oram, and one of the reasons was you didn't lie to her." She folded her hands over her ribs; it'd been a long, long day and there was still a lot to do before she could rest. "I want the same deal." She smiled at him. "I need you and anything that cuts you down, cuts me. If I use them as my body-guards, will that be seen as a slap at you?''

''Those that want to see it that way, will.'' He dug his fingers into the pepper-and-salt beard trimmed close to his jaw. ''That doesn't matter . . . mmm . . . might even be useful if certain people think I've got something to resent. Zdra, where's that gyes? Let's get this over with.''

''In the garden. . . .''

Serroi spoke from the corner. ''I'll go. Adlayr would attract too much attention, the way he isn't dressed. No one notices me.''

After the Healer left, Jestranos dug in his beard again and looked uneasy. ''Isn't dressed?''

K'vestmilly stared at him a moment, then started giggling as she realized the source of his anxiety. When she could speak again, she said, ''Nik, Oram, that's one complication you don't have to deal with. He's a shapechanger. The Healer's idea of an inconspicuous guard.''

''At least she's got sense. Going down there, saaa! Tonight of all nights.''

''He's my father, he had the right to hear it from me. And don't say you didn't know, because I won't believe you.''

''Marn, those visits, they have to. . . .''

She interrupted him, the anger that still churned in her putting an edge on the words. ''They have to stop. I know that. Going there would get him killed as dead as Mother. I know that isn't what you meant. If that was all, I'd say zhag with snobs and sneerers, he's a better man than the lot of them. But it isn't . . . it isn't. . . .'' she sighed. ''I haven't had time to visit him, how's Vyzharnos doing?''

Jestranos snorted. ''Young idiot, that burn on his

arm is still draining, but he wants to go home. Home! That hole in a warren. Maiden Bless, the sekalari aren't listening to him yet.''

"Doesn't he realize he's a target now, like all of us?"

"Zhag knows what he realizes."

K'vestmilly swung her legs over the side of the day-bed and sat with her hands folded in her lap as she ran tired eyes along the arc of faces carved from the dusk by the single lamp, glanced up at Jestranos Oram standing beside her, then fixed on the broad face of the big man who'd taken the center of the arc as his right. "There are certain things that custom and ritual require, but the timing of those things is important and how they're managed can have long-standing effects. The first of these is just how and when we announce the Marn's death. And . . . mmm . . . what we say when we do. Oram?"

"The announcement can't be delayed," he cleared his throat, clasped his hands behind him and stared at the shadowed ceiling. "But to detail the circumstances would be a mistake, an admission of weakness. If the guard can't even protect the Marn, who can they pro-tect? Once that notion spreads widely enough, the next step is obvious: What good is the Marn? Why not find someone who can do a better job? There are seeds of trouble in the Land where those questions can find focus. And as I know I am alive, I know the Enemy is poised to use these things and I don't want to give him a free ride."

Camnor Heslin leaned forward, the chair creaking under him. "Not only a free ride, but a boost into the saddle if you go that route. I don't know this Land, but I do know politics. The Mijloc has made just about every mistake possible during the past two centuries, but we've survived and we've learned and one thing the Grand Council has had rammed up its poz, rumors are always worse than the truth. I sympathize with your grief, Marn, but you've got to use your mother's death to claim solidarity with your Nerodin who've had kin and neighbors killed or wounded in these raids and explosions. Make them your brothers, your sisters, let them share your grief—and give the lie to those who'll be saying you did it yourself out of ambition and greed.''

''What!'' Jestranos Oram took a step forward. ''No one would dare. . . .''

''Oh, yes they will, and if they say it often enough, people will start believing them.''

''They won't say anything when I get my hands on them. Mad's Tits, what kind of mind do you have?''

''The kind that's been polished in a rough-and-tumble you people here have no idea of. With one thing and another, you've been protected until you haven't a clue. Listen to me, Marn, that kind of talk feeds on heavy hands and breeds in darkness. What you do is drag it in the open, hold it to the light, and laugh. Make those provocateurs look like fools and all they'll provoke will be giggles. Try to suppress them and you'll just end up convincing Rodin and Nerodin both they're telling the truth. What you need are a dozen men and women with clever tongues; let me have them a day or two and I'll show them the kind of patter they'll need and if they're good enough, they'll be worth more to you than a hundred guards.''

''And we'll look weak as blind baby mice.''

''If you sit around moaning, you certainly will. That's only one side of it. The other . . . how well do your people know you, K'vestmilly Vos?''

''The Families somewhat, as to the rest, they've seen me ride by and that's about it.''

"I thought so. You've got to change that and fast. Give them a grand show so they'll feel good about you. A public funeral with all the color and music and oratory you can cram in. Distribute food to the poor, declare the day after the funeral a holiday for workers. Use Serroi, send her into the warrens and the local clinics, let her heal the burned and maimed from the explosions, let her help the children who are sick. Go to the clinics yourself to visit the patients there. Go with her into the warrens at least once, wearing the Mask, with Adlayr pacing beside you in his sicamar form, he's a magnificent beast, he'll impress the zhag out of everyone who sees him." He chuckled at a snort from Adlayr, sobered. "Give them a sense of mystery and magic, that's your greatest strength, Marn."

Jestranos snorted. "And the Pans will howl to high heaven that you're interfering with their privileges. Custom and law says it's the Treddekkap that declares holidays. There's another complication. The day after the Funeral is usually the day of the Masking of the new Marn. It's a private ceremony, only the Families are there. They'll fight against changing that."

Camnor Heslin grunted. "So, keep the Masking private, but after it's over, start a new custom. Present the Marn to the people, have her declare a Day of Rejoicing, a New Age born. The queen is dead, long live the queen. If you have to have the Treddekkap endorse that, tweak their strings and get it through. It's important."

"Even if I agree with you, K'vestmilly hasn't the holds that Ansila had. The Treddeks will delay and argue and generally act like vycherts in heat."

"How many do you need to make that declaration?"

"Six of eleven."

"How many you sure of?"

"Three. Maybe four."

"Then do a little trading and do it fast. Before the sun's up, if possible, by noon at the latest. Get hold of the ones you can count on, nail them down, figure out what you can offer to the waverers and do it. And the minute you know you've got the numbers, you call your Treddekkap into session and you ram the holiday through. And you'll get a bonus, K'vestmilly Vos. You'll have rooted an idea in their little brains. You're the Marn, you're the one who holds the reins, not a mare to be ridden or driven."

She chuckled softly. "Ah, Heslin, my mother was right, you could talk a lappet into skinning itself for stew." She tilted her head back. "Sit down, Oram, here, beside me. You make me nervous, towering like that. Good. What do you think of Heslin's plan?"

"I'm one of those skinned lappets. You're right about one thing, Vorbescar, I have no gift for what you call politics. I think K'vestmilly is going to need me and what I do, but it's best I stay as deep in the shadows as I can. And you'd better stay shadowed yourself. If the Mijloc isn't hated among the Families, the feeling that's there is a close cousin to hatred."

"Vai vai, in a world like yours, my friend, new ideas are very dangerous indeed; any change means losing."

K'vestmilly cleared her throat. "You can discuss philosophies of governance later. Oram, Husenkil says Family Pen will back me up whatever I say or do. You said four. Who are the others?"

"Osk. I know you and Marazhney don't get on, but she's clever and she won't let the Marn down, whoever the Marn is. Hal. Shapatnesh is a lightweight, but he knows his limitations and he's loyal, he doesn't bother listening when the other Treddeks try to pry him loose. Zav. Poddridar will slide into the nearest hole if she's let, but if you get a commitment from her, she'll stick. She's like Shapatnesh, doesn't bother listening once her mind's made up.''

''And those against me?''

''Treddeks Ker and Ano. They'll follow their Pans' lead and fight you on everything and do their best to drag you down. The Pan Ank's loyal enough, but he never leaves the High Harozh, just sits in his library lost in his books. I doubt he knows what century it is, let alone what day. Vilavinet Treddek Ank would be happy to skin you and your mother before you alive over hot coals, ambition, jealousy, or maybe she's madder than Treshteny but it doesn't show.''

''And the others?''

''Treddeks Sko and Bar will try dragging their feet; they're ambitious but they don't have the nerve to go against you, not yet anyway. If you can get to one of them, the other will follow. Vyk. The Pan spends most of his time sailing round the Skafarees, leaves running the Paperies to the Panya. He's here now, but he won't be for long. Dukladny Treddek Vyk says nothing and does less, waits and votes with the winning side. Nov. Tecozar Treddek Nov may be Prime among the Treddeks, but he does what Zavidesht Pan Nov tells him. How the Pan'll come down, only the Maiden knows. The Marn . . . ah, Ansila Vos reamed him out more than once for the condition of his warrens and the number of enforcers he employed. For a while it was getting to be quite an army. But he's been careful to back her on policies that got at other Families. I'd say what he does depends on what he sees as his best chance.'' He hesitated, scratched at his jaw. ''There's another thing. He's a man who fancies himself with women and his second wife died six months ago. His mourning time's over and he's looking around; it might be he'll have ambitions that way. As your consort. . . ."

K'vestmilly wrinkled her nose. "Some hope. Hedivy took me through the Shipper warren. That's enough to put anyone off that man."

"It wouldn't be a good idea to let him know that."

"You're not suggesting. . . ."

"Nik! I say this both as your Inquisitor and your friend, K'vestmilly Vos, it would be the worst choice you could possibly make."

"Prak, come sunup, then, we run the Deathflag up on the Marn's Tower, tie the white ribbons on the Mask pillars and . . ." she smiled at Camnor Heslin, "see to the distribution of more ribbons to the warrens, free to any Nerodin who wants them—man, woman, child. The Proclamation will be made in the Temple and copies sent to the clinics, the warren Chitelhouses, the schools, the mills, carried to the Zemyadel and the Hayadels . . ." she waved a hand, "zdra, everywhere, I can't think of all the places now . . . which means I'd better see the printmaster as soon as possible, so he can get the presses moving . . . Heslin, the wording's important, so I'd like you to work on that with me."

"Of course, O Marn."

"The funeral. Custom says in three days. Will that be long enough? I want that holiday, I want food distributed, lengths of cloth, needles and thread, in the name of Marnhidda Vos." She passed her hand across her eyes. "Oram, something even you don't know. Mother wrote a detailed account of her dealings with the Treddeks and the Pans, plus an assessment of each of them; she told me about it the night before she died. Was that Treshteny's doing? Never mind, you can tell me later. I've glanced through the book." She lifted a small black diary, grimaced. "Her handwriting's

even worse than mine. I picked up enough to know
Sko will not be a problem. He won't like it, but all he
needs is a hint that I know what Mother knew and
he'll come in line and salute with the rest.'' She
dropped the book in her lap. ''The problem is, how
do we get that hint to him?''

Camnor Heslin shifted in his chair. ''I have a sug-
gestion on that.'' He smiled. ''Another double, if you
will. You say Marazheny Treddek Osk is personally
hostile but loyal, and clever with it. The cleverness is
what's important. Bring her here. Tell her what you're
planning and why. Ask for her help. Show her that
book, tell her it's a private memoir that your mother
left you and that when she talks to Sko, she should
mention she saw you reading it and recognized the
writing. That should be sufficient to prod him into line.
Marazhney Osk will feel flattered by your recognition;
I don't know what there is between you, but that should
help smooth it out, and a clever counselor on your side
is not to be despised. And if she's as good as the Inquisitor suggests, you'll get your holiday through so
quickly there won't be time to organize against you.''
He got to his feet. ''There's another thing. I'll be
moved out of the Pevranamist by noon. . . .'' He
blinked. ''Today. You don't want to give any occasion
for talk. There should be a house ready, the Marn was
going to arrange it?'' He raised a brow, smiled when
Oram nodded. ''Good.'' He looked down at his wrinkled, stained clothing. ''I'll have to see a tailor and
organize proper furnishings before I start looking about
for trade.'' He smiled again. ''You may have noticed
I enjoy this chop and change. If I can help in any way,
I'll be delighted. I'm sure the Inquisitor here will be
able to set up discreet meetings if they seem necessary
or useful. Now, you'd best send for Marazhney Osk.
I'll go set down some notes and come back when she's

gone so we can work on that proclamation." He reached for the chair to move it out of his way, straightened. "Pen and Osk. Oram, I don't want to tell you your business, but I'd have them warned and watched. Within the hour, if not sooner. If I were your Enemy, they'd be my next targets."

When they were alone, Jestranos Oram stood looking down at K'vestmilly Vos. "You'll be a good Marn, K'vestmilly Vos. To tell you true, I thought you were too heedless and . . ." He sighed. "Too stupid. Like Pen's brother."

"Maiden Bless, what a compliment that is."

"You said you wanted the truth. The truth is I was a fool."

"Nik, Oram. The way I acted, t'huh! You had plenty of evidence for it."

"Are you all right? Do you want me to find Bozhka Sekan and send her to you?"

"I'm just tired. The little Healer took care of everything when she pulled me back, even the bruises from this afternoon. I wish Mother had . . . zdra zdra, I suppose she had her reasons."

"That she did. If you want, I'll talk to you about them when we have the time. Where's your maid? I don't like leaving you alone."

"Puzhee? I don't want her here fussing me. Don't worry about me. If we're going to hold this together, you've got things to do. Besides, I'll have Mother's book for company, then Marazhney as soon as you can get her here. Then Heslin for the proclamation."

"He makes me wonder about the Mijloc."

"He is a piece, isn't he." She swung her feet up onto the daybed, opened the diary. "Marazhney, Oram. We need to get started."

18. Funeral and Furor

The rider sped north along the River Road, cutting across the bends through fields of kurice and shen and stretches of bremba vines, driving his mount as long as he could; when the macai squatted, he beat it back onto its feet, cut to the nearest farm, took a new mount at gunpoint and went racing on.

> > < <

Dressed in heavy white silk robes, veiled with a cloud of white lace, a great black sicamar pacing at her side, K'vestmilly Vos walked before the Bier that held her mother's body wrapped in a white silk winding cloth, moving down the Mask Way into Charamanac Street, the broad avenue that led to the Maiden Temple and the court where the Pyre waited. The walks on both sides of the street were crowded with Nerodin, most of them with white ribbons tied around their arms or in their hair. Nerodin women and men lifted children like flags so many fluttering ribbons were tied about them, held them up so they could see the Bier pass and be a part of this Moment; more leaned out of upper story windows, Rodin cousins along with Nerodin families who could afford the price of the window.

What's that beast?

A sicamar, I think. I saw a picture of one once.

*It's just walking there. How do they get it to do
that? I thought it was a wild thing.
I dunno. Maybe it was SENT, you know.*

Men and women drifted along the back of the crowd,
whispering, suggesting, insinuating, dropping their
poison and moving on.

*Witch, look at her prancing along with her
demon familiar . . . hasn't the courtesy to hide
her perversion . . . killed her own mother,
didn't the maid see her sliding into the room
before the table dressers went in . . . blaming
those poor folk, Oram's got them in the
dungeons, torturing them . . . I know it for a
fact, I've got a cousin works in that pile . . .
suffering for what she did . . . isn't that what
they all do, cursèd Rodin, make you pay for
their crimes . . . the Marn was going to set her
aside . . . I heard that from someone who has a
brother working as a waiter, he said they were
quarrelling all the time, that sometimes guards
had to pull them apart . . . Sakariva Vyk, that
was the one the Marn favored . . . I heard it
was Ochanary Bar . . . nik, it was Bratinny
Osk . . . nik, she wouldn't go outside Vos, I
heard she was grooming young Selimna Vos and
would've made it official in another month. . . .*

Drummers, harpers, pipers followed the Bier,
dressed in white from cap to heels, playing the Marn's
Dirge, the Mourning music that pulsed to the stamp
of the feet of the Honor Guard carrying and escorting
the Body. Down the wide, tree-lined Charamanac
Street the procession went, Nerodin boys in the trees
waving white ribbons.

Near the Temple there was a crowd of working men,
standing shoulder to shoulder, some of them holding
ladders with their children standing on the steps—

ladesmen and bargeveks from the Shipper's warren, workers from the mills, the glasshouses, the papery, the leatherworks, the potteries, there because K'vest-milly Vos had wrung that concession also from the Treddekkap, sending runners with paper tickets to all the workplaces, tickets that gave them a right to a place there—leathery men with gnarled hands, stained and bent bodies, many of them with tears streaking down their hard faces. The Marn had been their defense against the Families; she was FOR them; they knew it in their bones and they were afraid. They didn't know K'vestmilly Vos, they didn't know what turn their lives would take now that Ansila Vos was gone.

In the Maiden Court the Pyre rose higher than the tall double doors of the Temple. The wood was Aromatic Cherdva that grew only on the Marn's Reserve. Each time an Heir was born, Cherdva trees were selected and cut, stripped of their bark and air-dried, marinated in a special naprezh oil made by macerating certain herbs known only to the Preörchmat, then sealed in wax to wait their moment. The Setras had spent the past three days breaching the wax and rubbing each log until the wood glowed; men chosen from each of the warrens had piled the logs into the Pyre, cutting notches to lock them together, trimming the lengths until they had the final platform laid out with all the square bits of wood heaped about the stand that would hold the Bier.

The Pans marched behind the Bier, wearing the Family colors in long flowing scarves, white ribbons blowing from their tall felt hats, white ribbons tied to their long, carved staffs, their faces covered with white mourning masks.

*". . . seven, eight, nine, ten, Granda, there's
s'posed to be 'leven of 'em.
There is, Lishalee, you learned the colors just
last month, count them off for me, mm?
Red, that's Nov. Blue that's Pen. Russet, that's
Bar. Saffron, that's Sko. Violet, that's Zav.
Orange, that's Vyk. Gold, that's Osk. Olive,
that's Ano. Emerald, that's Ank. Copper, that's
Hal. Ker is rust . . . it's Ker, he isn't there.
He must've been down south, wasn't time for
him to get here, you're seeing what a Family
Pan is missing, Lishalee, and you won't see it
again till you have grandkids yourself. . . .*

Treshtal and Fialovy followed the Pans, dancing the
Sorrows of Cadander and behind them, more musicians came, playing softly, more dancers came, singly
and in groups, then the Chitveks of the warrens and
representatives from the Workers Guilds and Merchant
Associations.

The whisperers moved on, weaving past light-
fingered boy thieves lifting everything loose, past children playing games in the dust, freed for the day from
their schools, moving to back streets as the walks grew
too crowded, walking parallel to the procession.

*Witch . . . killed her mother . . . it's time . . .
time the Marn and the Families paid for their
crimes . . . torturers . . . thieves . . . steal
everything . . . even sweat . . . from the
workers . . . from honest men . . . rape your
wives . . . daughters . . . debauch your sons
. . . witch . . . blood crimes . . . sacrifice . . .
get worse and worse. . . .*

Mostly the Nerodin were too concentrated on the
procession to bother with them, brushing them off like
the black biters that swarmed in the Spring, but now
and then a man or woman would take in what they

were saying, yell and slap at them, punch them, or
merely curse them. If they were knocked down, they
scrambled to their feet and went on, slaps they ignored
as they ignored the curses.

But there were those that listened. . . .

Her long, thick white hair streaming free, her arms
outstretched, the heavy white silk of her robe falling
in graceful folds about her tall thin body, the Preörchmat stood before the pyre, the logs a shining amber
behind her, echoing the gold and amber pectoral with
the Maiden's interlaced diamonds that hung from a
heavy gold chain about her neck.

When the Dedach reached her, the Preörchmat
brought her hands together in front of the pectoral,
palm pressed against palm.

The drums, the harps, the pipes fell silent. The Rodin crowded into the court sighed and went still.

"Who is it that comes to the Maiden?" The
Preörchmat's deep voice filled the Court.

K'vestmilly Vos folded the Veil back. "Marnhidda
Vos comes to seek the Blessing of the Maiden and the
cleansing peace of the fire."

"Come then and receive Her blessing. Her arms
embrace the world."

> > < <

Starting from the attics and working her way down,
the meie Zasya Myers led the search of Pen House,
the agents Tratch and Zepatos with her as skeptical
witnesses. Oram didn't believe in Ildas and thought
Zasya was crazy as Treshteny, but his own men had
already searched the House and found nothing. He
didn't believe that either.

The House was empty; the Nerodin servants who

hadn't had leave to watch the procession were gathered on the hillside behind it.

Flicking her antenna, searching for anything strange, Honeydew flew above the Fireborn, watching as Ildas trotted from room to room, sniffing and nosing into every corner. Zasya followed, alert for the slightest sign of discovery; she'd seen the ravaged Gold Room and she intended to take no chances on another explosion with her and Honeydew in the middle.

They reached the bedroom floor and went into the Pan's Suite.

Ildas nosed at the Pan's bed, stiffened, his spine arched, his tail quivering erect. Honeydew dropped to the floor by the bed and crouched there, peering underneath it.

Zepatos pushed past Zasya. "What is it? What has the little one found?"

"We don't know yet. *Honey?*"

Honeydew hear. The sprite edged farther in, vanishing beneath the linen valance, the white lace cover; her mosquito hum came back, echoing in Zasya's mind. Zaszas, Honeydew feel a hot thing. Not hot like fire, but hot like Honeydew don't know what.

A moment later she emerged, fluttering to Zasya's shoulder. There's a thing Dasdas sniffs, Honeydew sees it, like a piece of wood it is, hot hot baaaad!

Zasya Myers swung round, said, "Get the Inquisitor up here. We've found something, I'm not sure what, but it could be dangerous. And a rope. We're going to have to move the bed, but no one should go near it."

"We looked under there an hour ago, before you even got here. Saw nothing, nothing happened."

Zasya scowled at him. "There's something now, I promise you. Ildas and Honeydew say so and I believe

them. If somebody's going to lie down on that bed . . .
ei vai, better be your best enemy you try that with.''

"Prak, so we clear the room. Tratch, tie the rope's
ends to those footposts, then get back over here. Zep,
go get the others, we'll need more weight pulling, that
thing's big as a boat.''

The huge bed groaned and squealed forward a few
inches, then the footboard pulled free and the end of
the frame hit the floor—and the room went up, part of
the blast funneling through the open door, driving the
guards and the meie against the far wall of the sitting
room outside.

Zepatos rolled onto his feet and ran to the hole
where the door had been. "Spoggin' zhag, if Pen'd
laid down on that, there wouldn't be a smell of him
left.''

> > < <

The drums, harps, and pipers played, the Setra choir
on Temple steps chanted, the bearers climbed the
wooden ramp, set the Bier on the stand and came
clumping down again. Two young torchbearers came
round from behind the Pyre to stand beside the
Preörchmat who opened her arms, spread them wide,
the heavy silk falling like butterfly wings and again
there was silence that the ritual words might be spoken
and heard.

> > < <

Ildas found another camouflaged bomb beneath Vedouce the Heir's bed, the guards pulled the footboard
loose again and that one exploded also; they finished

the sweep of the House, then moved to the next hill
and Osk House.

> > < <

The macai groaned its protest, started to squat. The
rider brought the crop down hard alongside its nose
and drove it on, though even pain couldn't coax more
than a balky walk from the exhausted beast. The fields
stretched to blue mountains on both sides of the river,
with no sign of habitation except a few whitedust roads
winding through the green and tan. He rounded a small
grove of javories and brellims, gasped with surprise.
"Mad's Tits!"

A boat was nosed into the mud of the riverbank,
turned on its side, its sail sagging into the water; it'd
apparently been there for several days without being
discovered.

He used the macai to right the boat, then turned the
weary beast loose to graze in the fields, bailed out the
water, and in less than an hour was on his way upstream.

> > < <

"Treshteny Falladin . . ." Bozhka Sekan stood.
"People call her crazy, but I don't think so." Her eyes
were weary and sad; she wore grief like a shawl about
her shoulders. Serroi wondered why she wasn't at the
funeral, but she didn't ask. "She acts the way she does
because the world's too much for her. It's an explosion
of ghosts out there, battering her, if you can imagine
being battered by ghosts. In here, we keep things simple." She opened the door and stood aside to let Serroi move past her, following her into the silent empty
hallway. "Now and then, though, even this is too

much.'' Their feet echoed on tiles polished to a high gloss, painfully clean. ''She curls up and doesn't talk or eat for a day or two. Day before yesterday something happened that sent her off again. Turn left at the next crossway. That's why her family brought her to us some . . . oh . . . let's see, how long ago was it? Years and years ago. She was just a child, down to skin and bone and she wouldn't talk or move or open her eyes.''

Bozhka Sekan unclipped a ring of keys from her belt, opened the door at the end of the side hall. ''She's been face to the wall for a few days, even her nurse couldn't get her to eat and talk, but she came back to us this morning and asked for you. She's in her garden; the . . . the Marn had it made for her, the walls, the plantings. Sh . . . she came to talk to her there. Treshteny has these spells, you see, visions of will-be . . . nik, better to say might-be.'' She stopped at the end of a tall wooden screen elaborately carved and pierced. ''Go on, I'll wait here. Too many people confuse her.''

Serroi walked around the screen and into a long, narrow garden.

It was a simple garden, no flowers, just grass and trees, vines climbing up the walls, a section of a stream cutting across the far corner, the high thick walls shut out everything but a wandering breeze and a sky with a few shreds of cloud drifting eastward.

A white-clad nurse hovering behind her, a young woman sat on one of several benches. There was a javory sapling by her foot and another, older javory a short distance behind the bench, tall enough to cast lacy shadows across her face. She was thin with a ravaged beauty built from elegant bones and huge dark blue eyes. The hands resting in her lap twitched and shook as she watched Serroi approach.

"Treshteny? You wanted to see me."

Treshteny trembled, then steadied as she fixed her eyes on her visitor; she drew an extended breath, let it trickle out, her stiff body relaxing. "You are a long one, strong and steady as a stone. Sit beside me. Take my hand."

When the thin cold fingers touched Serroi's, the garden fell apart around her as if she were looking at it through multiple lenses; she fought the spreading, brought everything into focus again.

Beside her Treshteny sighed with pleasure. "To see singly and solid, it is joy so sweet. . . ." She sat silent a moment, then pulled her hand away. "But like candy, more than a little is too much. I am surprised to find I have an attachment to my manyness; I thank you for that, Healer. I would not have known it without you." She folded her hands in her lap. "They asked to see you. I watched them born. They want to meet their mother."

Serroi closed her eyes. "Three nights ago, yes?"

Treshteny shivered, her face going pale at the memory, but she didn't answer, just reached down and tickled the sapling by her foot. "Come come, wood sprite, come see, dryadita."

The baby javory shivered. The first glimpse Serroi got was of huge brown eyes, then a translucent little girl shape as tall as a man's hand came shyly from the trunk. She shimmered a moment on the gravel, then walked timidly toward Serroi, glancing back every few steps to gain reassurance from her tree.

She touched Serroi's leg; her hand was cool like a leaf blowing against the skin. She giggled. Serroi felt it in her bones though she heard nothing. The dryadita lifted her arms, waved her tiny hands.

Serroi scooped her up, settled her in her lap, and sat looking down at her wondering what to do next.

The baby sighed with pleasure, nestled against her, cooing in her magical way that reached inside Serroi and made her feel adoring and fluttery as if this truly were a baby she'd birthed that she was holding in her arms.

One by one the adult trees in the garden gave up their inhabitants and the dryads gathered about the bench, squatting on the gravel staring up at Serroi.

> > < <

K'vestmilly Vos stretched out her hands, touched finger to finger with the Preörchmat, then the old woman stepped to one side and stood waiting. The young torchbearers came toward K'vestmilly, faces pale with concentration. They gave her the torches, dropped to their knees. A drum began to beat, a pipe picked up the rhythm, then one of the harps. The Setra choir on the steps began a soft chant, the meaningless syllables getting louder and louder. A rich soprano voice climbed to a high note—and K'vestmilly plunged the torches into the base of the Pyre.

> > < <

The rider left the boat at the Pevranamist landing, walked wearily through empty streets, confused and disturbed by that emptiness until he began to see white ribbons and crowds ahead, until he looked up and saw the Death Flag flying from Marn's Tower; when he did, he swore and tried to move leaden legs faster.

A flash of a card got him through the Pevranamist gate and he ran panting toward the Guard quarters, crashing into Hedivy Starab as he rounded a corner.

"Lisk, what. . . ."

"Where's Oram? Get me to him quick."

"He's pulling teeth."

"Huh?"

"Come into office 'n tell me about it. I'll roust the Rat into sending a runner to find him."

> > < <

"So you're my children?" Serroi leaned forward, touched a smooth cool cheek, smiled as the dryad's palm flattened over her hand, holding it against her face. "I am pleased to see you."

They looked at each other, the slender girl-women from the trees, then they moved closer, arms weaving over shoulders, linking them multiply, the dryads on the ends, setting their hands on Serroi's knees. *Dark and Terrible looked at us when we were born, Dark and Terrible hated us. We were afraid. In you there is darkness, in all earth walkers, there is a seed of darkness, there is no darkness in us and we fear you a little, even you, O Mother, but this Other is all dark with no seed of light within it, Mother. Keep it from us. We are afraid. Find it and take it away, Mother, or we will die. It will eat us, it will eat all there is and never find peace. We want to be, Mother, and take joy in the life you have given us.*

> > < <

The sweet smell of the burning oil-soaked logs filled the court, flowed over the walls and into the streets beyond. A vast groan passed over the watchers as they breathed in the vapor and saw rise before them an immense figure sketched against the blue sky with its wisps of clouds, the Maiden with the Marn in her arms.

The image wavered, and vanished; the crowd sighed again and began to disperse.

$$> > < <$$

Ildas found another bomb tucked under the dinner table in the wing of Osk House where Marazhney Treddek Osk and her family lived. Before trying to explode this one, Jestranos Oram had the servants clear the room, moving out all dishes and other ornaments, stripping it down to the bare walls.

The guards used a rope to tip the table over; as soon as the top hit the floor, the bomb blew.

The runner banged on the gate at Osk House. "The Inquisitor," he yelled, "I've got a message for him from the Pevranamist. Important."

Irritated at being stuck here on duty while most of the other workers from the House were at the Funeral, the guard leaned out the gatehouse window and grinned at the messenger. "Important is it? Prove it."

"You stickin' your nose in Quisitin' business? I tell you this, you don't open that gate 'bout the next two seconds, Oram'll kick your butt so hard you'll be lookin' out y' asshole."

There was a loud bang from the house. The guard winced, then sourly set himself at the winch, winding up the gate. The runner slipped under the moment there was space enough for him.

Oram came scowling into the office, his scowl growing blacker as he saw Lisken. "What more!"

"Takuzhone's dead, blown to bits, Govaritil is crazy mad and Takuboure's on his way north with an army."

19. Mother Death

Come to me, Belovéd, come.

Treshtal stirred, pushed up and sat a moment, his hands pressed against his eyes. His knees and hips still burned from the long dance during the procession yesterday and after the Masking that morning. Even without having to work on hard pavement, the fire in his joints came more often these days, frightening him when he thought about it.

Fialovy stirred, muttered and came groggily awake. "What is it?"

"Nothing, go back to sleep."

"Your knees?"

He dropped his hands and stared at them for several breaths. "I'm going out," he said finally. "I need to walk."

"Tresh. . . ."

"I don't want to hear it. Go to sleep."

He stepped into the clearing among the sighing dark-needled bovries and stood a moment watching moon shadows shift over the bleached limestone of the ruined shrine. There was an old story that demons were born of the moon shadows; he wondered briefly if he were one of them. There were times when he didn't understand what he was doing, times when he was tired and sick and nothing mattered, when his hate

turned to ash and all he wanted was to die. He pulled
loose a handful of needles from a branch brushing his
head, rubbed them between his palms and sniffed at
them, the acrid odor clearing some of the fog from his
head.

He dropped the crushed needles, wiped his hands
on his shirt, and walked into the shrine.

Moonlight coming through the rotting roof and
playing about him, he knelt at the altar, resting his
elbows on the worn surface of the stone. "I'm here,"
he said. "Nothing went right. Did you know? They
found the ardors, I don't know how, exploded them
when no one was in the room. And the Dedach didn't
do what you said, at least not yet. There've been no
arrests. In the proclamation she laid out exactly what
happened and claimed sisterhood with the others
who've died, she called the Treddekkap into session
and got everything she wanted from them. Several of
the whisperers we primed were beaten bloody by angry workers. When she came out after the Masking
this morning and spoke . . . they're saying already
she's going to be one of the Great Marns." He dropped
his head on his arms. "I'm only one man," he said,
weariness groaning in the words. "I can't lift the world
on my shoulders."

*You are not alone, O Belovéd, though you are my
first and dearest. There are raiders and landfolk working in their small ways to bring the purge of evil from
the Land. And I shall bring you helpers, true-believers
who will work for us and take some of the burden from
you, O Belovéd.*

It was a strange feeling that took him then, a sense
of confusion and loss, of melting outward as if his skin
had broken. He said nothing, just knelt on burning
knees and wondered what had gone wrong with him.

Come, Belovéd, come to my embrace, leave your

pain and your disappointments. Every day and every death blesses us. There are forces that think they work against us, Belovéd, but our strength grows with everything they do. Come, Belovéd, come to me, feel how strong we are. . . .

When he levered himself on the altar and lay in the hollow, the rapture that raced through his veins was so potent the exultation it carried was almost more than he could bear. If it grew stronger yet, it would make a conflagration of him greater than the Marn's funeral Pyre.

The buttery light of the Glory was nearly opaque. It surged and pulsed, extruding branches and knobs as if it struggled toward shape and solidity. *Touch me, take me within you. Will you consent, Belovéd? Will you receive the last gift?*

"Yes, yes. I'm tired . . . so tired."

The Glory shivered and surged—and waited.

"I consent. Do what you want."

The Glory came into him and this time it wasn't pleasure but pain, wrenching terrible pain that was more wonderful than the pleasure had been, cleansing pain.

She filled him, pushed him into a warm corner of himself.

For the first time he knew the Glory was SHE.

He nestled against HER breast.

"Mother Death," he murmured, not with his mouth but with the tiny seed that held what was left of him.

Yes, Belovéd. Now be easy. You've done what was needed. All that was needed. I will do the rest.

20. War

"Doby, do look a that." The boy straightened from the row where he and his brothers and cousins were pulling weeds from around the bremba vines, lifting the huge, triangular leaves to loosen the dirt above tubers almost big enough for harvest. He pointed at dust and smoke rolling above the line of windbreak trees. "Watcha think that is?"

Doby glanced up, wrinkled his snub nose. "I dunno, but you do better get your tail back to work, Trub. Ol' Jiz, he'll cut you a swish keep you standing f'r a month."

"Jiz, phah!" Trub spat at a green crawler, giggled as he pinned it. "Choooo, Dob', look, riders. Mad's Tits, lots and lots of riders."

About fifty men had burst through the line of bushy kerov trees. They came on into the field, the claws of their macain tearing up the brembas. The Overseer Jizraim came running, cursing and waving his arms—until one of them lifted a longgun and put a bullet through his head. As if that were the signal they'd been waiting for, the rest of the men began shooting.

Trub gasped and crumpled, the back of his head gone. Brains and blood splattered over Doby. Around Doby the other boys were screaming and trying to run, wounded, dying, dead. He scrambled across Trub's body and pulled bremba leaves over him, lying hidden, stiff with fear and horror as the men slaughtered everyone they saw. A stray shot burned across his leg, but he bit on his thumb and kept the groans in his throat. A macai loped past, swerving round Trub's body, but the rider didn't see him.

The men rode on. Doby started to crawl out, but huddled back as he heard the honks of more macain, the thudding of their feet, heard men shouting, laughing, mocking the dead, tens and hundreds of men riding through the bremba field, churning it to mud, going round his bremba patch to avoid the bodies scattered about him. After the men there was the steady slow thudding of orsk hooves and the creak of axles as huge drays rumbled past.

It was almost dark before the field was quiet again.

Doby rolled from under the leaves, staggered to his feet and looked around, then bent over, vomiting until his throat burned. He wiped his mouth, limped around Trub and over Brosky, Stek, Mapel and the rest of his cousins and brothers, heading toward the village, trying not to think of what he might find when he got there.

>><<

When K'vestmilly Vos turned the corner on the narrow hall, she heard the noise coming from the Setkan, angry shouts rising above the rumble of voices; she stopped.

Jestranos Oram snorted. "I told you, you should've let me go in there ahead of time and calm them down."

"You know what Heslin said. If they see me leaning on you. . . ."

"Hmp! You act like he's an oracle."

"Zdra, he's been right so far." She looked over her shoulder at Zasya and Adlayr with Honeydew riding

Adlayr's shoulder. "That's what I'm throwing you into, my friends; I appreciate your courage."

Adlayr grinned. "All part of the job."

K'vestmilly Vos touched the Mask. Though she wasn't used to it yet and the feel of it on her face bothered her, it was also oddly comforting as if her mother were going in with her.

The Setkan, the Treddekkap's Meeting Chamber, was a large room, a long table in the middle and a raised platform at the end with the Marn's Chair on it. The Treddeks were seated round the table, Tecozar Nov as Prime in the end seat, the one facing the Marn's chair, the others on stools along the sides. The rest of the room was filled with Nerodin visitors, chairs brought in for them, though most of them weren't using them at the moment; they were on their feet yelling at each other and at the Treddeks—representatives from the Workers Guilds and the Merchant Associations, Chitveks from the warrens. They were here on the Marn's invitation, something some of the Rodin Treddeks were visibly resenting, voicing that resentment with yells of their own.

K'vestmilly Vos walked across the platform, settled in the Marn Chair, the meie taking position at her right, the gyes at her left. Oram walked down the steps at the side and stood by the near end of the table, scowling, his arms crossed.

She waited.

Embarrassed, the yellers fell silent, dipped bows, then found their chairs.

Tecozar Treddek Nov rose to his feet. "We welcome you to the Treddekkap, O Marnhidda Vos. We congratulate you on the style and facility with which you have assumed the Mask, and it is with . . ."

K'vestmilly Vos leaned forward. "Let me thank you

now for your good wishes, O Prime, and acknowledge the grace with which you would have presented them, but there is a gravely urgent situation confronting us and compliments are for quiet times." She stood, walked to the front of the dais, paused a moment. Camnor Heslin had scripted this with her, rehearsed it with movements and voice changes, showed her what to look for so she could intercept objections before they came out.

"You may have heard rumors," she said, and was pleased with the sound of her voice, steady and full. "Let me tell you they are true." *A slight pause here, a turn of the Mask, side to side, gathering them in.* "With the help of our friends from the Biserica we have discovered a way to locate the bombs that have caused so much trouble and trigger them without losing lives." *Another pause, then a quick addition.* "Property, yes. Lives, no." *Pause, deepen the voice, add a touch of solemnity.* "We have crafted a proclamation to be sent to every public place in the cities, to the plants and mills, everywhere we could think of that might be in danger." She saw restlessness gathering, used another rapid series of words to acknowledge and counter it. "Nik, no questions yet, the Inquisitor has men waiting with copies of the proclamation to pass out to you when you leave." *Slow again, matter of fact speech, hands coming out just slightly, a sketch of an embrace to gather them in.* "The bombs have more than a touch of magic to them, they conform themselves to their surroundings, which makes them difficult to locate. On the Pan Pen's bed, for example, the bomb was an extra brace that looked exactly like the rest of the wood, stain and all. You could not tell it was there unless you knew what the underside looked like and realized that something new had been introduced."

She smiled behind the Mask. She had their attention now. "What we propose is this. We are going to sweep the warrens first." *Ah! Heslin was right, this is where I need to come on strong.* "Silence! Hear me out or leave. Good. We begin with the warrens since the most lives are at risk there." *Slow again, matter-of-fact, calm.* "We will have two teams, one will be headed by the meie Zasya Myers and her mystical companion, one by the gyes Adlayr Ryan-Turriy with the sprite you see on his shoulder. They will begin the work this afternoon, as soon as we're finished here. While we're doing this, shop owners, overseers, and workers should be examining their work areas, looking for anything that has been added without explanation, the material doesn't matter. What looks like an old box, an extra steel brace or a discarded bit of lumber might be one of those bombs." *Pause, yes, that's got them sweating, now ease up a little.* "This inspection should be safe if it is done quickly and without moving anything. A heavy jolt would explode the bomb, and many of you have seen what happens then." She spread her hands, inclined her head, beginning to use the Mask as her mother had. "We understand quite well that there will be panic and false alarms." *Voice soothing, understanding, motherly—which is a joke of jokes. Heslin was right, though, look at them relax.* "We rely on all of you to counter this, it was one of the reasons you were asked to come here. Since we have only two teams capable of verifying a sighting, it will take several weeks to work our way through the cities, but once the sweep is completed and people are warned, there is less chance of new bombs being planted on us. We cannot promise complete safety but at least you and everyone else will no longer be helpless."

As she paused, once again turning the Mask from side to side, Tecozar Treddek Nov rose to his feet, raised his arms. "A salute to the Marn," he cried, "to the Mother of our Land and her care for us all." He clapped his hands with a loud slapping sound. The other Treddeks and the visitors rose, stood clapping rhythmically, slap slap, slap slap slap, slap slap, slap slap slap.

K'vestmilly bowed, cried out, "Enough. I thank you, but there is more I must report and this is not so pleasant. One of the Inquisitor's agents arrived from Govaritil yesterday, he came as fast as he could without stopping to sleep, eating on the move, to tell us that Takuzhone—one of the Val Kepal's twin sons, for those of you who don't know the name—to tell us Takuzhone was killed in an explosion as his father was only a few weeks ago." *Pause. They don't know what it means, they're beginning to worry again. Zdra, woman, move it along. Heslin said this bit should be as quick and easy as I can make it.*

"Govaritil exploded with rage; they blame us for both deaths. The other brother Takuboure is now the new Val Kepal; he has gathered an army and is marching north with it, burning and killing as he comes." *It starts getting delicate now; hit them with it, he said.* "It is not a large army, two or three thousand is what the agent said, but they are well supplied—suspiciously well supplied; our informant tells us that Takuboure opened some warehouses, brought out uniforms and weapons, produced trained fighters to wear the uniforms and carry the guns." *They're getting restless again. Hurry it up and get to the sticking place.* "That's the core of what's coming at us, but it's not all, there are also irregulars who've armed themselves and managed some sort of supplies, perhaps a thousand of those, angry men who don't care what they do as long as it inflicts damage." *Louder now, hit the words hard. Hands chopping to emphasize each*

one. Project power and determination. "After I called
you here, I sent a notice commandeering ten barges,
nik, Tecozar Nov, we'll discuss this later, let me finish. Barges that were empty or nearly so. I've sent five
hundred of the Marn's Guard south on them along with
supplies from the Marn's Reserve and enough macain
to mount them. It isn't enough." *Passion now, you feel
it, make them feel it.* "It isn't nearly enough!" *Quiet
again, sad.* "But they were what I had to hand."
Steady, hands out. "They have orders to stay alive as
long as possible and do what they can to delay the
Govaritzers until we can train a true army and get it
in place. A number of the Inquisitor's men went with
them as scouts, taking with them several of the communicators Ansila Vos ordered from the Biserica."
*Lean forward, bring them in, hands coming together
then spreading again, you're flattering them by making
them a part of your inside knowledge.* "This was done
secretly, paid for from the Marn's Purse; you are the
first to be told beyond the Inquisitor's men. You know
what they are, Oram has been after them for more than
a year and he's told you what they do. They will keep
us informed as to what is happening and where the
army is. It is one advantage we have that they do not."
She took a long breath, straightened her shoulders,
stood with her head up, her arms at her sides, light
gleaming on the painted ivory of the Mask as she
turned her head slowly from side to side, then back to
face the table. "To you, the Treddeks of Cadander, I
hereby declare a War Emergency and call upon you to
render your accounts in men and gold according to
Law and Custom."

K'vestmilly Vos dropped on the daybed, took the
Mask off, and rubbed at her eyes. "If I'm not deaf
after that. . . ." She ran her fingers through her hair

until it was a wild cloud of red tangles about her narrow face. "That's done, Maiden Bless. Now, the rest of it. Heslin's program. If anything comes up, I'll be at the hospital with the Healer for the next two hours. You really think Pen's Heir can handle the army?"

Oram stroked his beard. "Vedouce grinds his way from point to point, but he gets there and you can trust him. No flash, just lots of solid base. He's done a good job with the mills, cut out a lot of waste and effort. And the men know him, they like him because he listens to them and does something about their complaints. Which is a lot more than you can say about most Heirs. Add that to the fact that the gritz have as little experience with war as we do."

"Good. I don't want flash, I want men who get things done. And I'd better get myself started doing right now. We need to keep the cities quiet. Maiden Bless Camnor Heslin." She got to her feet, put her hand on Jestranos Oram's arm. "Which isn't to lessen you, my friend." She smiled up at him, eyes crinkled to slits. "No flash, but lots of solid base." She patted the arm and turned away, saying over her shoulder as she walked toward the bedroom, "And you've got the harder job. Find the man or woman here who's directing these attacks; we'll have to let the source go until we've got more time to deal with it."

"Hmm. About the source, Marn."

She turned, brow raised.

"The Healer came to me with an odd story, I don't know what to think of it. That she's somehow responsible for the Enemy. She offered to leave and draw Its attention away from us."

"What? These attacks started months before Mother even thought of sending to the Biserica."

"It was complicated. Bad dreams and magic mixed in a stew I don't pretend to understand."

"You do know who she is? What she is?"

"Nik. And I don't really care." He lifted his cloak off the back of the chair, draped it over his arm. "I doubt you had the mind for it the day your mother died, but I watched her work. Doesn't matter what burden she carries, Marn. With this war coming, we need her." In the doorway, he turned again. "Take care, Marn. Don't let her touch you and have people around you always."

> > < <

Doby crouched by the rail fence, shaking with sobs as he looked at the bodies of the vul calves and macai foals, shot and left for the flies. Ahead of them, inside the sheltering lines of kerovs, the village was burning; he'd seen flickers of red in the rolls of smoke rising above the bushy trees, but there were no noises except the distant crackle of the fires and he knew his people were dead as these beasts. He pressed against a post, trying to hide in its shadow. Since he couldn't hear any voices or macai hoots, the raiders must have passed on, but he was afraid to get closer, didn't know if he could anyway. His leg was stiffening, still bleeding a little from the bullet burn when he moved.

A hand dropped on his shoulder.

He yelped, began struggling and hitting out until he recognized the voice creaking in his ears, old Mama Charody, the Wise Woman who lived in the hills.

"Come, boy. Stay with me a while and a while. I need strong hands to dig m' herbs and you need food and a place. Can you walk?"

He nodded, limped after her as she stood and started off; the pain in his leg was awful, but his fear was gone.

> > < <

"The worst of the burns are down this way, O Marn." The sekalari glanced at Serroi who was pale and sweating. "Maiden Bless, there haven't been any more for several days. I don't know what we'd do with them."

As they turned into the corridor, K'vestmilly heard a soft fall of harp notes soothing as a water flow, then a voice singing though she couldn't make out the words.

"That's young Vyzharnos." The sekalari smiled fondly. "He's moved into the convalescent wing, comes across here every day." She nodded her white-coifed head at the door they were approaching. "The music seems to help." She sighed. "There's so little we can do for them."

The room was filled with moaning and sighing figures like cloth dolls crudely shaped in human form, lying on sheets of rubber clamped to iron frames. The smell was indescribable. Vyzharnos sat with his back to the door, a harp cradled in his arms, singing an old song, a tale of lovers betrayed and then revenged and reunited. The sekalari crossed to him, touched him on the shoulder. He nodded, but the harp and his voice went on without faltering.

K'vestmilly found that her memory of him had faded, but once she saw him again, the ache and the need came rushing back, stronger than before. *Ah, Poet, you won't even turn to greet your Marn. Maiden Bless, why did you happen to me now? It's impossible. . . .*

The little Healer stood in the center of the ward, turning slowly, as if she groped for the one who needed her most, the flesh in her arms and her hands going translucent and beginning to glow like green-glass lamps. She moved to one of the beds, bent over the silent, motionless form. The glow spread from her hands, embraced the body, pulsing, never still, thicker over the torso—then abruptly flowed back into the Healer's arms. She turned to the next bed.

K'vestmilly watched and decided Oram was right; even if Serroi were the danger he thought, and she didn't believe that, Cadander did need her. She moved quietly to Vyzharnos, stood with her hand on his shoulder as Serroi went from bed to bed, each healing quicker than the last until she seemed to do little more than touch, glow and move on.

When Serroi left the last bed, her face was drawn and so pale the throbbing green eyespot was the only color left in it. "Take me outside," she whispered. "I need to be outside, on the earth."

All around them the burn victims were sitting up, tearing loose the bandages, inspecting hands and arms that were free of pain, free of scars, with pale new skin, pink and soft as a baby's bottom.

After one quick look around, the sekalari yanked on the bell rope, then went to help unwind bandages. Over her shoulder, she said, "Vyzharnos, take them to the sun garden."

Serroi dropped onto the grass, sat with her eyes closed, her face turned to the sun.

"Like a slunicha plant," Vyzharnos murmured. "Who is she?"

"From the Biserica. The Prieti Meien sent her with the others Mother asked for."

"I'm sorry about your mother, O Marn."

"I asked you to call me K'vestmilly once; you didn't that time either."

"Better not," he said. "Listen, I said some stupid things then, forget them, will you? Anything I can do to help you, I will."

K'vestmilly closed her eyes. There was a stress on the *you* that she hadn't missed, but it meant only that he hadn't given up his disgust at the Families; the warmth in his voice was not for her, it was anger at the bomber who'd caused the pain in the burn room, the force that sent the raiders who'd killed his friends and nearly killed him. The hurt in her now was no sweet need, but she fought it back and when she spoke, her voice was steady. "When they let you out of here, Poet, go see the Mijlocker agent called Camnor Heslin. He'll know how you can help us, the Marn and your dear Nerodin."

> > < <

Hedivy climbed as high in the daub tree as he could, turned the longglasses across the fields; the flatness of the land made long distance reconnaissance feasible, but it also meant that a closer approach to the advancing army was difficult if not impossible. Swearing as he saw fires jump in a village that was a little dark blot against the horizon, and black smoke go boiling up to join other smoke columns farther south, he unclipped the com from his belt and used his thumb to cycle through the channels. "Pron, Duch, Ashal, Svoh, anyone who can talk," he muttered over and over, then waited, watching the line of red lights. One started blinking, he flicked to that one, spoke, "Go."

"Ya, Pron here. Go."

"Where are you? Go."

"Sitting on a bump behind a young kerov, watching a massacre. Wait. There's about four, maybe five, riders coming up, shooting as they come. Ker's men, I think. Five against a fifty or more. Good riders, and

those must be some of Ker's prizes they're sitting on,
Mad's Tits, you should see them weave; the gritzers
got some new kind of longgun, faster fire than any of
ours, but that's not doing them much good. They're
milling round, gettin' in each other's way, now the
leader's yellin', gettin' them into shape, going after
the Kers. One's down, there goes another, the last
three, they're off, nothing the gritz are riding gonna
catch those flyers. Haaah! One of the Kers wasn't
killed, just dumped when his mac went down, a bullet
in its head I think, anyway it's dead meat, he's socked
in behind that meat and spraying the gritz. Saa, they're
backing off, circling . . . ahhh, sproch! they got him.
Not before he took down couple hands worth. Five,
six dead, some wounded, three four of 'em pretty bad
it looks like. Did more'n just crunch some gritz, those
Kers. The villagers, they're scattered all over the fields,
keeping low and making time. 'Less they run into another bunch a gritz, some of 'em may get away. Hev,
I can see a dust cloud down south a ways, I think that's
the main body, I'd say half a day back. No one's come
this far yet or spotted me, but I got an itchy feeling.
I'm shuttin' down and gettin' outta here.''

> > < <

The city guard banged on the door. When it opened
he said, ''We found one, get yourself and your kids
outta here.''

He left them scurrying about the room, collecting a
few clothes and family treasures, went to bang on the
next door.

Adlayr stood in the doorway of this floor's lavatory,
watching Honeydew flutter over the table pushed up
against the window. She dropped and hovered over an

old box, waved her hand at it, then zipped back to his shoulder, talking all the way.

The guard Horvath came running up the stairs. "Everyone's out. What is it?"

"Box there." Adlayr pointed. "Under that soap and stuff on the table." *Honeydew, you think you could drop a cord around it?*

Honeydew don't think so. Honeydew think maybe even the littlest touch, box go boom.

"Ei vai. Horvath, Honeydew says it's touch that does it. I was going to drop a cord round it and give it a pull through that window so we could save these rooms, but it looks like that's no go."

"Same as the rest, right? Too bad. You'n and the sprite go join the warreners, I'll knock a pane out the window to mark it and try hitting the box from outside. Hmm?"

"Yeh." *Honey, let's go.*

The guard found the broken window, settled his longgun against his shoulders, collected his breath and squeezed the trigger.

The side of the warren disintegrated.

> > < <

The camp on the west side of the river was growing every hour with supplies and men arriving from Dander and Calanda. A large double pavilion was set up near the north edge of the neat lines of smaller tents. Inside the front section there was a folding table with stools around it. Vedouce Pen sat at the head, one of the communicators by his right hand, looking down at a map of Cadander, making marks with a pencil as he, Drittal Shar who was head of the Marn's Guard, and a recording secretary listened to Hedivy's report com-

ing through the communicator. Vedouce was a broad,
solid man, the thickness of his shoulders hard muscle.
His eyes were a dark brown, deceptively mild, with
droopy lids that made him look half asleep. Shar was
a little wiry man with a face like a ferret. He, too,
had a map in front of him, but his pale blue eyes were
moving restlessly from the communicator to Vedouce
and back.

". . . keepin' on the east side of the river." The
voice was clear and crisp, even the Zemyadel lilt re-
produced, but strange coming from that black rectan-
gle with something of its humanity stripped away.
"The main body is staying with the supply wagons,
of which there are ten. Big twelve wheelers they are,
drawn by triple hitches of orsk. Advance bands are
clearing the way for it, they do kill everything that
moves and burn everything that stands still for the
fire." They heard Hedivy drew in a breath, a creaking
as he shifted position in the tree.

"Tween twenty-five and fifty men each and there are
three or four bands sent out, though not always the
same men. Duch pulled off a ticky trick two days ago.
He has been watching the main body for us, so he have
a better guess that most about where it'd stop for the
night. He took a wild chance and went to ground in a
grove and won his bet when the camp went up less'n
a stade away from him. He called back a description
to me in case he was nailed before he could get away,
how they organize things, and how they decide who's
going on ahead. Seems they draw lots and the ones
who get the markers are the heroes for the day, strut-
tin' and boastin' like clowns." Hedivy paused. "Have
you any questions so far? Go."

Vedouce lifted his heavy head, tapped the speak-
button. "Later. Go." He returned the mode to report
and made another note on the map.

"Ker's men have been doing good work, they are sniping at the gritz each day, four, five raiders are hittin' the advance bands, shootin' and runnin'. They have not been able to stop the bands from burnin', but they've covered the escape of many a Bezhvali and they have killed more gritz than they have lost their own. It is fleabites, though, that is all." Hedivy cleared his throat. "One place the gritz are sure to be, it is at the villages ahead and these would make good traps. Let the bands come in close, then wipe them out. Once the gritz get into the Zemyadel, where the land is not quite so flat, if you find locals who know the ground, you can set up ambushes as long as they keep sending their killers out. And you can follow Ker's lead, you can push it farther, you can get at the orsks that pull those supply wagons. Plant longguns in trees by the Big Bend where the main body'll almost surely stay close to the river for at least twenty stades. It should be at Bend in about a week, the way it be movin'. A few sharpshooters could lay out half a dozen of orsks in as many minutes and have a chance to get away, should there be a fast boat handy. The more we whittle off, the fewer we will have to face when the real fighting starts. Go."

Vedouce tapped the speak-button. "How many in the main body? Go."

"Duch did a reasonable good count. More than first reports have said. Four thousand fighters, divided into four bitaskas, each with its own supply section, the bitaskas into navstas of twenty men with a vudvek in charge of each, discipline's good, morale is high. And they are well supplied, food, weapons, remounts. They make twenty miles a day without straining macai or orsk. That is in the Bezhval, though. They will be slowing once they hit the Zemyadel, there are more people and the land is cut up, not so flat." He shifted again, there was a sharp snapping sound that came through the speaker. "No problem, just a poison terk getting too close. Too many of them in this spojjin' daub. About a thousand irregulars, Duch says, though they're harder to count because they mill about a lot. They have their own supplies, most of it on pack vuls. They have been staying close to the army so far, but Duch says he can see them getting restless when the bands come back at night and boast about their kills. He thinks it will not be long before they break away and start raiding on their own. Have you any questions? I've a call coming in from one of my men which I'd better take. Go."

Vedouce spoke briskly, "Good work, Hedivy. You and your men. We'll be sending a small force down this afternoon. Be looking for them. I'll be here for another hour if anything comes up. Out." He made a few more notes on the map, then looked up. "Three hundred, Shar, five barges for transport. Three communicators, destroy them if there's a chance they'll fall into gritzer hands. We can't spare more. Do what you can. It'll be at least another week before we can hope to start moving south."

21. Things Get Worse

Serroi went to Treshteny's garden after she left the warrens. She was beginning to feel like a machine, pull the lever and out pops the glow. And she was getting waspish because she was essentially a side show in the drama that was playing here, subordinated to Heslin and K'vestmilly Vos, left out of consultations, having to pick up snippets of gossip to find out what was going on. Even when she tried to do the right thing and tell about the Fetch, Oram might as well have patted her on the head and told her "go way, little girl." Her pride was hurt. It was idiotic, but that was the truth.

She sat on the bench, watching the dryads play, the dryadita cuddled on her lap, humming baby songs that vibrated in her bones and warmed her soul. As to the rest that were born of her healing—it was going to be hard to claim the nixies as her own and the carnivorous trees were beyond her at the moment. As for the Fetch . . . she didn't want to think about It. Maybe It was like the trees and didn't count, she didn't create them, they simply changed. The nixies . . . they had a casual cruelty about them that frightened her, a cold alien quality . . . but if she wanted the delicate dryads as her children, she had to take those others, the dark as well as the light. As that thought slipped through her idling mind, it plucked a chord in her that said this is

important. She tried to pin down how, but the sweet
voices of the dryads washed over her and she let it go
and leaned back, the dryadita drowsing against her.

Treshteny drifted round the carved screen, the silent
nurse following her. The timeseer glanced at Serroi,
smiled at the dancing dryads, and began walking
around the garden, moving from tree to tree, touching
each of them and murmuring something that only she
could hear. She stood a while watching the stream,
started to sway back and forth as if the water pulled
her. The nurse touched her arm. Treshteny blinked,
gave her a cloudy smile and wandered on.

She sat down on the bench beside Serroi and held
out her hand. Serroi took it, fighting the disintegration
that she'd felt before when this happened. The long
thin fingers grew warm in hers.

After several breaths, Treshteny sighed and pulled
her hand away. ''My brother's dead.''

''Ei vai, I'm sorry to hear that. Were you close?''

''We were twins, but he changed, I changed. He's
changed again. His body's still walking. He's dead. It's
not so bad. Dead is comfortable.'' She looked around,
eyes vague. ''I wish I had children like you do. They
won't let me. My father had me cut before he sent me
here. You've so many around you, a whole family of
weirdings.'' She tilted her head, pursed her lips, cautiously extending a forefinger to touch the dryadita,
beaming when tiny fingers closed about hers. ''Bébé.''

The two women sat in a peaceful drowse, the warm
afternoon sun touching them lightly through the lace-
work of shadow from the javory on the far side of the
path. The water burbled in the corner, an intermittent
breeze ruffled the leaves of the javories and brellims,
hummed in the needles of the single cherdva growing
by the stream. The dryads settled to quieter games,
cats cradle with subtle strings they pulled from their

own nonsubstance; nimble fingers dancing through the patterns, they passed the strings back and forth in an endless exchange they seemed never to grow tired of.

"Oram is annoyed," Treshteny said.

"Mmm, why?"

"Since you came, I've only had one premoaning fit and he missed that one. When the Marn died, it was."

"That's bad?"

"For him it is. In times like this." She twisted her fingers together, looked through her lashes at Serroi. "I used to see things . . ." A sigh. "Things that were . . . maybe . . . going to happen." A shiver as if something cold and unseen brushed her shoulders. "So the Marn and he could do this or that and make it come out better."

"And none since the Marn died?"

"Nik."

"Are you sorry?"

"Nik, nik, nik, nik. . . ."

> > < <

"Spider one to Spider three."

"Three here. Go."

"You've pulled a big one. Fifty-three breaking out, heading your way fast. Be there in half an hour. Waste the notneys, yah! Go."

"Do our best. Out."

Zatko clipped the com to his belt and walked into the other room. "They're coming. Half hour, latest. Fifty-three."

The Trivud Throdal nodded. "Send a runner to the outlayers and let them know." He turned to the Bezhvali village starod. "You'd better go join your folk, it's gonna get hot round here."

"Nik. I won't get in your way, Vudvek, but Pan Ker expects me to watch his property."

"Up to you." Throdal left the room and went to check his men.

The Govaritzer fighters came charging through the fields of shen, trampling down the knee-high leaf blades, the thin stalks with heads just beginning to set. They raced through the single street of the small village, howling with rage at the sight of the deserted houses, emptying their longguns into silent, unresponsive walls.

They stopped by empty corrals, reloaded and fired up the torches they carried strapped to their saddles, kicked their macain into a run and started back.

And ran into a storm of lead that cut two-thirds of them down before they had a chance to react.

The quickest and luckiest flung themselves from their mounts and scrambled for cover, some with minor wounds, some untouched.

A Govaritzer broke from an alley between two houses, scrambling for the line of kerov trees. He got two steps, fell when a bullet tore away half his head.

That was enough for the rest of the survivors. They dug in and began shooting, trying for as many of the Guard as they could get.

"Spider three to base."

"Base here. Go."

"Rozummy village clean, fifty-three gritz hit it, fifty-three dead, two of us grazed, but no dead. How'd the others do? Go."

"Spider four, twenty-five in, twenty-four dead, one had a lame mac, lagged behind, got away, they sent two after him, they said he came on outriders from the main army before they could do him. Spider two, thirty, clean kill like yours. Go."

"Up the Guards! Whoop! Thanks, base. We're mounted and ready to move out according to plan. Go."

"Spider five. Shar here. Spider six reports a stirring in the main army, ten navstas organizing up front, getting ready to take off. Take your navstas and ride west ten stades, meet up with Spiders two and three near Petinol village, go to ground there, and wait for the gritz. You'll be three hundred to their two, but they'll be ready for you this time, with reinforcements close to hand, so it won't be any walkover. Wait for orders, then you crunch those notneys, yah. Out."

> > < <

Vyzharnos Oram scowled at Tingajil. "You're the Marn's oslak."

"And you're Oram's droozh." She smiled sweetly at him. "Ready to sell out with the rest of us."

Vyzharnos raised his brows. "So she has teeth."

"And a limited amount of patience before she bites. Shall we get busy?"

They were in one of the workrooms down the hall from Oram's office, a small bare cube with a table, two chairs and a window. Tingajil's lute case sat at one end of the table, beside some overstuffed folders filled with scribed copies of reports and summaries; there were two pads of lined paper, a cup with several stylos in it, and a bottle of ink. Vyzharnos moved along the table, flipped open one of the folders, and took out a report. "Saa! There's still idiots saying the Marn killed her mother."

She moved around the end of the table and stood beside him, looking down at the closely written sheet. "I'm surprised the Inquisitor hasn't arrested them and dumped them so deep they wouldn't see shine for a year.''

"Father got some good advice and for once he took it. Make them look like fools, get people laughing at them and cheering the Marn. Which is what we're supposed to help do.'' He grimaced. ''Marn's one thing. You do what you want, but I'm not about to celebrate any spojjin' Family.''

Tingajil lifted the sheet of paper, set it aside, and began reading the next; as her eyes moved down the lines, her face grew pinched and pale. She looked up, handed him the paper. ''This is what I want to work on.''

He looked at what he held. It was a list of villages destroyed, an estimate of the number of people killed. ''Yes,'' he said. ''Yes. You're right.'' He dropped the paper, closed his eyes, moved his fingers over the bandage around his arm where the vuurvis burn was slowly healing. ''River of blood,'' he said. ''Drowned in a river of blood, a river of fire.''

Tingajil reached for the lute case, humming a tentative tune as she did so.

> > < <

K'vestmilly Vos the Marn walked in her garden with Sabbanot Treddek Ano. ''Reports have been coming in from the South,'' she said, ''they tell me the Govaritzers will be in the Zemyadel by the end of the week. Pan Ano has done well getting as much of the harvest as you can salvage into Nov's warehouses, but I haven't seen you pulling people and livestock out. I would like to think you're caring as much for your people as you are for your pocketbooks.''

Sabbanot Ano reddened with anger, the lines in his

narrow face deepening, his thick lips dragging down. He said nothing.

She could feel his hostility, the resistance he was throwing up against whatever she said. Her own anger rose in her throat; she wanted to take his hide off, tell him exactly what she thought of his cupidity and callousness. She moved beside him, the Mask heavy on her face, reminding her of her mother's words: *you'll coax and you'll wheedle, you'll bribe and you'll punish, secretly and openly, you'll do the twisty dance the rest of your life.*

She walked through flowering sliva trees, pink-tinted petals falling around her, their delicate perfume drifting gently about her; nesting modaries sang among the branches and high overhead, wild jessers screamed as they glided in long ovals above the city. The peace here was almost painful because she couldn't get out of her mind the things she'd read that morning when Oram brought her reports from the Bezhval, transcribed from the communicator and gaining power from such immediacy.

She moved on, circling back toward the entrance. There was one more thing she had to say to the Treddek and she wanted to get rid of him as soon as she finished saying it. A gesture brought a guard from the shadows of a bushy young daub. The guard was nearly as young and as green, one of the boys Oram was training so he could release the veterans to other work. He opened the door and stood at attention.

She stepped aside, turned the Mask on the Treddek. "I have heard rumors," she said. "Very disquieting rumors about hoarding and plans to squeeze the cities by raising food prices to the clouds. Ano will have losses because of this war and has a right to recover some of them. I will accept a doubling of current prices, and consider a tripling in extraordinary circumstances—which will have to be proven—but if I hear of prices being yanked higher than that, the offending individual will have his stock seized with no compensation; if he is acting as agent, his employer will be fined. The same will be done to those found hoarding. Good day, Sabbanot Treddek Ano.''

> > < <

"Spider six to Pack.''
"Pack here. Go.''
"Gritz had second thoughts. They're sending a scout party to check the lay. Two men ridin' together, double timin' it. Be on y' twenny minutes, maybe less. Out.''

"Kinnet, you got 'em?''
"Yah, Vudvek.'' The voice came from the top of the tallest of the trees in the kerov hedge. "Dust cloud moving more or less in a straight line, heading right toward us.''
"Vykon, Nariz, you ready?''
The two guards lifted their coiled whips.
"Get moving.''

Vykon and his brother Nariz walked with care through the thickly scattercast plants, brushing past them without flattening them; when they reached the line the riders were taking, they crouched in the shen about ten feet apart, pulled the coverts they'd woven over them and waited for the scouts to come past them. They'd been chosen for this because they came from a drover family in the High Harozh and they'd learned the whip almost before they could walk and stalking tricks when they were boys going after the shy, swift jelen with knife and noose.

* * *

The two gritzer scouts came at a steady pace across the fields, riding long racy macain with the dark warty hides of mountain breds, scanning the shen for trampled areas and traces of riders passing through it, heading for the village beyond the kerov hedges.

Vykon and Nariz rose from their nests with their whips snapping out; they had the invaders off their macain, necks broken before they had a chance to shout or loose off their longguns. They caught the macain, stripped the bodies, and rode back to their navsta.

Thirty navstas of the Marn's Guard were deployed in a double arc half a stade in front of Petinol, the village nearest the advancing force, the men concealed by kerov hedges, or lying beside their macain in pits they'd dug, half in the forward ranks, half in the reserves.

Vykon was in one of the frontline pits, waiting for the horn. He and Nariz had spent the past year guarding ore shipments from the mines—hard, dangerous work where they were targets for raiders who could come at them any time, anywhere; now it was their side choosing time and place and he was more than ready for it. He stroked his macai's horny nose, scratching the softer skin in the folds, soothing him, keeping him quiet. "Easy, Rhuzho," he muttered, "You're no spojjin' equine t' have to yell g'dday to your spojjin' kin. Good ol' Rhuzho, not much longer, I can hear them coming, make more noise than a herd a drunk vuls. Just a little longer . . . just a little. . . ."

The horn sounded. Vykon rolled into the saddle, had Rhuzho on his feet and jumping from the pit an instant later.

> > < <

The macai limped up the Mask Way, its head low,
foam dripping from its mouth. One ear was shot off,
the blood from the wound crusted over the skinfolds
of its neck; a crease on its haunch oozed sluggishly as
the thrusting muscles of the powerful hind legs kept
cracking the scab over the shallow wound. Its rider
was even worse off, bending low over the macai's long
neck, a rag tied around his head, his face pale and
sweating, one arm hanging stiff.

The gate guard rang the alarm as soon as he saw the
rider, then leaned out of the window, hands cupped
about his mouth, yelled, "Help's coming."

Shaking his head as the rider paid him no attention
and kept the beast struggling up the Way, he opened
the Gate for two Guard cadets, watched as they met
the rider, swore as the man shook his head, kept urg-
ing his macai along.

When they finally passed through the Gate, the rider
straightened. "Take good care of her," he said, his
voice hoarse from the long effort. "She's a good 'un."
His eyes rolled back and the young guards caught him
as he fell.

"Marn . . ." He tried to sit up.

K'vestmilly put her hand on his shoulder, eased him
back. "Nik, friend. You've done enough. Tell me."

"Hal . . . the mines. . . ." He closed his eyes.
"Pan Hal says send what help you can. The chovan
have linked up with Majilarn raiders, they've stopped
going after the shipments and are hitting at the villages, even the mines themselves. Killing, burning,
throwing bombs. Don't know why, getting nothing
from it. Coming at night. Almost every night. Food's

running out. Ammunition's almost gone.'' He lifted a hand, let it fall. "That's all.''

K'vestmilly touched her forefinger to his lips. "Maiden Bless,'' she said. "You've done well, now rest.''

"Sadra . . . my macai. . . .''

"She's fine, drank a gallon and is scarfing down grain like there's no tomorrow.''

"She. . . .''

"Yes . . . I know . . . rest, we'll take care of everything. . . .''

"Take care of everything. Saaa! How in zhag am I going to do that?'' K'vestmilly flung her hands out, went back to pacing across the Marn's sitting room. "People are pouring into the cities, north, south, we've got to feed them, find housing for them, jobs if we can. The sweeps are saving lives, but there's no way to get the bombs out without exploding them and that means more folk on the streets, their homes gone. The sekalari don't have time to sleep, the clinics are stuffed, people in the halls because there aren't enough beds. Serroi helps, Maiden Bless, how she helps, but she's only one and she has to rest sometimes, and I have to send her South tomorrow where she'll have wounded fighters to deal with, zhag! How she's going to handle it, healing them and sending them back to get killed. And it isn't only the mines, Majilarn are raiding the Harozh, and they've got their own chovan to worry about, and where are we going to find guards to send there when we need every man in the South? We've just had a battle in the Bezhval, we call it a victory because three of theirs went down for one of ours and we ONLY lost seventy of our best fighters. So where are we going to find guards for Hal?'' She glanced at Marazhney Treddek Osk sitting in the shadows, her long thin face enigmatic. "And how long is it going to be before Osk is in the same danger?"

It was late, after midnight. Once again there was only a single lamp burning; oil supplies were being drawn down more quickly than they could be replenished through Tuku-kul. It was another worry that pushed at K'vestmilly each time she looked at the lamp, a little itch added to all the others that were making her feel besieged.

Camnor Heslin and Jestranos Oram sat beside the Treddek, watching her, waiting for her to finish her rant.

She drew in a long breath, felt the Mask tighten against her face. With an impatient shrug she slipped it off and tossed it on the daybed. "Oram, how many men can we pull out of the cities?"

"The real answer to that is none." He leaned forward, lifted a hand to cut off her protest. "I've got ancients called out of retirement putting a little gloss on boys so they won't shoot themselves in the foot or murder trees. So I can put them on the walls here and free up guards to keep the Red Dan open and build up the army. If we take some of the older men who're volunteering to go South and use them to handle the influx and keep the peace, I can shake loose maybe a hundred."

"I see. Then we leave the Travasherims to the raiders and bring the people in. The Harozh—they'll have to take care of themselves. Unless any of you have a better idea?"

Marazhney leaned forward. "And the Merrzachars?"

"If Osk starts getting hit before we finish with the Govaritzers, there's not much we can do. If he wants to keep the mines going, that's up to him, but he should think about sending the women and children someplace safe, and anyone else he doesn't need out there. If I were him, I'd send them to the fisher villages on the Stathvoreen, they'd do better there than they would here.''

"Supplies?''

"You know the problems as well as I do, Marazhney Osk.'' She dropped onto the daybed, ran her hands through her hair, breaking it loose from the gel. "We're not used to war here, any of us.''

Camnor Heslin tapped fingers on a massive thigh. "The point in having a focus of power is having a focus of responsibility.'' His voice was dry, that rich deep voice that had coaxed her out of spasms of anger and fear so many times already; he wasn't going to coax this time. "You don't need an enemy if you defeat yourself. You can't let fleabites distract you. What would happen to Dander and Calanda under sack by an army of men looking for revenge? And if Dander and Calanda fall, the rest fall after them. The greatest good for the greatest number. Not pretty or simple, but the truth seldom is. Do what you can about these other things, but deal with that army. Deal with it or let someone else try.''

K'vestmilly combed her fingers through her hair again, then shook her head at him, laughing a little. "Spanking me, Heslin?''

He shrugged. "However you see it.''

"My call in that, too?''

"You're the Marn. Remember it.''

"Prak. Oram, find those men for me. Commandeer all the boats in the River Quarter that can go up the Papery canal and start them on their way to the Travasherims. Use the canal as a gathering point, shove the miners in those boats, and get them down here. It's the quickest way I can think of to clear out that situation. Anyone who gets left behind, well . . .

they'll have to fend for themselves. Marazhney, talk
with your Pan, see that he knows the situation and
we'll deal from there. And we'll keep men and supplies flowing South. And I'll prod Vedouce to finish
the training and shift himself.'' She stood. ''Any
questions? Nik? Then let's get some sleep.'' Her mouth
twisted into a brief half-smile. ''Even you, Oram. If
you crash on me, I don't know what I'd do.''

> > < <

The Govaritzer army closed in on itself and moved
massively northward, a ring of sharpshooters on the
outside with the new longguns that shot faster and
whose range was greater than any guns the Guards
had. There were no more advance bands burning and
killing, but the army itself passed over the deserted
villages, over the fields around them and left nothing
behind but ash. The Ker raiders used the kerov hedges
as cover and did some minor damage, but mostly they
died, the Govaritzers collecting their macain and adding them to their own remounts.

The navstas from the Marn's Guard attacked the
night camps, hit and run raids. . . .

Vykon, Nariz, and half a dozen neighbors and cousins from the High Harozh crept through the darkness
after TheDom-set, only an hour till dawn, moving on
toes and elbows across the trampled ground, keeping
their progress smooth and silent as cloudshadows; the
sentries were mostly citymen who hadn't an eye for
emptiness, but they weren't stupid. A jerk instead of
a flow or the wrong silhouette would bring a bullet
and an alarm.

Vykon reached the rope corral, went still as the macain stirred restlessly; the wind was in his face, so his
scent wasn't troubling them, but macain had better than

average nightsight and weren't fooled by shadows. A crawling man was a strange thing and strange things at night made them nervous.

A low whistle. He was up, knife slicing through the rope as he leapt at the nearest macai, caught hold of the spongy growth on the long neck, and pulled himself astride. He slipped the coiled whip from his shoulder, snapped it out and ticked the flanks of several macai near him, brought the butt down on his mount's flank with a warbling whoop, bent low as the beast went charging through the gap in the rope, half a dozen other macai following him. On either side of him, the others were doing the same thing.

Alarm whistles were blowing behind him, guns popping. One of the macai running with him grunted and fell over. There was a stinging on his arm and a squeal from his mount, the sound of the shot lost in the uproar; hooting with rage the macai extended itself, its gait turning so rough in its urgency he had a hard time staying on.

Gradually he got the beast calmed and turned in the direction he wanted. The other macain were slowing, following docilely behind him, three of them. If the others had done as well, they'd gotten away with nearly fifty of the gritzer remounts. And with a little more luck, the gritz mounting up to chase them would be boiling and careless with it and would follow the raiders right into the guns of the navstas waiting for them.

> > < <

K'vestmilly moved restlessly through the Marn's suite, talking to herself, trying for some kind of resolution of the whirling thoughts that wouldn't let her sleep. "Delaying action. Delaying! He keeps saying the men aren't ready yet; if we attack before they're

ready, we haven't a chance. When by zhag are they
going to be ready! The gritz will be in the Zemyadel
by tomorrow. Three weeks and they're in Dander.
K'milly, you're doing it to yourself again. You don't
need Heslin to tell you. Sleep? I can't sleep. I need to
talk to someone. Not Oram. I know everything he'd
say, I know how his nose twitches and when he's going
to rub at that scrubby beard.'' She closed her eyes.
''Vyzharnos, ah my love who doesn't know it and
would be appalled if he did. Maiden Bless, I wish I
could slip over to you and you'd hold me and tell me
everything's all right as long as I'm there.'' She moved
her shoulders, laughed, an unhappy sound. ''I wonder
who I'd have to kick out of your bed if I was stupid
enough to go to you. Tingajil, probably. Pretty and
gentle, enough edge to be interesting. Everything I'm
not. Mother, Mother, I wish you were here. Hus!
That's it. I'll go talk to him. Thank you, Mother. One
of the blessings of the Mask, you said. People forget
your face or never knew it.''

Adlayr Ryan-Turriy opened the door, blinked at her.
''Marn?''
''Come with me.''
''Anything you want me to bring?''
''What you brought when we went to the pottery.''
''Ah.''

Though it was very late, there were knots of people
in the streets, milling about, laughing, arguing, fighting, pairing off to vanish into the shadows. And there
were children everywhere, children that should have
been abed long ago, most of them belonging to families camping in the covered sideways and the work-
yards, refugees and people from the warrens who'd
had their homes blown up. The street people were out

in force, gamblers, acrobats, singers, beggars. More than once she heard Vyzharnos and Tingajil's song, *River of Blood,* accompanied by the slapping of hands, banging of fists on walls. The kavarnas were bulging, the anger thick as lampsmoke, sometimes anger at the Families or at the Marn, mostly anger at the Govaritzers and the Majilarn.

A hand clamped on her arm, pulling her around. A red drunken face was thrust close to hers, nearly choking her with the stench of cheap slivach. "Eh milach, ga' somefin f'r y', look't sa, goo' siller." He clinked a battered fist by her ear, used his weight to shove her toward one of the sideways.

A dark form swooped from the darkness above, razor talons raked the side of his head, then the thing was gone. K'vestmilly wrenched free and hurried on.

"You have sudden friends." Husenkil locked the door behind her. "Let's go upstairs."

"I didn't think it'd be a good idea to beat on your door."

"Nik, you're right. The Tailor's got his nose in everyone's business these days. I didn't trust him when he was just snoopy, now that he's an Elder. . . ." He glanced at her, grabbed her shoulder, brought the lamp closer to her face. "That's blood."

"Not mine."

He started up the stairs again. Over his shoulder he said, "Tell me."

"It's nothing. A drunk with ideas. Adlayr dissuaded him."

"Chert! It wasn't really a bright notion this, though I'm glad to see you."

She joined him on the landing, walked past him as he held the door for her. "I needed to talk to someone I don't have to coax or manipulate."

"Hmm." He dropped the bar into its hooks, took her arm, and led her into the sitting room.

Wrapped in one of Husenkil's old robes, Adlayr was sitting on the floor, his back against a wall. He started to get up as K'vestmilly came in, but she waved him back. "If I can't trust you, gyes. . . ." She let Husenkil seat her on a couch, pulled off the scarf, and shook out her hair.

"I'll put some water on to heat." He stepped through a door, left it ajar.

It was the first time she'd been in his living quarters. As she heard the rush of water into a kettle, the clank as he set it on the stove, the rattle of coals and paper, the snap-hiss of a match, she looked around. It was a comfortable room, almost painfully neat, an old cut-wool rug on the floor, curtains woven from unbleached yarn. There were four chairs and two small tables with simple lines and close attention to grain and surface; she was sure she knew who'd made those. Interwoven boxes hung on one wall, made by the same hand. In the boxes were a collection of pots and tiles, small glows of pure bright color. She found a peace in this simplicity that didn't exist inside the Pevranamist, and some of the tension she'd brought with her slipped away.

Husenkil brought the tray in, a chocolatier on it made of rough terracotta with green drip-glaze, mugs to match and a plateful of thin waffle wafers. He looked tired and older than she remembered. What was it, two weeks? three? since she'd seen him?

"I shouldn't have come," she said. "Waking you up in the middle of the night."

"Nik, Kimi. It's good to see you—and you certainly couldn't come in daylight." He filled a mug and brought it to her, took another to Adlayr, then settled himself in one of the chairs, sipping and smiling at her.

The mug was warm against K'vestmilly's palms, the smell of the chocolate sweet and dark. "Mother loved hot chocolate. Did you catch it from her or was it the other way round?"

"Neither, Kimi. It was one of the few things we shared that we never argued about."

"Are you all right? I've had reports, things are difficult in the cities. Do you get enough to eat? Are you safe here, living alone like this?"

For several breaths he didn't answer her, just sipped at the chocolate and stared at the wall behind her shoulder. He set the cup on the tray and leaned forward, hands falling over his knees. "It's just as well you came tonight, Kimi. This is probably the last time we can talk, at least until the war is over and things are straightened out again. Narazha, you remember her? Her father and her older brothers, they're signing up for the fighting. Her mother and her aunt-by-law who's living with them because her husband and sons have already gone, they're moving in with me tomorrow, no more quiet, the house will be full of women." He looked around and sighed. "It's suited me, living alone. Would've suited your mother, if she could've. I'll be spending my days in the warrens, Oram's made me one of his peace keepers, so at least I'll get out the house."

K'vestmilly started to protest, closed her mouth and dropped her eyes. "Be careful," she murmured.

"I'm not a rash man, Kimi. We all have to do our part and I wouldn't want yours, it's far harder than mine." He was silent another few breaths, then said, "Don't try to send extras to me, I know you want to, but I won't take it."

"You won't let me do anything?"

He laughed. "Zdra zdra, if I go sick, I'd like that Healer of yours to do her act on me. Seriously, I don't need much. And having the Glory this close," he sighed, "it keeps the prowlers away. So it's good for something. We never did get a chance to go to one of those meetings like you wanted. Too many things happening."

She frowned. "They're really pulling in the members with all these people crowding into the cities. Oram hasn't got . . . zdra, call them what they are, he hasn't got the spies to keep track of what's going on. He doesn't think much of them, but they worry me." She wrinkled her nose. "I'm my mother's daughter for sure. Anything I don't know worries me."

"The Tailor keeps trying to get me in there; if you want I. . . ."

"Nik!" She grimaced at the chocolate she'd spilled on her skirt, set the mug down, and rubbed at the stain with the napkin he tossed her. "They seem to be giving comfort where it's needed. The Preörchmat wouldn't agree, but their gain is her loss. That's something we'll have to look into, too, what it means that people aren't turning to the Temple." She smiled at him. "I suppose you'll have something to say there."

He twisted his wide mouth into a down-curved grin. "Be sure of that, Kimi love."

She closed her eyes, the word love warming her heart, chasing away the loneliness that had been eating at her. He didn't have to say it. He wouldn't have said it unless he meant it, she'd learned that even in the brief time she'd known him. "My mother was a wise one," she said after a short silence, then got to her feet. "I hope I do as well for my daughter. Zdra, you need your sleep, Hus, and I've got to get back."

"Marn." Adlayr got hastily to his feet, stripping off

the robe as he rose. "Give me five minutes or so before you step out the door. I need time to get set."

K'vestmilly hugged her father hard and slipped into the street; when she heard the bars chunking home, she slapped the door for a last farewell and started up the street.

She stopped a moment outside the House of Glory, listened to the sounds coming muffled through the door, a steady monotonous chant: Glory Glory Glory.

Shaking her head, she went swiftly on, leaning forward as if she pushed against a wind.

22. Death and Creation

The Darkness vibrated.
In her sleep Serroi moaned and sweated; it was
pressing on her, closing in around her.
Darkness and terror. She pushed at it and it
was like touching warm wet rubber. Revulsion
filled her.
*A shape congealed in the Heart of Darkness, a
focus that sucked the essence of Darkness into
it. A woman came toward Serroi, arms curved
to embrace her, a woman whose face changed
and changed again, elements of Yael-mri and
Tayyan were there, Raiki Janja and something
of every woman she'd known, fleshing the bones
of the Fetch. "Mother," it said, voice sweet
and insinuating, confidence growing, but not yet
reaching to demand. "Come to me. Let me love
you like I love my children, come to me, be
part of me. Come. . . ."*

"Spider six to base.
"Base here. Go."
"Shooters in position. Van's almost in sight, I can
see the dust and the smoke from the fires they're set-

ting. Unless something's come up, I'm headin' for the boat. Go.''

"Good work and good luck. Out."

The army came over the shen fields like an amoeba oozing across the land, eating everything in its path and leaving destruction behind. There were tiny pops and crackles around the fringes where the Kers were still attacking, driven to crazy daring by the blood of their kin and the destruction of their homes. When that got too annoying, the amoeba put out a pseudopod and smeared the attackers into the ground, then withdrew into itself and moved on.

It was a blind amoeba—it no longer dared send out advance bands and single scouts never came back, the spotters watching them and the Marn's Guard saw to that—and it was slower, having lost a third of its re-mounts to guard forays, but it was not appreciably weakened.

When it reached the deep incurve of the Great Bend and the groves of brellim, daub, and javory that grew along the river at the northern border of the Hayadel Bezhval, it extended several pseudopods and swept through the trees searching for ambushers.

It found none and oozed on.

Vykon eased from the blind high in the crown of the brellim, swung down the trunk and dropped to the ground, nodded to Nariz who came from the shadows to join him. On both sides of the brothers more silent Harozhni left their nests and moved toward the edge of the grove and the trees they'd marked yesterday while there was still light, big old trees, daubs and brellims that would give them the angle and the cover they needed.

On the plain outside, the ragged tail of the amoeba had moved past except for the slow, ponderous supply wagons that were creaking by the ambush, the orsks plodding stolidly along, six to a hitch, their horns lopped and capped. Vykon sighted on his first target, a slab-sided wheeler with a mottled red and white hide; he waited for the signal from the whistleman.

It came.

He squeezed off his three shots, dropped from the tree and ran for the river, ignoring the yells and the squealing protests from gritzer macain as the tailgritz wrenched them around and prodded them into a full run.

He reached the river a few mac-lengths ahead of the pursuers, dived from the low bluff, hit the water and churned toward the boat, pulling himself in, turning in time to see his brother Nariz go floating off, half his head shot away, and his cousin Plino jerk in mid-air, splash down and not come up. He howled. The boat rocking under him as the other snipers clambered in, shots from the gritzers on the bluff lancing past him, he brought up his longgun and squeezed the trigger. Nothing happened. Cursing, he went to his knees, yanked the clip, dropping it in his haste. He forced calm on himself, dug into the oiled pouch at his belt and pulled a dry one out.

The helmsman pulled the anchor over the rail, the boatboy hauled up the sail, yelled, ''Head down, we're getting outta here.''

Ignoring the men crawling about, the shifts of the boat, the burn on the side of his head where a gritz had almost sent him after his brother, Vykon began shooting, slowly, steadily. On the bluff a macai went down, a man tumbled into the water and floated away, another swayed and retreated, then the boat slid off to the far side of the river and fled round the bend, leaving the dead and the invaders behind.

Vykon slid the rifle into the sheath on his back,

banged his head on his crossed arms again and again, crying for his brother and his cousin, his hands clenching, opening, clenching again. Around him other men wept and groaned for brothers and cousins; in the High Harozh everyone was related to one degree or another.

"Spider seven to base."

"Base here. Go."

"We really put the boot in this time, the whole thing's stopped and milling about. I'm behind 'em but even with glasses, it's hard to see how bad the damage is, too many riders crowding in. There's some orsks down, one wagon's tipped over, one of the orsks was wounded and went into a panic, panicked the others. Bit a luck there. Zdra, it's a lovely mess. Go."

"Anyone nosing down round your way? Go."

"Nik, quiet as the morning after a long drunk. What's the count on our side? Go."

"Six lost, presumed dead. Two scratches and a broken leg. Soon as you think it's safe, come in. Time you got linked into General's web. Go."

"Waste the notneys, yah! I'm going to wait till dark, they're in a mean mood out there. See you in the morning. Out."

> > < <

Treshtal dozed inside the body he no longer owned, the life it led his only remaining dream as the remnants of his self flaked away, reducing by infinitesimal decrements the last remaining seed of identity.

The Dancer moved from House to House, altar to altar, dancing joy and passion—the joy of destruction, pain and death, the passion to join with others and move as one, renouncing the misery of individual thought. As men died in the South, as the refugees fought and killed each other or themselves in their despair and restlessness, the Fetch in him grew stronger and the Dancer reached out farther and farther, touching the dark seeds in every soul, bringing them to bloom. Gathering the blooms to Herself, creating her own army.

Cadander was an old land, layered with traditions so ancient most people never thought of them as having a beginning: they were and they had always been. It had been a peaceful land, prosperous and healthy with only the restive Govaritzers as enemies and a few Majilarn raiders who were a seasonal problem like winter storms and summer droughts—and a part of the long tradition themselves, training-partners in their way for the youths of the High Harozh, trading-partners when it wasn't Raiders Moon.

There'd always been strains beneath the surface, people never fit neatly into boxes however strong the drive to push them in, but there was enough give in the system, especially in the unspoken but eternal struggle between the Marn and the Families, to allow an illusion of freedom to the majority of the Cadandri, faceless Family cousins and Nerodin alike, and the really unhappy could always go somewhere else.

The Dancer sought out those fault lines and played on them, working without words, setting dream on dream until dream became fact in the mind of the dreamer and the refusal of daylife to conform to the dream seemed a conspiracy of those with power to steal possibility and keep the dreamer crushed underfoot. That some of the conspiracy actually existed, that the Families maintained their power by deliberate limitations set on the Nerodin, nailed in place by law and custom, all that had nothing to do with the rage that simmered in those who lived on the lower rungs of the Cadandri Ladder.

Illusion had an emotional power that truth never reached to.

Clad in Treshtal's body, the Fetch danced on the altars of the House of Glory and spun chaos from illusion.

And life in Dander and Calanda grew darker and more dangerous as the days slid past.

> > < <

Husenkil recoiled as the stench rolled out of the shed. "Chert! Kosta, where's that cib root? Light it up so we can smoke the place and get in there without puking our innards out. Hinker, bring up the body bags." He frowned at the boy who'd brought them to the shed on the Steel Point wasteland, one of the growing packs of stray children running the streets. "Tomal, you did good. Here." He tossed the boy the copper medza that was the standard reward for such reports. "You better get on, this isn't going to be pretty."

The boy's dark brown eyes were as empty as a nixy's, with some of the same chill, alien quality. After a minute he shrugged and strolled off.

"Saa saaa, what we're coming to." Husenkil took the cib torch his deputy was waving through the crack and pushed the door open wider. Body fragments lay everywhere, blood was thick and stinking on the floor, on the far wall someone had written the glyphs for the word KAZIM, a word he'd seen before and knew with a sick feeling he'd see again. "Agh! This is the worst yet. Where's that lantern? Let's get busy."

It was hard to tell how many bodies were in the shed, the fragments were torn that small. As they slid the decomposing bits into the bags, they took a count of the feet they found and agreed in the end there were

two women and three children, impossible to tell
whether the children had been boys or girls. The worst
part of it were the teeth marks. When Hinker picked
up a small forearm and saw the curved red stigmata
embossed into the pale skin, he dropped it, rushed
outside, and emptied his stomach.

They loaded the bags onto a litter and took them
across the river to the Temple for cremation. There
was no chance of identifying the victims, just five more
Cadandri Nerodin gone lost in the stew that churned
through the cities.

> > < <

Zavidesht Pan Nov stood in an office in the attic of
one of his warehouses looking out a dormer window
at the river; his wharves weren't empty, but the activity he could see was an anemic ghost of what it had
been and very little of it was bringing him any profit;
most of those barges were packing in men, mounts and
supplies for the army, the rest unloading cargo to be
transferred to the Pevranamist storehouses, supplies
the Marn was bringing in through Tuku-kul, paying
for it with taxes she collected from the Families. He
held a small knife and was drawing the blade across
and across the sill, scoring the hard wood, breaking
loose splinters. Under his breath he cursed K'vestmilly
Vos, cycling the epithets repeatedly, monotonously. He
was losing money by the fistful, his plans were coming
apart in his hands, the Glory was ignoring him; the
cities were in ferment, ripe for anyone with the brains
and nerve to seize them. *Brains? Stupid! Depending
too much on other people to do things I should've taken
hold of myself. Prak, that's going to change. That bitch
is going to learn her place. Under my foot!*
He slipped the little knife back into the sleeve sheath

and crossed the room. He brushed his hands off, straightened his tunic, smoothed his short curly mustache, pulled the door open. "Rav, get in here." He seated himself behind the work table as a thin man slipped through the narrow opening and used his skinny flank to push the door shut.

"Yah, Pan?"

"First thing, what's the news from the Zem?"

"Vedouce's got the army dug in. 'S waiting for the gritz to get there. He got the best ground but 's outnumbered two to one and they got better guns, more 'xperience. 'S gonna be a bloody 'un, 's not a chet in th' cities willin' to take odds on who wins, even Telmas and he were bettin' on his ma's last breath."

"When?"

"Hard t' say. Two days, three. Less'n a week for sure."

"What's the Marn got on Sko?"

"Dunno. Word is old Marn left a notebook fulla dirt."

"Any chance we could get hold of that?"

"If you c'd figure a way to get hold a that maid of hers. Elsewise, none."

"Hmm. That's been tried before." He frowned, thumb smoothing along the right half of his mustache. "I've an idea about it, though, maybe. . . ." He waved a hand as if he brushed the thought away. "Ker's been hit hard, he won't be much in sight. With Vedouce gone, Pen's a bag of air, stick a pin in him, he'd . . . ah. Marazhney Treddek Osk. How much would it take to remove her?"

"Might be hard to get at her. Since the bomb in Osk House, she move to Pevranamist. Gettin' in's a poss, gettin' out not. An't no hod gonna risk his neck for no pile a coin. Not for no klent he don't know. If y' c'n dig 'er outta there, that's som'n else."

"Zdra, we leave that. Get hold of your spies in the Pevranamist, have 'em ready to move once I hook the maid. And start thinking how we can pry Treddek Osk loose." He got to his feet, walked round the table and set his hand on Ravach's shoulder. "When we're in, you can have Jestranos Oram to play with. And his job. You'd like that, mh?"

Scaly eyelids blinking, a small smile lifting the corners of his mouth, Ravach stared at him a moment, then he nodded. "I serve," he said.

"Zdra, I know. Before you do any of that other, find me the dancer Treshtal and bring him here. And keep it quiet."

The Dancer walked in and the room vibrated with his presence.

Zavidesht Pan Nov blinked, then a motion of his hand sent Ravach out the door, leaving the two of them alone. He folded his hands and glared at the Dancer. "You've been precious little use so far, for all your promises. Your whisperers either get laughed at or booted off and the Marn hasn't done a single thing you said she would."

"It's Heslin you should blame for that last." The Dancer's voice was so mild and low it was hard to hear what he said, though there was no meekness in him, no response to the implied threat in the Pan's voice.

"That fat fool?"

The Dancer shrugged. "I've told you. Believe it or not as you choose."

The color of his eyes had changed; they had been a light hazel, now they were yellow as egg yolks. He moved constantly, fingers twitching, shifting from foot to foot, shoulders swaying, head turning. Watching him made Zavidesht Pan Nov feel itchy and uncomfortable.

"Whatever," Zavidesht said. "It's time for something real from you. I want control of the Marn's maid Puzhee."

"Why?"

"It's my business."

"It's mine if you want my help."

"You're saying you can do it."

"I'm saying why should I?"

"You want the Marn gone?"

"As do we both. So?"

"I don't want your bombs, she's got those spojjin' bisracs around her all the time and getting at her that way has about as much hope as an icicle in a furnace. She's got something I want . . ." he hesitated, shrugged and went on, "a book her mother left her. If I can get that, I can use it to strip her support from her and when she's alone, that's it."

The Dancer flowed to the window; there was no other way to describe how he moved—as if he no longer had bones or flesh beneath his skin. He ran a finger across the scoring and for an instant the sill glowed, then was just wood again with peels of varnish coming loose. "How soon?" he said, his head turned so his profile was visible, with the enigmatic smile that made the Pan want to kick him.

"Yesterday." Zavidesht scowled. "What do you think, blec? As soon as you can do it. I want that book!"

"Tonight?"

"Good enough. Who's going to win the battle down South?"

"You. What else matters?"

"Explain."

"If the Govaritzers win, the Marn is gone." The Dancer moved away from the window, his hand trailing along the wall leaving faint glowing tracks like slug slime. "The Families will be looking for a strong leader to defend them; with the Glory behind you, you'll have the fighters to do it." The voice was soft, insinuating. "Even if the Govaritzers lose, there'll be so many of the Guard killed, the Marn won't have her army and with a little luck . . ." he turned to face the Pan, eyes empty, mouth still curved in that meaningless smile, ". . . or planning . . . Vedouce will go down, too; if you're ready, you can take her."

"Zdra, let's hope this prediction is more accurate than your others.

> > < <

The wharves were a swarm of noise, torchlight, voices, stamp, scrape, shuffle of hundreds of feet, fire-reddened faces moving in and out of shadow, light gleaming off longgun barrels, off the buttons and straps of uniforms, macain hooting, barrels rumbling. This was one of the last levies heading south to stand as reinforcements when the battle began.

One of the bargeveks looked around. "Eh, Poet! Thought you was dead."

Vyzharnos lifted the arm with the bandage, waved it back and forth, tapped the black patch over his bad eye. "Almost was. Give us a hand, Mouk, that barge is as good as any." He stepped aside, took Tingajil's arm and eased her up the planks onto the deck. " 'Lo, Pommer, you lookin' good. Torg. Akshee. Gonna play you some songs. 'S Tingajil here, you heard of her. Give us a boost up on the cabin roof, we'll use that as a stage."

Disregarding the danger and the commotion, with Zasya, Ildas, and Adlayr guarding her, torchlight gleaming on the ivory Mask, K'vestmilly Vos moved through the crowd, touching arms and shoulders,

speaking to the men, wishing them well, telling them
how important they were, guardians of Dander and
Calanda.

Tingajil sat, tuning her lute, waiting for the Marn to
finish; Vyzharnos stood behind her, the harp ready.

K'vestmilly Vos looked up as she reached the barge,
lifted a hand to them and passed on.

Cloak huddled around her, the hood pulled forward
to hide her face, Serroi stood at the mouth of an alley
between two warehouses, watching K'vestmilly Vos
and the lines of men moving onto the barges. The
Marn was worried about her, she knew that—Healer
confronted by mutilated soldiers to be pieced together
and thrown back to be torn up again. K'vestmilly didn't
see how she could endure that. She was so young, so
green—so sheltered. Memories came back of another
time, another war. When there was no choice, you did
what you had to. Healing the men would be exhaust-
ing, but it was necessary, she'd do it and the only thing
that really worried her was the uncertainty about what
else she'd be birthing onto this Land. Or calling into
it. She smiled despite her misgivings. Two hundred
years from now, maybe all this would be as distant
and unreal as the Son's War was to these people. *I
doubt I'll be round to see that happen. Two lives is
more than most get and three would be overdoing it
for sure.*

Tingajil and Vyzharnos started singing, a new song,
a song about a soldier going to war, saying farewell to
his lover, finding his young brother hidden on the
barge, a sentimental song that brought tears to the eyes,
set the men on the wharves to clapping in time with
the beat. When they finished, a man called out, "River
of Blood, sing River of Blood." More joined him, feet

stamping on the planks of the wharves, hands clapping.

Serroi sighed. That song was everywhere; she was getting desperately tired of it. Apparently it'd hit something very deep in the Cadandri soul, especially among the Nerodin, and worked to reseal the powerful link between the Marn and her people.

Camnor's idea, that. Heslin, Heslin, you remind me so much of Hern. Maiden Bless, how I miss him. I've got to get away. Camnor isn't Hern. Have to remember that. CAMNOR. ISN'T. HERN. But when I look at him, when I hear him talk, when I see him think, it's like Hern's there, inside him. . . .

She shook her head and moved away from the busy wharves, walking in the shadows on the Ladesman's Way, heading for a quiet place where she could sit and contemplate the river and the nixies. With the battle coming up and the flood of wounded she expected, she needed to come to terms with these dark children of hers.

The last wharf was smaller than the others, built round the turn of a shallow bend, so it angled away from the busier ones, the jut of the warehouse blocking her view of the barges when she looked over her shoulder a last time. "Good enough," she said aloud and settled on the end, leaning against a worn bitt, her feet dangling over the edge. *Come talk to me. You called me Mother, let me know my children.*

Behind her, round the edge of the warehouse, she heard small scrabbling sounds, probably from rats or the chinin packs that ran wild down this end of the Shipper's Quarter. She ignored them and fixed her eyes on the river flowing past, dark and silent with ripples of red and streaks of yellow from the distant torches, an almost full Nijilic TheDom scrolling lines of tar-

nished silver on water beyond the reach of the torchlight.

The water bulged around the pilings, heads formed,
facetted and shining, eyes deep in dark hollows.
Mother! It was a liquid shout crashing into her like
the surf she remembered from her days as a child on
the Sorceror's Isles; if she hadn't been clutching at the
bitt, it would've knocked her over. The wild gurgling
laughter that followed dismayed her; even Ser Noris
was less strange than these feral things.

*If you're my children, what is it we share? Tell me.
I need to know.*

We are you, Mother. We arrrreee. The dozens of
faces below shifted and in seconds she was looking at
replicas of herself. *We are your anger, your need and
your greed, the waterweeds of your soul.*

Nay! she cried, drew her legs up and shifted round
so she was kneeling, looking down at them, her hands
closed on the plank's edge. *I won't accept that, you're
more than weeds. Anger, yes, I see that, but let it be
your own. If you are my children, you are also your-
selves. Be free. If it means anything, I tell you be free.*

There was a gurgling wail from the nixies, they
crowded closer, crying *We are your children, don't
abandon us. Love us, Mother, love ussssss.*

Serroi shivered, closed her eyes. They knew in-
stantly what she'd tried not to see. What she called
freedom was a candy-coating on rejection, an attempt
to disown them for her own comfort's sake. Ashamed,
she stretched out on her stomach, reached down and
touched a hand straining up at her.

The nixy laughed wildly, wrapped its fingers about
her wrist and tried to pull her down. *Motherrrr,
commmme. . . .*

She could feel anguish, an emptiness that cried out
to be filled, and a equal need inside her responded.

The dryads had been lovely and loving and she'd grown
fond of them all. This was something else, this was
all her own anguish, all the sorrows of her life brought
to flesh . . . of a sort . . . this was danger and demand
. . . and . . . she didn't know what else. Despite her
lingering fears, though, that touch was a claiming, and
a link was forged between them. It would not be broken. They were still strange, these waterborn, most of
the time she wasn't going to like them much, or many
of the things they did, but love them she would. She
must. They were her children.

The fingers that clasped her wrist and tugged so
strongly at her turned warm and slid away. Another
hand came up to clasp hers, another, then another, on
and on till all the nixies were touched and warmed;
they went swimming off, playing and giggling—in their
dark way, momentarily at least, as joyfilled as the dryads.

She sat up, drained but happy, wondering if—after
all—the only thing she had to do was touch the Fetch
as she had touched Ser Noris. That had helped end
one war, would it help with this one?

More scraping sounds, footsteps behind her.

She tried to get up, hands closed on her arms, someone grabbed her hair through the hood of her cloak.
She couldn't move, she couldn't see who it was, they
lifted her off her feet, rushed her down the wharf toward the deep shadows at the end of the warehouse.
"Don't . . ." she cried, "let me go! I don't want to
. . . let me go!"

Feet stamped louder, the hands holding her shook
her and shook her, until her teeth jarred together and
she couldn't speak. And the chant began, hardly louder
than a whisper, but all around her, breathing over her:
Kazim, kazim, kazim. . . .

She didn't know the word, but the hunger, rage, and

greed in it terrified her—and the sense she got that all those hands belonged to one body, one soul. Terrified, she reached out and **TOOK.**

Her captors dropped around her.

She stumbled back a few steps and looked down, her head swimming, her stomach clenching.

There were three of them, two men and a woman, dressed in rough, dark brown robes with pointed cowls, and they were very dead.

Mother, Mother, give them to us. Give them, give them, give them give them. . . .

Serroi swung round.

The nixies were back, splashing vigorously, thrusting themselves up out of the water, bringing their arms up, long fingers writhing. *Mother, Mother, give them to us, give them, give them, give them to us.*

Why? What good would it do? Do you eat them?

Gurgling laughter. The nixies slapped at each other, submerged and came shooting up to curve over in a glinting arc and slide into the water again. *Nay nay, grooooosssss. They are shape, Mother. They teach us how to be. They are toys, Mother, we have fun with them until they come apart and then the bones are nice.*

Serroi shivered. She looked down at the dead. They weren't something she wanted to explain. "Why not?"

She dragged the bodies to the edge of the wharf and rolled them into the water. "Ei vai, my dark babies, enjoy." She wiped her hands on her skirt, let it fall. "This miserable war first, Fetch, then I'm coming for you."

> > < <

When he heard the steady pad of macai feet coming behind the rocky knoll where the navsta lay waiting for the gritz, Vykon eased his hand over Rhuzho's nose, pinching the nostrils slightly to warn the beast to silence.

Vedouce Pan rode up the slope and stopped his mount behind them. "Vudvek Severn," he said quietly and waited.

Vykon watched Severn uncoil and stand erect. He didn't salute. That wasn't the way of the High Harozh; only the Marn and their own Pan got more than the courtesy of equal to equal. "General," he said and waited.

Vedouce smiled grimly. "Harozh, all of you, you've done well and given much and I'm asking more. The gritz are moving already, they'll be here with the sun and here we have to say to them, this far and no further. Maiden Bless and keep you whole while you give them what they've earned." He grinned suddenly. "A boot in the balls and fire in the hole." He touched his hat, turned his macai and rode down the hill.

He knows us all, every spojjin' one, name and place. Vykon scratched in the folds on Rhuzho's face. It made a warm feeling in his gut. *Mad's Tits, we're gonna do 'em, we're gonna do 'em good.*

> > < <

Tingajil climbed the stairs in the Mid-Dander warren, Vyzharnos following close behind. When they reached it, the third floor was dark and quiet, with a single nightcandle burning near the head of the last flight.

Vyzharnos stopped her, his hand on her shoulder. "Are you sure, Jil? It's so late, they're probably asleep."

"Nik, Poet. No one's going to sleep tonight. Harez was in that levy. We have to be with Retezhry and her children.'' She moved the last few steps and knocked at the door.

"Who is it?'' The words were muffled and quavery.

"Tinga. Let us in.''

Vyata Vyloush opened the door, smiled determinedly at Vyzharnos. "Welcome,'' she murmured. "Maiden Bless.''

"I thank you, Matka.'' He took her hand, bent over it with graceful courtesy, eased her around as he pulled the door shut, then escorted her to her chair.

Tingajil hurried across the room to her older sister, hugged her, then knelt beside her. "Are you all right, Tezhry?''

"Did you see him, Tinga? How did he look?''

"I saw him. He was with Chetnery's brother and Doro and Hazal and oh, lots of folk we know. He'll be fine, Tezhry. They're backup, you know, just in case things go bad. Nothing like that's going to happen. Vedouce is a smart man. Didn't Zav tell you that? Shouldn't he know? He works at Steel Point.''

Halinny's eyes were red, her young face drawn, she was forcing a smile to reassure her mother and her grandmother. "Sing for us, Tinga. Not something sweet or silly.'' She looked suddenly fierce, her fingers tightening on her mother's shoulder, hard enough to make Retezhry wince. "Sing 'River of Blood' for us. So we can remember what it's for that my father had to go.''

> > < <

K'vestmilly Marnhidda Vos paced back and forth across the room, the highest chamber in the Marn's Tower, the Room with Nine Windows, moving round the wide bed that took up most of the middle section,

running her hands through her wild red hair until it
stood out in a tangled halo about her face. All the
lamps were lit, glass and silver lamps with huge round
reservoirs, enough oil in them to last the whole night.

It was tradition. In times of trouble, the Marn
Watched from the Tower, so Rodin and Nerodin could
look from their windows and see the light in the tower
and feel protected.

The knock she'd been waiting for came. She closed
her eyes briefly, closed her hands into fists. *Maiden
bless and help me.* She let out the breath she'd been
holding, crossed to the door and opened it. "Thank
you, Adlayr. Come back just before dawn, will you?"

He nodded and turned away, his bare feet soundless
on the stones.

"Come in, Camnor Heslin, sit and talk to me. And
thank you for coming."

He looked around, crossed to a bench beside the
window and settled himself on it, leaning forward, his
hands on his knees. "It's tomorrow?"

"Vedouce says around sunrise." She glanced at the
Mask lying on the table by the bed; for the first time
she missed its comfortable concealment. "He didn't
say how long before we'd know the outcome."

"Hern's journals said the Sons' War lasted for
weeks, the hot part of it. Of course there were more
fighters involved on both sides and the Biserica had
the Wall to help with their defense."

"Ah!" She turned and strode to the window, stood
staring out over the cities without seeing anything,
even her own reflection. "How can we . . . Maiden
Bless, Heslin, how can we endure anything like that?"

"Don't jump, K'milly. You're fighting yourself
again."

"I HATE waiting. I LOATHE waiting." She swung
round, began pacing with short agitated steps, back

and forth, back and forth, wringing her hands. "Waiting . . . you feel so helpless . . . MY people, MINE, Heslin . . . when they die, I die . . . a little. . . ."

He left the couch, took hold of her shoulders, and shook her lightly, then pulled her against his massive chest and held her till the shaking stopped.

She pulled away, went back to the window. "Sit down, please, Heslin. And don't look at me."

"Ei vai." There was a hint of amusement in his voice.

She looked over her shoulder, frowning, annoyed and warmed at the same time by the twinkle in his dark blue eyes. She turned her head back and once again stared at the window. "I . . . do you know about the Marn . . . nik, don't answer, not yet . . . I know you understand the constraints I'm . . . the Marn has one freedom, she can choose her consorts without interference . . . it's a private decision . . . who fathers . . . fathers her children . . . one man or a dozen . . . the sons . . . they go to the man . . . men . . . that's important . . . a Marn's got to know she can trust. . . ." She leaned forward, rested her brow against the cool glass. "It's time. I can't wait longer. Love me, Heslin. Give me a child."

K'vestmilly slipped from the bed and stood looking down at the sleeping man. *Each time we meet, you surprise me, Camnor Heslin.* She stretched, deliciously tired, so relaxed a touch would send her into a puddle of goo, smiled fondly at Heslin, then slouched across the room to kneel on a couch, her elbows on the windowsill, staring out at cities where there were many others waking and waiting; there were lighted windows dotted all over the dark masses of Dander and Calanda.

"We Watch together." Her breath made a small

round patch of fog on the glass; she wiped it away,
looked down at her hands. She'd coveted Heslin's sharp
mind, wanted it for her daughter, though she hadn't
found his body exciting, nothing like the ache she felt
whenever she looked at Vyzharnos. She was fond
enough of him to expect a pleasant experience, but no
passion. Now she was confused. Heslin had found
things in her she'd never known were there. What was
love anyway?

She left the bench and went to look at him again, to
draw her fingertip down his long nose and along the
curve of his mouth without actually touching him. Very
gently, so she wouldn't wake him, she smoothed the
soft soft black hair back from his brow, murmured,
''You cunning man, what else are you hiding beneath
that fat?'' She laughed softly, went round the end of
the bed and crawled beneath the covers again, snuggling against him, drawing comfort from the soft
yielding warmth of his flesh.

> > < <

The Fetch stalked back and forth, flesh melting,
snatched back to cover the bone when the
exposure went too far. When it spoke, there was
agitation in the voice, a growing stridency and
anger. ''You acknowledge THEM,'' it flung at
Serroi, ''those clowns, those gobbets of filthy
water, you acknowledge them, why do you
scorn me?

23. Battle

Vykon felt them before he saw them, a vibration in the earth pressed against his sternum; a cloud of dust and smoke mixed with the low lying morning fog and it was several minutes before the front riders took shape.

They came in half a dozen columns, riding five abreast, the columns staggered from the point riders, like a huge lance-head, the supply wagons tucked in between the tang-columns—reduced from ten to four with captured draft vul from Bezhval farms added to the hitches ahead of the orsks that the raid had left alive. The gritz had tried sending out scouts again, relying on stealth to get them past the Guard watch, but the Mys spotters were tracking them with long-glasses and when they saw men riding off, they used their coms to give numbers and descriptions of the would-be scouts. The scouts met lethal Harozhni whips and didn't get back to the gritz army.

The army came rolling on, nervous and alert, but moving blind, with no idea where the Guard was or what lay ahead of them.

Vykon lay with his navsta on the rocky knoll to one side of the path of the approaching army, the wind hitting the side of his face. *Even the wind fights for us. Quiet, Rhuzho, not much longer, it's a trap, old son, look at the notneys ridin' like they own the earth, stick your spojjin' noses in just a little farther. . . .*

A horn sounded.

Vykon slid his longgun forward, balancing the barrel on the low barricade of rocks he'd built in front of his post and covered with dirt; he squeezed the trigger, shouted his brother's name as he saw a gritz fall, then began shooting steadily.

> > < <

"Puzhee?"

The big woman was on her knees, rocking back and forth, her eyes wild, her face working.

K'vestmilly started to touch her shoulder, snatched her hand back, and ran from the room.

She caught her breath, opened the door. "Adlayr, send the hall guard for Oram, quick, I need him. Wait a minute . . ." she rubbed her fingers over the furrow between her brows. "Is Honeydew around?"

Adlayr stared at the corridor's ceiling a moment. "She's coming. It'll take a while, she was in Treshteny's garden. Is time important?"

"I don't know, but I want her as fast as she can get here." She touched the Mask, grimaced behind it, but left it in place. "I think someone's got at Puzhee."

"How?"

"Good question."

Jestranos Oram clasped his hands behind him and scowled at the rocking woman. "According to the gateguard, she went out midafternoon. Down to Dander. No one knows where. It's close to hopeless trying to find out with that swarm in the streets, but I've put Zep on it. If there's any way, he'll nose it out."

Honeydew fluttered in from the bedroom, the mosquito buzz of her voice drilling through Oram's deeper tones; she landed on Adlayr's shoulder and he translated.

"Honey says there's no boom about the place, not in the gardens or anywhere, so that's not why."

"Then what. . . . Wait here." K'vestmilly hurried into the bedroom, shutting the door behind her. She was back a moment later, the Mask gone, her mouth compressed into a thin line.

Oram took a step toward her, stopped when she shook her head.

She stood a moment with her eyes closed, then moved quietly around Puzhee, knelt in front of her.

"Dama, nik."

"Quiet, Oram. Puzhee, Puzhee . . ." She crooned the name several times more without getting any response. "Not to worry, little mother, it's no problem, no one's going to ask you any questions, you didn't do anything wrong, not a thing, nothing. I'm going to stand up, I want you to stand with me. I'm not going to touch you. No one's going to touch you. Stand up, little mother, I've got a job for you. I neeeed you to do something for me." She got slowly to her feet and stood waiting.

Puzhee stopped rocking. Eyes still eerily blank, a line of drool dripping from the corner of her mouth, she got slowly to her feet.

K'vestmilly fluttered her hands, encouraging the maid without touching her. "That's good. That's right. Now, I want you to go to Bozhka Sekan and tell her she's to let you see the woman Treshteny. I want you to watch that woman and see everything she does until it gets dark. Bozhka Sekan is to give you a bed and you can do the same thing tomorrow." She waited, tense, then relaxed as Puzhee blinked, then shook out her skirt, smoothed her apron, resettled her hair bands. The maid dipped a curtsey, walked toward the door, her face reassembling itself as she moved. By the time she walked through the door, she seemed almost as usual.

As the door clicked shut, K'vestmilly let out the

breath she'd been holding, blinked angrily as tears of relief gathered in her eyes. "Puzhee! Even her." She passed her hand over her face. "Adlayr, get to Bozhka Sekan, tell her about no questions, no touching, she'll know why; stay there until you're sure Puzhee's not going to hurt anyone."

Oram scratched at his beard. "So?"

"Simple. Someone wanted mother's diary. They got it." She dropped onto the daybed, lay against the raised back. "Maiden Bless! Something else to cope with. I know you're handicapped with so many men sent south, but this could be a break. It's the Enemy did this to Puzhee, but it's a Pan who wants that book. Someone has found himself an ally. The moment you get a hint of who's moving, take him. If you need written authorization, you've got it."

She watched him leave, then swung her feet up and lay back, eyes closed, exhaustion like weights piled on her body.

> > < <

Vykon emptied his longgun into the line of gritz charging at the knoll, heard Hurbay spacing his shots as he slapped in another clip, reminded again that it should have been Nariz, but Nariz was dead, the memory cold air on a rotten tooth.

This was the third charge they'd faced since dawn and their stocks of ammunition were getting low. *Spojjin' gritz still coming on, they going to roll over us this time if there was only a dozen left of them.*

Grunt as a gritz bullet creased his leg, another clipped a hank of hair before he got behind the daub trunk. He dug into his pouch, found some loose cartridges, plugged them into the clip and shoved them home. While Hurbay reloaded he was shooting again, rage cold and hard in his belly. No time for real aiming, but the gritz were so close by now, six shots gave him six hits . . . then he was on his feet, swinging the butt of his longgun into the jaw of a macai, taking a shot in the shoulder, not even feeling it in his fury, his drive to get his hands on a gritz.

He woke on a canvas cot in a ragged line of other cots, his head burning, his shoulder an agony that pulsed with every breath he drew. He groaned, then sank his teeth in his lip and swallowed a second groan, closed his eyes so he could hold everything inside.

A few moments later, he felt a warmth and the pain began to diminish. Startled, he opened his eyes. A small woman in white was bending over the cot next to his, a faint green glow leaking around her sides. She straightened, turned; her eyes had a distant look, a green spot between her brows was throbbing, her hands were transparent green lamps. She set them on his body; the glow spread over him. He stopped thinking, stopped feeling.

When he was aware again, she'd moved on, was already two beds down.

The burn was gone, the pain was gone. Cautiously he moved his shoulder. Nothing. He sat up, touched the wound on his head. The skin was smooth; he knew it was the right place because the hair was gone in a long groove. "Spros!"

Hurbay was in the cot next over. He yawned, blinked, looking startled. He pushed up. "Vyk, wha' happ'n?"

"Dunno. You see Sev round? We turn 'em back?"

"Dunno." Hurbay swung his legs over the edge of the cot, got to his feet. He stretched, felt at his body, stamped his left foot. "Choo! She somethin' that Healer."

"Zdra, let's hit camp. I'm hungry. And I want to know what'n zhag happened."

> > < <

The Tradurad's windowdoors were open, shadows of javory leaves dancing across the walls and floor, across Adlayr leaning against the wall, his longgun propped against his thigh, across the Marn's work table and the two women sitting there listening to Hedivy's voice coming through the com. Honeydew knelt beside K'vestmilly's pad reading what was written there. On the trip north Adlayr and Zasya had taught her how to read and make letters and everything written and printed fascinated her.

". . . hit us hard, but we held the lines against them. Vedouce set up half a dozen navstas as rovers with coms and sent them where the spotters were telling him there was a threat the gritz would come breaking through, a problem here and a problem there, but it mostly worked."

Marazhney Osk was a tall, lean woman with an abundance of grey-streaked black hair and large blue eyes; she'd been beautiful as a young bride, though rather shy and abrupt in her speech, the daughter of a wealthy Nerodin merchant who'd bought her one of the Osk cousins for a husband so her children, his grandchildren, would be Rodin. All that was a long time ago. She wasn't shy these days; though she had the same brusqueness of manner, it came from impatience and an unwillingness to tolerate fools, among whom she'd classed K'vestmilly Vos, afraid the Marn was going to foist an empty-headed kapkit on them. She'd changed her mind about K'vestmilly, though she was still not overly fond of her.

"The gritz did make one breakthrough, but after a

good hard fight, we cut 'em down and we pushed 'em back. Gritz went to lick their wounds; they were cut up pretty zhaggin bad. We are better off with a lot of wounded and not many dead, thanks to the Healer.''

Marazhney Osk tapped her fingers on the table, nodded with satisfaction. ''Vedouce was a good choice, Marn.''

K'vestmilly poked the end of the stylo beneath the Mask, scratched at her cheek, smiling at the grudging approval in the Treddek's voice. She eased Honeydew aside, made a note, touched the speaker button. ''Hev, any judgment about the outcome? Go.''

''Zdra, given they lost a pile of men this morning, there are still more of them than us. Vedouce is wearing them down, holding them till their supplies run low, so he won't attack for another day or so.''

K'vestmilly noted that, smiled again as she watched the sprite wriggle round so she could see what was written on the pad.

''The way he has things set up here, we can keep turning them back, unless they spring something we don't expect. Which I do not expect. The gritz, they're cursed with a crazy man running them, Takuboure is worse than a koch in heat, he has his fingers everywhere, it was him who kept the attack going after any fool could see it was a cause long lost. Spotters say it cost him an extra hundred dead, more than that in wounded. Gritz they can't move without us knowing, the coms make a big difference. It is going to take a while, though, maybe another week. . . .''

The door slammed open, the Pan Nov strode into the room, followed by Pans Sko, Ker and Ano, with Bar hanging behind, looking frightened. Honeydew flitted from the desk, huddled behind the top folds of the drapes hanging beside the windowdoors that led into one of the Pevranamist's many gardens.

Adlayr left the wall; he didn't seem to move fast but he was at K'vestmilly's side with the longgun up and pointing at Pan Nov before the delegation was completely in the room. K'vestmilly tapped the send switch on the com, started to slide it off the table onto her lap.

"Nik, Marn, hands on the table where they were. We'll all be happier that way." Nov turned to Adlayr. "Put the gun down, gyes, or the Marn will have your brains in her lap."

Marazhney Osk was facing the window. She went stiff, her hands clenching into fists.

K'vestmilly glanced over her shoulder. "Stand easy, gyes. For now."

Ravach slithered in through the windowdoor, hand-gun aimed at Adlayr's head. He reached a skinny arm around Adlayr, took the longgun and sidled around the table to stand beside Pan Nov.

Armed men were filing through the door behind the Pans; they lined up against the wall, guns out and ready.

Nov snapped his fingers. One of the guards came forward, holding something wrapped in cloth. He set it on the worktable.

"A present for you, Marn." Nov smiled, rubbed his finger over the dark curls of his moustache. "Un-wrap it, why don't you. Now."

K'vestmilly ignored him and scanned the faces of the other Pans. Ker watched her with a feral intent-ness, the rage in him so strong she could almost smell it. A tic twitched beside Ano's eye and he wouldn't look at her, though he wasn't as uneasy and shrinking as Bar. Sko was pale, staring at the wall behind her. *That's why the book went. Chert! Why didn't Oram. . . .*

"Your present, Marn. Peel it."

She looked at the unappetizing bundle, grateful

again for the concealment the Mask offered. *Mother, keep me strong. . . .*

It was Oram's head inside the cloths, mouth open, eyes wide in horror.

She folded the strips of cloth back around it, contempt in her voice when she spoke. "Only a man without honor would so dishonor the dead. Why?"

"Because you're weak and a fool, like your mother before you. If the Marn had crushed those gritz when they started getting resty, none of this would've happened. We're going to make sure it doesn't happen again. We're going to level Govaritil, plow salt into the ground and any gritz left alive after we're finished will spend the rest of their miserable lives in bond, paying for the damage they've caused."

"Slaves. Hmm, so you're a slaver now, Nov. I can't say I'm surprised, having seen your warrens."

Ker pushed forward. "Prisonerss, not sslavess. O Belovéd Leader, you're a fool. All thiss'ss going out to zhag knowss who." He hooked the com unit to him, crashed it down on the desk and swept the fragments off the table. "Get on with it, the way we planned." He moved past Nov and took his place beside Ano.

"He's right," Nov said briskly. "Enough talking. The Mask." He held out his hand. "You don't want to make me take it."

K'vestmilly pushed the chair back, stood. She looked at the blood on her hands, Oram's blood. "Nik," she said. "You'll have to lay your murderer's hands on it if you want it, Pan Nov. You will have to lay your hands on it and strip it from me. I am Marn by oath and anointing. You may strip me, rape me, beat me, even kill me, but you can't change that. I will not be your accomplice in dishonor."

She watched the blood purple his face and knew he

wanted to do all those things, but he needed those other Pans and even Ker wouldn't follow him that far.

"Prak," he said. "We'll see. Ravach, do it."

The skinny man moved with angular swiftness behind Pan Nov, snatching a cushion from one of the chairs; the cushion came up, slapped against Marazhney Osk's head, the shot that followed was muffled—an absurdly small sound. Marazhney looked startled, fell over onto the table, a narrow trickle of blood oozing from the small hole above her ear.

K'vestmilly swallowed; her mother's death had been horrible, but in a way, not so horrible as this. A bomb was a mechanical thing; you couldn't blame a bomb for exploding, it'd be like blaming a cloud for moving between you and the sun. This was a man—or supposed to be—killing with less feeling than a viper striking.

Nov stroked his mustache. "Still not going to give me the Mask?"

"Nik."

"Ravach."

Ravach lifted the cushion, shook it out, circled behind her to stand beside Adlayr. "On y' knees."

Adlayr looked at him, then at K'vestmilly. "You had it right, Marn. No honor in this whole stinkin' lot. You, rat, you want to shoot me? Reach." He began unbuttoning his tunic, moving slowly so he wouldn't startle anyone into acting before he was ready.

Ker intervened again. "Nik! The Biserica can shut too many doors."

Nov's blue eyes turned slatey, but he held onto his temper. "The Biserica's a long way off."

"Yess, but there are otherss of that sspawn closse by. We'll do thiss like we planned, Nov, or I'm out now."

Nov shrugged. "Prak, like we planned. Marn. . . ."

Her stomach knotted again at the contempt in his voice, her knees shook; she stared at him, saying nothing—because there was nothing to say, because she didn't trust her voice.

"We're going to lock you and this oslak of yours in the Marn's Tower. When you're hungry and thirsty enough, I figure you'll be ready to cooperate. Look out the window in an hour or so, I'll have another little treat for you. Oh, yes, take your present with you. Don't be ungrateful, girl."

> > < <

"Spider six to base."

"Base here. Go."

"Force about two hundred moving out, trying to sneak, looks like, heading direct east, moving fast and quiet, speed about half a stade an hour. Go."

"Got it. We'll douse their ambitions. Out."

Vedouce made a few notes on his map, frowned at it a moment, beckoned to one of his runners. "Stin, I want the trivuds Throdal, Drit, and Frohat, and that Zemmer guide Tulom. Go."

Before the boy left the pavilion, Vedouce'd reached for the measuring stick and was ruling off a fan-shaped area on the map.

"Tulom, take a look at this. We've got two hundred riders coming north somewhere in this area, passing between the villages of Unava and Podsu. Where's the best place to stop them?"

Tulom was a small, shy man, vanishing into a healthy crop of gray-streaked brown face hair. He glanced at the map, came round the table, Vedouce making a place for him. "That there's Unava?"

"Yes."

"Zdra, zdra." Tulom drew a chalky fingernail in intersecting curves above the dot that represented the village. "There's these couple rock croppeys riz up here, maybe fifty foot the highest point, good f'r nothing but snakes. They burn 'em off to chase the snakes out. Been a couple years since they did it last, should be a sizable stand a brush by now. Land's poor round there, not much water, mostly grazing. Easy ridin', though. Over here . . ." he slid his nail down a hair farther. "Orchards, sliv, broshk, jab'l. Wouldn't be fast gettin' through there, but y' could make it. Here, vineyard, lotsa wire, posts. Bad ground for chargin'. Prob'ly give it a miss, I would, 'f I wanted to make time."

"If you had a local guide to give you the lay and you wanted to circle round so you could come on us from behind, with a good likelihood you wouldn't be seen, how would you do it?"

"I'd come round the far side of Unava, so . . ." He took the pencil Vedouce handed him, held it awkwardly and drew a shaky line around the dot and continued outside the fan that Vedouce had ruled in. "Go past the croppeys, so. Keepin' an eye on them and stayin' as near outta shootin' range as I could. Come round this way, all pasture here, hills, some ravines, but none of 'em big enough to bother. Ano's Plantings here, daub, javory, cherdva, some fancy woods the Ano 'fore last brought up from the Zemilsud and got to grow here, plenty a cover. I'd keep on north till I was sure we'd got past Guard lines, then I'd cut across here, more orchards, but they'd give enough cover to fool the longglasses. And there y' be." He finished the line at the camp.

"As easy as that."

"Not so spojjin' easy, it's a good day'n 'af ride,

comin' that way, but 'f y' got the men and the time. . . ."

"Prak." He sat back in his chair. "Trivuds. Any comments?"

Throdal looked at the others, then spoke, "The Plantings. They'll be watching the croppeys, that's too obvious an ambush, and they'll relax a little once they're past that and the village. On top of that, they'll be tired, take 'em all day to get that far. Closer to us, we'll be there first and rested. No too close either, so if any gets by us, you'd have time to be ready for 'em."

Frohat scowled. "Any way to check if they're really coming at us or just a decoy to draw us down?"

Drit chuckled. "Gloom and Doom at it again." He sobered. "He's got a point, General. I don't see how we can ignore that lot, but sending us, that'll make some sorta dent here, what if they just turn round and the whole lot of 'em come at us again?"

Throdal cleared his throat. "That's why the Planting ambush's best, it's only a few hours' ride. We take a com and if it's a fake, we head back, turn their trick on them, and hit 'em from behind."

Vedouce leaned forward, his mild brown eyes twinkling. "Prak. So I'm a brilliant general. Do you know what that means, my friends? I'm smart enough to steal from the best. Listen, this is what I want you to do. . . ."

"Spider seven to base."

"Base here. Go."

"There's a string of barges coming upriver. Want three guesses why? Go."

"How far? Go."

"Can see sails of three barges for sure, maybe another behind them, first hull's just coming in view. Half a day off maybe. Go."

"Keep 'n eye on them, Seven, let us know zemzem they head for shore. Out."

Vedouce scanned the lined leathery faces of the bargeveks, nodded with satisfaction. "Pommer, Torg, good to see you. And your name is?"

"Akshee. And this is Jerst 'n Kouss."

Vedouce nodded at them, clasped his hands over his solid belly. "Gritz has a line of supply barges coming north. Seven says maybe four, maybe more, half a day south. Think you could take 'em, bring them to us instead?"

"What we got to work with?"

"Your pick of the boats and barges unloading now. A navsta of Harozhni sharpshooters."

"Two boats, six more bargeveks to sail the prizes back, let us pick 'em. For boardin' and seizin', Harozhni who know somethin' about boats, cull the rest. Coming back, one boat to follow, one to lead, with the Harozhni shooters keepin' heads down on shore."

Vedouce nodded, scrawled a few lines on a bit of paper. "You handle it, Pommer. Show that where you have to. Sooner you do it, the better I'll like it, hmm?"

Hedivy blinked as the receive-signal cut a word in half; he shrugged, made the switch, and waited. There was a loud crash, then a voice he recognized. Pan Nov. *Marn, hands on the table where they were. We'll all be happier that way. Put the gun down, gyes, or the Marn will have your brains in her lap.*

He scooped up the com, ran from the tent, heading for the General's pavilion, swearing under his breath as he listened to the exchange that followed.

24. Ploy and Counterploy

> *Far to the south Serroi moved between the beds*
> *of the wounded, touching, healing—and the*
> *overflow from the forces flowing through her*
> *spread out and out, filling Cadander and*
> *changing the land. . . .*

"Oh." Treshteny sat bolt upright, then she tilted forward, rolling gently off the bench to lay with her face in the gravel, her body twitching slightly.

The nurse ran round the bench, knelt beside her, checked her pulse, then trotted from the garden to call Bozhka Sekan.

A green shimmer oozed from Treshteny's body and took shape as a baby fawn who nestled in the curve of her arm, translucent as stained glass, warm and vigorous with the life she'd given him. Overhead, the overflow of Serroi's healing spread even to patches of light; these found shape as golden ariels with shimmers for speech. And all around tiny mouselets were born of shadow and scampered away to find shelter among the roots and branches.

Treshteny got to her feet, brushed off her face and the front of her dress. She smiled fondly at the faun dancing by her knee, his curly horns glinting like glass in the sunlight. He pointed at the wooden screen. She squinted to shut out the more peripheral of the maybe-ghosts, nodded and followed him to the door into the Hospital.

As she'd expected, it was locked; Bozhka Sekan and the Marn had arranged that to be sure curious idiots didn't come to disturb her. The faun danced impatiently, slapped at her leg and lifted his hands so she'd pick him up. When he was sitting on her arm, he leaned impatiently toward the door, kicked at her to get her to move closer. He slammed a horn against the lock and the door flew open.

Treshteny giggled. She bent, set the faun down, followed him as he clicked importantly along.

At first the hall was empty, not even nurses hurrying along with their trays and their brooms, then Treshteny heard voices, footsteps; the faun darted into the nearest room. She followed him and pushed the door closed until only a fingerwidth of space remained; through the narrow opening she watched the manifold Bozhka Sekan go rushing past, the manifold nurse beside her.

The faun darted out again, went hurrying down the corridor. Treshteny followed, tears dripping disregarded down her face and onto her blouse. In all the maybes she'd seen in her premoaning fit, Bozhka Sekan died, sometimes swiftly, sometimes in great pain, and there was no way she could see to stop it.

She left the hospital and walked down the long slope into Dander, eyes watching her from trees and under piles of leaves, ariels flitting by overhead. The earth seemed to bubble with new sorts of folk who came to greet her as she passed.

In the city a wall developed lips and blew her a kiss. She waved and walked placidly past, forcing her way through the maybe-ghosts swirling thick as soup about her. At any other time the chaos would have sent her curling into a ball, but the bright green faun trotted steadily along ahead of her, its single thread a steady-

ing clew that kept her on course so she didn't have to
worry about what was *NOW* and what was not.

She could feel a faint throb coming up through the
walk, vibrating against the soles of her bare feet; it
was a sickening thing, part of the evil that'd filled her
fit. It was also part of the purpose that drove her.

She passed through one of the entrances to the Mid-
Dander warren, climbed to the third floor.

The man who opened the door was tall and lean with
a bandage on his right arm and a patch over his left
eye; he held a stylo and there were smears of ink on
his fingers and alongside his nose. "Yes?" He frowned
at her. "Do I know you?"

"I am Mad Treshteny. May we come in?"

"We?" He looked past her, saw no one, shrugged,
and pulled the door wider. "I didn't know you left the
hospital. Tinga, is there any tea left?"

Treshteny walked in, settled on a chair, and smiled
at the blonde young woman who handed her a cup and
saucer. "I thank you, Tingajil. You will either die tomorrow or marry twice and have a granddaughter who
will be Marn."

"Oh." Tingajil blinked. "You interest me. How am
I supposed to die tomorrow?"

"Men will come looking for you. You will hide and
be betrayed by your sister. They will slit your throat
and throw you into the river. You are dangerous. 'River
of Blood' has got too great a hold on Nerodin hearts."

Tingajil blinked, one slim hand coming up to stroke
her throat. "And how do I avoid the knife?"

"You leave now, within the hour, and go to Oskland, OskHold. Take only what you can carry yourself
and plan for a long stay. You tell no one, not your
mother nor your father, and especially not your sister,
that you are leaving."

"Treshteny the Mad."

"That is me." She bent down, stroked the soft curls between the little faun's horns. "And . . ." she bent closer, listened, smiled, straightened. "This is Yela'o. He's a faun and just born. We're gong to Oskland, too."

Tingajil blinked again, glanced at Vyzharnos who was watching the madwoman with intense concentration, then she flung her hand out, impatience in the gesture and in her voice when she spoke. "Why would my sister do such a thing?"

"She has been touched and taken by the Fetch, the Enemy, Mother Death." Treshteny turned to Vyzharnos. "Your father is dead, Poet. They took his head and showed it to the Marn. It was a present. They're shooting her father right now. You probably thought he was long ago dead, but he wasn't, not till now. They think they've closed their hands tight about the Marn, but they haven't."

"What do you read for her?"

"I may not say that. The words are in my head, but they will not come to my tongue."

"Why did you come here? Why warn us and not others?"

"You are the father of the son Tingajil carries in her womb. He will wed the daughter the Marn carries, their child will be Marn if this fate comes to be."

"Tinga!"

"I'm not . . . I don't know . . . why do you believe her?"

"My fath . . . father and the last Marn did and neither of them w . . . were naive or gullible. Who's this Fetch? Who's Mother Death?"

"I may not say that. I know and do not know. There is pain. I do not want to know." She got to her feet. "I must go, the killing will begin soon." She stared past them as the wall unfolded before her and she

SAW. "Yes. Yes. Yes." Her smile widened. "It is good. Tingajil will not die now."

The baby faun had been titupping about the room; he rushed past her and danced impatiently before the door.

"I'm coming, Yela'o, I know, time is."

Leaving a taut silence behind her, she went down the stairs and passed out into the street and the bewildering confusion there.

When she reached the Bridge, it was several moments before she could argue herself into stepping on what seemed little more than mist; the span was there and not there, the past short, the future shorter. Yela'o had to dig his horns into her leg until it bled before he could get her to move.

Her stomach calmed a little as the planks stayed solid under foot no matter how they looked, but by the time she reached the Calanda bank her nausea was so strong she had to sit on the ground with her eyes closed until she had enough control of herself to go on.

The faun crawled into her lap and nestled against her, crooning to her. She remembered Serroi cuddling the dryadita and smiled with satisfaction; now she, too, had a baby, he was hers to cherish.

When she was able, she began walking east along the Mine Road.

> > < <

"Spider six to base."

"Base here. Go."

"Gritz starting to shift, lots of in and out the big tent. Saddling up. Think they gettin' ready to hit. Go."

"I'll tell him. Report every ten minutes. Break in with anything that looks urgent. Out." The Aide got to his feet, clapped his hand on his companion's shoulder. "Watch my com, I got to see the General."

Vedouce sat hunched over, listening as Hedivy finished.

". . . no names except the one, Nov. I am sure indeed that was Pan Nov, I know him from way way back; the one who smashed the com, that might be Ker. He's had time to get there even if he had to cut round the gritz and the way those esses whistled . . ." He shrugged.

Vedouce tapped a broad thumb on the map. "She'll be alive, they don't dare kill her, not till she's declared an heir." He looked up, eyes bleak, white spots by his nose. "They'll be purging the Families. They wouldn't go after the Marn before they'd got Oram. I . . ."

The Aide came in, glanced at Hedivy, advanced to the table. "Report from Mys one, tuhl General. Gritz're stirring, Mys thinks they're getting ready for another attack."

"Just stirring?"

"Not mounted up yet, but they're saddling."

"Oskliveh!" Vedouce stood. "Prak. Thanks, Stoppa. Bring me the reports as they come in." As soon as the Aide was out, he turned to Hedivy. "I can't give you any men," he said, "not even your own agents. I need them as spotters. You'll have to make do with any of Oram's men who escaped the knife." He found a scrap of paper, scrawled some words on it, and signed it. "Anything that floats, you can have that and the bargeveks to sail it."

> > < <

Honeydew fluttered through the window and landed on the table beside Camnor Heslin, her wings drooping with exhaustion, her body trembling.

"Trouble, Honey?" He found a small pencil and a pad, pushed it towards her, read over her shoulder as she managed shaky letters, cutting the words to the bare minimum. "N-o-v Nov. S-h-o-t shot. M-a-r-a-zh—Nov shot Marazhney? Murd! The Marn? P-r-i-s prisoner. Where? M-a-r-n T-o-w Marn's Tower. A-d-l Adlayr p-r he's a prisoner, too? Then he's alive. At least that's something. Nov and who else? K Ker, A-n Ano, S-k Sko, B-a Bar. That's all? G-u-a not the Marn's Guard? N-o-v Ah, Nov's thugs. What about Oram, why . . . ah d-e-a dead. N-o-v g-v h-e-a-d t-o M. You rest a minute here, Honeydew." He yanked on a bellpull. "We'll have to do something about that."

"Tomcey, I need messengers. Jemny and Zakus. Dressed in their off-duty clothes. Send the rest of the servants home, tell them to keep their heads down, there's trouble coming and this's going to be a hotspot."

The Domcevek was a tall lanky man with gray eyes so pale they seemed blind; he glanced at the huddled sprite, nodded. "We've heard talk, tuhl Heslin. Some of it against foreigners. There's several who'd stay if you asked."

"I thank you for that, Tomcey, but best not. I'm going to ground myself. It'll be easier for all—and most certainly not lack of trust—if you and the others don't know where."

"Zdra zdra, take care, tuhl Heslin." He bowed and left.

"A good man, Honeydew, caught in a bad time." Heslin opened a drawer of the file at the left end of the worktable, took out two shortguns, loaded them and set them on the table, and began writing.

He'd just finished the second note when the Dom-cevek returned carrying a tray with a pile of sand-wiches, some of them cut very small, a steaming cha pot and cups; the two men followed close behind him. He set the tray on the table and left without speaking.

Jemny looked at the shortguns. "You think it's go-ing to be that bad, tuhl Heslin?"

Heslin folded the second note, set both of them in front of him and put a gun on each. "I'll tell you what this's about. Pan Nov, with the backing of Ker, Ano and Bar, has already taken the Pevranamist, made the Marn prisoner, killed Jestranos Oram. What I'd like you to do is take these notes to Pen House and Osk House. Maybe it's too late already, but there's a chance, those notneys could have wanted to secure the Pevranamist before they went after smaller targets. And this is a favor I'm asking you, not an order."

Zakus sniffed, picked up the gun and the note, tucked them in his shirt. He touched a finger to a brow, turned, and strode out.

Jemny grinned. "Me, too," he said and followed his friend.

> > < <

K'vestmilly Vos paced restlessly, moving round the end of the big bed and back to the window, glancing repeatedly at the heavy Nerodin woman sitting in the chair by the door. She'd stopped looking out the win-dow, it made her sick to see the bodies scattered about the courts and gardens, loyal servants and the boy guards. Adlayr was seated on the floor with his back set against the wall; his eyes were closed, his face placid. She frowned at him, wondering about Zasya. The meie would have been in bed, resting for her shift as night guard. Did they catch her asleep? Was she still alive? *Aaaaah! I can't ask him anything as long at that creature's listening.* She halted in front of the woman. "What's your name?"

The woman looked up at her, yellow lights in her muddy brown eyes. She stared at the Mask for several moments, then looked away, having said nothing.

K'vestmilly sighed and went back to her pacing.

"Look out one of the east windows, Marn." The woman spoke in a monotone, a touch of triumph the only seasoning in her voice.

"Why?"

There was no answer. The woman's face went blank as the wall.

"Gyes." When Adlayr opened his eyes, K'vestmilly pointed to the window next to hers. He nodded and joined her looking into the court below.

A group of men led in Husenkil and Narazha, bound their hands behind them, and forced them to stand with their backs against a wall. Narazha's skirt was torn and bloody, she was naked from the waist up, her small breasts bleeding and torn. Husenkil's face was bruised and bleeding; he'd walked bent over, an arm dangling loosely; there was a wooden plug in his mouth, held in place by leather straps.

The count came up to her, *five, four, three . . .*

A sharp whistle.

A scatter of shots.

Her hands closing so tight on the windowsill her nails dug gouges in the wood, she watched Husenkil and Narazha fall, continued to watch as the shooters walked out again.

Behind her the woman spoke again. "Every hour."

K'vestmilly Vos turned slowly. She looked at the woman, then she looked at Adlayr.

He nodded, started across the room.

The woman hoisted herself to her feet, opened her mouth to yell for help.

He was on her before she got a sound out, his hands around her throat.

"Is she dead?"

"Nik, just unconscious." He squatted beside the bulky body. "I'll keep her out; it's not hard. Honeydew's got to Heslin already, he's sent to warn the Pens and the Osks. He thinks it's maybe not too late. Ildas warned Zas and she went to ground, hasn't been able to get clear. . . ." The woman stirred; he sent her out again with a quick pressure of his fingers. "Waiting for dark, I think. Hard to tell. Ildas is . . . most times he won't talk to anyone but her." He shook his head. "No matter. Heslin has had supplies cached, macain ready, in case something like this happened. He'll be waiting for us on the East Bank. All we have to do is get to him."

"You and the sprite can talk this far apart?"

"A lot farther, now we're used to each other. This is your Tower, Marn. Any bolt holes?"

She scratched at her arm, smiled behind the Mask. "Not exactly. One of the first Vos Marns had an itch to be clever and a fear of being locked in anywhere; if you know the trick of it, you don't need a key to open the door from this side. We can go when we want to. The Marns don't talk about it except to the Heirs."

He applied pressure again. "Hmm. About that out there." He nodded at the window. "Is your actually handing him the Mask that important?"

"It legitimizes him and he needs that." As she spoke, she moved to the bed, stripped back the covers, peeled a sham off a pillow. "Without it . . . zdra, he's strongest at the moment, but it won't be long before one or two of the others get together and move against him." She pulled the Mask off, wrapped it in the sham and dropped the bundle down the front of her shirt, hurried past him, began feeling about the lock-plate. "Forget about her. You'd better shift to the sicamar. There'll be guards, be ready to take them out when I get the door open." She moved her fingers hesitantly across the heavy decoration on the metal plate, her face thoughtful.

There was a thud behind her; she glanced over her shoulder and saw him carrying the woman to the bed, a red blotch on the side of her jaw; she smiled and went back to exploring the plate. "When I was nine, Mother showed me how to work this. That was a while . . . ah! You ready?" She got to her feet, grinned fiercely when she saw the black beast crouched on the floor. "Good. Let's go!"

Sicamar at her heels, K'vestmilly Vos strode through the backways of the Pevranamist, dusty corridors, dim rooms long closed up and unused, desiccated gardens and crumbling arcades, places where she'd played when she was a prepube spolz' hiding out from her tutors. Empty rooms, empty corridors—even when they reached the Warren-in-the-Mist where the servants and minor functionaries lived. They were all gone, fled or dead or part of the conspiracy. She couldn't think about them, couldn't think about anything but getting away; each time the image of Husenkil falling flashed into her head, she pushed it away before the pain could start. If she let it come, she'd curl in a ball and howl.

The sicamar growled softly, angled in front of her, nudging her toward an alcove. She slid behind dusty curtains as two men came tramping down a cross corridor.

They stopped at the intersection. "You hear somethin'?" The voice was a rough tenor with the river roll to the r, had to be one of Nov's wharfliks. K'vestmilly held her breath and waited tensely.

"Prob'ly 'nother rat." Hoarse laughter. "Near shot y' foot off last 'un."

There was the sound of scuffling, then the two men stomped off again, arguing about the reward they expected once Nov was firmly in place.

K'vestmilly slammed her fist against the wall, sneezed at the dust she knocked down and swore helplessly at this glimpse of what was coming down on her people.

The sicamar rubbed his head against her leg, nudged her toward the curtains.

Near the back of the main building Zasya emerged from shadow and loped along with them, grim and silent, a small throwing knife in one hand and a lead weight in the other.

K'vestmilly eased a battered door open, gritting her teeth as it creaked and scraped across the stone; she looked out into an empty stableyard, and let herself relax a little. "Zdra, the two of you, the mews are just ahead. If we can get past there without trouble, we're out." She glanced at the sicamar, managed a half smile as the black beast showed its teeth in a feral grin. "Easy for you to say. Let's go."

She trotted past the empty stalls, went along the fence of the riding ring beyond the barn, across the last of the courts and onto the patch of wooded hillside where the mews was built.

The jessers in the open hutches began screeching when they saw the sicamar, beating as high into the air as their tethers would allow. The Keeper heard them and came from his cot. He stood staring at her as she walked toward him.

Forcing a smile, she said, "Good day, Drez, I came to see how Rishi's wing is healing. Don't mind him," she nodded at the sicamar, "he's tame."

He didn't answer, didn't move.

She took another step toward him, not surprised by his silence. That was the way he was; he left chatter to the jessers, spoke about two words a month. Then she saw the buttery yellow shine of his eyes, and threw herself to one side as his hand came round with a long knife. He leapt at her, went flying as the sicamar crashed into him, clamped long curving teeth into his neck and shook him until his spine cracked.

K'vestmilly got to her feet and stood watching Adlayr shift to man; it happened faster than she'd thought—there was a shimmer and the black beast was a naked man.

Zasya touched her arm. "I've sent Ildas scouting, but I don't think there's anyone else around."

As Adlayr began unbuttoning the Keeper's trousers, he looked over his shoulder, said, "Help me, Zas, I need his clothes. I can't go down the hill in fur and four-footed, it's too limiting."

> > < <

"Base to Throdal."

"Throdal here, go."

"Any show? Go."

"They comin', scouts say round a half hour 'fore they get here. They ridin' easy, but comin' fast, nice 'n bunched up. We got 'em. Go."

"Do it fast as you can without losing more men than you have to. The gritz're mounting an attack, just sticking their noses out right now. Come round back-

side when you're finished, hit the zhaggin' gritz where
they don't expect it. Go.''

"I'll pass it on. Out.''

Vykon bent over his mount's neck, scratching the
soft places inside the folds of skin. "Easy now, Rhuzho, easy, not long now.''

His navsta had been withdrawn from the lines; they
were waiting in the trees atop one of several rocky
knolls near the Planting that shielded the gritz camp.
Vedouce had asked for volunteers for a mission that
would probably get most of them killed and nearly got
himself trampled by the response. He shouted with
laughter, snatched a hat from an aide, tore strips from
a notebook, signed one of them, and called the vudveks to draw.

Severn pulled the marked strip and rode whooping
back to his men.

Hurbay was up a tall daub with the longglass. "They
comin','' he called down. "They drivin' one a the
supply wagons ahead a them, got a sorta shield
spreadin' across the front, bunch a riders round the
orsks to keep 'em covered. A mob behind. Comin'
slow, but steady. Vedouce is ready for 'em, he's already got navstas right and left, must be waiting for
Crazy Tak to show. Gritz're going straight for the
camp. Two more wagons pokin' their noses out. Mad's
Tits, you should see them, they think they got us. Yaa,
there he is, Crazy Tak, he's on the second wagon, can't
miss all that red. Come on, potresh, we gonna have
your ass . . . yaaaa, there goes the Zemmer fire over
the far side, mowing those notneys like summer shem.
Now it's Shar and his Dandri this side. Now the gritz
are turning the wagons, makin' a arc, chert! they've
done it, shields touching, get those orsks, you nijas.
Spojj! they're forming up again, fightin' back. . . .''

Vykon fidgeted as the battle developed, a mix of hate and fear sour in his throat; sweat trickled down his back, cold and sticky. He piled pebbles in front of him, shifting them from pile to pile, whispering a litany of dead, his brother and cousins, stopping now and then to murmur to Rhuzho, scratch in the skin folds of his neck, rub the macai's nose when the beast caught the twitches from him.

Severn squatted beside him. "Almost time," he muttered, squeezed Vykon's shoulder near the neck, "you too tight, loosen up." He tapped Vykon on the back, moved on.

Riding at an easy lope, metal parts muffled, they moved through the trees, passed into the fringe of the Planting, Vykon remembering his first solo hunt. It'd felt like this. Smells, colors, sound, everything intensified . . . the pressure of the saber sheath against his thigh, the longgun's stock rubbing against his back, the dark dank smell of the thick loam kicked up by Rhuzho's claws, the whumpf of the macai's breath, the dusty sunbeams slanting down from breaks in the canopy, the hum of the black biters, a scrap of distant birdsong, the silence close by. Not the same as the attacks he and his brother had been in when they had served as shipment guards, that was just business, this was for the Land. And for the Blood.

They reached the markpoint; Severn lifted his hand to call a halt, looked over his shoulder to make sure they were in phalanx. His mouth curled in a wild grin, he brought the hand down like the chop of an ax and they were out of the trees, their macain booted into full gallop, holding their places in the arrow they'd pointed at the wagon where Crazy Tak was yelling orders to his men.

At the same time, warned by the watching Mys, the

Zemmers and the Dandri provided a distraction by
charging the wagons.

In the resulting chaos the navsta almost reached their
target before they were spotted.

Crouched low over Rhuzho's neck, Vykon swung the
saber, jerked it loose, swung again. The macai
screamed, fought with his lethal forefeet, muscled on
through the gathering gritz, screamed again as a bullet
from the wagon that had burned along Vykon's ribs
gouged a long hole from his flank.

Severn's Zelly dropped, head blown half off. He
managed to scramble clear, recovered his saber, and
went at the gritz until they cut him down.

Leg and ribs bleeding, one ear a stub, a river of
blood running down the side of his neck, soaking his
shirt, Rhuzho's teeth and claws and his saber clearing
the way, Vykon drove toward the wagon, yelling his
brother's name over and over though he wasn't aware
of it, couldn't hear his own voice in the roar around
him.

Rhuzho clawed his way up over gritz and wood and
with a last surge of his hind legs reached the wagon
bed; he stumbled as a dozen bullets caught him in the
chest and fell forward, faithful even in dying, his
struggles throwing down the gritz ahead, opening a
path for his rider. A bullet burned along the top of
Vykon's shoulder, another clipped off a flying lock of
hair, the others missed him completely. Weaving and
slashing, he fought his way forward.

Hurbay jumped from his dying mount and made the
wagon, driving after Vykon, keeping gritz off his back.
Tiskov and Zalban were fighting the gritz who surged
toward the wagon. The rest of the navsta was down,
dead or dying.

Vykon jumped a dead man, took a bullet in the arm from Tak's shortgun; he didn't feel it except as a dull blow, which he ignored because it wasn't his sabre side. Takuboure was yelling and cursing, he didn't hear that either. The saber hilt slipping in his hand from the blood on it, he leapt and lunged and skewered Crazy Tak. He twisted the blade, shouting his triumph as blood sprayed onto his face and arms, then fell as a gritz's sabre nearly cut his head from his shoulders.

> > < <

K'vestmilly Vos followed Adlayr and Zasya down the path she'd taken so many times before, riding to the hunt in her heedless days and later going secretly to visit her father. She fought memory off, focused her thoughts on what lay ahead. They had to get through Dander and across the Bridge, link up with Heslin, and ride south to join Vedouce and the army.

Over and over she played out the plan in her head as she trotted through the silence of the Marn's Plantings, sun rays slanting down around her, touching to jewel brightness the fur on the modaries, varabecs, skarivas and v'lashers as they flew about among the trees, snatches of their songs drifting on the cool breeze that rustled through the leaves. Instead of strengthening her, the serenity and beauty of the place ate away at her concentration, let the anguish of the past hours seep through. Tears stinging her eyes, she fought that weakness, there was no time for grief, no time. . . .

The ground pulsed, leapt against her foot, catching her in mid-stride, nearly throwing her down, rejecting her. She thought for a moment she was crazier than Mad Treshteny because even the air brushing past her felt hostile.

She staggered a few steps, slapped a hand against a tree trunk, snatched it away as a force in the tree nipped at her palm. "You, too?"

She stood staring at nothing, swaying with the shift, consciously aware for the first time—through the abrupt loss of that tie—how intensely personal was the Marn's connection with Cadander, like the blood tie passed from mother to daughter generation after generation.

And now the Land was dead to her, a dislocate comparable to the deaths of her mother and her father; she reached out, groping at nothing as she struggled to understand what was happening.

When Adlayr took her hand and urged her on, she heard his voice as a distant rumble, but let him lead her, hollow woman, her mind empty.

At the edge of the Planting, Zasya touched K'vestmilly's arm again. "Wait."

While Adlayr stood guard, the meie pulled the sham from K'vestmilly's blouse. Letting her hold the Mask, Zasya tore strips from the sham and used them to bind down her hair. "This mop of yours, Marn, it's a shout saying here I am. It's going to be all right, Marn, this beat, whatever it is, it's just part of the attack, we'll find out what's doing it and we'll stop it. Now, I'm going to pull this strip across your mouth, it'll look like a gag, but it's more of a mask, the effect I'm going for, you're our mad sister we're taking home to get her away from all that's happening. Here's the rest of the sham for the Mask, wrap it up and tuck it away . . . good . . . and this strip goes round your wrists; I'm not going to tie it, I'll just hold it in place. It's all right to cry now, that'll help the effect, you can grieve, Marn, leave all the rest to us."

* * *

As they entered the city, moving south along Charamanac Street, the throbbing grew louder as if a demon's drum beat beneath the pavement; answering to the beat of that drum were thousands of murderous ecstatic dancers.

Adlayr and Zasya led K'vestmilly around and away from a woman with a knife who was dipping and weaving through a long bloody spiral, the knife slicing flesh, cloth, everything that came within her reach. Some died, spraying blood from slashed throats, others lost hands, others bled and ignored it, turning through their own spirals of death with knives of their own and bludgeons and other weapons improvised from whatever came to hand.

"Kazim," they chanted. "Kazim, kazim, kazim."

Adlayr kicked and shoved, moving through them, clearing a way for the others. Zasya jerked K'vestmilly again and again away from the blind sweep of death. It wasn't difficult, keeping clear, it only took alertness and speed. There was no focus to the blows; the dancers struck at random, bruising air as much as they bruised flesh.

When they reached the Bridge, it was almost empty—as if the nixies swarming below, agitated and noisy, had provided a sort of insulation from the maddening throb.

Calanda was quieter, probably because there were fewer people there; many of the men had gone south with the army, at least double what Dander had sent if one didn't count the Marn's Guard.

Dusty and disregarded, K'vestmilly followed meie and gyes south along the River Road, leaving the worst of the hostile throb behind her, only weariness left and a grief that lumped inside her like a bad meal that wouldn't go away.

* * *

Camnor Heslin stepped from under restless trees and stood at the edge of the shadow waiting for them.

Honeydew fluttered to meet them, settling on Adlayr's shoulder, chattering into his ear, rubbing her tiny hand against his whiskery cheek.

Heslin unwrapped the straps from K'vestmilly's wrists, pulled down the strip wound loosely across her face. He wiped away tears and dust. "Honeydew told me about your father. If I'd known. . . ."

She leaned against him, needing that familiar solidity to give her back some of the warmth, the connectedness, that she'd lost.

He held her for a few breaths, moving a hand gently up and down her back, then he moved her away. "We'd best be going, they'll be looking for you soon, if they aren't already."

As she settled the Mask over her face, she felt her mother comforting her as Ansila Vos never had when she was alive—and she had a sense of eons, the power of blood and history. She tore the covering from her hair, combed her fingers through it until it stood out from her head, then she kneed the macai into its travel lope and headed south, the others following silently behind her.

> > < <

At the feral grove, Heslin used his com to call Hedivy to them. While they waited, the greenish purple aura throbbing over the trees grew darker and stronger than before. Out in the river the nixies were agitated, noisy, rushing at the east bank, merging once again with the thick yellow-brown water that gave the Yellow Dan its name.

The wind tore at them, erratic gusts that surged and fell with no discernible rhythm. The land ba-boomed with a steady beat heard in the bones rather than the ears. The sky grew dark and ominous, lightning walked all around them, though it couldn't seem to reach them, deflected by the trees and the nixies that crowded thickly about the landing. The trees began to writhe and thrash about, the smallest on the outside of the grove bending almost to the ground. The landing groaned and shifted under the pressure of wind and water, threatening to tear from its posts and slide away downstream.

Hedivy stepped onto the landing. "Marn." He blinked as the wind blew rain in his face, but stood stolid and immovable, braced against the shoving of the storm gusts.

"Hedivy Starab." K'vestmilly raised her voice, almost shouting so he could hear her over the storm.

He looked past her at the others. "Oram?"

"Dead. Nov had him killed."

"Ahhhh."

K'vestmilly smiled behind the Mask when the lightning showed her the flat chill look in his eyes, then she shook her head. "There's nothing for you in Dander, Hedivy Starab. You wouldn't get near him. It's bad there. Half the Nerodin are killing the other half, I don't know why. The Pevranamist is swarming with wharfliks. And Nov's no doubt rooting through Oram's files and planning what to do with the agents he finds listed there. How close is Vedouce to finishing off the gritz?"

"Attack came when I was leaving." He squinted against the grit the wind was blowing into his face. "If Vedouce pulls off the plan he has worked out, this time he'll break them. If not, might take another week."

"I see." She took off the Mask, looked at it, slipped

it into the front of her blouse. "Come south with us. I ask it, I don't order you."

He thought about that a moment, then he nodded. "Boat," he said.

"In that?"

"You need someone to tell 'im you coming."

"Yes, you're right." Her voice was hoarse with the strain of struggling to be heard. "Zas, go with him. Tell Vedouce what you know and when we'll get there." She coughed, wiped her mouth. "If he has questions, have Ildas pass them to Honeydew. More private that way. Adlayr, bring my mac and give me a hand up, let's get started."

> > < <

"Spider two to Base."

"Base here. Go."

"The gritz barges are coming round the bend, I can see a bunch of Harozh on deck the first one. They should be tying up before the hour's done. Vych! Bunch of gritz coming out of the Planting, they're scattered, no more than two or three together, and they're going fast and going light. There's more of 'em. Choo—eee. Looks like they not going to stop till they hit the Horn. You want me to keep watching or what? Go."

"General said to tell you watch another hour, then come in. Go."

"We got 'em that good? Go."

"Yeh. Enough blood in that field to drown a herd of orsks. Out."

> > < <

Serroi walked along the cots, her bare feet cool on

the shadowed earth; they'd arranged the wounded the way she wanted, the worst at the beginning. She set her hands on men with bellies laid open, arms, legs mangled or even gone—and as she did so the flow from the earth came welling up through her like a vast quiet stream—it wasn't her at all that did the healing, not any longer, she was only a conduit—and she felt the power flowing out from her as well, a perfume on the wind, or dandelion seeds scattering—and at the edge of her awareness she felt other lives welling up, shapeless things given shape through her—her children who looked nothing like her, but were hers nonetheless—reaching out and out, even to the mountains where stones came to life and awareness, walking into the mines and out again, wading through earth and stone as men waded through water. No more hungry trees, she was pleased at that, though she had no idea why these trees did not respond as those had, perhaps the dryads that filled them now kept them sweet.

And she felt the Fetch throbbing around her, unable to touch her, but wanting, wanting, almost demanding . . . she could taste the desire, shuddered from the demand. If she'd had time for fear, she would have been afraid.

She walked and healed. And more of the long-absent magic flowed through the Land, spreading beyond Cadander, across the seas, wind-blown around the world.

* * *

Vedouce left his pavilion and walked to look over the wounded who lay in cots between a double row of trees. The first of them were already sitting up, feeling at themselves, grinning and looking surprised. He strolled along the line, slapping shoulders, laughing and joking, calling names when he knew them, especially when he recognized someone from Steel Point.

Later he'd have to go inspect the dead lying out in that trampled field, get their names, the Families they were affiliated with. It wasn't something he looked forward to, but he'd do it, and make sure he got the stories of how they died so he could pass these on to their kin.

By the time he reached the end of the line, Serroi was sitting cross-legged by a tree, her face blank, her mind somewhere he'd never understand. He stopped by the medic standing a quiet guard between her and the healed. "Give the Healer my blessing and my thanks when she's ready to hear it."

He moved on to talk with vudveks and trivuds, to calm them down, to make sure that the camps were organized, the men ready to move out in the morning, driving south after the running gritz, that spotters were sent out to make sure no vengeful gritz circled round to hit them in their sleep. It was nearly sundown by the time he got back to the pavilion and settled wearily in his chair, the Aide Stoppah pouring him a cup of kava while Shar reported the status of the Guard.

"What are you doing back here!" Vedouce surged to his feet, blood darkening his heavy face.

Hedivy nodded at the others. "Send them out, this is for your ears only."

Vedouce stared at him a moment long, then he turned to Shar. "Wait outside, will you please?"

Shar's pale blue eyes shifted restlessly, then he shrugged. "Yell if you want us."

"So?"

"The Marn's broke free, she's riding here with the gyes and Heslin."

Vedouce straightened his back, his face relaxing a little. "How do you know?"

"We met up by the Patch Farms." Hedivy stood

slumped, left thumb rubbing across the back of his right hand. "I was right about Nov and Ker." He spoke slowly, his voice a low growl as he watched Vedouce's face closely. "The meie came back with me, she's with the Healer if you want to talk to her. What she told me, the others involved are Sko, Ano, and Bar. Ank, Vyk, Zav, and Hal, don't know. Osk is definitely out. Nov had Marazhney shot. Heslin sent warning notes to Pen House and Osk House, told them to head for Osk Hold in the Merrzachars. Don't know if the warnings were in time or not."

"Zdra." Vedouce leaned back in his chair, closed his eyes. "When will she get here?"

"Early tomorrow morning if they ride all night. They have remounts, so I do expect they will. If you've got questions, you can talk to her."

"You left the com with her?"

"Nik." Hedivy jerked a thumb at the entrance to the tent. "She said tell the meie Zasya Myers. Her familiar Ildas will pass word to the sprite. More private that way she said."

"Ah." Vedouce got to his feet, circled round the table and thrust his head past the door curtain. "Stoppah, find Trivud Chol, he'll be with the Harozhni, bring him here, will you? Move!"

Vedouce leaned forward, brown eyes narrowed and intent. "Chol, the Marn's on her way here. I want to send a guard force north to meet her. But," he held up a hand, "that's trickier than you might think." He repeated what Hedivy told him, finished, "Choose twenty men, men you're sure you know." He got to his feet. "Then we all head north and twist some tails."

26. The Dancer Rises

I spared you, Mother. I have left you free. No more. It's time you understood. It's time you came to me. All you have to do is reach out to me. I will touch your hand, bring you here to me, I will give you the world and all that is in it. Cadander is mine now. It can be yours, Mother. To do with as you will. All that I ask is that you love me. Give me at least what you've given those creatures you spawned. Call me Daughter and Belovéd. That's all I ask.

The Dancer turned from the window and stood waiting for Nov to come to him. He no longer moved constantly, he didn't have to, his whole body seemed to vibrate.

"Where is she?" The suppressed fury in Nov's whispered words gave them more force than a shout. "You said you'd find her. Where is she?"

"On the River Road a few hours from the army."

"Bring her back. What good are you? Bring her back."

"It wasn't me who let her escape."

"She took the Mask, the bitch. If I don't have the Mask. . . ."

"If that's your only problem, you have no problem." The Dancer held his hands out, cupped, the palms facing each other as if they held a sphere between them. The space filled with yellow light, the light surged and flowed and a moment later the Dancer held a Mask between his hands. "Take it. Even the Preörchmat will not know it is a copy."

> > < <

K'vestmilly Vos huddled inside the cloak the Guard had given her; her thighs were aching and her back wasn't much better—it'd been a long time since she'd ridden this far and this hard. And in such miserable weather. The rain had stopped yesterday, but it threatened every moment to let loose another flood. She could do without that, the wind and the lightning were bad enough. *The Enemy was at it again, couldn't strike at them directly, Maiden Bless, but he could wear them down.*

The escort Vedouce had sent were all around her, silent figures flashing from the dark with each lightning strike, the creaks, grunts, thump of the macai pads lost in storm noise and that miserable, exasperating beat.

She was so tired; she couldn't remember the last time she'd slept a whole night. Some of those nights, though . . . she smiled behind the Mask she put back on when the guard arrived, glanced at Heslin and sighed, he made it worth losing sleep. The brief flush of pleasure slid away without alleviating her exhaustion. Just a little bit longer now, a few hours and she could rest, safe for a while, the responsibility for running things loaded onto Vedouce's back. She couldn't leave it there long, she knew that well enough, but just for a breath. A free breath, a rest.

"Marn."

The word came at her out of the dark with an ur-

gency that jerked her from her weary drift. A macai's
head moved past her knee, then Adlayr was riding beside her. He leaned closer, yelled, "Marn, problems.
Have to talk."

K'vestmilly held up a hand, brought her mount to a
halt.

Camnor Heslin and Trivud Chol crowded into a tight
circle with K'vestmilly and Adlayr so they were close
enough to hear above the wind and thunder and the
throb of the earth.

K'vestmilly leaned toward Adlayr, yelled, "What is
it?"

"Zasya . . . warning, through Honeydew." Adlayr
opened his cloak and as lightning flashed again, they
saw the sprite huddling in his shirt pocket. "Twenty
minutes ago, everything was quiet, men were sleeping, except for sentries. Then the ground started to
thump worse than this here and men got up and started
killing everyone around them, like we saw in the cities,
Marn. Shar was one of the Taken, he almost killed
Vedouce, but he wasn't strong or fast enough, Vedouce broke his neck, got out and saw what was happening, he woke one of his aides, had him blow the
horn, keep blowing it so the men who hadn't gone
crazy could gather round him. They're fighting back
now, but it's bad, having to shoot folk who'd been
fighting beside them just yesterday. Worst thing is nobody knows what's going on."

"Zhag!" K'vestmilly touched the Mask, turned her
head to look back along the road. "If we. . . ."

Heslin interrupted her before she could finish. "Nik,
Marn. That won't solve anything. As long as the army's intact, the Enemy's under threat. And since he
seems to've linked with Nov . . ."

"Prak. So what do you suggest?"

"Adlayr, could you fly in this weather?"

Hands closed into fists resting on his thighs, the gyes lifted his head, the wind whipping his loosened braid, a light in his eyes as wild as the storm. When he looked down again, he was smiling, a fierce, humorless grimace. "Yes."

"If you went up till you saw the camp, you could find the safest way to get to Vedouce, if there is any safe way. Leave Honeydew with me and tell her how we should go. Is that acceptable, Marn?"

K'vestmilly closed her eyes a moment, knowing the Mask hid her revulsion. *No rest, none at all—am I to send him to his death?* She swallowed, took a deep breath and said, "Yes, of course. As long as the gyes is willing."

Adlayr swung from the saddle, tossing his reins to the Trivud Chol. He edged around to Camnor Heslin, passed Honeydew to him, protected from the wind by the cloak Heslin swung around them.

"Adlayr, I'm going to keep my hand where she can reach it; tell her to pinch my thumb if we're supposed to turn left, my forefinger for right turns; if we're supposed to stop, to scratch whatever she can reach with all four fingers. Anything we need to add . . . mmm . . . if you want us to slow down . . ." he grinned, "she can pull back on my thumb."

Adlayr glanced at Honeydew who was perched on Heslin's massive thigh, fluttering her wings to work the wrinkles out and running her hands through her tangled mop of thistledown hair. He shifted his gaze back to Heslin. "She's got it; she can hear and understand you."

"I know, but I wanted to make sure. There's a lot resting on her."

Adlayr glanced at Honeydew again, grinned. "She says you forgot something. When it's time to get

started, she'll give you a kick. I'll leave my clothes
with you. That all right?''

> > < <

Her movements jagged with anger, the Preörchmat
strode into the Tradurad, stopped just inside the door,
her eyes passing over the two armed guards, shuddering away from Ravach whose reputation she knew too
well, finishing on the face of Zavidesht Pan Nov. Behind her she could hear the rapid, frightened breathing
of the two Setras on service duty with her. ''Why did
you send those . . . those thugs for us?''

''The Marn has been killed. Two gritz slipped past
the guards and got to her.'' He waved a hand at the
worktable and the body wrapped in clean white linen
that was stretched out on it.

The Preörchmat hurried across the room and drew
back the shroud to view the face. She sucked in a
quick breath, looked up. ''This is not the Marn.''

''What does that matter? It is who you say it is.''

''Zavidesht Pan Nov, what are you saying to me?''

''I am saying you will burn this body as the Marn's
tomorrow and you will Mask my daughter Motylla day
after.''

''I will not.''

Nov snapped his fingers.

Ravach set his handgun at the base of the elder Setra's skull and pulled the trigger, taking a quick step
back so she wouldn't fall on him. Another step and he
had the muzzle of the handgun pressed against the
temple of the younger.

''One by one,'' Nov said. ''We'll bring them in and
you can watch them die. If we finish the Setras, we'll
start on the sekalaries. One by one.''

The Preörchmat stood with her hand pressed across

her mouth, gazing at the threatened Setra who had her eyes closed, her lips moving in whispered prayers. She was very young, just out of the Novitiate.

"Well?"

"If you gain what you deserve, you will spend eons in zhagdeep whimpering in pain."

"Rav."

"Nik. I'll do it. Send the girl to me tonight so I can prepare her."

Nov thumbed his mustache. "With two guards who will not leave her side."

"If you feel it necessary."

"Don't the Songs say avoid the occasion of temptation?"

"We would not harm a child. It's not her fault you're her father."

> > < <

The great black trax spiraled upward above the scattered trees along the River Road. Lightning leaped around him without touching him despite his immense wingspan; he rode the angry wind as if it were a zephyr wafting from bloom to bloom.

Honeydew kicked at Heslin's thigh.

He clicked his macai into an easy lope; several of the Harozh guard closed around him, the others gathered about K'vestmilly Vos, longguns resting on their thighs, heads turning as they scanned the surrounding ground as far as they could see in the intense gloom, taking turns to keep their eyes closed so the lightning wouldn't destroy the nightsight of all at once.

The beat in the soil got louder and louder, the road seemed to bump and sway under the feet of the macain. K'vestmilly's mount hooted and complained, threatened to squat, but kept on moving because the

unnatural mobility of the earth frightened him. She
could feel him trembling, see his head jerking up and
down, side to side as he moved. She leaned forward,
murmuring words lost to the wind and the beat,
scratching his neck folds, trying to reassure him; he
was tired already and his fidgets were wasting energy.
"Just a little more, my druh. . . ." Her mouth
twitched. "Sheee! K'vestmilly Vos, you better stop
saying that sort of thing, every time you do, something
horrible happens. . . ."

Heslin turned, turned again, winding through a maze
of hedges and rocky knolls, plantings and windrows.
The rain broke and came hard into their faces, the
wind hammered at them, the earth humped under
them, up and down, up and down like ocean surge.

K'vestmilly was too tired to shiver; she just clung to
the saddle and ached. She knew she should be thinking
what to do when they got to Vedouce, what to say, but
her mind had found a rut that she couldn't break out
of. She kept seeing her mother exploding, her father
beaten and broken, falling dead, she kept seeing the
shop exploding, feeling the power of the bomb as it
hurled her across the street into a wall, seeing again
and groaning again at the blood and death, worse than
death, the men women children still alive but torn until
they were not recognizable, screaming, burning, she
heard their screams in the beat beneath the earth, that
demon heart drumming away louder and louder. . . .

Heslin stopped.
The trax spiraled down, landed clumsily, and
shifted.
"I came to warn you," Adlayr shouted, "you're going to have to fight through to Vedouce, there's no

clear way. I brought you to the thinnest part but there's a mix of gritz and crazies ahead. Zas will tell ours where we are so they won't get us by mistake, she says just use your sabers, otherwise you could hit some you don't want to.'' He shifted again and went loping ahead of them, a black sicamar with werefire crackling at the ends of his fur.

The sicamar screamed his kill-cry and leapt into the mass of crazies, lashing out with claws and teeth; the Guards were close behind him, sabers swinging, macain squealing and striking out. Struggling for every inch of ground gained, the wedge of riders drove toward the flicker of Vedouce's fire, intermittently visible as a spark between trees. As the crazies closed with them, the Harozhni guard began using handguns, shooting down so they wouldn't hit the defenders. K'vestmilly Vos and Heslin rode knee to knee, handguns ready for anything that broke past the Guard ring.

On and on—till they burst through the defending lines to a shout of welcome from the beleaguered fighters. "Marn, Marn, Marn, Marn."

They were answered by cries from the crazies. "Kazim, kazim, kazim, kazim."

Marn. Kazim. Marn. Kazim. Marn. Kazim.

The twined chants fought with rain and wind and the throb of the earth, shots, groans, screams, grunts, all the noises of death.

Vedouce crouched beside the fire in an improvised shelter made of panels from the pavilion stretched between three trees, another tied above them in a crude roof. He spoke into a com, thumb on the wheel, changing channels repeatedly, gave orders through the com and to the boy runners that scurried in and out, barely pausing to catch their breath.

He looked up as K'vestmilly Vos and Heslin stepped into the circle of light. "Marn."

"Vedouce Pen's Heir."

He nodded to Heslin, turned back to the com. "Burning? All of them? Go."

Hedivy's voice came, small but clear. "Most of the bargeveks were caught by the madness, they fired their barges and joined the mob. Got Pommer and Jerst here, they're clean, you want us to shift supplies to you, we'll need ladesmen and shooters, can you send us anything? Go."

Vedouce glanced around, saw one of his runners crouched by a treetrunk. "Find Chon, tell him to collect ten of his fighters and bring them to me." As the boy trotted out, Vedouce tapped the speaker button. "Marn's got here, I'll send over ten of the Harozhni that fetched her. Out." He ran his hand through his thinning brown hair. "Heslin, if my people live, I've got you to thank for it."

Camnor Heslin shrugged. "It cost me nothing but a little time and less ink."

"You know as well as I how many would bother. You advised them to head for OskHold. Why?"

"Given what Honeydew told me, it seemed probable that Osk was loyal and I couldn't be sure of anyone else." Camnor Heslin fumbled under his cloak, eased the sprite onto his shoulder; she clung to a strand of wet hair and drooped wearily against his neck. "OskHold is far enough from Dander and well enough defended that there'd be a reasonable chance Nov would leave it alone. At least for a while."

"I see. Marn, the meie told me the same thing as this . . ." he waved a hand toward the chaos outside, "was happening in Dander and Calanda."

K'vestmilly was standing near the front of the shelter, staring into the night, listening to the sounds of the fighting; she turned, drew the shaking fingers of one hand down the side of the Mask, plucked at her skirt with the other. "Crazies here, crazies there, dancing in circles, killing whatever they touch. Chanting the same word, kazim, whatever that means. If Adlayr and Zasya hadn't kicked them away from me, I'd be dead as the rest. It's worse than the bombs, Vedouce. Bombs we could fight. This, I don't know. And I'm afraid I brought it on you, it follows me, that beat. Do you hear it? Of course you do, you have to hear it. The Enemy calling his Claimed."

Vedouce glanced at these nervous hands, ironed expression from his face. "Then I think we had better follow Heslin's notion and head for Oskland. Marn, the Healer's in a tent back of this shelter, you can get some sleep there; you might as well, it'll be a few hours yet before we're ready to move. Heslin, if you don't mind staying, I'd like to talk to you a while. You can stretch out on my cot," he nodded at the back of the tent, "once we're finished."

K'vestmilly groaned in nightmare, sticky, sweating, rigid with night terror, caught half-awake (enough to know she was dreaming) and half-asleep and unable to escape from the endless unreeling of death and torment.

A small, cool hand touched her brow, stayed there, spreading calm into her straining body. Gradually she relaxed into full sleep.

> > < <

Motylla was a dark-haired pretty child, ten years old and frightened, but she had courage and held her head high as she listened to the chant of the Setras and looked without flinching at the unwelcoming face of the Preörchmat.

The day had barely begun outside, the sky was still

heavily shrouded in dark gray clouds, so the altar chamber of the Temple was lit by the sacred silver lamps, but it was so huge that shadows clung everywhere like sooty cobwebs and it was nearly empty, most of the Families absent. And there were only a few Setras, just enough for the choir and to assist in the ceremony.

The chant reached its peak, the Preörchmat lifted the Mask high. It caught the light from the lamps and gleamed eerily.

Motylla knelt, bowed her head, spoke the words she'd been taught, then rose again to receive the Mask.

When it came down over her face, she bit her lip so she wouldn't cry out. It burned like fire. Then it nestled against her and she felt a force come from it and flow into her. When she turned to face the Families and speak her first words as Marn, her eyes shone butter yellow.

> > < <

K'vestmilly Vos woke to silence. The little tent was empty, the flap pulled back to let in cool, green, morning sunlight. She crawled from the blankets, groped for the Mask and slipped it on, found her comb and dragged it through her hair, swearing at the tangles, impatient with the need to keep up some kind of front. But that and the Mask was all she had now.

The comb broke. K'vestmilly swore again and hurled the pieces at the tent wall, then scurried on hands and knees to collect them—it might be a long time before she got another.

She shook out her blouse and skirt, pulled them on, then ducked from the tent, straightened up and looked around, astonished.

The ground under the trees swarmed with men carrying loads, leading macain back and forth for reasons she couldn't fathom. The young day was bright and clear, the air dry, the bits of sky she could see through the leaves was as blue as any morning she could remember. Last night's attack had melted into nothing.

Zasya Meyers stepped from the shadows, the Fireborn at her heels. "Marn."

"Meie. What happened?"

"Just before dawn the drumbeat changed, I can't say how, but you could feel it was different. The crazies, they backed off and started marching north. And the gritz that're left, they took off same time, too many of us left for them to do anything but get killed."

"Vedouce didn't go after them?"

"The men wanted to. He had to talk hard and fast, saying they needed time to get ready to retake the cities, that by now those who were alive would stay alive and there was nothing they could do for those that were dead; he lost some men spite of him making sense, they were too worried about their families, but he kept most of them together, the Steel Pointers and the Harozhni and a lot of the Zemyani—the ones that weren't Claimed. The Enemy didn't get many Harozhni, we don't know why. We're starting for Oskland as soon as we've got the supplies packed and the march organized. We're almost ready, maybe an hour or two more. He said when you woke, I should take you over to the Healer's work shelter, you can have a wash there and something to eat."

"Adlayr?"

"Flying, watching the crazies march north. Vedouce wants to know the minute they change direction. If they do."

"I see. Breakfast sounds good. It's been a while since I've had even a smell of food."

> > < <

The Dancer sat in the Marn's chair as Nov and his daughter along with the other Conspirator Pans came in answer to his summons, a hook in their heads that would not let them rest until they were where he wanted them, standing beside the Treddekkap Table looking up at him.

Nov's face purpled with fury as he saw what he thought was his tool in his daughter's place. Growling, he lifted his fists and started toward the dais.

The Dancer lifted his left hand, palm out, and Nov stopped as if he'd run into a wall.

The Dancer held up his right hand, snapped thumb against forefinger.

Motylla cried out, tried to pull the Mask off, but she could not. She fell in a heap by her father's feet, sobbing with pain and fear.

The Dancer snapped his fingers again and the pain stopped. Motylla rose and walked blindly toward the dais, avoiding her father's hands when he reached for her; she turned, set her back against the dais, folded her arms across her narrow chest.

The Dancer's voice was a contented purr when he spoke. "I am Mother Death, I am the Glory. You are MY Masks, the lot of you. You rule the Land and I rule you. What I say is law, and you will pass that on."

Ker screamed and leapt forward, his rage carrying him through the Dancer's barrier; he got close enough to touch the Dancer's leg—touch and scream.

The Dancer closed his right hand into a fist.

Nov fell to his knees. Sko, Ano, and Bar went down behind him.

Unable to move, they watched Ker die.

It took four hours. When it was over, the Dancer stood, opened his hands. "The lessoning is finished." A snap of the fingers and Motylla moved along the dais to the stairs, climbed them, and stood beside the Dancer, closed in the thick yellow aura that glowed around him. He laughed, hag's laughter, cackling and ugly. "Walk away, little Masks. We'll talk again."

> > < <

After the noon meal, the vudveks took their navstas into the positions they'd have on the trek to Oskland, the outriding scouts were checking their coms and Adlayr flew like a great black shadow above the muster.

The Harozhni who'd brought K'vestmilly Vos into camp had claimed the right to be called the Marn's Own; they escorted her to the hastily constructed platform, the Trivud Chon himself lifting her to stand beside Vedouce Pen. She wore clean clothing scavenged for her by her Own, a black cloak of heavy silk that Vedouce had contributed. The bright noon light gleamed on the Mask and her wild red hair.

"Marn, Marn, Marn. . . ." the fighters chanted and clapped their hands together in Cadander's rhythmic salute—slap slap, slap slap slap.

She quieted them and spoke first of her faith in them, her pleasure in seeing so many alive and well and in their right minds, then she paused, stretched her hands wide, the cloak falling in graceful folds over her arms. "This will not end here," she cried. "Nor will I be the last Marnhidda Vos. I tell you something now that no one else knows, except the Healer Serroi who it was told me the best part of it. I have taken a consort, a man of wisdom and strength, and in my womb the next Marn grows. The line continues and the land will be ours, yours and mine and my child's."

EPILOGUE

As Serroi rode with the Marn's Army, the Fetch walked in her mind's eye. It was no longer alone, Its hand rested on the narrow shoulder of the girl child walking beside it, a girl with long silky black hair and a Mask twin to the Marn's.

You see, Mother. You see my daughter, my own claimed child? You see how sweet and lovely she is? This Land is Mine and Hers. Those dull earth worms you prefer to Me, they'll do nothing but die and be mine in the end. I am Death, Mother. All things come to me.

She wrinkled her nose and refused to acknowledge the image. Under her breath, she said, "Death? We'll see who dies."

Honeydew stirred on her shoulder. Serry? You talking to me? She yawned and stretched, her wings tickling Serroi's neck.

Nay, Honey. Just wishes on the wind. Go back to sleep. We've got a long way to go.

DAW

Jo Clayton

The Wild Magic Series:

☐ **WILD MAGIC: Book 1**   UE2496—$4.99

Faan was a mortal, kidnapped by the mightiest of goddesses, and trapped in a war between gods. Could she learn to master her own powers before the rival gods destroyed her?

☐ **WILDFIRE: Book 2**   UE2514—$4.99

Faan embarks on a difficult and daring search to find her mother, refusing to remain a pawn in the deadly games being played between gods and wizards.

☐ **THE MAGIC WARS: Book 3**   UE2547—$4.99

When universes meet and the wild magic is unchained, will Faan and her comrades survive the chaos of a sorcerous war?

The Drinker of Souls Series:

☐ **DRINKER OF SOULS: Book 1**   UE2433—$4.50

She was Brann, the Drinker of Souls, from whom all but the very brave and the very foolish fled in fear.

☐ **A GATHERING OF STONES: Book 3**   UE2346—$3.95

Trapped by the Chained God's power, can Brann and her allies find the magic talismans to set the god—and themselves-free?

Mercedes Lackey

The Novels of Valdemar

THE LAST HERALD-MAGE

☐ MAGIC'S PAWN: Book 1   UE2352—$4.99
☐ MAGIC'S PROMISE: Book 2   UE2401—$4.99
☐ MAGIC'S PRICE: Book 3   UE2426—$4.99

VOWS AND HONOR

☐ THE OATHBOUND: Book 1   UE2285—$4.99
☐ OATHBREAKERS: Book 2   UE2319—$4.99

KEROWYN'S TALE

☐ BY THE SWORD   UE2463—$5.99

THE HERALDS OF VALDEMAR

☐ ARROWS OF THE QUEEN: Book 1   UE2378—$4.99
☐ ARROW'S FLIGHT: Book 2   UE2377—$4.99
☐ ARROW'S FALL: Book 3   UE2400—$4.99

THE MAGE WINDS

☐ WINDS OF FATE: Book 1 (hardcover)   UE2489—$18.95
☐ WINDS OF FATE: Book 1 (paperback)   UE2516—$4.99
☐ WINDS OF CHANGE: Book 2 (hardcover)   UE2534—$20.00
☐ WINDS OF CHANGE: Book 2 (paperback)   UE2563—$4.99
☐ WINDS OF FURY: Book 3 (hardcover)   UE2562—$20.00

The Novels of Darkover
(with Marion Zimmer Bradley)

☐ REDISCOVERY (hardcover)   UE2561—$18.00
